# Jenny Pitman

# *The Vendetta*

MACMILLAN

First published 2004 by Macmillan
an imprint of Pan Macmillan Ltd
Pan Macmillan, 20 New Wharf Road, London N1 9RR
Basingstoke and Oxford
Associated companies throughout the world
www.panmacmillan.com

ISBN 1 4050 0616 1 HB
ISBN 1 4050 5118 3 TPB

3 5 7 9 8 6 4

A CIP catalogue record for this book is available from
the British Library.

Typeset by SetSystems Ltd, Saffron Walden, Essex
Printed and bound in Great Britain by
Mackays of Chatham plc, Chatham, Kent

*To my husband, David,*

*and my sons, Mark and Paul,*

*for their continued love and support*

# Prologue

'Why the hell're you so late with this?' the voice of Tim Farr's boss, Jim Tree, rasped. 'We've already got the story off the wires. This accident happened, what – six hours ago?'

'Yes, I know, but I followed the recovery vehicle that carted the wrecks away. Then I went to the hospital. I did phone in to keep you in the picture, so to speak.'

Jimmy snorted.

'Well, you should've spoken to me. OK, I'll tell you what I want. A colour piece, five hundred words, faxed over to me by midnight. That's in thirty-five minutes' time, so you'd better move your arse, son. And don't make this story too poncy.'

The reporter's fingers paused, reached for a styrofoam cup of coffee, raised it to his lips. He looked at his watch. Eleven twenty-five. He hurriedly put down the cup and pounded on, trying to summon up a mental picture of the drama he had watched unfolding on Cleeve Hill earlier that evening.

> Jan Hardy was the National Hunt heroine from the uncon-
> sidered Edge Farm yard, who burst onto the racing scene
> only a couple of seasons ago and whose horse Magic Maestro
> had just sensationally won the Cathcart Chase. I had seen
> her face radiant in the winners' enclosure, and her broad
> smile lighting up the presentation ceremony. Now, as they
> carefully shuttled her on a stretcher to the waiting ambu-
> lance, the pretty features were obscured by the oxygen mask.
> And lodged in that bell of blonde hair were tiny granules of
> shattered glass, which shone under the lights like glitter dust.
> The knot of lookers-on, marshalled behind the police barrier,

uttered a collective sigh as the crew hoisted her through the ambulance doors and we saw her, unmistakably, move her arm, then her head. At least she was alive.

But from a distance I couldn't be sure about her companion, apparently the driver of the car. They took another forty-five minutes to get the young man out. He was covered in blood and appeared lifeless. I asked a policeman who he was. He just shook his head, but later I learned it was Eddie Sullivan. He's a close friend of Mrs Hardy and many fans of the jumping game will remember the race he rode as an amateur rider in the Foxhunters' Chase at Aintree's Grand National meeting two years ago on a horse she trained. The name of Jan Hardy was then virtually unknown, but in a sensational race Sullivan, on Russian Eagle, approached the last of the great fences certain to win, until under bizarre circumstances he came to grief when his saddle slipped on landing . . .

Ten minutes later Tim had finished the story. He had included almost everything he knew about the accident except for one small fact, something he had noticed about Eddie's smashed car. It was a small detail, which indicated there was something about the accident that was not quite straightforward. It might lead nowhere or, on the other hand, it might lead to a terrific story. But that would have to wait until tomorrow.

He scrolled back to the top of the piece and thought about the headline. It was always worth putting one in, though the sub-editors usually considered they knew better. He rejigged it:

JAN HARDY: FATAL TRAGEDY MARS DAY OF TRIUMPH

Then he added his byline:

*By Tim Farr*

# 1

Numb from shock, drowsy from drugs, Jan drifted in and out of consciousness. She understood she was in bed. But there was a background of buzzing and occasional cheeps, like a hedgerow in summer. Periodically her mind came into focus and the hedgerow dissolved into the hospital. She was besieged by medical paraphernalia – drip stands, tubes, wires, bleeping monitors. She shut her eyes. Her body felt as if it was bobbing weightlessly in warm water. Opening her eyelids again, she knew she was staring at the ceiling, where the strip light seemed to her as sharp and real as anything she had ever seen in her life. She understood for a moment it was the source of the buzzing. Her hearing seemed selectively amplified. She heard a voice in some other room or corridor call out the word, 'Doctor!'

Much less clear were the figures in white and blue flitting around the blurred periphery of her vision. She tried to move her head. Someone touched her arm. A needle went in and she returned to semi-consciousness. Now she was at the same time in a hospital ward *and* in the corner of a ripe June hayfield. Something rattled and she heard the harness of a horse, smelled the leather. A door hinge whinnied, a trolley clattered exactly like her pony's hooves on the cobbled surface of the yard when she was a girl. Somewhere down the ward a shaken pillow snorted like a horse going to exercise in the early morning.

A little later images of the previous day began to form in her brain, messages she could not read properly. They floated past her like a surreal landscape viewed from a ghostly train. Eddie insisted he would drive her home. She picked up a race card.

She stood in the centre of the paddock, giving Finbar Howlett, the jockey, his instructions. She placed a two pound bet on the Tote for the kids. The crowd shouted at the start of the Gold Cup – the Cheltenham roar. She handed Magic Maestro's passport across the counter to the declarations clerk. Leading the horse from the pre-parade ring, Joe Paley looked as grave as a chess player. Finbar got a leg up into the saddle and Magic Maestro skittered for a moment before walking on. Drumming hooves. Virginia Gilbert queening it in the trainers' bar. Eddie insisted he would drive her home. The last fence. Excitement. Whoops of joy. The winners' enclosure. The trophy presentation, with cheers and clapping. The face of Harold Powell snarling at her by the weighing room. A.D. O'Hagan in the hospitality box, beckoning the waiter to pour more champagne. Eddie insisting he would drive her home . . .

These impressions seemed unconnected, like a randomly shuffled pack of picture cards. Her mind fumbled with them for a while, and then she fell back into a deep sleep.

A woman in a white coat and with glossy dark hair was beside her bed. It was early morning.

'Nurse, what's happened?' Jan asked. 'Why am I in hospital?'

He throat and mouth were dry. She could manage no more than a creaky whisper. The woman leaned nearer.

'It's Dr Pierson, Jan. Penny Pierson.'

'Are you a doctor?'

Jan found she could shift her head, and it didn't hurt. She looked sideways and saw the folded earpieces of a stethoscope protruding from a pocket of the white coat.

'Oh, yes, so you are. Sorry.'

'Are you feeling better?'

'Better? I don't know. Can you tell me what happened? I don't . . . I can't remember.'

Dr Pierson perched herself on the bed beside Jan.

'Well, you've been in a road accident. Coming away from the racecourse, so I've been told.'

'An accident? Did I smash up the Shogun?'

'No, it wasn't you driving.'

'Oh.'

Then her brain sparked a connection. *Eddie insisting he would drive her home.*

'Eddie. Eddie was driving,' Jan said. 'Something . . . some car hit us.'

'Is it coming back to you?'

'Bits of it.'

'Good. You'll remember it all in time. Bit by bit.'

In her mind, fog still swirled around the previous night, but it was true that more and more was coming back to her. It was dark. They were in Eddie's old two-seater Morgan. Its throaty engine was coughing bronchitically as he accelerated up the hill.

'Some other car was there, going fast,' she said as a whole chunk of memory cleared the mist. 'Eddie went off the road and we crashed . . . Then, nothing, until I woke up – *When? – Last night? This morning?* – and the car was a complete wreck. Eddie was knocked out. At least, I thought he was. I was talking to him, and he didn't reply. And then I thought maybe he wasn't knocked out. I mean, I thought . . .'

She felt a sudden panic and began shaking. She snapped her head sideways to look at Dr Pierson and this time the suddenness of her movement caused pain in her neck and the side of her face, which she now realized was bandaged. Her voice was little more than a parched croak.

'He *is* OK? He wasn't moving. I think I thought he was dead.'

The doctor smiled again.

'No, Jan, it's all right. Eddie's still with us. But he's very poorly. He's in the intensive care unit.'

'Thank God.'

Jan raised her hands, still trembling violently, to her face. Dressings covered her cheeks and temples. Her hands too were bandaged. She let them fall back to the covers and suddenly the tears came.

'Thank God. Oh, thank God . . .'

Physically, Jan had come off lightly, with superficial face wounds, a throbbing bump just above her right temple, and bruises where the car's impact had thrown her body against the seat belt. There were also cuts to her hands, caused when she had tried to brush away the crumbs of window glass that had showered down on her. Otherwise, incredibly, she seemed unhurt.

No longer needed, the drips and monitors were wheeled away and one of the nurses, a sympathetic Scottish girl, gave Jan a mirror.

'See?' she said. 'It's no so bad.'

Jan saw that dressings wrapped her head from the crown to beneath her chin, making a square white frame for her even whiter features, the eyes hollow and sunken from shock.

'I look like a nun in a horror film,' she commented disapprovingly.

At half-past nine her parents were the first visitors to arrive, her father holding a big bunch of bananas and her mother, practical as ever, carried a holdall with a change of clothes and Jan's toilet bag.

'We stopped at Edge on the way to pick them up,' she said. 'Fran will be down with the children in a few minutes.'

'But what about school?' Jan asked.

'Oh, they can miss the first hour. It's more important they see you – they wouldn't be able to concentrate anyway.'

Perched on the bedside chair, Mary Pritchard looked pale and strained, though she would not have admitted it. Reg made a more convincing show of cheerfulness.

'You look fantastic, girl.'

His daughter knew it was a well-meaning lie, though she could tell also that Reg was mightily relieved to see things were not a great deal worse.

'Don't be daft. How can I look fantastic, Dad? I'm a bloody mess.'

'A few cuts. You did worse trying to gallop your pony through that copse as a child, remember?'

'Well, I'm not a child now. And what's the news about Eddie? They won't tell me anything.'

'Eddie'll be all right. He's young and strong.'

'Then why's he in intensive care?'

She caught Reg and Mary exchanging a doubtful glance.

'Mum? Dad? Please, I need to know. I'm sure he wasn't wearing his seat belt. I thought he was dead. Dad, can't you try and find out how he is? I can't stand the way they're not telling me anything.'

Reg said he would ask about Eddie if the chance came up. But Jan knew her father too well and it was obvious he already had more information than he was letting on. She did not pursue the matter, for now Fran, the woman who acted as her nanny and general helper around the house, arrived with Megan and Matty. The children approached their mother with serious faces. The sight of the bandages and the dark blue bruises frightened them. After a few moments' consideration, Megan turned to her grandad.

'Mummy looks like a mummy. She's frightening me.'

Jan blinked back her tears.

After three-quarters of an hour, during which Reg reassured Jan that all was well in the yard, and that he'd been told by Annabel how well Magic Maestro had come out of his race and eaten up his feed, Mary Pritchard saw that her daughter was exhausted and began to shoo the family out.

'These children are due at school,' she told her daughter, 'and you need to rest.'

'No, I don't. I have to go home. I thought I would get out today, but now they're telling me not until tomorrow at the earliest. It's the bump on my head they're concerned about, though of course it's nothing.'

Mary placed the palm of her hand across her daughter's forehead, in a gesture she had always used to soothe Jan as a small child.

'Nothing is important after an accident like that, child. You need to look after yourself. Get your strength. Annabel will be all right at the yard for a day or two, I'll have the little ones and your dad can drive them to school.'

Jan lay back on the pillows and closed her eyes.

'All right, Mum, don't go on. I'll try. I just wish I knew something about Eddie.'

Later in the day, after Jan had been moved out of the A and E department and into a room off a general ward 'for observation', she awoke from what was probably the deepest sleep of her life. Her bandages were now removed and replaced by smaller dressings, and she was beginning to feel more herself. Her face, although it was swollen, was otherwise surprisingly lightly damaged with, as Penny Pierson told her, no danger of any permanent scarring.

'Your skin will be pristine again in a few days,' the doctor said. 'The bruises will last a little longer, but I'd say you'll be at least presentable by the end of next week. It's just that bump on your head that we want to keep an eye on.'

'Please tell me how Eddie is. Is he bad?'

Dr Pierson studied her patient for a few moments, weighing up how much to divulge.

'Mr Sullivan's got problems,' she said judiciously. 'We're doing all we can for him.'

'What do you mean – problems? What problems? Is he conscious? Can I see him?'

The doctor shook her head.

'I'm afraid not. He's not fully conscious yet.'

'But I could *see* him, couldn't I? Just for a moment?'

'I don't think it's advisable, Jan. Not just yet.'

Jan knew it was pointless to continue the argument. Instead she broached the subject that had been nagging at her ever since she'd woken up in the morning.

'I vaguely remember there was another car – in the accident, I mean. Was it overtaking us? Or coming the other way? I'm still a bit muddled. Was there another car?'

'Jan, I'm just the doctor. But I can tell you someone else was brought in.'

'The driver of the other car?'

'He was apparently driving another car, yes.'

'And? How is he?'

Dr Pierson laid a hand on Jan's briefly, and said in a soft voice, 'I'm really sorry to say this, Jan, but he didn't make it. He was pronounced dead on arrival.'

'Dead on arrival,' Jan repeated dully.

'In fact, I believe he was killed instantly.'

'I see.'

Closing her eyes, Jan breathed deeply in and out, feeling the seat-belt bruises around her left collarbone. The life of a stranger cut off in an instant, and she had been there.

'Do you know his name?'

'No,' said Penny Pierson, 'and I don't think it's a good idea for you to worry about it. Don't make me regret that I told you, hey? You've got to be strong. Your family needs you at home, so don't go and make yourself worse.'

She stood up and bustled towards the door, but then spun round, reminded of something.

'Oh, yes, I forgot, there's a Detective Inspector Hadfield who's been wanting to see you. He called in this morning and said he'd be back this afternoon. Shall we stall him? I can get the consultant to tell him to go away if you like.'

Jan waved her hand, dismissing the idea.

'No, no, it's OK. Let him come in. I'd like to see him.'

*And find out what he knows*, she added to herself.

DI Brian Hadfield, of the plain-clothes branch, turned up within the hour. He tiptoed into the room, as if afraid to waken the occupant, though he could see Jan was awake and expecting him. He was of medium height, with a thatch of grey hair and blue eyes twinkling out of a ruddy complexion. A small uniformed woman constable was in attendance.

'Mrs Hardy, may I say what a fan I am of yours? That Irish National with Russian Eagle, what a finish. Great win.'

'Thank you,' Jan said mechanically. 'Would you like to sit down? How can I help?'

Jan tried to assess the policeman as he shifted the bedside chair into a position closer to her. He looked innocuous enough. But that 'what a fan I am' stuff was a warning sign. Maybe he really was a racing enthusiast. On the other hand, maybe he'd done a spot of research just so he could butter her up. Jan had never had anything against the police, but she was instinctively wary about a complete stranger paying her compliments, particularly a policeman.

'We're investigating the serious road traffic accident on Cleeve Hill last night – as you've probably guessed . . .'

He gave a slight hiccup of a laugh. Was he nervous?

'And obviously we want to know exactly what happened, so at some point we're going to need to take your statement about the incident.'

'My statement?'

She hadn't visualized this. She'd thought it would be DI Hadfield briefing *her* on what had happened.

'Yes,' he said. 'There's nothing to worry about. It's just your version of events.'

Jan hauled herself into a slightly more upright position in the bed.

'My *version*? I thought you'd come to tell me what happened. Now you're making it sound as if there's something suspicious, as if I did something wrong.'

Hadfield's cheerful face wilted slightly. He held up his hand.

'Oh, don't get me wrong, Mrs Hardy. You see, unfortunately a man has died: the driver of the other car.'

'I heard just before you arrived. I'm sorry.'

'You were in Mr Sullivan's car, the Morgan?'

Jan nodded.

'So the thing is – obviously – there now has to be a full police investigation, and as Mr Sullivan's in no state to speak to us, you're the only one who can throw any light on the situation at the moment.'

Jan frowned. Alarm bells were ringing. The truth was that she had not yet fully constructed her memory of the previous night. In fact, subconsciously, she'd probably been avoiding doing so. Her memory was still only jumbled fragments. And she was quite sure she shouldn't give Hadfield a statement consisting of fragments. She would have to be certain of the truth before she could tell it.

'I guess I'm still shocked – I did have a nasty blow on the head, you know. I can't really remember what happened fully. Not yet anyway.'

'Can't you tell me *anything*?'

He spoke gently, regretfully.

'Sorry, Inspector. I've got lots of rather fuzzy impressions, nothing concrete. It'll all come back eventually though, I'm told. The doctor will explain . . .'

🐎

The policeman had to accept Jan's polite refusal to give a statement, and he withdrew, tiptoeing out of the room in the same bizarre way he had come in. Later that afternoon there seemed to be a lull in ward activity. Jan was hardly breathing as she slipped out of bed and put on her dressing gown. She opened the door of her room and looked out: the corridor was deserted. She quietly crept out and headed for the stairwell. Holding the banister tightly, she went down one flight. Her legs felt weak and wobbly but they held her.

On the next floor she saw a sign with an arrow pointing to the intensive care unit. She padded in its direction, and after what seemed like an age came to the unit, which was entered by a pair of swing doors. Amazingly nobody challenged her as she eased her way through. Now she was in a corridor which ran past a suite of dimly lit rooms, furnished with beds that looked more like operating tables, each surrounded by batteries of high-tech equipment. Each interior could be seen from the corridor through a double-glazed window, although the rooms had slatted blinds. Some had been drawn shut on the inside. The patients' names were written on small cards posted on the doors.

She counted six rooms before the corridor was broken by the nurses' station. The first room was empty. The second housed a patient who was, as she could see through the slats, encased in bandages. She checked the name on the door, but it meant nothing. The third room was occupied by a female, but on the door of the fourth she found what she was looking for: 'Edward Sullivan'.

The blinds were lowered but not fully shut, so Jan could peer between them. The lighting was dim, but sufficient to give a view of the bed and the patient. He lay there, heavily bandaged around the head, arms and midriff, encircled by the latest electronic machinery and drip stands. His bare chest, rising and falling as he breathed, was the only movement he made. She could see the electrodes that fed the cardiograph machines and other monitoring devices. The black hair sprouting above the head dressing seemed like Eddie's. But this man had a huge head and face, a bulbous nose, bloated jowls and lips like frankfurter sausages. This man was not Eddie. Had they moved him and forgotten to change the name card? If so, where was he?

'Can I help you?'

A blue-uniformed nursing sister had bustled up without Jan noticing.

'Er, I don't know,' said Jan, startled. She instantly collected herself and indicated the intensive care room. 'Actually I'm wondering about Eddie Sullivan. I'm Jan Hardy and I was with him, you see, in the car.'

'Oh?'

'Well, see it's his name here on the door, but this isn't him. Can you tell me what's happened? Where is he? Have you moved him? Has he come round? Is he able to see anyone?'

The sister gave a faint smile.

'Oh, this is him all right.'

Jan jabbed a finger in the direction of the patient.

'*That's* Eddie?' she asked in disbelief.

'Large as life.'

'But it can't be.'

'Oh, no doubt his face looks a bit different from when you last saw him. It often happens after car accidents. I've had mothers in here unable to recognize their own sons. Don't worry too much, I can assure you his face will return to normal.'

Shocked, Jan studied the supine patient again, and now realized that it was indeed Eddie, his features so grossly distorted by swellings and a large haematoma as to be unrecognizable.

'He came off much worse than me, didn't he?' she said quietly. 'Is he unconscious?'

'Yes, I'm afraid so.'

'In a coma?'

'That's just a term for it, but don't be too worried. It's amazing how quickly young people can recover.'

'When will he wake up?'

The sister shrugged.

'You can never be sure. He's quite heavily sedated, but we think the signs are good.'

'So he'll make a full recovery?'

The nurse smiled again, a professional and practised smile, but comforting all the same.

'We take one step at a time around here, Mrs Hardy. The first thing is for him to be fully conscious. The doctor thinks he might, just might, come round in a day or so. Then we can reassess him.'

On her way back to her own bed, Jan began to have thoughts of a kind she had not entertained before. What if Eddie didn't come round? What if he stayed in a coma for years? What if he died?

As she climbed the stairs, Eddie's voice suddenly came back to her, as he gunned the spluttering engine of the Morgan. *I bloody love you, Jan Hardy.* Yes, he really had said that last night. And what was more, she'd said the same thing back to him, the only time she'd said those words since the death of her husband, John.

*Oh, Eddie, you stupid, stupid, irresponsible idiot! You didn't wear your seat belt and now look at you.* Silently she wept.

# 2

'God, I feel shit,' Jan whispered to herself early on Saturday morning. At eight-thirty the trauma specialist appeared in her room on his rounds. His manner was reassuringly decisive.

'Did you sleep well?'

'Not very. I feel like I've been run over by a steamroller.'

'But the headache's eased?'

Jan nodded.

'Good. How's your memory of the accident?'

'I've got most of what happened, I think, though not necessarily in the correct order.'

'That's quite a usual pattern. The pieces will slot into place sooner rather than later. In the meantime . . .'

He looked at the medical notes, asked a few more questions as to how she felt generally. Then he spoke to the nursing sister and scribbled something on the notes.

'Well, Mrs Hardy, I see no reason to keep you in. Go home. But you need to rest for a few more days. That can be done as easily there as here – more easily, maybe.'

'What about riding?' she asked.

'Riding? I wouldn't consider that resting, myself.'

Jan took him to mean that if *she* thought riding was resting, then she could go ahead and do it.

'Please could you tell me about my friend, Eddie? Yesterday he was still unconscious. Has there been any change?'

The doctor shook his head regretfully.

'No change overnight, I'm afraid. These things can be unpredictable, but I think we can say his condition has stabilized. We are still monitoring him closely and that's all I can say at the moment.'

It was one of Jan's stable lads, Joe Paley, Magic Maestro's work rider, who drove down in the Shogun to collect her. Despite a shaky start, Joe had proved to be one of Jan's most loyal members of staff.

''Lo, Mrs H,' he mumbled when she met him in the hospital lobby. 'I'm sorry for your trouble.'

It was the only mention he made of the accident. Joe was not a garrulous young man except when talking to, or about, horses. So on the way back to Edge Farm he let himself be questioned about the yard: how Maestro had come out of his race, the trouble they were having with Russian Eagle's foot, and the well-being of a possible future star hurdler, A.D. O'Hagan's Wexford Lad, who'd had sore shins. They were just coming to the prospects for today's racing and Jan's two runners at Uttoxeter when Joe turned off the road and up the track that led to Edge Farm Stables.

As they drove up the tarmac drive to the house, passing the newly completed stable yard, her heart lightened as she saw her three dogs, Fred, Tigger and Fly, come pelting out of the office to greet her. They were followed a split second later by the slender figure of her assistant trainer Annabel.

🐎

'I can't tell you what a shock it was,' said Annabel. They were sitting at the big kitchen table with mugs of tea.

'We didn't know anything until the police called, about nine-thirty, tenish. When you and Eddie didn't come home, we thought maybe you'd gone off to a hotel for a celebration dinner or something. You know, an impulse thing.'

'Dinner, *or something*? Bel, as if I would without phoning.'

Annabel giggled. Relief at the early return of her friend and boss had made her effervescent.

'Eddie would. I thought maybe he'd talked you into it.'

But the thought of Eddie quickly dampened their spirits.

'How is he?' Bel continued, sensing Jan's gloom.

'I saw him in the ICU. He's completely unrecognizable. Bel, *never* drive without wearing a seat belt. He's a complete mess: his nose is broken and his jaw. Everything in his face is huge; even his bruises have bruises. He's still out of it. I don't think they really know how badly he's hurt, I mean the extent of his internal injuries. I guess they'll wait until he wakes up . . .'

She let the sentence hang, but the unspoken words *if he ever wakes up* were understood between them. Suddenly Jan felt a welling up in her chest and her eyes prickled. Annabel reached for her hand.

'Are you OK? Come on, I'm sure he'll be fine. You know Eddie.'

Jan nodded, swallowing the emotion and taking a deep breath. She was not going to cry now. At least she was alive. Eddie was alive. That was all that mattered at this precise moment. The future was the future and she would climb whatever mountains came her way – she knew that also.

Jan rose briskly, ripped off a sheet of kitchen paper and blew her nose. 'Have you spoken to the Sullivans?'

'Yesterday morning. I couldn't tell them much because I didn't know much. So I just said Eddie's in hospital and we'd call them with an update later today.'

'OK, I'll do that in a minute. Now, what about Uttoxeter? I don't think I'm quite up to going racing, not with this face anyway. Can you cope?'

Annabel nodded.

'No problem. It's already sorted. I'm taking Roz and Con. The rest of the crew will be here, so there's no need for you to roll up your sleeves.'

Annabel had made a list of the well-wishers who'd called to ask how Jan was. Most of her owners had rung yesterday, after reading about the crash in their morning papers – Johnny Carlton-Brown, Bernie Sutcliffe, Lady Fairford, Colonel Gilbert and, of course, Toby Waller the banker, who was Jan's most constant loyal friend and adviser.

'What about A.D.?' Jan asked.

'Phoned last night from Switzerland. Wants you to call him as soon as you're well enough. If you can't get him, he says can you talk to Jimmy O'Driscoll at Aigmont.'

Jan wrinkled her nose. She didn't much care for A.D.'s racing manager, who ostensibly oversaw the huge equine operation that was centred on the billionaire's estate in County Wicklow.

'I'll call the owners later and reassure them,' she promised, 'when things are quiet. They're entitled to know what's going on.'

'Oh, and Tony Robertson called this morning. He said he'd be over to see you about four-thirty.'

Jan smiled. As her family doctor, Tony paid her rather more attention than might be expected of a busy GP. But then, he was also her most persistent suitor; he had asked her to marry him as recently as last Christmas. She liked the man. She even rather fancied him. But could she persuade herself to think of him as anything other than a friend?

On that question might hang her whole future.

🐎

Jan waved the horsebox off to Uttoxeter, then curled up on the sofa with the phone. First she called Eddie's parents in Queensland. His father Ron came on the line first.

'Wotcher, Jan,' he barked. 'You OK?'

'I'm all right, thanks, Ron. I just had a couple of nights in hospital, nothing too serious.'

'Good girl. Now what about my boy? Smashed himself up, has he?'

'I'm afraid he's not too well. He's still unconscious and it's impossible to say any more until he comes round. Hello?'

Muffled fragments of a tearful argument could be heard at the Sullivan end and then Sue Sullivan was speaking.

'Jan, Jan are you still there? Oh, good. Where exactly is Edward?'

'Cheltenham General, in the intensive care unit. Shall I give you the number?'

She rummaged in her bag and pulled out a bit of paper.

After Jan had recited the number, Sue continued, 'I'll be getting a flight over, but I don't know exactly how soon that will be. But be sure to tell Edward I'm on my way.'

Jan spent the rest of the morning working her way through the list of other callers. She spoke to Lady Fairford and Colonel Gilbert, assuring them of her basic well-being, and left messages for Johnny,

Toby and Bernie. At last she dialled the Swiss number that, so she had been told, would connect her with A.D. O'Hagan.

O'Hagan was a phenomenon. Thirty years before he had been a mere building-site hod carrier from Killarney. Now he was a big-time currency dealer, international poker player, and the owner of a string of more than fifty (mostly very expensive) racehorses, as well as the proprietor of a renowned stud. At first he had been a complete enigma to Jan, originally taking an interest in her after they'd met at the Doncaster Sales nearly four years ago, when she was an unknown trainer of point-to-pointers. Her early fears that A.D. might be just another chequebook Romeo had disappeared when she saw him with his beautiful opera-singer wife Siobhan, to whom A.D. was single-mindedly devoted. In fact, as Jan had gradually come to understand, single-mindedness was A.D.'s outstanding trait, and it had made him what he was today. He had made several fortunes by spotting opportunities that no one else could see, and then by watching them with all the concentration of a falcon on a field mouse. But oddly, though he had a raptor's eye, he did not have the manners of a predator. He was, in fact, unfailingly courteous and could on occasion be extremely generous.

But A.D. never relaxed his grip on his business interests, which included his racing operation. Although nominally the racing manager, Jimmy O'Driscoll was in reality not much more than an office boy, a glorified gofer. Leaving as little as possible to chance, A.D. gave his personal attention to the career of each and every one of his horses just as meticulously as he timed the trades he made on the world's financial markets. He also moved quickly once his mind was made up. With little evidence to go on but Jan's feat in successfully training one difficult hunter-chaser, Russian Eagle, he had decided to act as the guarantor in her application for a public trainer's licence. He had then got Edge Farm off to a flying start by sending her half a dozen good National Hunt horses.

Of course A.D. was a tough man to please. Jan knew that the Irishman had, at times, been more than a little disappointed by her yard's record with his horses during most of the current season. Apart from Galway Fox winning a two-mile hurdle in January, and Magic Maestro's fantastic performance two days before at Cheltenham, there had been little to put out the bunting for. As she dialled his number, she wondered what he would think of her capping their hard-earned victory at Cheltenham by almost getting herself killed in a car with Eddie Sullivan.

'Hello Jan. I'm on the golf course, so I hope you'll excuse me if I'm brief. You're all right?'

'Yes, I'm fine. I've probably suffered more damage falling off horses. I got away with a few scratches and a bump on the head. Eddie's badly smashed up, though.'

'Eddie again, is it? I'm beginning to regret I ever gave that young man the means to get back from Australia. When will you be back at work yourself?'

'I only got home a few hours ago, but I'm fifty per cent back already. It'll be a hundred per cent by next week. And as you know I've got the best team working for me, so you have no need to worry.'

'I never worry, Jan. Are my horses all right? What about Maestro after Thursday?'

'Never better, A.D. He's been demolishing his feed.'

'And Wexford Lad's shins?'

'On the mend.'

'Grand. Look after yourself, I'll be in touch soon.'

In the afternoon Jan dozed off and on and watched television in between. It was the Saturday after the Cheltenham Festival, and she reckoned racing was still suffering from a monumental collective hangover, which meant it was a perfect time to nick a couple of races when nobody was looking. She watched as her first runner, a strong, intelligent horse called Blue Boar, named after the owner's cordon bleu restaurant in Bath, ran well into third place. Two races later, after she had watched one of Virginia Gilbert's hurdlers prevail in a tight three-way finish, an old-timer whom Jan trained for Virginia's father Colonel Gilbert, Wolf's Rock, ran the race of his life to take the two-mile chase.

Jan was well aware that Virginia Gilbert did not like her, so she appreciated the colonel's gesture of friendship in keeping Wolf's

Rock with her instead of transferring the horse to his daughter's yard. Wolf had originally been regarded as a staying chaser in the making, but a breathing problem had restricted him to the shorter distances. He couldn't quite compete at top level with the two-mile specialists, but here, in a modest race run to suit him and on ground that had been softened by overnight rain, he was able to dictate the pace. Under young Luke Lacy, he powered over the last with four lengths in hand and held on to defeat the favourite's late thrust. Jan smiled at the cheering she heard emanating from the office, where her staff always gathered to watch the TV races: somebody had had a bet. She was pretty sure she'd seen the colonel and Annabel in the background during the televised paddock preview and, though she knew he was no heavy gambler, she hoped the old man had had at least a small bet himself. At twelve to one, it had not been a bad touch.

But Jan's mood of elation evaporated when, five minutes later, she opened the front door to be confronted by the smiling face of Detective Inspector Brian Hadfield. At his right shoulder was the small, thick-legged woman police officer she had seen before.

'Mrs Hardy,' said Hadfield with apologetic formality, 'may I say how very pleased I was when I telephoned the hospital to learn you had been discharged?'

He swayed around and gestured a little theatrically with his arm towards the stable block. 'And may I add what a delightful and impressive place you have here?'

'Thank you, Inspector.'

She decided it was best to be polite, though, if Hadfield's remarks had been intended to charm, they had had the opposite effect. 'What can I do for you?' she asked rather more sarcastically than she had intended.

'It's that little matter of your statement again, I'm afraid. I was wondering if the events of Thursday evening are a little clearer to you now.'

Jan suddenly felt weak and very confused. She put a hand against the door frame to steady herself, looking from Hadfield to his companion.

'I don't know . . . it's a bit of a surprise, you just pitching up. You didn't phone to say you were coming.'

'You see we were passing the end of your road and we thought: might as well drop in on the off-chance. You know how it is. My job's a bit like yours Mrs Hardy – a policeman's work is never done, as they say.'

She suddenly felt drained and light headed. She would not be able to make much of a statement, but she felt unable to fight Hadfield's smiling persistence.

'You'd better come in. Go right through.'

She stepped back and gestured them inside. As they filed past and disappeared into the kitchen, she realized that now a second car had drawn up outside the house, and bounding from it was Tony Robertson with his medical bag.

'Jan! For goodness sake, you're as white as a ghost. What's going on? Who are those guys?'

'Police,' she hissed. 'They've come to take a statement. They just turned up out of the blue.'

'About the accident? I don't think you look up to it, old girl. Want me to have a word?'

She hesitated, then gave a fractional nod of the head. Tony strode ahead of her into the kitchen.

'Look, I'm Mrs Hardy's GP.'

Hadfield, with his hands stuck in his trouser pockets, was deep in contemplation of Jan's pinboard, stuck with postcards, photographs of her horses in action, and the children's pony club rosettes. He swivelled round.

'Oh! How d'you do, Dr . . .?'

He pulled his right hand from his pocket as if to hold it out, but realized just in time that there was a chance Tony would refuse to shake it.

'Dr Robertson, Anthony Robertson, from Winchcombe. Now you know perfectly well, although I understand why you're here, that Mrs Hardy has been through a very traumatic experience—'

Hadfield tried to interrupt, but Tony held up his hand.

'Please let me finish. A very traumatic accident *less* than forty-

eight hours ago, and furthermore she has just returned from a stay
in hospital. So I really think it's inappropriate for the police to be
pressuring her to make a statement before she has fully recovered
her senses and strength.'

Jan stood there, with her back to the Aga and her fingers gripping
the towel rail, worried at the aggressive tenor of Tony's speech.
Nothing Hadfield had done really justified it. On the other hand he
bloody should have phoned to say that he was calling. Just for a
moment, he bristled with indignation. Then his shoulders dropped
and the smile returned.

'Fine, fine,' he said. 'I merely thought it might be easier for Mrs
Hardy here in her own home, you know.'

'It would be. But not now, not today, and not until I say she's
medically fit to talk to you. All right?'

Hadfield glanced at the constable and tipped his head towards
the door.

'We'll make ourselves scarce then, Doctor. Mrs Hardy, I'm so
sorry if you think we've been heavy-handed. That was not my
intention, I assure you.'

Was there the faintest insinuation in his voice, the merest hint
that he thought he had sensed something suspect about this patient–
doctor relationship? For a moment Jan thought there was, then she
told herself she'd imagined it.

'That saw them off,' said Tony in triumph as he closed the door
on the two officers.

*How very like a man*, thought Jan, as Tony took her blood
pressure, and questioned her about her sleeping and appetite.
Everything had to be win or lose, biff or be biffed. But she was very
grateful for the way he'd kicked Hadfield into touch, knowing she
would not have been able to do it on her own with such effect.

'Thanks, Tony, but you were a bit hard on the poor sod. He was
doing his job, if a bit clumsily.'

The doctor smiled as he folded away his blood-pressure monitor.

'I know. But I feel a compulsion to protect you, Jan. I feel so . . .'

Jan cut him off.

'Tony, please don't. Not now, this is a professional visit.'

He closed his bag of tricks.

'OK, you're right. But it's difficult. I'm wondering if I should go on being your GP, actually. Medical ethics and all that.'

Jan did not respond, but as she watched him drive away a few minutes later she was thinking about the problem that faced her. She didn't want to encourage Tony, but she couldn't decide which course of action was preferable. If she agreed to register with another doctor, would that tacitly acknowledge Tony's idea of their relationship? On the other hand, if she remained his patient, that might give him the same message. The rule-of-thumb formula, *if in doubt do nothing*, was not generally Jan's preferred way. But in this case she thought it was best.

Jan lay down on the sofa and dozed off, waking only when she heard cheering coming from the yard and somebody clapping. The horsebox had returned in triumph. She hurried as best she could out into the yard to congratulate everybody, but most of all the horses. Back in his stable, Wolf's Rock snorted and shook his head as she gave him a Polo mint. As he crunched appreciatively, she ran her hands up and down each of his legs to feel for any heat that would indicate he had taken a knock or somehow jarred himself up – though the latter was unlikely on the soft ground he had raced on today. He was sound, and there was nothing amiss with Blue Boar either. Relieved, Jan gave the horses one last kiss on the nose before bolting the doors.

'I saw Virginia Gilbert at the races,' said Annabel casually as they walked back to the office after evening stables. 'She was looking nauseatingly pleased with her hurdles winner.'

'She had two winners as a matter of fact,' said Jan gloomily. 'Another at Warwick. It's been quite a day for the Gilbert family.'

'Well, she couldn't resist making a snide remark aimed at you.'

'Oh? What?'

'Asked how you were, of course, in all sincerity, apparently – I don't think. Then she said: "And how's Eddie 'accident-prone' Sullivan?", making the apostrophes with her fingers in the air. So insensitive, so stupid. I wanted to spit.'

'That woman!' said Jan, patting Annabel's shoulder. 'She loves to gloat, but we mustn't let it upset us. We must rise above it. We've the dear old colonel to think of. He's been a very good friend to me unlike his daughter, and he's a fantastic landlord to my parents as well, you know.'

Jan knew this was an important point, and a paramount reason not to let the rivalry between herself and Virginia get out of hand. The cottage in which the Pritchards were tenants, and the few acres on which Reg ran some sheep ('Just to keep my hand in,' he insisted) were part of the Riscombe Manor estate.

'How *is* Eddie, though? Any news?' Annabel asked.

'I don't know, but I suppose he's holding his own as nobody's phoned me to say otherwise. I'll ring the hospital right now and get an update.'

When they reached the office Jan made the call, speaking to the ICU nurse's station.

'No change,' she told Annabel, as she disconnected. 'He's still out of it, I'm afraid.'

'Oh, the poor thing,' said Annabel, shaking her head slowly. 'Do you think he's going to be all right?'

Suddenly Jan, for the first time since the crash, felt brisk and strong. Something about the way Wolf had churned his way to victory inspired her.

'Bel, do you know? I'm going to stop being worried about him. I think he leads a charmed existence. Any day now he's going to wake up and ask for a glass of champagne. I just feel it – in fact, I *know* it.'

# 3

Jan had slept deeply enough with the help of some pills which Tony had prescribed for her, but she woke early, feeling a rush of anxiety that drove her out of bed and into her clothes before she realized she ought to be lying in and trying to rest. There were no 'days off' at Edge Farm, any more than at other racing stables, but even in normal times – and how she wished they could get back to those – Sunday was a more leisurely day. The staff clocked on two hours later than in the rest of the week and even the boss had a luxurious extra hour in bed.

On Sundays, only the horses due to run the next day or on a Tuesday would be given a canter. The rest generally stood in their boxes. The only other exceptions this morning were horses like Wolf's Rock and Blue Boar, who had raced the previous day. These would be led out to stretch their legs and ease their weary muscles, followed by a small trot to double-check that they'd come through their races in good shape. Jan had felt the two horses' legs yesterday, but she knew that problems could also develop overnight and it was this thought that had been nagging at her. No horse could tell you how it felt, but experienced horse people read the animal's state from numerous signs, often instinctively. Sometimes Jan surprised herself by being utterly certain that this or that horse was not right without being able to say exactly why she thought so, except that there was something about the animal. As often as not her intuition was based on little more than the look of the horse's eye, or the feel of its coat, but she was almost invariably right. Sometimes her hand picked up one of these early warnings even before her brain did.

It was twenty-past-six by the kitchen clock when Jan laced her boots and pulled on her coat. She took a last swig of tea from her mug and set off down the yard, with the dogs gambolling ahead of her. When she had first arrived at Edge Farm, almost three years before, the site was desolate. She had lived in a mobile home while her house was built on the foundations of the old demolished farmhouse. Her handful of point-to-point horses had been stabled in the semi-ruined stone barn. Now she had a roomy new house faced in golden Cotswold stone. The horses had new quarters too – a timber-built stable yard, with the walls faced with creosoted weather-boarding, arranged on the conventional pattern that had been used in racing for two hundred years and more: thirty-eight boxes, the tack room, feed store and office ranged on four sides of a square to form an enclosed, inward-looking quadrangle. Each box had the traditional door to allow the horses to look out as they wished. Jan's devoted builder Gerry had finished the last side of the square less than a year ago, topping off the building with a stately, centrally placed arched gateway surmounted by a weathercock facing towards the house, which stood in a slightly more elevated position on the hill.

Edge could not have been an easy holding to farm. Most of the fields sloped, rising in steepness to the top of a west-facing Cotswold escarpment, which was exposed to the weather but had a panoramic view across the valley. Beyond the stables, out on the hillside, were Jan's gallops. A good turf strip began in the top field and ran away just beneath the top of the ridge with another short strip of turf for Jan's run of schooling fences. She had recently added a new four-furlong all-weather gallop. Nearer to the house were half a dozen fenced paddocks, one of which contained a mini show-jumping ring with jumps of various coloured poles for Megan's use.

In two half-barrels, positioned on either side of the archway, the daffodils planted by Edge Farm's self-appointed gardener, Reg, shook and rolled with the wind. The weathercock swivelled on its axis, squeaking, as Jan unlocked the gate and walked to the centre of the yard. The stable doors had all been closed and securely bolted the previous night, but she could hear the horses nickering and pawing their bedding in anticipation as they sensed her presence. She was still some way short of a full complement. There were twenty-four boxes occupied, twenty-two by horses in training and the others by Monarch and Smarty, Megan's ponies. Jan knew that when she did fill the yard she would need more staff, but the whole enterprise had grown so naturally from its unpromising beginnings that she suddenly felt it was really good to be alive. This was her world. Apart from the love of her family and, if she was lucky one day, that of a good man, what more could she ask for?

It was around mid-morning when Jan rang the hospital. Eddie had not woken up calling for a champagne breakfast as she had predicted. In fact, Eddie had done nothing. He still lay there, 'out of danger', but not yet back in the land of the living.

Jan had seen Eddie's condition, and it was obvious he would not be coming out of hospital soon even after he woke up. And when he did, he would need a lot of aftercare.

'I think I'll go over to Stow, to Eddie's pub,' she told Annabel, who had arrived for work at nine. 'He's still paying for the room, which is a waste of money that he probably hasn't got in any case. I thought I'd settle the account and bring his stuff back here for the time being.'

Annabel looked at her friend doubtfully.

'Are you sure you're all right to drive? Why don't you let me take you?'

It hadn't occurred to Jan that driving might be a problem. She thought about it, then shook her head. Of course she was all right, she had to be. It was only like getting straight back on the horse that had thrown you.

'No, no, Bel. I'm fine, and you've got plenty of stuff to do here.'

A few minutes later Jan sat behind the wheel of the Shogun and turned the ignition key. The engine fired first flick, setting up a thunderous smoky roar and judder as she revved the engine hard to warm it up. She slipped it into gear and cautiously set off down the lane. There was no problem turning onto the deserted public road, where she confidently began to pick up speed.

After about three-quarters of a mile the road passed through a small wood and climbed steeply. Jan had still not seen another vehicle, but now, as she accelerated, she realized one was approaching fast from the other side of the summit. It came into sight, breasting the rise with the chrome of the radiator grille flashing, bearing down on her like a giant bird.

'Christ!'

Jan was suddenly seized by inexplicable panic. She braked and the tyres yelped as the Mitsubishi swerved to the right. The other car swished up to her and powered past, just missing Jan's wayward bonnet as she over-corrected and veered to the left. For a few seconds, just as she was breasting the summit, she was all over the road frantically wrestling with the steering wheel, until finally the Shogun came to rest on the grass verge, its nearside wheels a couple of feet short of a roadside drainage ditch.

She was breathing hard and her heart pounded so loudly it shook her whole body. The spot over her temple, where the bump had now almost subsided, was throbbing again. She sat in silence and thought about what had just happened. Both her vehicle and the other had been safely on their own sides of the road. There had been no danger whatsoever, except in her mind. But the sudden appearance of another vehicle had been so like the accident on Cleeve Hill that it had been shocking enough to make her lose control. Weak and trembling, she stayed in the driver's seat – she did not know for how long – her eyes shut but visualizing again the wreckage of the cars on Thursday night and Eddie's battered face covered in blood. After a while she opened the door and slid out. She walked up and down for a few paces, sucking in the cool spring air until her heartbeat returned to normal and the trembling stopped. Eventually she got back into the driver's seat, and with a determined effort to dismiss all her morbid thoughts, she drove on to the King's Head pub in Stow, where Eddie had been living.

When Jan arrived, she was invited into the manager Mr Whiteside's office. He was a trimly dressed man in his forties. When she explained her intentions, he replied, 'Yes, of course, Mrs Hardy, that will be perfectly all right. I had heard about the accident and was expecting someone to call.'

Reaching down beside his desk he yanked a rolled copy of the *Wessex Daily News* from his wastebasket and unfolded it to show

Jan the headline: JAN HARDY: FATAL TRAGEDY MARS DAY OF TRIUMPH.

'It's Friday's edition,' he went on. 'Everybody was very upset. Eddie's been rather a favourite around here, as a matter of fact. I do hope he's making good progress.'

Jan was too dumbfounded to reply immediately. She looked numbly at the bold-type letters. She had not foreseen that there would be publicity. Why had no one mentioned this article before now?

'Oh,' she said, as Whiteside's enquiry penetrated the fog she looked through. 'No, he's not really. I mean he's still unconscious, so from that point of view he's still not too well.'

'Oh dear. I'm so sorry, Mrs Hardy. It must have been a terrible ordeal for you. What a mercy you weren't badly hurt yourself.'

'Yes, thank you. I was very lucky, very lucky indeed. With Eddie, it's just a question of waiting till he comes round, you see.'

'Well, when he does, give him our best, will you? Now, here's the key to his room, and while you're packing his things I'll get his bill made up. He's paid up to the beginning of last week, so it's not a horrendous amount.'

Jan stood up and took the key.

'Do you mind if I keep the newspaper?' she asked.

🐎

Eddie's room was not one of the pub's four-poster suites, much vaunted in the publicity literature that she'd seen in the lobby, but a cramped, budget-priced single room with a low, sloping ceiling right under the eaves. The space had been carefully cleaned and tidied by the chambermaid, giving the illusion that Eddie was an organized, orderly person.

'Like hell you are, Eddie Sullivan,' Jan muttered under her breath.

She sat on the bed and opened the *Wessex Daily News* at Tim Farr's story. She read it, then read it again. Oddly enough, it did not torment her. It was like reading about something that had happened to someone else, not her and Eddie. But one detail did have a dramatic effect. The name of the other driver – the dead man – was

William Moorhouse. Until this moment she had been able to think of the man's death as something abstract, even though it had happened so close to her and so violently. But now she actually knew his name she thought about him differently, as a person with family, workmates and neighbours. William Moorhouse was a real person; now he was dead.

Slowly she refolded the newspaper and put it down, remembering why she was there. A large leather holdall was pushed into the narrow space between the top of the wardrobe and the ceiling. She stretched up and pulled it down, then set it open on the bed. She quickly packed Eddie's shoes and clothes, tucking in the alarm clock and the half a dozen paperbacks from the bedside table. Crossing to the basin, she swept Eddie's toothbrush, toothpaste, shampoo and shaving gear into his washbag, which she dropped into the holdall on top of the clothes, alongside a half-empty bottle of malt whisky she found on the window ledge. She could not help thinking about the physical associations of every object – the clothing that had touched his skin and still smelt of his aftershave, the brush his teeth, the bottle his hand – but she didn't linger over these thoughts. She worked swiftly and efficiently until the holdall was crammed full.

Jan looked about her once more. It was odd she'd found no personal papers, no chequebook or passport. She slid open the drawer of the bedside table, but saw only a few coins, a penknife and a packet of mints. She dropped these into the side pocket of the holdall and zipped the bag up. A final thought made her kneel to peer under the bed, where she immediately noticed a faint gleam of brass in the darkness. She lay flat, reached under and pulled out a black leather attaché case. Laying it on the bed, she tried the two sprung catches with her thumbs without success. The case was locked.

After trundling down the narrow, winding staircase, Jan thanked Mr Whiteside, paid Eddie's bill and handed the room key across the counter. The pub manager swivelled to hang the key on its hook, at the same time whisking an envelope out of the pigeonhole behind it. He flicked a glance at the address, turned back to Jan and handed her the letter.

'I nearly forgot this,' he said.

It was a blue airmail envelope, stamped in Australia, with a postmark ten days earlier and no return address on the back flap.

'It arrived on Friday morning, I believe,' Whiteside went on. 'Can I help you with those bags?'

Jan pushed the letter into her pocket.

'Thank you,' she said, picking up the attaché case and leading the way as the pub manager hauled the heavy holdall out into the car park.

As Jan drove away, the airmail letter began to loom large in her mind. Her affair with Eddie, if you could call it an affair, had started with a lot of flirting, as these things do, most of it on his side. But then, in Dublin, after Eddie had suddenly returned from his self-imposed exile with his parents in Australia, she had slept with him and the whole relationship became a more serious, more puzzling experience. For the first time they had acknowledged their mutual desire and Eddie had eventually even told her he loved her. But Jan still didn't know if he really meant it, any more than she could be sure that she truly loved him. The feeling was there, of course, but it was so unlike what she had felt for John Hardy. Now she wondered if her previous ideas about love and relationships applied to this one. Though her feelings for Eddie had not necessarily been better than her love for John, they were undeniably less inhibited and – she had to admit – far more erotic. But was their relationship also more brittle?

One Christmas Eve, long ago, as they drank wine and stuffed little Megan's stocking, Jan had whispered to John rather tipsily, 'You know, you're my man for life, not just for Christmas.'

It had been perfectly true at the time, but would she ever be able to say the same to Eddie?

These doubts were impossible to put out of her mind now there was the question of Louise. Jan vividly remembered how sick she'd felt on the morning she took the call from Australia, hearing the desperate girl begging to speak to Eddie, the hint of a sob in her voice. More shocking details had emerged in the course of that morning – Eddie's affair, the pregnancy, and Louise's absolute insistence that Eddie was the father were even worse. Afterwards

Eddie's abrupt departure for Sydney had come almost as a relief. Altogether he had been away for eight months, during which the baby was born, but there was no happy family life for Eddie. Louise had made it quite clear she had only wanted him around during the pregnancy and birth as an insurance policy; afterwards he was surplus to requirements. Worse still was Eddie's discovery that Louise – 'the slapper' as Jan thought of her – was notorious for sleeping around, and that the baby might not be his daughter after all. In the weeks before the accident, it had been decided that only a DNA test would resolve the matter. The result of this was anxiously awaited.

Edge Farm came into sight from the road, perched on its hillside and surrounded by green fields and white-painted railings. At the same moment, another fragment of Thursday night's jigsaw dropped jarringly into place. Moments before the accident Jan had taken a call on Eddie's mobile, a message left by Sue Sullivan, his mother, in Australia. 'I've got some very important news,' she'd said. 'Give me a ring as soon as you get a chance.' What news? Was it to tell Eddie the test result? If so, it hadn't happened as he'd had no chance to return the call before the crash.

Suddenly, Jan needed her children with her. She drove straight on past the end of the Edge Farm drive to Riscombe, where she picked them up and took them home.

🐎

The blue airmail letter was still in Jan's pocket as she settled herself in the chair beside Eddie's bed shortly after three o'clock that afternoon. A few minutes earlier the sister had greeted her with a serene smile.

'Eddie's doing well. He's been making noises.'

'Has he been *talking*?'

The sister shook her head.

'Oh no, not yet. But we do think he's turned the corner. He can hear you if you speak loudly enough.'

Now, as Jan watched Eddie's chest rise and fall in unison with his breathing, she wished she knew what, if anything at all, was going on in his head. None of the high-tech monitoring equipment stacked around him on trolleys, winking and humming, could tell her that.

'Eddie!' Jan said leaning forward to put her mouth close to his ear. 'It's Jan. Can you hear me? Your mum's coming over from Oz. She could even be here tomorrow.'

Jan straightened and studied his face, but saw no reaction. He lay still, eyes closed, bandaged hands lying outside the covers. She leaned down again, but spoke louder this time.

'Everyone at Edge has been asking for you. I got your stuff from Stow, from the pub. Your friend Mr Whiteside sends his best wishes. He said you were their favourite guest.'

There was still no discernible response.

'They obviously don't know you like I do. I even paid your room bill.'

Had his lips moved? She thought she'd seen the faintest twitch; perhaps it was her imagination.

'So that's a little matter of a hundred and seventy-five quid you owe me, Eddie Sullivan.'

This time she wasn't mistaken, she was sure. Eddie's lips were moving. They were forming words.

'What was that? Eddie? I didn't hear.'

She leaned right over him to catch what he was saying. It was the thinnest murmur, carried on the faintest breath.

'Try again, Eddie. I didn't get it.'

This time he put in more effort, though the words still seemed to be coming from another room.

'Tough luck, Jan Hardy,' he was saying. 'I'm skint.'

'Eddie. Oh, Eddie, you're awake!'

# 4

'Dec! What the *bloody hell* are you doing? Catch up!'

On Monday mornings the majority of the horses took light exercise, just walking or trotting. Relief about Eddie had at least given Jan a night of deep, satisfying sleep and she had awoken determined to ride out with her first lot. It felt wonderful to be out there on such a bright morning, with boisterous cotton-wool clouds chasing across the watery sun. She sat high on Supercall's broad back and had told Dec to trot Magic Maestro alongside so she could have a look at his action, but they kept lagging behind.

'Sorry, Mrs H,' said Dec as he came alongside. He had a grin across his face that would grate a carrot. 'I'll tell you what, it's just grand to have you back on form.'

Jan couldn't help smiling too.

'Don't be so cheeky, you little sod. Concentrate.'

Later, after the staff had scoffed their bacon and eggs in the kitchen, Jan scrubbed Matty's face for school and sent him off in the car with Megan and Fran. She gave a huge sigh and decided to go down to the office to tackle the heap of paperwork that had built up since last week. It was a job she disliked intensely, but it had to be done. She was half an hour into it when the phone rang.

'Mrs Hardy? Good morning, it's Brian Hadfield. How are you feeling today? Much better, I hope.'

This wasn't just the conventional greeting. It sounded like Hadfield really wanted to know how Jan was.

'I'm pretty well, thank you, Inspector. I'm back in harness now. Trying to forget about last week, and doing my best to get on with my life, you know?'

'Well, I hope you haven't literally forgotten about last week. I mean, I still need that statement from you – remember?'

'No, of course I haven't forgotten that.'

'Have you seen Dr Robertson today by any chance?'

'He said he'd drop round tomorrow morning sometime.'

'I fully understand his concern for you as his patient, Mrs Hardy, but could you discuss the urgency of this matter with him and call me back? It seems to me, if you *are* back at work, this might be a good moment for me to get the business of the statement out of the way and to let you concentrate on your horses, bearing in mind what Dr Robertson said on Saturday . . .'

Jan could see no point in delaying any further. Everything had become so much clearer and more positive to her now that she decided it was time to get on with it. Hadfield would have his statement eventually, so why not today? It was as good a time as any.

'I agree completely, Mr Hadfield. And as I feel so much better now, I don't think the doctor would have any objection. Why don't you come over later today?'

They agreed that Hadfield would visit the stables at two that afternoon.

Later in the morning Jan and Fran drove to the hypermarket four miles away, a weekly fridge-stocking expedition that they always made together. Jan particularly enjoyed the company of the house-keeper-nanny because she was the only person, apart from Reg and Mary, whom she could talk to about the children to her heart's content. Fran was a down-to-earth woman in her forties who took a keen interest in Megan and Matty's development.

'Matty got such a fright when he saw me in hospital on Friday,' Jan told her. 'Did he say anything to you on the way to school?'

'Oh, he's right as rain now, bless him. He and Meg were chatting about it quite normally, like it was an everyday event almost. You know how kids are – they soon recover. And you're hardly marked, you know, Jan, physically anyway.'

'I know, I was so lucky.'

The rest of the journey was spent chatting about the school as Fran reminded her of the social events in its calendar. Jan cringed and hoped she would be able to attend them all.

While Fran was queuing at the fresh-meat counter Jan was going round the tinned foods shelves. They needed sweetcorn, tuna and baked beans. She was hesitating between four or eight tins of beans when she heard a voice behind her.

'Hello, Mrs Hardy.'

The young man pushing the shopping trolley was familiar, but Jan couldn't quite place him. She glanced down at his shopping. Lager, frozen dinners, bacon, chocolate cereals – young bachelor stuff.

'Sorry, do I know you?'

'We met at your open day the year before last. Tim Farr, *Wessex Daily News*.'

The penny dropped instantly. Jan held her breath. She wanted to bollock him, but decided to temper her inclination.

'You . . . it was you who wrote that piece. Last week.'

'About your accident? Yes, that was me. How's Mr Sullivan?'

'He's better, thank you. Far from well, but certainly better than he was.'

'I'm glad.'

'Are you? Isn't it better news, from your point of view, if he's worse – and worse news if he's better?'

Farr looked uncomfortable.

'Mrs Hardy, there's a difference between what the paper reports and what I feel. Not all journalists are vultures, you know. At least, I try not to be.'

'I'm glad to hear it,' said Jan a little less sceptically. 'So you were there, on Cleeve Hill?'

'I was about twenty-five cars behind you.'

Jan turned back to the shelves and took down a four-tin pack.

'You got an exclusive then. Lucky you.'

'I wouldn't quite put it that way.'

'Well, you needn't look so hangdog and ashamed of yourself. It wasn't such a bad article.'

'The thing is, Mrs Hardy, I was going to call you, so it's quite a coincidence bumping into you here. I was wondering if you were aware of something. It's just that on Thursday night I had a chance to look at Mr Sullivan's Morgan at the garage they took it to, and I noticed the tax disc.'

He paused, as if to add more significance to what he had just said. But Jan couldn't imagine what this might be.

'Tax disc?' she enquired. 'So? All cars have them, you know. It's the law.'

'Um, I'm aware of that, but they're supposed to be fully paid up. Mr Sullivan's expired in December.'

Jan scowled at him.

'It must have been the old one you saw,' she spat out before she could regain her composure.

'But there wasn't another one, I'm positive. I looked. I was wondering if you knew whether he had in fact recently renewed his road fund licence.'

'Look, what are you trying to make out of this? I really don't think it's any of your bloody business, anyway.'

'Well, if Mr Sullivan was driving the car illegally—'

Jan snorted.

'Don't talk such damned rubbish. Of course he wasn't. Now, if you'll excuse me, I've got my shopping to do.'

She snatched another pack of baked beans, gave a sharp forward shove to her trolley, and left him in the aisle gaping after her.

❦

It was a few minutes after two as Jan spooned instant coffee into three mugs before adding hot water and milk. She shook half a packet of digestives onto a plate and carried the tray through to the living room, where a smug Detective Inspector Hadfield and his uniformed companion awaited her.

She was going to slide the tray onto the low coffee table, which was partly surrounded by the sofa and chairs, but it was already in use. DI Hadfield had placed a small battery-driven recorder there.

'I hope you don't mind this,' he said matter of factly. 'It's usual procedure nowadays, and it will help us put together an accurate statement for you to sign. I assume you prefer to do it this way. You do, of course, have the option of writing out your own statement of the events that took place on Thursday evening.'

Jan shook her head hastily and put the tray down on a chair.

'No, no, it's OK. I'd much prefer it this way.'

'That's good. It'll probably save time in the long run.'

As she handed round the coffees, she sensed it was obvious that the inspector also preferred to use the recorder since it allowed him to ask Jan questions. Jan sat opposite Hadfield, and he quickly got down to business.

'Now, let's just cover what happened prior to your leaving the racecourse. One of your horses had just won, I believe.'

'Yes, the Cathcart. Apart from the Irish National last year, it was the biggest win of my career.'

Jan told him about the success of Magic Maestro, and the celebrations in A.D.'s box afterwards. It was clear Hadfield was more interested in the latter.

'And you and Mr Sullivan were there in Mr O'Hagan's party?'

'Yes.'

'I imagine there was a fair amount of drink consumed. Champagne, was it?'

Jan could obviously see where this line of questioning was going.

'Yes, but Eddie didn't have any, well, hardly any. "A gnat's bladderful" was his exact expression, I think, when he offered to drive me home.'

'He offered?'

'Yes, it was his idea. He said it was my day and I should be able to celebrate it.'

'How long were you at the party?'

'Well, it didn't finish till some time after six, maybe six-thirty. I was popping in and out of the box. I had various things to do with the horse, getting him bandaged up before packing him off home with my assistant trainer and travelling head lad.'

'And they were?'

'Annabel Halstead is my assistant. The lad was Joe Paley.'

Hadfield asked Jan to describe the drive from the trainers' car park towards Cleeve Hill.

'It was dark. We were in Eddie's Morgan. It kept misfiring slightly, nothing serious, but I remember that quite clearly.'

'What age is the car?'

Jan shrugged.

'I wouldn't know. Old. But it is, or rather it *was*, his pride and joy. He tried to keep it in good nick.'

'What was the traffic like?'

'Most of the race traffic had dispersed by then, so the road seemed just about normal. Eddie was accelerating up the hill when a car appeared out of the blue coming the other way and going really fast. At the same time another car was overtaking us, going at a mad speed. That's when the crash happened.'

'I see. So you're saying there was a *third* car?'

'Yes. It was just passing us.'

'And are you saying then that this third car caused the accident?'

'I don't know, not for sure; but yes, I think so. It all happened so quickly, but I was aware of another car coming up behind, making the oncoming one swerve to avoid it. And at the same time Eddie's car was being bumped off the road.'

'He was *bumped*?'

'Yes, I reckon so. I think the overtaking car must have barged us in some way. Trying to make room to get through, I imagine.'

'What happened to the overtaking car after it barged you?'

'I really don't know. We were a little too distracted to notice.'

The woman police officer reached for a digestive while Hadfield scratched his head.

'So just to get this straight, you're saying that there was a *third* car, overtaking you very fast at the same time as the oncoming vehicle bore down on you from higher up the hill, but on its proper side of the road. And it was the overtaking car which forced the oncoming car to swerve and hit the tree. And at the same time you and Mr Sullivan were pushed off the road by this overtaking car barging into you.'

'Yes. That's how I remember it. You sound surprised.'

'Well, it's just that no one's mentioned this other car before, Mrs Hardy. It does sound like an extremely important detail – I'll look into it. Do you have any idea of the make of this third car?'

'A big car. Some kind of four-wheel drive, maybe?'

'Not a van or a small lorry?'

'No, definitely a car, but much bigger, I mean much taller, than us.'

Hadfield was taking notes energetically, the smile coming and going on his face as he concentrated.

'I think that's really all I can tell you,' Jan added, after watching him for a few moments. 'I was dazed for a while after that.'

Hadfield sipped his coffee and turned his ambiguous smile on her once again.

'There's just one more thing, Mrs Hardy. You say Mr Sullivan kept his Morgan in as good nick as possible, yes?'

'Yes, I would say so. Although the Morgan's not a cheap car to maintain and Eddie isn't that well off. He's only just come back from Australia and he hasn't a regular job or anything.'

'Did you know he hadn't paid his road tax, Mrs Hardy?'

Jan's heart thumped.

'No. No, I didn't.'

'And that his tyres were badly worn, well below the legal limit?'

'No, I certainly didn't know that.'

Holding the silence for a few seconds, Hadfield looked at what he had written, then snapped shut his notebook. He reached over and pressed the OFF button on the recorder, then stood up. Hurriedly the constable crammed the rest of the biscuit into her mouth, drained her mug and followed suit.

'We won't detain you any further now,' said Hadfield, still smiling as he picked up the recorder and handed it to the constable. 'Do call us if anything else occurs to you. In the meanwhile I'll have the interview typed up as a statement for you to sign.'

After Jan had shut the door on the two police officers, she turned and flopped back against it with her eyes tight shut. She felt as if she had been interrogated. Those last two questions had shaken her. On Thursday night Eddie was driving an illegal car and the tyres were bald. She could easily guess the thoughts behind *that* particular fact. What if the Morgan had had a blowout? What if Eddie was actually responsible for the crash and the death of the other driver?

The door bell rang nerve-janglingly above her head and she jumped. Opening the door again, she found Hadfield's constable standing on the step, carrying a plastic bin bag. She held it out to Jan.

'Sorry, Mrs Hardy. We almost forgot this. It's Mr Sullivan's effects – we recovered them from the car.'

Jan took the bin bag through to the kitchen and emptied it on the table. There was a small tartan travelling rug, the Morgan's service log, a battered road atlas, Eddie's cloth cap, an umbrella, a tin of toffees and his mobile phone. She shook the plastic bag and one last thing dropped out, a key ring with the Morgan's ignition key, among various others.

Jan picked them up and weighed them in her hand, wondering.

A few minutes later Eddie's attaché case lay open on the kitchen table beside the heap of stuff from the car. It had not been hard to identify the small key which would open it. Jan felt that she was prying, but the need to know was stronger than her integrity at that precise moment. Had Eddie renewed his road tax? Was he even insured? She needed to know, for God's sake. She hunted through the old envelopes and scruffy papers, finding a few unopened bills, Eddie's passport, and a book of travellers' cheques in Australian dollars. At last she came to a brown envelope containing Eddie's motoring documents. The car registration was there, but there was no hint of a tax disc, and the MOT was hopelessly out of date. At last, she turned over the insurance document.

It confirmed her worst fears. Unless Eddie had fixed something up verbally in the last few days, it did not look as if he had renewed the policy when it expired five months earlier. Jan knew that it was a criminal offence to be driving uninsured, and obviously you were in dire straits if you got involved in a fatal accident. Would this lead the police to prosecute Eddie for the death of the other driver? Would they prejudge his guilt?

Something else about the way Hadfield had behaved was bugging her. When he questioned her about the third car overtaking, he had almost seemed to disbelieve her. Now it occurred to her for the first time how much they needed to identify that third car. Without it Eddie was going to have to take the whole blame for the accident full on the chin, for the wrecked cars, the injuries and, far worse, the death of an innocent man.

# 5

'I didn't know why I'm here,' said Eddie in a low, faraway voice. 'They had to tell me. The last thing I remember is that Magic Maestro won the Cathc—, the race. Unless I dreamt it.'

It was the middle of the morning, which had begun with Jan riding out first thing. She had then driven the children to school and kept on driving to Cheltenham General Hospital, where she found that Eddie had been brought out of the ICU to an observation ward. There were five other beds, three of which were occupied by immobile, heavily bandaged patients.

'No, you didn't dream it,' she said. 'A lot's happened since then so it does seem a bit like a dream, even to me. But he won the race all right.'

'Is he OK?'

'Yes, Eddie, he's fine. It's you we're concerned about at the moment.'

'Well, I do seem to have smashed myself up a bit. You look OK, though.'

'I had a couple of nights in here. A few cuts and bruises. But I was luckier than you.'

'I suppose the car's gone for a Brighton?'

'Gone to Brighton? What on earth for, Eddie?'

'No, the car, is it . . . smashed up?'

'Did you mean "gone for a burton"?'

'That's what I said.'

'No you didn't. You said "gone for a Brighton".'

'If you say so. But what about my *Morgan*?'

There was impatience in Eddie's voice. He looked at her quizzically.

Jan shook her head. 'I don't know. I'll try and find out.'

Eddie rolled his heavily bandaged head from side to side on the pillow. He grimaced.

'You all right?' Jan asked, concerned.

'No, my bloody head aches like a bastard.'

'I'll ask the nurse for some painkillers.'

'Forget that . . . the thing is I want to know the store. They're not . . . *telling* me anything, you see.'

'What are they not telling you, Eddie?'

'What's really wrong with me, how badly I'm messed up. I know I can't talk properly, keep making mishaps, misshapes . . .'

'Mistakes?'

'Yes. And I've got this permanent blinding headache and there's more . . .'

'Yes, Eddie, what more?'

'I can't move.'

'Of course you can't. They've got you immobilized.'

'Yes, I know. But, Jan, I can't even waggle my toes.'

🐎

'At first I thought he was all right,' said Jan half an hour later to Dr Matthews, the trauma specialist.

'But later he seemed worse?' he prompted. 'He probably got tired. That's normal. He will tire very quickly for the time being.'

'Talking to him's peculiar. He makes weird mistakes with words. Just now he said "gone for a Brighton" instead of "gone for a burton". Oh, and another one, "I want to know the *store*." He doesn't even know he's doing it. It's surreal. But what's more worrying is that he says he can't move his toes. He's afraid he's paralysed.'

Dr Matthews had a file open in front of him containing Eddie's medical notes. He consulted it for a moment, turning over two or three pages before unhooking his half-moon spectacles. He gave Jan an understanding smile, though his eyes were serious.

'Eddie has a fractured skull, Mrs Hardy, which will heal. But he also has a brain injury, which may take a little more time. If you want me to get technical, it's likely to be an acceleration-deceleration trauma, which is when the head is moving rapidly and then is stopped by something.'

He demonstrated by punching his right fist into the palm of his left hand.

'It's typical of a car accident. The brain whacks against the front of the skull, then recoils to hit the back. There'll certainly be bruising to the cerebral cortex. And a part of the brain called the temporal lobe, below the cerebral cortex, can be actually punctured by slamming into bony projections on the inside of the skull. There could be some particular areas of bleeding. So I'm not surprised he has a "bloody headache", as he put it and we would expect some degree of cognitive, behavioural and even motor dysfunction.'

'Which translated means?'

'Oh, sorry. What I mean is dysfunction of his mental processes, for instance, when memory and word selection are impaired. There could be some noticeable behavioural changes too. And motor dysfunction means that certain movements could become difficult, or restricted, as in the case of Eddie's toes.'

'So he *could* be paralysed?'

'It's much too early to say anything like that, Mrs Hardy. But the symptoms of traumatic brain injury can indeed mimic those of a stroke, including some degree of paralysis. On the other hand, Eddie also has a number of broken bones and other problems, which might include spinal injury. Obviously that could affect his lack of movement, so it's all going to have to be fully investigated.'

'How do you mean, investigated?'

'We'll have to arrange for scans and some other tests in a day or two. In the meantime the best thing we can do is to reassure him.'

🐎

Jan did some essential shopping in Cheltenham and had a quick sandwich for lunch at a coffee shop. Then, at Hadfield's invitation, she called at the police station to view her typed-up statement. It accurately reflected what she had told Hadfield on Sunday and she signed it. By two in the afternoon she was back in the hospital and at Eddie's bedside with magazines and fruit. But she could say nothing reassuring about the car. She had been to the garage and seen the wreck for herself.

'I'm afraid the Morgan's going to need completely rebuilding, at least the front end. New engine, the lot. I've been to the garage and that's what they told me.'

Eddie seemed unworried by the news.

'Oh well. Ins— in-sur-ance will pay up.'

He spoke the long word carefully, picking his way through the syllables.

'Will it?' Jan said. 'I'm not sure you had any.'

'Of course I did.'

'You may have had once, but I can't find anything that says you were covered last week. In which case the Morgan was uninsured and, what's more, the road tax and MOT were out of date and the tyres were nearly bald.'

'Nothing but problems!' Eddie groaned.

'Yes, problems. It seems the whole car was illegal, Eddie, and shouldn't have been on the road at all.'

'What about the in— the insurance?'

'Eddie, I've just told you. You didn't *have* any insurance.'

Eddie worked on the puzzle for a few moments, but eventually gave up the struggle. He shut his eyes and let his mind drift.

'I can't wait . . . to get back behind the wheel of the old car,' he said dreamily. 'Lower the top, wings in my hair.'

'Wind.'

'Sorry?'

'The usual phrase for when you're driving an open car: "wind in my hair".'

Eddie frowned and opened his eyes to stare at her, as if he suspected she was having him on.

'Yes, I know that Jan. What are you talk— talking about?'

She took his hand and stroked it.

'Nothing, Eddie. Wings are more poetic, anyway.'

Now he was looking back at her completely nonplussed.

'Never mind, Eddie, it's not important. You were talking about your beloved car.'

His bewilderment dissolved into a contented smile as he lan-
guidly closed his eyes again.

'My lovely Morgan, yes, the love of my life,' he whispered.

Jan leaned forward.

'Do you know something, Eddie Sullivan? You said I was that.'

'What?'

'You said you loved *me*. Just before the accident. But you don't
remember, do you?'

Jan kissed his forehead and got up to leave. If she hurried she
could be back at Edge in time for evening stables.

🐎

Jan's tour of the yard was an important part of the daily schedule at
Edge Farm. Once all the boxes had been mucked out, the horses
would be thoroughly groomed and their feet greased by the lad
or girl whose job it was to look after them. The bedding would
be refreshed and carefully spread around the stable floor, with the
walls banked about two foot higher. Jan and Annabel would go
from box to box, where the horses were 'stood up' wearing just
a head collar, their bodies stripped for a thorough inspection, to
decide on the exercise they would be doing the following day
and discuss their food rations.

Jan was particularly keen to have a look at Russian Eagle, who
held an entry in the Aintree Grand National, which was due to be
run in eleven days. After winning the Irish National at Fairyhouse
last spring, he was Jan's most prominent horse, and the obvious stable
pick of the big race. More than that, he was in with a big chance.

In assessing her horses' condition Jan relied on her eyes and,
equally as much, her hands. She looked into Eagle's eyes and
nostrils, then squeezed the top of his neck. She moved around him,
rubbing her hand along his ribcage and the top of his back and loins
– it was always her left hand, which she held loosely – gliding up
and down each of his legs, feeling for the slightest bump and any
sign of heat or tenderness. Over time, her hand seemed to form a
memory. Imprinted with information, it swept over each horse. She
was accomplished at detecting anomalies, or a slight variation from
what was normal for that animal.

Eagle had eaten up all his feed and was in pretty good all-round shape. Jan's hand detected nothing wrong with his legs.

'He's still a bit burly, we'll give him a good gallop in the morning. Finbar's coming over to ride out.'

Annabel made a note on her clipboard. Finbar Howlett would be partnering the horse at Liverpool and, since he had not ridden him before, this would give the two of them a chance to get acquainted. Jan rubbed Eagle's nose and broke a large carrot in two halves, which he crunched appreciatively. With a final pat on the neck, she left his box and moved on to the next.

The yard, in fact, had two Grand National entries. The second was Arctic Hay, who was one of the longest-standing residents of Jan's yard, although never one of its stars. His owner, the Brummie scrap-metal dealer Bernie Sutcliffe, had insisted Jan enter him, even though she told him the horse would have little chance.

'The National's a bloody lottery anyway, ain't it?' he had argued back in January. 'Or so I am led to believe.'

'Bernie, that's bollocks. Most years the race is won by one of the better horses. We all know that jump racing has an element of chance, and the National has more of it than most because it's four-and-a-half miles with a lot of runners and huge fences. It's not easy to be sure in advance if a horse will be suited to it or not. Of course, the chance is lessened if you have a good jumper.'

'So take the chance. I've got a feeling he might go well.'

Jan sighed with indignation.

'Bernie, the National's a uniquely demanding test. We'd be throwing Arctic Hay in at the deep end; he's an old horse and he might not appreciate it, quite frankly.'

'He *might*. As you said, we won't know till we've tried. And, remember, I'd still be the owner of that Russian Eagle if I hadn't kindly sold him to young Annabel – now he's one of the ante-post favourites. It bloody hurts when I think about that. Having my own runner will make me feel a bit better.'

Bernie had been determined to have his day out at Aintree – so Jan had no choice but to indulge him. She would never have agreed if it meant putting the horse at risk, but Arctic Hay was a wily old campaigner and a sound jumper. If he could keep out of trouble in the cavalry charge to the first fence, Jan thought he had a reasonable chance of getting twice round the Aintree track safely. Slowly, but safely.

Jan gave as much attention to Arctic Hay as she had to Russian Eagle, and she could find nothing amiss.

'You deserve your chance,' she told him, rubbing his muzzle before giving him a carrot.

Toby Waller, an old school friend of Eddie's, had for long been one of Jan's confidants, and had helped her out of more than one difficulty. He was a rich young man, not super-rich, but well used to handling large sums of money, both as the son of a wealthy family and as a successful merchant banker in his own right. He also happened to have a very cool, shrewd head on his shoulders, at least in matters of finance and the law. So when he rang later to enquire how both Jan and Eddie were, she realized he was just the person to unburden herself to.

'Toby, you're not free tonight, by any chance?'

'Well, yes, I could very easily be,' he said. 'And, if it's for you, I already am. Are you coming to town?'

'God, no. Don't be silly, you know how I hate it. I was wondering if I could tempt you down here and we could have dinner. I desperately need a sympathetic ear.'

It was rather a naked appeal, but Toby understood perfectly.

'Into which you will pour your woes?' he said. 'I'd love to and what's more . . .'

She heard him turning the pages of his diary.

'I don't have any meetings tomorrow morning, at least nothing that can't be postponed. So, that's settled. I am inveigled. Shall we say eight-thirty in the Fox?'

Toby was single and did not have a girlfriend, or at least not one he owned up to. He was tangle-haired and tubby and held not a shred of sex appeal either for Jan or Annabel. Jan welcomed this because it made his loyalty and friendship even more valuable, something solid and uncomplicated. For Annabel, the matter was slightly different. Toby had been distantly and pessimistically in love with her for years, but Annabel was well used to the type of man who blushed like a postbox and lost the power of speech when he came into her presence. But she treated Toby as he was – one of the nicest of the breed she had ever met.

The village of Stanfield, a brisk twenty minutes' walk from Edge Farm, was lucky in its pub. The Fox & Pheasant had long practice in hospitality, having provided beer to thirsty travellers and farm workers since the reign of Charles II. It had a few clean, comfortable rooms for overnight accommodation and provided proper country fare.

When Jan arrived, Toby was already perched on a bar stool, in heated discussion with a group of locals about football. He leapt down and greeted her with a big hug.

'What shall we have?' he asked, as he ushered her into the dining area. 'A bottle of the bubbly stuff, I think, to celebrate your good fortune.'

'Good fortune? Is that what you call it?'

'Yes, Jan, I do. You're unscathed, thank heaven. By all accounts it was a dreadful crash.'

'Yes, it was. But Eddie—'

Toby held up his hand.

'We'll talk about Eddie later. Let's deal with you first. Are you really all right?'

'Yes, I'm fine. I was wearing the seat belt, so I didn't hit anything and, miraculously, nothing hit me except broken glass. Mind you, my boobs are rather bruised.'

'So no breakages?'

'Only to my peace of mind. But then racehorse trainers don't get much of that at the best of times.'

'Well, for someone who's had windscreen glass showering into them, you look wonderful. Now, that drink.'

Toby went back to the bar, ordered a bottle of Dom Pérignon, and returned with two menus.

'A big steak for me, I think. I'm starving. What about you?'

Jan chose poached salmon with a side salad. While they waited for the food they sipped the chilled champagne, as Toby told her about his recent week's fishing on a stretch of the river Tay in Scotland.

'It never ceases to amaze me how some blokes just have to spit in the water and a bloody great salmon rises to it.'

'Did you catch anything?'

He shrugged.

'A grayling or two. But who cares? What I really like is standing in my waders in the gurgling stream, hundreds of miles from debentures, corporate bonds and scrip issues. It's pure therapy. Talking of which, how are my horses?'

Jan looked vague and didn't answer. It was obvious to Toby that her mind was only half engaged, when normally she was completely focused on her work.

'OK, Jan,' he said after a few moments. 'Tell me what's on your mind. It's about Eddie, isn't it?'

'Yes. I think he's in real trouble, Toby.'

'So I gather. But at least he's awake.'

'Yes, thank God for that.'

'I can just imagine him lying there, wrapped up like Rameses II, with tubes going in and out and a face like a half-eaten sherry trifle.'

The image made Jan snigger.

'Stop it, Toby. Don't mock the afflicted. The poor chap's badly hurt, with head injuries and God knows what further down.'

'Further down?'

'I mean his spine, idiot. At the moment they don't know how bad it is.'

'But bad on what scale?'

'On a scale from making a full recovery, and being able to ride a horse with all his old panache, to being stuck in a wheelchair for the rest of his life.'

Toby became more serious.

'I see,' he continued. 'That bad. I'm really sorry.'

'Anyway, when I say he's in trouble, I'm not just talking about his health.'

She told Toby about the conversations with Tim Farr, Hadfield's reference to the Morgan's bald tyres and her own researches in Eddie's attaché case.

'I felt awful poking around amongst his private things, but I had to. He had motor insurance documents all right, but they expired some time last summer.'

'I see. And there was no sign that he'd paid the road tax or had the MOT done?'

'None whatsoever. In the meantime, the police are investigating the accident further.'

'I think you'd better tell me about what happened that night, and I mean every little detail you can remember.'

She described it as fully as she could, beginning with A.D. O'Hagan's celebration party and ending with her waking up in hospital the next morning. Then she handed him a copy of the statement she had signed for Inspector Hadfield, which Toby read carefully.

'Given what you've told me,' he said, handing back the sheet of paper, 'this statement seems reasonable. Anyway, the important thing is that you're in the clear. You were a passenger and in no way responsible for anything that happened. I imagine the police are interested in Eddie, though, and they may prosecute him for driving an untaxed, uninsured and perhaps unroadworthy car. I don't know how bad that can be in legal terms, but it's certainly made far worse by the fact that there was an accident and that a man died. They will also have been very interested as to how much he had to drink at A.D.'s party.'

'But Eddie wasn't responsible. It was the driver of the other car, the one that overtook us – it caused all the mayhem. It's him they should be looking for.'

'Oh, they will be. You can be sure of that. But it all happened very quickly in the dark. Do you know if there are any independent witnesses who saw this other car, the four-wheel drive?'

'Which I'm now pretty sure was a Range Rover.'

'The Range Rover, then?'

'No, I don't. But the journalist I mentioned – Tim Farr – he might, I suppose. He was behind us on the road and it may have passed him. Or he may have spoken to other witnesses who saw. Apparently he stayed around at the scene for quite some time.'

'Right. I think it might be worth having a word or two with Mr Farr. Can you face it? I would do it, but you already know him, so—'

'Yes, I'll be all right doing that.'

'Has Inspector Hadfield said anything about an inquest?'

Jan hadn't thought of an inquest. She shook her head, new panicky thoughts whizzing through her mind.

'No, no, he never mentioned it. Will I have to give evidence?'

'Possibly. When you next speak to Hadfield, I suggest you ask him. Or you could contact the coroner's office directly, if you prefer. In the meantime I'll have a word with my solicitor. The drink thing may not arise because, as Eddie was unconscious for three days, he can't have given a blood sample for testing. But it's best we know the worst they can fling at him.'

'Eddie's mother's due to arrive from Australia any time now and . . .'

She was on the verge of telling Toby about Louise and her baby daughter, but she held back. This was Eddie's secret, not hers.

'Well, it's just that I'd like to be able to put her in the picture if I can.'

Toby smiled, creasing his fleshy, well-fed jowls. His eyes had the sparkle of a supreme optimist.

'Look, don't worry, Jan, I promise I won't hang around. I'll make that call tomorrow. Now drink up your champers and let's order pudding. I thought we might have a nice dessert wine to go with it.'

🐎

Getting ready for bed, Jan felt intensely grateful that she had friends like Toby. There had been many moments since John's death when she had been isolated, a woman in a man's game, a pauper in the world of the rich. But she had never actually felt lonely – with such good friends and family behind her, how could she?

A while later, as she was lying in the dark drifting off to sleep, the bedside phone rang sharply. Jan jerked awake and fumbled for the light, squinting as the room came to life. It was eleven o'clock. Instead of letting the answering machine take the call, she grabbed the phone, thinking the caller might be Sue Sullivan arriving from Australia.

'Hello?' she said.

There was silence, no one answered.

'Hello, hello . . .'

Still no one spoke. Jan tried a third time.

'Who's there? Hello, who is it?'

Getting no response, she hung up, turned off the light and lay staring into the darkness. It was extremely unsettling: either the caller wanted to speak to her but for some reason couldn't get through, which was tantalizing enough at this hour; or it was a wrong number. Or perhaps there was someone who deliberately wanted to frighten her. If so, they had been successful.

She waited for the phone to ring again. She was awake now, her senses and nerves fully alert. She gulped water from the bedside glass, composed herself and fifteen minutes later she was convinced the call was a wrong number.

Until it happened again.

'Hello, who is this?' she gasped, her throat so tight she almost choked.

This time she was positive she could hear background noises, a car sweeping past, or wind in trees, or maybe just someone breathing. Whatever it was, there was definitely someone on the other end of the line now, she was certain.

'Look, speak now or I'll hang up. And I won't pick up the phone again.'

# 6

As a faint ribbon of light appeared along the heights above Edge Farm and the morning routine of the racing stable began to unfold, Jan's common sense reasserted itself. The anonymous phone calls must have been a wrong number, she told herself. There had been no heavy breather. Just a hiss on the line.

At five to six the staff began arriving to muck out. Roz Stoddard and her sister Karen had already been in since five-thirty, going round the boxes with a small morning feed, checking the manger and water pots and that the occupants had come through the night without mishap. Annabel had driven up, looking her usual stylish self, and giving a lift to Emma, one of Jan's local stable lasses. Declan and Connor, having moved from the old caravan into a room in the village, arrived on a pair of violently rattling old bikes that they had persuaded Jan to buy for them. The two Irish lads rarely communicated with anyone first thing in the morning except in grunts. It was not until they got up on a horse's back that their good humour returned and the banter started. They were followed by the local boys Darren and Tom, rider and pillion on Darren's scooter, and finally on foot by Joe Paley, who was his usual five or ten minutes late.

Wednesdays and Saturdays were work days, when those horses in full training were given a serious gallop to test their wind and stretch their muscles to the limit. The amount of work Jan gave her horses depended to some extent on their physique but also on their temperament. Some horses were grafters and soaked up as much exercise as she cared to give them. Others would sulk if she galloped them a single furlong further than they liked. This did not apply to either of her Grand National horses, and she had planned to work them together this morning, with Arctic Hay's rider weighing a stone less than Russian Eagle's, just to even things up.

With minutes to spare before seven, the time Jan's first lot always pulled out, Finbar Howlett drove up to ride out the big horse.

'He gave me a great feel, Mrs Hardy,' said Finbar, as they walked back into the yard, where the jockey slipped off the horse's back. 'Fantastic long stride he's got. He should fly the big Aintree fences.'

'He already has,' said Jan. 'I want you to look at the video of his Foxhunters' before you go. He jumped Valentine's like a pole-vaulter that day.'

In a more modest way Arctic Hay had done his stuff, too, but had been predictably unable to match Eagle's loping stride and finished ten lengths behind.

After breakfast Jan settled Finbar down with the videotape showing the Foxhunters' Chase of two years earlier, when Russian Eagle had been ridden by Eddie and damn near won the race. Then she phoned the hospital. Eddie, it seemed, was feeling better. His headache had eased and he was speaking more coherently. She decided to drive down to visit him at midday, and then go straight on to Chepstow, where Teenage Red, owned by the rock group Band of Brothers, was to run in a bumper and Penny Price's Arrow Star had an engagement in the three-mile chase.

She decided to take the Australian letter with her. She would have to judge whether Eddie was in a fit state to talk about his possible child in Australia; at some point he would have to face up to this. But when she arrived on the ward any thoughts of solving the problem vanished. Sitting beside Eddie's bed was the slim, upright figure of a woman in her early sixties: Sue Sullivan.

The greeting Eddie's mother gave Jan was poised perfectly between the kiss of near strangers and the enthusiastic hug you might give to a family member.

'I flew into Heathrow early this morning and hired a car,' Sue Sullivan said. 'I was just going to phone you. I can't tell you how grateful we are to you for looking after Edward so brilliantly.'

Her tone was bright, but there was an edge to it that revealed the strain she was obviously feeling.

'It's not a problem. I know he would have done the same for me. But you must be very tired, Sue.'

'I must confess I am a bit. It's such a long flight. But I was desperate to see my boy.'

'Well, look, I've got to go on from here to Chepstow racecourse. We've got a couple of runners there. But, please, go back to Edge and rest. I'll phone my housekeeper, Fran, to let her know you're coming, and she'll make up a bed for you. That is, if you don't mind Megan's room. I haven't got a spare.'

'Jan, you have plenty to deal with, don't mind me. I can stay in town – there must be a hotel that's reasonable.'

'Sue, I wouldn't hear of it. You're staying with us.'

'Well, that is really kind of you.'

Jan dragged up a chair on the other side of the bed and gave Eddie the latest news from the yard, what little there was. He questioned her about a few things, still speaking deliberately, but already hitting fewer wrong words. Amongst other things, she mentioned Russian Eagle's good work earlier in the morning.

'Yes, Russian Eagle,' said Eddie, giving the impression that a particle of memory had just dropped into place. 'I'm riding . . . riding him in the National, aren't I?'

'What, you? Don't be silly. Finbar's on him.'

'No, I am. I'm his jock, his . . . jockey. And I'll be up and about in a couple of days. I won't have any . . . problem doing the weight. I've hardly eaten a thing, it's such crap they feed us here.'

'Eddie, you're *not* riding him. Not this time.'

Jan and Sue exchanged a rueful smile at Eddie's wind-up.

'Jan! *I'm* riding him, OK? That's . . . my . . . bloody horse and I'm bloody riding him.'

Jan was shaken. She now realized this was not meant to be a wind-up, Eddie was genuinely agitated.

Sue took his hand and stroked it in a motherly way.

'Darling, you're too badly hurt. You can't ride in any races at the moment, Edward. You've been in a car crash.'

'Yes, I know I've been in a *sodding* car crash, Mother. I *know* what happened. All right?'

Sue Sullivan was astounded by her son's vehemence, and even more startled when she saw tears welling up in his eyes.

'Hey, Eddie,' said Jan, 'it's OK. It's OK. You're going to be fine, though it may take a little longer than a couple of days. You will just have to be patient.'

Eddie was breathing hard and looking in turn from Jan to his mother, swivelling his glistening brown eyes from side to side, as if it was too painful to move his head.

On a sudden impulse, Jan added, 'Tell you what, though. You can ride Eagle in next year's National. I promise you'll be fit enough by then. What do you say to that?'

Eddie looked at her to gauge whether she could be trusted. Jan didn't particularly like or understand the look. Distrust did not become Eddie. It was not in his nature, any more than he was given to sudden outbursts of irrational rage.

'All right,' he mumbled. 'It's a deal. You've given your word.'

🐎

'Jan! It's great to see you back racing again. And so soon.'

The ruddy-faced Captain Freckle, the clerk of the course at Chepstow, beamed at her as she handed in the passports of her runners at the declarations office.

'Yes, I was very lucky.'

She clung to this phrase throughout the afternoon. Everywhere she went, when people said how wonderful it was to see her, how well she looked, she replied how lucky she had been. Was all this just passing bonhomie, she wondered. Of course, much of it was, but although the bonhomie was fleeting it didn't stop it being true. The numerous handshakes, pats on the back and pecks on the cheek were signs of the racing tribe welcoming back one of their own, one who had been through an ordeal and survived and Jan took genuine pleasure from it. Hers was a small, out-of-the-way yard, only three years in business and still struggling to establish itself. But she felt she had been accepted into the tribe now, well, by most of them at least.

Arrow Star was owned by one of Jan's nicest and most enthusiastic owners. Penny Price was a local woman, of about thirty, who worked in the daytime as a secretary and at a chicken factory during the night to help meet the training fees. She had bred Arrow Star herself and he was her only pride and joy. Things had become a little easier for Penny after her parents had signed up as joint owners. They were small, uncomplicated farmers, people like Reg and Mary, not well off but the salt of the earth.

Jan felt the least she could do was to try her damnedest to make the big horse pay his way. He was huge – 'a bit of a hippo' was how one jockey had described him. Nevertheless, he had landed third place in the unconventional cross-country race at Cheltenham back in November. Even though he faced more conventional steeplechase fences today, it was not beyond the bounds of possibility that Willy Summers, the experienced jockey Jan had engaged to ride him, could repeat the success and bring in another few hundred pounds in place money.

To the delight of the Price family, Arrow Star did even better. The horse plugged around the circuit at a moderate pace, putting in mighty leaps at every obstacle, which kept him on terms with the slicker, faster animals. Then, unexpectedly after the turn for home, there was a pile up. The runners were approaching the penultimate fence halfway along Chepstow's demanding home run, with Arrow Star racing on his own a few lengths off the field. Suddenly, out of the blue, a loose horse appeared alongside the bunch. Instead of running round the fence, as most do, he swerved left and right like a world-class rugby player before jumping the fence diagonally across the leaders. He cannoned into the front two, bringing them down, which in turn hampered the other horses and left their jockeys clinging round their necks. Arrow Star, travelling behind with a wet sail, pricked his ears in amazement and pinged the fence. He didn't shirk his responsibility and galloped to the last; hurling himself over it, he churned his way to the line, passing it a length and a half clear.

The famous gap-toothed grin of Willy Summers was a joy to behold, though it was the delight of Arrow Star's owner as she led her horse into the unsaddling enclosure that lit the whole place.

For Jan this was one of her best moments in racing, to win for owners who were also good friends. She knew Arrow Star was never going to set the world on fire, but there would never be a more genuine horse in training. Now there was definitely not a happier or more deserving owner than Penny Price anywhere in the world.

🐎

Jan and Annabel were drinking coffee in the crowded owners' and trainers' bar when Jan noticed Virginia Gilbert come in with a wiry sort of man, just above average height and dressed in a tailored tweed suit and check cap. He removed the headgear as he stalked through the door to reveal a sleek head of black hair. Jan's heart sank – it was Harold Powell. She quickly turned her back and, tapping Annabel on the arm, indicated the new arrivals with a movement of her head.

Jan's dealings with Harold Powell had developed over the previous four years and every new turn in them had been unpleasant.

'He's obviously got plenty of money still,' commented Annabel.

'I know. It seems people like him always have lots hidden away somewhere.'

'But what's he doing here with Virginia?'

'Plotting my downfall probably,' said Jan gloomily.

'You mean, after what he said to you at Cheltenham?'

Jan looked at Annabel blankly.

'What? He was at Cheltenham?'

'Don't you remember? You said he confronted you near the saddling boxes. He told you that you'd ruined his life.'

Jan narrowed her eyes and strained to get the memory. *Near the saddling boxes*. Yes, that was it. Harold quivering with rage. Harold actually believed Jan had deliberately done him down, that she'd waged a personal campaign against him. Harold snarling his contempt and promising her, 'You'll get what's coming to you.'

She flicked an anxious glance across at Harold and Virginia. They were sitting at a table on the far side of the room, deep in conversation and did not appear to have registered Jan's presence in the bar.

'Come, on, Bel,' she said. 'We're getting out of here. I'm not staying in the same room as that man.'

🐎

Teenage Red did not give Jan a double that day. He had been a little short of work, but Jan and Annabel agreed on the way home that he would be a live contender next time out.

After the ritual of evening stables Jan had started making supper for the children, when Sue Sullivan appeared, looking surprisingly alert for a woman with jet-lag.

'I didn't want to sleep too long. Ron says you've got to reset the body clock after a long flight and you can't do that by giving in to sleep at the wrong time of day.'

They sat at the kitchen table and ate beans on toast, while Megan entertained Sue at great length with an account of her riding exploits in the world of junior eventing with Monarch, the pony that Colonel Gilbert had lent her.

'One day I'm going to be the new Lucinda Green and Matty's going to be the new Murty McGrath,' she announced, with the blind certainty that only a child can have.

'That's good,' said Sue. 'You must always aim for the top.'

An hour later the children went off to bed while the two women settled down with a bottle of wine in front of the fire.

'Were you shocked to see Eddie?' Jan enquired.

'Yes, a little. Even though I'd spent the whole journey imagining he'd be even worse.'

'Yes, I know.' Jan sighed. 'That's the curse of motherhood, imagining the worst.'

'It's odd, but he seems different. I know he's all bandaged up and in pain, but the Edward I knew always laughed off his hurts – always.'

'Yes, making light of things was his way, wasn't it?'

'But what I want to say is, he's so lucky to have you, Jan. I couldn't wish for better. In fact I am very much hoping that—'

'There's precious little I can do for him at the moment,' Jan interrupted, fearful of hearing what Sue Sullivan was hoping for. 'He won't be up and about for weeks, so the doctors are saying.'

'But there's so *much* you can do, Jan. Don't you see? I mean, after he's had all the hospital treatment? And even during it he's going to need lots of support if he's ever to get back to his old cheery self. He's going to need a good woman by his side. I know Ron agrees. You two are made for each other.'

Suddenly Jan felt wildly nervous about where this was going to head. She tried to steer the conversation into another channel.

'Is he like Ron? In character, I mean.'

'In some ways very. Ron's hopeless on his own, too. I mean, he doesn't look after himself.'

Sue laughed.

'I should think right now he's sitting down to a boiled egg for breakfast. Then he'll have more of the same for his tea. Terribly bad for his cholesterol, but that's all he ever eats if I'm not there. Either that or cheese, possibly a few beans.'

Jan smiled, thinking of the meal they'd had earlier.

'Anyway,' Sue went on, 'that is why I said what I said, about you and Edward. I just can't hang around in England for too long. Ron needs me. That's why I went back, you see, back to the marriage. You knew we'd separated shortly before Ron's business went for six?'

Jan nodded.

'Well, when that Mafia gang or whoever they were went after him and he had to scarper to Australia, I knew I couldn't let him go on his own. Even though we'd been living apart for eighteen months, I was still doing his *laundry*, for goodness sake. We'd been married for thirty-five years. I suppose we couldn't manage apart, either of us.'

'You too?'

'Yes, me too. I guess I must still be hooked on him. He really is a good man, Jan – not always the most reliable, I know, not always the most sensible either, but good underneath all that.'

Jan understood that Sue wasn't only talking about her husband, but about her son. She was appealing to Jan on Eddie's behalf, an appeal that Eddie would rather die than make for himself.

'Yes,' said Jan as brightly as she could, 'of course he is. Now, I haven't told you about how we got on at Chepstow, yet, have I?'

Jan told Sue about the runs of Arrow Star and Teenage Red, and promised to take her down the yard to see the horses in the morning. Suddenly she was suppressing yawns. It was time to tidy up before going to bed.

Jan had just switched off the light and was settling down to sleep when the phone at her bedside gave a loud shrill. She reached out, without turning on the light, and picked up the receiver.

'Yes?'

Was it that fluctuating hiss again, or breathing?

'Who is this, please?'

She was doing her best to sound authoritative, in control. But this had no apparent effect. Whoever had dialled her number had either not got through or was deliberately keeping silent.

After twenty seconds Jan put down the receiver, switched on the light and swung her legs out of the bed so she was sitting. Suddenly she felt almost sick with anger. Who the hell was it? How dare they disturb her like this? She felt along the lead of the phone and pulled the plug out of the Telecom socket. Then she went downstairs to the hall and did the same.

Back in bed, she breathed deeply and tried to quieten her pounding heart. Of course, she had heard of people being plagued by anonymous malicious phone calls, but it had never happened to her. Sometimes the calls meant nothing at all because they were done by harmless nutters. *That must be it*, she thought. Some prat who had lost money on one of her horses. They'd soon give up, or bet on another horse and start bothering the trainer of that one.

The thought, and the knowledge that the phone could not ring again until she reconnected it, calmed her and she eventually fell asleep.

# 7

'Hello, Jan. It's Toby. Are you busy?'

'I'm doing my entries, but it can wait.'

It was mid-morning as Jan took the call in the office, where she had been dealing with a fistful of paperwork which she'd generated as she searched for suitable races for her horses.

'It's about the discussion we had on Tuesday night. I have talked off the record to a lawyer friend about Eddie's little problem.'

'I hope you're going to tell me it *is* a little problem.'

'Well, not exactly, I'm afraid.'

'Not good news, then?'

'Mixed, I'd say. The first thing is that, because someone died in the accident, a thorough police investigation is inevitable, which we more or less predicted. Have you found out anything else?'

Jan had called the coroner's office the previous afternoon.

'Yes, the coroner's already opened the inquest but adjourned it. Apparently if there's a proper trial, the inquest might not be needed as all the evidence will be presented in court and they won't want to prejudice it.'

'Which is as I thought. What about the post-mortem?'

'By all accounts they've done one already. What do you think that means?'

'Obviously the family will want the body released for burial. But first the coroner needs to establish if the guy was drunk, had taken drugs or had a heart attack whilst driving.'

'I see. So where does this leave Eddie?'

'Right. Eddie has several relatively minor driving offences to face, namely driving without valid documentation, which he is obviously guilty of, and driving an unfit vehicle, which he may well be guilty of. Normally they would attract fines and might mean he's disqualified from driving.'

'But *was* the Morgan unfit?'

'I can only go on what you've told me, but my friend says that if the car's tyres were as you described them then it was demonstrably unfit for the road and that's an offence. But having discovered this, and knowing that Eddie didn't have a current MOT certificate, the police will take a closer look at the whole car, or what's left of it, especially at the things checked in an MOT test, such as the brake pads. If they find these were badly worn, or there were any other dangerous defects, they can say the accident was a result of these faults, and that it was his responsibility. Then if the police thought they could make it stick, they'd charge him.'

'But what with, Toby? I'm really scared. What if they try to implicate me?'

'They won't, Jan, but Eddie could be accused of death by reckless driving, that's my best guess.'

'The best? You're joking.'

'Sorry, Jan, not the right word. Anyway, here's the serious bit. If he's found guilty, he could be looking at a custodial sentence, anything from a few months to five years.'

'*Five years, for Christ's sake,*' Jan gasped as she clutched the desk to steady herself.

'That's reserved for extreme cases. The average is two to three years.'

'Two to three *years*? Dear God, Toby, please tell me this isn't real.'

Toby's voice, usually so humorous, remained low and serious.

'Jan, please don't be so upset. It hasn't happened, not yet. And it may never. My friend agrees with what I told you on Tuesday night and the circumstances of the accident mean that the police will find it extremely difficult to establish exactly what happened for sure.'

'Toby, for fuck's sake, I *know* what happened. Why won't anyone believe me? It had nothing to do with Eddie's brakes, or his tyres. The Range Rover forced both of us off the road – *that's what happened.*'

'Jan, it's going to serve no useful purpose getting angry and losing control. I know what you said in your statement and that you were with Eddie and saw it all. But the police will definitely want an independent witness, or some other kind of evidence.'

'You mean they will never believe me?'

'I don't know. They may, they should. But don't forget we pay them to be suspicious about things like this. Anyway, the positive point is, if they really can't be sure how the accident happened, they are hardly likely to prosecute Eddie, except on the minor charges.'

'And if they find the car that barged us off the road while making the other poor sod hit a tree, they'll go after him,' Jan continued weakly.

'Exactly. But there's something else my friend mentioned.'

'Go on. I might as well have it all.'

'Have you thought about the dead man? Or rather, have you considered his family and his insurers? Theoretically Eddie shouldn't have been on the road in that car, should he? So what are they going to make of his liability?'

Jan suddenly saw what Toby was getting at.

'Oh my God, the insurance!'

'Yes, the insurance. There will undoubtedly be a claim, which Eddie almost certainly wasn't covered for. In which case the family might feel entitled to damages. So Eddie could be sued for everything he's got. And more.'

'I suppose that's all right, then. He hasn't got a pot to piss in.'

After putting down the receiver, Jan went up to the house, to find Sue sitting in the kitchen writing postcards. While she made a mug of tea, Jan very gently gave an edited version of her conversation with Toby, leaving out the mention of prison and of the possible claim by relations of the deceased.

Sue took it all calmly. 'I think it's far more important to get him better than to worry him about all this legal stuff.'

'Do you know if he's seen Hadfield yet?' Jan asked, handing Sue a mug.

'The policeman? No, I don't think so.'

'He'll want Eddie's statement about the accident.'

Sue waved her hand dismissively and smiled.

'Waste of time, dear. Edward can't remember a thing about it. And he's got memory blanks going back weeks. He says that the whole time since he came back from Australia's a complete fog.'

'What about before he came back?'

'What do you mean?'

Jan took a deep breath and fetched the airmail letter which she had still not delivered.

'This arrived for him at the King's Head on Saturday. I haven't given it to him because I thought it might be something to do with that girl, her baby and the DNA test.'

Sue looked at her sharply.

'You know about the test?'

'Yes, Eddie told me.'

Taking the envelope Sue looked at it casually.

'And you were worried it would upset him, you mean? It's OK, the letter's from me. It's mostly about what his father and I'd been up to, but there *is* news about Alice, the child, in it. And I've been wondering when you'd ask about her.'

'I've been wondering if I should.'

'That's funny. We've both been skating around the subject, haven't we? It's like something that shouldn't be mentioned.'

'Nevertheless, it's still been on my mind.'

'Mine too. But with Edward being so badly hurt, I've not had the heart to mention it to him. I'm not sure he'd remember it, anyway.'

Jan sat down opposite Eddie's mother. 'What's going on? I think I've got a right to know if Eddie really is a father.'

'Jan, I agree with you entirely.'

Sue laid the letter on the table in front of her, looking fixedly at it as she spoke.

'The fact is we still don't know. We're waiting for the result of the test to come through, or we were when I left. As it is at the moment, Alice might be our granddaughter, or she might not be.'

She tapped the envelope on the table with a forefinger capped by crimson nail varnish.

'I wrote that she's in foster care. I suppose it's for the best, for the time being. The mother doesn't want her now, probably never did.'

Sue's last remark was loaded with contempt.

'Well, Eddie does,' said Jan. 'I mean, if he's the father, he does. He told me as much.'

'Yes. And if the little mite's his, then we'll have to take her, won't we?'

By Sunday, ten days after the accident, Jan had begun to count the reasons to be cheerful. She was feeling and looking more like her old self. There had been no more weird phone calls. And the stable had a winner for A.D. O'Hagan at Newbury on Saturday. When she visited Eddie on Sunday she realized how much he had improved, at least physically. He could sit up in bed and the head dressings had been simplified to a white cap of crêpe bandaging around his cranium. His bare face was decorated with the dark little knots of his stitches, which weren't pretty, but it seemed like progress. The bruising, though, still looked like the colours of a sherry trifle, but the puffiness in his face had mostly subsided.

However, Eddie himself was anything but cheerful.

It was late afternoon and Jan was alone with him.

'How are you feeling?' she asked.

'Not very clever,' Eddie answered in a grumpy manner. 'Still, at least I can talk properly even if I can't bloody walk.'

'You're starting physiotherapy next week, aren't you? That'll help, I'm sure.'

'Not if I'm paralysed it sodding won't. That'll be me, for life.'

'Don't talk such rubbish, Eddie. You sound like someone who's given up, and that's not like you.'

There was a pause. Eddie was staring straight ahead.

'A policeman was here,' he said.

'Hadfield? Yes, I met him. He's investigating the accident. What did he want?'

'He wanted me to tell him all about it. Which I couldn't as it's a complete fucking blank. He kept going on about the poor state of the Morgan and accused me of not keeping up the insurance, MOT and the rest. I told him it wasn't true, it couldn't possibly be.'

Jan caught her breath.

'You mean you *did* renew them?'

'I've no idea.'

'Oh. It seems you didn't, Eddie. I can't find anything and I've searched everywhere.'

'Perhaps I forgot to. That's a laugh. Now I've forgotten that I forgot.'

'Look, stop worrying about it for now. It'll all come back, I'm sure, but it will take time. What's the last thing you do remember?'

'Sun, surf, Foster's lager. Australia. Everything after that's blurred. I do remember stuff, but none of it makes sense.'

Driving back to Edge, Jan suddenly found her eyes filling with tears. She pulled into a lay-by and tried to control the wave of emotion. Eddie's moroseness was like a pall of gloom hanging over them. Then, as she reflected, she realized her feelings were not so much pity for him, as self-pity. What could he remember about her? Could he recall the reason he'd come back to England? Did he remember they had been passionate lovers? And if he didn't, where did that leave her?

'Stop this right now,' Jan scolded herself.

Rummaging in her pocket, she found a screwed-up tissue; she blew her nose several times and drove on, determined she would overcome this problem, however big it was.

As she let herself into the house, Fran was in the hall holding the phone. She quickly put her hand over the mouthpiece.

'It's a reporter – Tim Farr?' she whispered.

Jan sighed and took the receiver.

'Hello, Mr Farr. How are you?' she asked.

'Tim, please.'

'What can I do for you?' Jan continued.

'It's in connection with the accident, I mean Cleeve Hill. Do you have a few moments to talk?'

'I might have. Go on, spit it out.'

'The police have put out an appeal for witnesses. They are

particularly interested in the driver of a vehicle that may have left the scene before the police arrived.'

Jan sat down on the upright chair next to the small telephone table.

'What kind of car?'

'A big four-wheel drive evidently.'

'Like a Range Rover?'

'Yes. To quote the press release, "possibly resembling a Range Rover". Registration number, not known. Colour of car, ditto.'

Jan tried to sound matter of fact, but she was electrified. It seemed that Hadfield's interviews with other motorists at the scene might have corroborated her statement.

'Mr Farr, Tim, do you know how the police got hold of this?'

'No, they just call it "information received".'

'But you were driving behind us. Were you passed by a Range Rover going really fast, driven by a lunatic?'

'No, Mrs Hardy. But I was quite a long way behind you, remember. The police were already arriving when I turned up. What about you? Do you know anything positive about this other vehicle?'

Jan hesitated.

'No, Tim, I'm sorry I don't. I've really got nothing to add. I suppose your best bet is to get on to Hadfield.'

'I already have. He won't confirm if it's a positive or not.'

It was not yet six o'clock the next morning, with *Farming Today* still on the kitchen radio, when Jan heard the clatter of running feet outside, followed by a furious ringing on the front-door bell.

'Jan! Come quick!'

It was Roz, Jan's head girl, who always arrived for work first. She was jumping up and down on the doorstep and clearly agitated.

'Quick! It's Eagle!'

They ran like Steve Cram and Seb Coe, helter-skelter back down to the yard.

Russian Eagle was lying upside down, with his head towards the stable door and his legs fast against the right-hand wall. He was breathing noisily, the great barrel of his thorax heaving up and down. His big eyes were watery and bloodshot, rolling around with distress. Blood trickled from his nostrils and his mouth dribbled sticky saliva.

'He's cast,' said Jan in despair. 'We've got to get him up, *now*.'

Jan ran and unhooked a lunge rein from the tack-room wall. She knew this was something that happened from time to time, though it seemed inexplicable to anyone not close to horses. Eagle had got down for a roll and got wedged in a position he could not get free from. In a blind panic, he would have struck out with his hooves, desperate to release himself, and banged his head on the floor several times. He might have lain there for several hours, occasionally renewing his struggle until he was completely exhausted. Jan knew he could have done himself untold damage.

'You'll have to come in with me,' she told Roz, whose face was frozen with fear. 'And for Christ's sake don't get crushed.'

Jan grabbed the head-collar from a hook by the stable door and went into the box. She immediately knelt beside Eagle's head, talking to the horse, soothing him like a hypnotist. She stroked his neck and he feebly lifted his head off the floor. Slowly she worked the collar over his nose before pulling the long leather strip behind his ears and buckling it.

Jan instructed Roz to hold Eagle's head tight to the floor while she fixed the lunge rein to his hind leg. She knew this was a precarious move – if Eagle renewed his fight for freedom both she and Roz could be seriously injured. Thankfully Con and Dec appeared at that moment and helped Jan give an almighty tug on the lunge rein, flipping Eagle back into his correct position. The battered horse lay quiet for a moment before staggering drunkenly to his feet.

Jan looked him over carefully and knew straight away they were in trouble, but, to confirm it, she asked Roz to walk him gently into the yard. Instantly, they could both detect the horse's lameness.

'Off-hind,' Roz said.

Jan carefully ran her hand down all his legs in turn and felt that somehow or other he had got off lightly. The problem in the off-hind leg was obvious by the extra heat and swelling, but she would need the vet to diagnose the underlying injury. Miraculously, the other three seemed normal. Jan felt sure Eagle's injured leg wasn't fractured.

'It's bad enough, though,' she said as the big horse stood swishing his tail, feeling as subdued as she did.

At that moment Annabel, Eagle's co-owner with A.D. O'Hagan, appeared out of the gloom. As Jan told her what had happened, Bel stood looking at her horse in disbelief, then burst into floods of tears. Jan handed her a tissue and felt like joining her.

'I suppose that's his chance in the National gone,' said Annabel. 'Give him to me, I'll take him, Roz. He needs washing down and a drink of warm water. You can give me a hand, if you like.'

'I'll phone the vet,' said Jan, already heading for the office.

Later, in the kitchen after the first lot had come in from the gallops, Megan was unusually quiet over her bowl of cereal. 'What does it mean, cast in his box?' she asked.

Jan dropped some sliced bread into the toaster.

'It means they lie down in their box and they can't get up.'

'Why can't they get up? I've seen Smarty roll and he always gets up.'

'Well, it depends on the position they're in. Horses have rather stiff spines. Much stiffer than dogs or cats. So they're less flexible and if they're in certain positions, like, for instance, getting too close to the wall of the box or having their bottom wedged in the corner, they can't bend their backs far enough to twist over onto the other side.'

'Why don't they just get up, though?'

'It's by rolling over that they get their hind legs under them, which is the only way they can get up again.'

'And if they're too close to the wall they can't roll?'

'Exactly.'

'Is Eagle going to be all right?'

'I hope so. We'll know when the vet gets here, which will be soon or I'll throttle her.'

The ebullient Shirley McGregor was in the yard by nine-thirty. She examined Eagle and confirmed that he had got off lightly.

'I've seen loads of them with their jawbones fractured, where they've bashed their heads on the concrete floor.'

'I always make sure the floor's covered all over with plenty of bedding,' said Jan.

'Good, it's probably saved us a lot of grief. And I'd say the leg's going to mend OK, but it'll take time. This one's in the National, isn't he?'

Jan shrugged and sighed at the same time.

'Yes, he was. Not any more, though. What's more, I'm going to have to ring A.D. O'Hagan and tell him. He isn't going to like it . . .'

'I'll take an X-ray just to be sure we know what we're dealing with. I've brought my portable with me. If we'e not happy in a day or two you may have to bring him to the surgery, but I really wouldn't want to travel him at the moment.'

Forty minutes later Shirley bounced into the office to give Jan her prognosis.

'I'm sure it'll mend completely, but you won't be able to do much with him for a while. So . . .'

She beamed at Jan.

'It's an enforced holiday for him.'

There was always a collective sense of loss when a fancied horse had to be taken out of a big race through injury. Shirley's noisy cheerfulness was normally popular around Edge Farm, but the young vet was not sensitive to atmosphere, and seemed oblivious to the sombre mood that had settled over the yard.

'Can you do me a written report as soon as possible? In simple language, please,' Jan asked. 'I'll need all the details. A.D.'s a stickler and with this particular horse I'm going to have to give him chapter and verse.'

'That's all right, no problem. Any other patients for me to look at while I'm here? How's that splint? Has it settled?'

On her regular Thursday visits Shirley had been treating Miller's Lodge, one of Johnny Carlton-Brown's horses.

'It's much better. We thought he'd be back doing a little light work next week.'

'Want me to have a look?'

Jan shook her head.

'No, it's OK. It'll wait till Thursday when you do your rounds.'

'By the way, how's Eddie?'

Shirley had asked casually enough, but Jan couldn't help remembering the previous year, when Shirley had made a play for Eddie.

'Eddie?' Jan said crisply. 'He's enjoying an enforced holiday too.'

# 8

As soon as Shirley McGregor had left, Annabel burst into the office. After her initial tears, she had been monosyllabic while riding work on the gallops and later back in the yard, doing her duties with grim-faced efficiency. But a forceful storm had been brewing inside her; now it was about to burst.

'I can't *believe* you let this happen to my beautiful Eagle,' she lashed out, choking with emotion.

Her outline was framed in the doorway, and Jan could clearly see that she was shaking.

'What on earth do you mean, Bel? I didn't "let this happen". It just did – all by its bloody self.'

'But Eagle was in the very best shape of his life in the biggest week of his life. You should've been more careful.'

Jan was astounded. Annabel had always been Jan's closest ally. She was an invaluable assistant. Was she now turning against her too?

'For Christ's sake, Bel. It wasn't a question of being more careful. How could it be? He was cast in his box. I wish to God it hadn't happened, but it did. It affects me as well, you know. It was just an awful random accident.'

'No, it's that bloody car crash!' Annabel's voice was quavering. 'It's taken your mind off the job.'

'Bel, no! That's unforgivable! I won't have that.'

Jan pushed back her chair. Getting to her feet, she faced Annabel, an entirely new, completely unexpected Annabel. Jan understood her friend's passionate regard for the animals in their care and her even more partisan love for, and pride in, Russian

Eagle. But this need to blame someone for what was an unforeseen, unforeseeable even, disaster seemed so unlike her.

'I tell you what's really unforgivable, Jan. It's unforgivable that Russian Eagle can't run for the biggest honour there is for him. It's unforgivable that you didn't put a round-the-clock watch on his stable.'

'Now just wait a *minute*, Bel.' Jan couldn't help raising her voice. 'No one, but *no one* could have predicted this. You're not bloody thinking straight. You're pissed off, you're disappointed, but—'

'Disappointed?' Annabel's voice was shrill. 'Yes, I'm disappointed all right, Jan, in *you*. Eagle was going to win, I just know he was. And now he won't even get the chance.'

Jan felt her own temper surge up to the same level.

'Now *look*, you're right out of order, young lady, and you'd better get your head together, if you want to go on working here. Do you understand? I will not put up with the accusations you've made. Not from you, or anybody else for that matter.'

But Annabel had already turned and stalked out. Jan shot to the open door and watched her 'friend' cross the yard towards the main gate. The dogs, who had been lolling around under the archway, sprang to life, as if energized by Annabel's irrational anger. They scurried after her, leaping around her long striding legs. Through the arch, Jan could see Bel jerk open the rear door of her car to let the dogs pile in. With squealing tyres, she drove off as fast as she could, clattering the loose stones which edged the drive, and disappeared up the track leading to the top of the ridge and the gallops.

'That's all I bloody needed,' Jan muttered. She shook her head in disbelief and returned to her desk. She was aware that it was not unknown for the big yards to keep a round-the-clock watch on horses prior to an important race. There had been cases of Derby favourites being threatened by criminals, and consequently requiring that kind of protection. But Jan had only ever kept vigil for a mare about to foal, or for horses with a life-threatening illness. It was wholly unreasonable – and completely beyond her means – to mount a twenty-four hour guard on a healthy horse just because he had a big race coming up. A.D. O'Hagan, Annabel's partner in the ownership of Russian Eagle, would agree, Jan was certain.

Otherwise he would have insisted on the precaution himself. He had not, of course, because it was absurd.

With a swift intake of breath Jan remembered that A.D. still did not know Eagle was out of the National. As she lifted the phone, her hand still trembling at Annabel's reaction, she wondered what A.D.'s response would be like. If there was one thing as certain as sunrise, Jan knew that he never, under any circumstances, became hysterical.

She called his mobile, but an automatic voice informed her politely that the number was at present unavailable. She joggled the phone cradle and dialled Aigmont, getting through immediately to A.D.'s secretary.

'Mr O'Hagan's away, Mrs Hardy. I can't reach him at the moment, I'm afraid. Is there a problem? Can I help?'

'It's about—'

Jan checked herself. She must be discreet. Almost anything connected with A.D.'s racing activities was potentially sensitive, but when it concerned a well-fancied runner just a few days before the Grand National thousands of pounds in ante-post bets could be at stake. And quite a lot of that would probably be A.D.'s. It would be best if no one at his end knew about Russian Eagle before he did.

'It's OK, but could you ask him to contact me as soon as possible, please? It is rather important.'

🐎

Three hours later Annabel returned. The yard had no runners today and Jan was in the house, arranging some of Reg's daffodils in a vase, when the blonde head of her assistant passed the kitchen window. Annabel let herself in through the front door and wandered quietly into the kitchen, where she headed straight for the electric kettle, which she shook to check if there was any water inside.

'I went for a walk along the ridge.' She spoke in a subdued, contrite voice. 'I needed to clear my head.'

'And have you?'

'Yes.'

'I'm very glad to hear it.'

Annabel switched the kettle on. She bit her lip as she concentrated on making two mugs of tea, while her eyes looked anywhere rather than meet Jan's gaze. She brought the steaming mugs to the table and placed her elbows on it, propping her chin on her hands.

'I'm really sorry, Jan,' she said at last. 'It was completely unprofessional of me to lose it like that. You're right, of course. No one could have foreseen what happened. I was just so disappointed that I let it get the better of me. I was thinking like an owner who knows nothing about the job, for God's sake!'

'Well, I'm sorry too that I raised my voice and yelled like I did, and I'm terribly sorry about Eagle. I do understand how personally you take everything about him. Of course you were thinking like an owner because you are one – well, half one. But, honestly, everyone's depressed about this. Don't you think I was desperate for him to run? Don't you think I could do with the ackers if he had won, or was placed even?'

'He must be feeling pretty sorry for himself, poor sod. All wound up to go and then nothing. What a let-down.'

It was not until the evening that Jan's phone rang and she heard A.D.'s even, measured tones.

'Jan, I'm sorry I couldn't get back to you earlier. I was involved in rather a long poker game.'

Jan took a deep breath. 'I've got some bad news, I'm afraid, A.D.'

'What's that, then?'

A.D. listened without interruption as she explained the morning's sequence of events.

'You've taken him out of the race?'

'No, I wanted to talk to you first. But I'll have to do it tomorrow. No choice. I'll send you a copy of the vet's report, of course.'

'Yes, do that. And you can refer any press enquiries to me, if you like. What a damnable thing. There'd be no chance of a crack at the Irish National again, I suppose?'

The Irish Grand National at Fairyhouse was two weeks after the

Aintree event and Russian Eagle had a precautionary entry in the race he'd won the previous season.

'No, A.D. I think it'll take a bit longer than that. I really am sorry.'

'Would he be ready to run again before the summer? Uttoxeter maybe?'

'Oh yes, I hope so. He'll be as sound as a bell in a month, with any luck.'

'Oh well, these things happen to most horses. They're not machines you know, even if some people treat them as such.'

'Will you still be at Aintree?'

'Why wouldn't I be? I'll be there all three days for sure. 'Bye Jan.'

He hung up abruptly.

🐎

Sue had established her own routine. She drove down to Cheltenham to see Eddie each morning, always asking Jan whether she could get anything from the shops on the way back. Jan had come to rely on her for odd loaves of bread, pints of milk, jars of coffee or a bottle of wine for their dinner in the evening.

On Wednesday morning Jan had asked if Sue would drop into the bank and pay in a few cheques, then gather some extra groceries from the supermarket, while Megan had requested a pony magazine from the village store. Sue always carried out her small commissions to the letter, so it was a complete surprise when she arrived back at lunchtime empty-handed, with a dazed expression on her face.

'Oh, Jan,' she said, slapping her forehead. 'I've completely forgotten Megan's magazine, and the tea and things. How stupid of me.'

'Never mind, they're not that important. What about the bank?'

Sue fished in her bag and drew out the bundle of cheques, neatly tucked into Jan's paying-in book. She handed them back to Jan.

'Sorry, I forgot those too.'

'Sue, is something the matter?'

'I had a row with Edward, you see, or rather he picked a fight with me. It was horrible. I could think about nothing else all the way back.'

'Why on earth did he do that?'

'Well, it's something I haven't told you yet, but you should know anyway. I was speaking to Ron last night and he told me about the DNA test on the child.'

Jan had been leafing through the cheques, making sure they were all there. Now she froze. The cheques had suddenly lost all interest for her.

'The DNA test? Why? What did Ron say?'

Sue took off her coat and went to hang it in the hall. Returning, she paused in front of the kitchen mirror to check her hair.

'Well, as you know, we've all been on tenterhooks, haven't we? And the result should have been through by now, according to what we were told earlier. So Ron telephoned the lab to ask what was going on and they said the certified sample Edward sent them, I think it was a few hairs off his head or something, got lost. They couldn't find them. Would you believe it?'

'Was this before or after they did the test?'

'Oh, before. Apparently the sample went missing more or less immediately on arrival at the lab. So now they say we have to get another one certified and sent over.'

'Did you tell Eddie?'

'That's what caused the ructions, I'm sad to say. Edward still can't remember deciding to go ahead with a paternity test or providing the original sample. He remembers all about the baby, and he remembers that good-for-nothing Louise, but he got quite worked up and cross about her – he called her a slut, which I wouldn't disagree with, by the way. I think he really hates the mention of her now.'

'Is that what you argued about?'

'No, it was about the replacement sample for the DNA test. He suddenly said he'd lost all interest and couldn't give a damn. He wasn't going to go ahead with it, didn't think he'd be able to look after a child in his condition, and he said she would be better off being adopted. Of course, I told him not to be silly and that Ron and I would have her, if that's what it came to, until Edward was ready to take her on. But he shouted at me that he thought he was *never* going to get better. He said, "I'm going to be an effing basket case, Mum, and you might as well get effing used to the idea." He was shouting at me so loudly that the nurse came in to ask what the matter was. I told him it was stuff and nonsense, of course he's going to make a complete recovery, even if it does take a little time. And then, of course, I went too far and said that, even if he doesn't get better, everything would be all right. He really didn't like hearing that – it seems all the negativity has to come from him. He doesn't want to hear the rest of us saying he might not recover. But the point I was trying to make was that Ron and I would be only too happy to raise our granddaughter, as best we could, if we have to.'

'I know you would and I'm sure Eddie will too, in time.'

Sue shrugged.

'Well, we may never know because he won't have the test now, not at any price.'

'Not at the moment,' Jan said gently, 'but he may some day.'

Sue's face was twisted with the pain only a mother feels at the thought of her son's distressing behaviour.

'I don't know. He's so very angry, Jan, it's frightening. He's never been like this before. He called me all sorts of names, said I was interfering in his life and I should eff off back to Australia and his dad, and he didn't want to hear another word about the sodding baby ever again. He's washed his hands of her. As far as he's concerned, she's history. He told me to get out and as I was leaving he shouted, "You're all history."'

Jan usually managed a visit to Eddie every second afternoon and found him quieter than before and oddly disengaged, except when he became irritable over trivial things – the nursing, he claimed, wasn't up to standard and the hospital food was total crap. Today, as she crossed the hospital car park, she wondered how he would be after his appalling row with Sue. He had raised the bar with that one. From being merely tetchy and depressed he had completely lost his self-control, shouting, swearing, not caring a single jot what he said. And what was even more puzzling he had changed his mind about the baby. Why?

As she pushed through the swing door of the reception area, she saw a familiar figure advancing towards her.

'Mrs Hardy!'

It was Brian Hadfield, evidently on his way out.

'Inspector. How are you?'

'Never better, thank you. I've been in to see Eddie. Afraid he wasn't too pleased to see me, though.'

'Was it about the accident?' Jan asked innocently, knowing perfectly well it could be about nothing else.

'Yes, as a matter of fact. And now that I've bumped into you, perhaps we could have a word. Cup of tea in the cafeteria?'

Jan followed Hadfield down a corridor, through another pair of doors and into a bright, pleasant room with a dozen or so tables. Hadfield bustled over to the counter and came back with tea in two styrofoam cups.

'I must say,' he remarked, with that trademark smile playing ever pleasantly over his lips, 'Eddie's looking very much better, isn't he?'

'Yes, I think he is.'

'But he's not feeling better, that's the trouble. When he thinks about the future he's only looking on the pessimistic side. But that's a no-win policy, in my opinion.'

'So what brought you here to see him, Mr Hadfield?'

'I needed to get the signature witnessed on his statement. Not that the statement gets us very far.'

'What do you mean?'

'He really hasn't got anything to say. I mean, for instance, he won't confirm your allegation that the accident was brought about by a third vehicle overtaking and forcing both his and Mr Moor-house's cars off the road.'

'Inspector Hadfield, it's not an allegation. It's the truth. And of course Eddie won't confirm it. He doesn't remember anything. He's got post-traumatic amnesia.'

Hadfield sipped his tea before slowly lowering his cup.

'Has he now?'

'Of course he has. If he could remember, don't you think he'd tell you?'

'I'm sure he would if there *was* another car, Mrs Hardy.'

Jan felt herself growing hot around the neck and face. How dare Hadfield cast doubt on the truth of her statement?

'I told you, there was. I'll repeat it until I'm blue in the face, if you like. And I've read in the press that you've put out a call for any witnesses who saw a four-by-four driving away. So why are you continuing to doubt this? I'm sure one of the other drivers must have noticed it passing them, the way it was being driven before it caught up with us.'

Hadfield shook his head.

'Not necessarily. I've questioned all of them. No dice, I'm afraid. If the car exists—'

'Don't go there again. I've *told* you it exists!'

Hadfield held up a finger. 'What I was hoping for was a witness further up the road who saw this vehicle driving away from the accident. It could have been parked up and only come onto the road after you drove by.'

Jan considered this for the first time.

'I see, yes. I didn't think of that. Following us, you mean.'

'Following you in a manner of speaking, yes.'

'But presuming it was following us on purpose, suppose it was trying to get to us to run us off the road deliberately.'

Hadfield frowned.

'You've lost me, Mrs Hardy. Who would want to do that?'

'A man called Harold Powell, he might. He had already threatened me at Cheltenham racecourse a few hours before the crash. *And* he drives a Range Rover.'

Hadfield looked startled and the smile left his lips for a moment. He reached for his notebook.

'I think you'd better tell me a bit more about this, Mrs Hardy.'

Hadfield listened carefully to the saga of Stonewall Farm and the death of Olwen Hardy, making a few entries in the notebook. When Jan had finished, he asked if she knew Harold Powell's address. He jotted it down and drained the tea from his cup.

'I wish you'd told me all this before, Mrs Hardy.'

'I couldn't tell you about Harold threatening me because for a long time the five or six hours before the crash were a complete blank. I couldn't even remember my own horse had won. I had to look at the video to convince myself it was true.'

Hadfield's smile returned.

'Well, it can happen in these cases,' he conceded. 'And you say that, since then, you've been receiving anonymous phone calls?'

'Yes. Two.'

'When exactly?'

She told him the date and times.

'And did whoever it was say anything, anything at all?'

'No. I kept asking who it was. Then I hung up.'

'How long before you hung up?'

Jan shrugged.

'Twenty, thirty seconds.'

'But you heard breathing?'

'I thought I did. I presume the object of the exercise was to freak me out.'

'That's a possibility. Some men get a sexual thrill out of doing just that, you know – particularly to a good-looking woman like yourself.'

Hadfield's clumsy gallantry seemed grossly out of place. Ignoring it, Jan pressed on.

'So you are saying the phone calls had nothing to do with the accident.'

'I'm saying neither. They may have or they may not. It might just be a case of a wrong number. But I'll certainly look into it. In the meantime I'll enquire into Mr Powell's movements on the day of the accident, and I'll have a quiet word with Dyfed and Powys Constabulary about your mother-in-law's death. Don't worry, Mrs Hardy, we'll get to the bottom of this and if Harold Powell's behind any of it, we'll have him sooner or later.'

Going into Eddie's room a few minutes later, Jan found him staring morosely into space.

'Here, I've brought you some reading to improve your taste.'

She dropped the latest *Country Life* on his bed, then leaned over and kissed him. Eddie's head did not move and his lips were unresponsive and cold.

'Well, aren't you even going to say hi?'

'Hi.'

'Did your mum tell you about Russian Eagle?'

'Yes.'

'Is that all you're going to say?'

'What is there to say?'

'Look, Eddie, what's the matter? I need to know. What's happened to that "larky lad" I used to love so much?'

'He was in a car crash, remember? Not that I can. All I know is I'm completely fucked up. I can't walk. I'm never going to be able to walk. And the police think I'm a fucking criminal.'

'That's such a load of crap. I've just seen Hadfield and he confirmed he's looking for the third car, the Range Rover that shoved us off the road. You know what? I think it might have been driven by our old friend, Harold Powell. In fact I'm convinced it was.'

'Who's that?'

'Harold Powell – you know, he threatened me at the racecourse, said I'd get what's coming to me.'

'Never heard of him,' Eddie replied in an even more truculent manner.

With a sigh, Jan flopped down on a chair beside the bed and changed tack.

'Never mind. It'll all come back eventually, I know it. And as for this rubbish about being paralysed, I saw Dr Matthews in the corridor just now – you remember, your doctor? He said, when you're fit to travel they'll see if they can get you into Stoke Mandeville, the spinal injuries rehab centre. They're brilliant down there, they work wonders.'

'They'll have to.'

Jan wanted to shake him.

'Look, I just wish you'd snap out of this, Eddie. We've all had enough of it. You're going to be fine. So just stay focused and keep that thought in the front of your pea brain.'

Eddie didn't even muster the faintest smile. Before he would have risen to the bait immediately with a swift riposte, now he just scowled.

'Your mum said you had a bit of a row,' she went on, trying to speak more gently. 'Is that why you're so miserable? Are you thinking about the baby in Australia? Is that it?'

'No,' said Eddie. 'That's not it. I'm thinking about spending my life in a wheelchair. My whole life in a wheelchair – in *prison*.'

# 9

It was a fine spring day, with the daffodils in full bloom and a bright blue sky, as Jan breathed, with relish, the crisp air. No matter that her horse had little chance in the race, there was something magical about Grand National day. Jan entered the course at long last, after being in heavy traffic for what seemed like an eternity. Not that Dec and Con minded at all as most of the women on Merseyside were dolled up in skimpy fashion dresses. Jan noticed, much to her amusement, the lads' eyes swivelling round like fruit machines at the delights passing by.

One of the first people Jan met was Bernie Sutcliffe, the owner of her only runner, Arctic Hay. The Birmingham scrap dealer made no concession to the countryside way of life and was resplendent in his shiny grey suit, camel-hair coat and flashy grey shoes.

''Ullo, Jan. What'd yow think orr chances orr?' Bernie asked excitedly. 'Shall I back 'im?'

'Hang on, Bernie, I've only just arrived myself. Let's go and see Arctic first, then you can walk the course with me.' Jan thought this would get Bernie back down and also settle her nerves, as well as killing a bit of time before the famous race.

'Bloody 'ell,' said Bernie as they approached Becher's Brook, 'I feel as sick as a dog. I didn't realize the fences were this big.'

Jan smiled at Bernie's discomfort. 'I know,' she said. 'And remember we'll be safely in the stands when the horses are careering over these fences at about thirty miles per hour.'

As they continued their walk, Jan poked the ground with one of Reg's old walking sticks, paying particular attention to the take-off and landing sides at each fence. After two days of continuous rain earlier in the week, the going was still soft.

'This'll be fine for Arctic,' Jan panted, 'and there's less chance of the faster horses having their own way. It'll definitely favour the better jumpers.'

'Is 'e a better jumper?'

'He's a careful, steady old lad, Bernie, but don't get counting your chickens.' After the shock of Becher's they rounded the Canal Turn, when Jan noticed Bernie's stride had shortened dramatically as they approached the next fence, Valentine's Brook. Bernie reached for the running rail like a punch-drunk boxer would reach for the ropes and peeled off one of his shoes.

Jan stifled a giggle. 'Isn't it wet enough for those crocs, Bernie?'

''Ere, yow taking the piss out of my shoes, Jan? I might 'ave bought 'em on the market, but they still cost me a 'undred and fifty oles. They're ruined and me feet are soaking. Look, even the colour's run out of me socks. Can't we get a sodding taxi back to the stands?'

Now Jan laughed out loud at the sight of Bernie's foot. 'Never mind,' she giggled, 'a couple of stiff whiskies in the owners' and trainers' will soon anaesthetize them.'

'I bloody 'ope so, Jan. I'm crippled.'

🐎

The buzz in the trainers' bar was electric, with everyone excited and nervous at the same time. Several of Jan's owners were already there, to add their support, they said, whilst A.D. was ensconced in a private box which he had hired for the whole meeting. He had phoned Jan on the way to the races and asked if she would join him for a drink before racing started. After a quick drink, Jan left Bernie with the rest of the gang and made her way through the thronging crowd in search of A.D.'s suite.

Standing beside her husband, Siobhan O'Hagan beamed a welcoming smile.

'Come in, Jan. It's great to see you. You look fantastic considering the accident.'

'You mean the crash or the fact that Eagle didn't make it here? I don't know which hurts the most,' Jan said ruefully.

A.D. gave Jan a peck on each cheek.

'Ah well, I remember someone in racing wrote a book once called *The Glorious Uncertainty*, which describes this game to a tee – you should read it. Now, what will you have?'

🏇

As the afternoon unfolded and the first three races were run, the big one approached. As the tension in the crowd was rapidly reaching a crescendo, Jan looked at her watch. It was time for her to make her way to the weighing room to collect the saddle from Finbar Howlett, her jockey. This time she had insisted Finbar's valet provide them with brand-new leathers and irons and a new girth and surcingle to keep the saddle securely in place. She wasn't taking any chances, but still she was still racked with nerves at every stage of the saddling process as she remembered the time that Russian Eagle's tack was sabotaged when Eddie rode him in the Foxhunters'.

'Come on, get a grip on yourself,' she chided. 'You've done this hundreds of times before. What's the difference today?'

In the tense period between the emergence of the forty runners onto the course, to parade in front of the stands, and the moment when the starter would press the lever to launch them hurtling towards the first fence, Jan knew her job was over for now. She could do no more for Arctic Hay. She scanned the crowd and realized the entire mass were seized by a collective nervousness with calls and bursts of anxious laughter breaking out from various sections of the packed stands. The bookmakers shouted last-minute prices from the rails and out on the course the horses were jinking and jogging round in a disorganized circle behind the starting gate. Some of the jockeys dismounted, others had their girths checked one last time. Finally, as everyone's emotional temperature crept up towards the danger zone, the starter called the field into line. It was time for the off.

🏇

Arctic Hay was Jan's first-ever runner in the Grand National, but in her eyes he covered himself in glory. True, he finished in last place and was at least two furlongs behind the winner, but twenty-six of the runners had fallen by the wayside and he hadn't. Jan, who'd never hoped for anything better, was delighted, though she was a little worried about Bernie, thinking his self-esteem might be punctured by coming last. Yet Bernie seemed as close to contentment as his nature would allow.

'I never thought I'd actually enjoy watching an 'orse of mine bringing up the rear. Now 'e knows 'is way round we can come back next time and win it.'

'Steady on, Bernie, don't get your hopes up too high. I love your horse too, but he's still more of a Land Rover than a Ferrari, you know. The old boy will be rising fourteen and I wouldn't want to risk him at that age.'

'Uh, we'll see about that,' muttered Bernie.

A.D. O'Hagan had asked Jan to rejoin him in his box for a drink after the big race. Some of the hospitality boxes at Aintree overlook the course in a perfect place to watch the battle to the winning line. With Russian Eagle out of action, A.D. had no National runner this year, but his party turned into a celebration anyway as one of his Irish-trained stars had taken the highly prestigious Aintree Hurdle with irresistible authority.

When Jan returned, the box was in uproar.

Dermot O'Hare, A.D.'s Irish trainer, spotted her first, and raised his glass of Guinness.

'How's me girl?' he called out.

'I don't know how your girl is, Dermot – ' Jan smiled sweetly – 'but I'm very well, thanks.'

Jimmy O'Driscoll, who was standing beside Dermot, had just been taking a swig from his glass. He snorted with laughter and came up with his face splattered with creamy froth.

'Give it up, Der, you're wasting your time,' he said loudly. 'I don't think the lady's interested.'

A.D. crossed the room, beckoning to a waiter with a tray of drinks. Jan took a glass of wine and he guided her to a quiet corner.

'Don't mind those two chancers, Jan,' he murmured. 'Congratulations on the performance of your horse, by the way. Now, I'm afraid I didn't ask you back here just for social reasons. I was wanting a little word. But first, how's Russian Eagle?'

'Still a bit sore, but he's improving.'

'That's grand. Well, what I wanted to say was I've another horse for you. He's a four-year-old gelding that we picked up privately in the winter. Very good-looking, well-bred type which I paid a good price for, probably a bit too much as it's turned out. I was expecting him to be in all the top novice hurdles. In fact, I liked him so much I was thinking he'd be the successor to the horse that won today. So far it's not working out too well.'

'Why, what's the problem?' asked Jan.

'He's impressive enough on the gallops when he's got friends and relations around him, but he's a disaster at the races. Fights the bridle, won't settle in a race, only wants to run like the blazes.'

'Still, it's a bonus he wants to run. Not all of them do.'

'I know, I know, but flat out – that's all this fellow wants to do. He's no brakes. Treats the jockey like a passenger. We've had three runs out of him and in the first he blazed away in front for a mile, ten, twenty lengths clear. In fact, Murty thought he was going to be carted all the way to Cashel Rock, but he'd galloped himself into the ground, done too much too soon and finished tailed off, so in his next two races we put a citation bridle on him. This, as I'm sure you know already, is one of the most severe bits available for anchoring uncontrollable, headstrong horses.'

'Really – a citation? He's that bad?'

A.D. nodded. 'He is, but the fact is, it's not really helped. It's stopping him all right, but he fights it like the devil and, as you know, that hurts. So now he's refusing to race at all and on top of that he's jibbing at the horsebox and is difficult to travel. I'd say he needs a change of scene and some sympathetic handling.'

'It sounds like the kind of challenge I relish and I shouldn't turn it down,' said Jan.

'OK, that's great. I'll make the arrangements.'

🐎

Back at Edge Farm on Sunday, Jan walked up to the house after evening stables. The day before a beautifully packaged bottle of champagne had arrived by special delivery, with a note saying, *Dear Jan, This is so that you can toast Arctic Hay's homecoming. Well done. Love, Tony.* Jan had been touched by his thoughtfulness and she agreed the horse thoroughly deserved to have a glass raised to him.

The house was unusually quiet. Sue Sullivan had left the day before in a hire car to visit her sister in Cornwall, while Megan and Matty had been despatched to spent the weekend with their grand-parents. As she passed through the hall, Jan noticed the light on the answering machine was blinking and pressed the play button. 'Hello, Jan, it's Tony. I've got news about Eddie. Give me a ring when you get a moment, I'm at home.'

She dialled Tony's number.

'Jan, what a great run from Arctic Hay. You must be delighted.'

'Thanks, Tony, we all are. And now I've got just the thing to celebrate with. That was just so thoughtful of you. As a matter of fact, I'm just about to get it out of the fridge and take it down to the yard. But what's this about Eddie?'

'I was over at the hospital this morning and bumped into Frank Matthews, Eddie's consultant. You know that they've been uncer-tain how much of his problem is spinal and how much is down to the head injury? Well, now the scans have confirmed it. He does have a degree of spinal damage.'

'Oh God, Tony. How bad?'

'Not as bad as it sounds. There's been a certain amount of what they call spinal shock, which is indicated by the swelling and bleeding in tissue around where the spine has been put under stress. That generally goes away. However, there may, just may, at this stage be some underlying damage to the spinal cord itself which can't be properly assessed until the effects of spinal shock have subsided. Either way, Eddie will have some hard work to do in the rehabilitation unit when they transfer him to Stoke Mandeville.'

'God, that's awful,' Jan gasped. 'When are they moving him?'

'They'll take him over there by ambulance next week. Appar-ently, the sooner his therapy gets started the less danger there is of some long-term or irreversible disability. I understand Mrs Sullivan's going in for a chat with the team at Cheltenham on Monday, but she won't have heard about the latest results. I thought you both might like to know in advance.'

'Thanks, Tony. I really appreciate it. Eddie's mother will too. She's away for the weekend, but I'll tell her the minute she returns.'

🐎

As Jan carried a fistful of assorted glasses and the champagne down to the yard, she wondered why Tony had called her. Was it really just the act of a friend? Or was it to make sure she knew he still cared for her? But he had already done that with the bottle of bubbly. On the other hand, Tony knew perfectly well that Eddie's reappearance in her life had been the immediate reason why she had said no to a close relationship with himself. She seriously hoped the phone call about Eddie's medical condition was not a disguised form of gloating.

🐎

On Tuesday, almost three weeks after the Cleeve Hill accident, Eddie was taken to the National Spinal Injuries Centre at Stoke Mandeville Hospital. The next day, Sue and Jan made the sixty-plus mile drive to see how he had settled in.

They found him propped up in a room on his own, not looking very different from how he'd been at Cheltenham – bandaged, bedridden and suspicious.

'This place is full of people in wheelchairs. They haven't fitted me for one yet.'

'Eddie, you're not going to need one,' Jan said, doing her best to reassure him.

'Or if you do it'll only be temporary,' added Sue cautiously.

'A guy came in and gave me a speech on spinal shock and something else. Anterior cord syndrome, I think that's what he said. I still don't know what it is. Why can't they give it out in words of one syllable? It was too much like hard work trying to follow what he meant.'

'Oh, Edward, you must at least try,' said his mother, doing her best to coax him.

'Anyway, it was all medical jargon,' Eddie said darkly. 'I don't think they want me to know the real facts. And they definitely know more than they are telling, that's for sure.'

The conversation was haphazard as Eddie seemed reluctant to join in and preferred to watch the television. Channel Four was showing the first races of the Newmarket flat season, the Craven meeting, in which the second race was a fairly low-grade mile-and-a-quarter handicap. Jan normally didn't pay particular attention to the rival racing code, but during the race build-up she was captivated by the sight of a handsome four-year-old bay gelding with a white blaze snaking down his nose called Velvet Dynasty, a name she thought she'd seen somewhere recently, though she couldn't recall where. He was in a muck sweat, almost pulling his lad's arm off with sharp jerks of his head, but she could see what a nice short-backed, deep-chested horse he was. During the race, which was easily won by the well-prepared favourite, Jan scrutinized the horse's every move. Velvet Dynasty ran a stinker, continually changing his legs and windmilling his tail like an animal out of sorts. His young jockey was obviously having a nightmare ride, which he made worse by trying to switch his mount from the inside of the field to the outside before veering back inside again, as if he'd lost his steering as well as his head.

Jan was musing on what a nice chaser the horse might make if he took to the jumping game. It might make a man of him, she considered – given the right handling he could be all right.

Suddenly the sister breezed in to announce that in ten minutes it would be time for Eddie's physiotherapy and made it abundantly clear that she wanted his visitors to make themselves scarce.

'Eddie,' Jan said as she and Sue got up to go, 'I'm afraid I'm not going to be able to come over to see you quite as often as I did when you were in Cheltenham. But I promise I'll come whenever I can.'

'But I'll be here,' said Sue brightly, glancing quickly at Jan. 'I thought I might put myself in a guest house in Aylesbury so as to be close at hand. You know, I can bring in some bits and pieces every day.'

Eddie's grunted acknowledgement and sour face made Jan reflect that that the old cheeky smile, which had been his most endearing feature, hadn't once lit up his face since the accident.

'Are you really going to stay in a B and B?' Jan asked Sue as they settled in the car a few minutes later. 'He won't be coming out for weeks, I shouldn't think.'

'Well, dear, I've got to head back to Australia before too long.' Sue sighed. 'Edward's out of danger now, and Ron needs me too, you know. Of course, I want to see as much of Edward as I can before I go, so I think a B and B's the only option, don't you?'

🐎

It took an hour and a half to get back to Edge. Jan parked the Shogun and Sue jumped out to greet Megan and Matty, who had pelted out of the house at the sound of the approaching car. Jan stayed in the driving seat for a while, pondering. Eddie still had a huge corner to turn. How could she possibly help him from this distance, with Sue going home and a tightly staffed racing stable to be kept going? Admittedly, things would get a little better in a month's time, when the horses were out to grass for six weeks and the staff began taking their holidays. But, even then, there was still loads to do around Edge Farm without having to make the long journey to see Eddie.

🐎

Four days later Jan took two horses to Worcester, A.D. O'Hagan's Erin's Jet and Toby's black gelding, Nero's Friend. Bordering the river Severn, Worcester is one of the most accessible courses in England and, on a day like this, with just a few clouds flying high and white across the undiluted blue of the sky, Jan felt it was the perfect place to go racing.

She had high hopes for both her runners. Erin's Jet was returning after winning at the course the previous year and, while Toby's big black horse was a newcomer, she was sure he would appreciate Worcester's flat, galloping track.

The double she had envisaged did not come off. Erin's Jet found a couple too good for him and finished third, but Nero at least confirmed the promise Jan had seen when she'd recommended

Toby Waller to lay out £35,000 at the Derby Sale in Ireland the previous year. He cantered to the start as if he felt he owned the place, and came back in a style that suggested he really did, jumping rhythmically and beating his field by six lengths.

After she'd sent Nero back to the stables on the far side of the course, Jan doubled back for the presentation of the prize. Toby's podgy cheeks were pink with excitement as he collected his trophy and he beamed with all the pride of an owner accepting the Cheltenham Gold Cup.

Afterwards he quickly made his excuses. 'Jan, I've got to shoot off. Got a meeting with some important clients. But that was a great moment. I could get really used to this.'

He kissed Jan enthusiastically on both cheeks and headed for the car park. Jan wandered back to the paddock, where she stood watching the runners in the next race as they circled.

'Jan, how very nice to see you,' a male voice called out.

She spun round and saw that Colonel Gilbert was heading towards her, accompanied by his daughter Virginia. The latter's grim face was looking every bit as sharp as a well-honed hatchet. *She must have swallowed the lemon from her gin and tonic*, Jan thought.

# 10

'Hello, Colonel! Virginia.'

Jan's response to the colonel's greeting was genuinely warm. Her acknowledgement of his daughter was a little cooler. Virginia's pale green dress under a matching jacket was clearly the expensive product of some couturier. The jacket had the exaggerated puffed-up shoulders that were in fashion and which Jan thought were particularly unsuited to Virginia's bony figure.

'Hello, Jan,' Virginia said, with equally muted enthusiasm. 'Busy as ever, I see.'

Jan had no time to think of a response to this remark, whatever it was supposed to mean, as Virginia immediately turned to her father.

'Daddy, I've got to shoot off. I've arranged to have a drink with Patrick Lamberhurst. I'll see you later.'

'Yes, fine,' Colonel Gilbert said good-humouredly. 'I'll stay here and have a dekko at the runners for the next.'

He watched his only daughter skitter off on her unsuitable high heels, and then turned back to Jan, who said, 'I saw your runner in the long-distance race, Colonel. I would be surprised if he didn't improve a lot for the run.'

'Which is exactly what Ginnie's hoping. He's a lazy old sod at home. But that's a bloody good-looking chap *you* won with.'

'Yes, he's special, isn't he?'

'You bought him yourself?'

Jan laughed.

'Not exactly. I don't have that kind of spare cash. But I told Toby Waller if he didn't stump up I'd have his guts for garters.'

The colonel sighed, but his eyes were twinkling.

'You have a good eye and a great natural touch with a horse, Jan. Somehow I don't think my Ginnie has quite the same talent. She needs to work at it a bit harder, I suspect.'

Jan found herself blushing. The colonel was a bony old boy with plum-coloured cheeks and a pronounced limp, but he had charm and knew how to deliver a compliment. He was also, as Jan knew, a staunch friend who, despite her rivalry with his daughter, had supported Jan's training career from the first.

'How's my old friend Wolf?' he asked.

Most of the colonel's horses – he owned half a dozen at least – were with his daughter these days, but Wolf's Rock, which the colonel had bred himself on his small stud at Riscombe, had always been trained by Jan. With his sporadic breathing problems, Wolf had been lightly raced this season.

'He's ready for a run. I've got a two-mile chase at Hereford in my sights.'

'Good. Fax me over the details, would you? Now, what's your total strength at Edge Farm these days? I remember last year you were aiming for thirty horses. Have you got there yet?'

'No, I'm still a few short. I nearly made it, though, until I lost some after the Gary West fiasco.'

'Oh yes, an unfortunate business that. Still, at least it means you'd be able to squeeze in another horse of mine, I hope. Do you remember I said I might send you another one or two?'

Jan took a quick look at the route Virginia had taken, worried that she might suddenly reappear.

'Oh, yes of course. But what about—? Well, what about Virginia?'

'Ginnie's got about as many as she can reasonably cope with at the moment. But a maiden aunt of mine finally gave up the ghost in her nursing home and left me a bit of dosh on the understanding I must put it to good use, so I thought of you. How about helping me spend it on a new horse?'

'Colonel, I'd absolutely love to. I'll be going to the July sale at Newmarket, which is for horses in training, so I can have a look at what's on offer there if you like.'

'Ideally I want a youngster that might develop into a top-class three-mile chaser, after having a bit of fun over hurdles along the way. I should think with your eye you might spot one that's been running on the flat, but really has a secret yen to go jumping.'

'If only I could read their minds that easily – ' Jan laughed – 'it would simplify things enormously. But I'm sure there'll be some decent candidates at Tatts.'

'That's good. So do your homework with the catalogue and, if you find anything suitable, let me have the details in advance. If I like the look of them, I'll give you the OK to bid. Shall we say up to £20,000?'

'Fine, but you know I will have to see the horse in person, so to speak, before I can recommend bidding.'

The colonel nodded.

'Naturally, Jan. I might even come to the sale myself. Four eyes can often be better than two in that situation.'

He turned towards the paddock and waved an arm in the direction of the horses, who were now being mounted.

'So, what do we think of this little lot?'

Driving back down the M5 with Declan in the lorry, Jan felt exhilarated by the colonel's request. Apart from the thrill of racing itself, there was nothing quite like the buzz from getting a new horse. Every one was a different challenge. In her eyes every one was a champion until proved otherwise.

When they pulled into the yard, Jan found a visitor waiting for her. Tim Farr was leaning against the bonnet of his car, smoking a cigarette. He dropped it like a scalded cat and quickly ground it out with his foot as the horsebox drew near.

'Hello, Mrs Hardy,' he said as she jumped down from the cab.

'Mr Farr.'

'Tim,' he corrected. 'Did you have a successful day?'

'Yes, quite satisfactory, thanks. I hope you've not come to be a nuisance. I've still got work to do, you know.'

Jan jerked her thumb towards the horsebox as Dec was busy lowering the ramp. Erin's Jet and Nero's Friend were shifting around expectantly – she could hear them nicker. *They are thinking about the warm mash in their mangers*, she thought and smiled.

'I was just wondering if I could put something to you,' Farr continued, oblivious to Jan's frustration. 'It's about the accident on Cleeve Hill.'

'You're not still worrying at that old bone? I'd have thought it's stale news by now.'

'The thing is, I've been wondering if maybe it wasn't an accident at all.'

Jan spun round and stared at him.

'How do you mean? Of course it was.'

'I'm thinking of that four-by-four, the Range Rover or whatever it was the police have been looking for. Maybe the driver is more than a potential witness. Maybe it was involved in the incident, but they drove away unscathed. Maybe it *caused* the accident.'

'Ye-es?'

'Is that what happened?'

Jan shook her head.

'No go, I'm afraid. Those are not my words. You're doing the talking, not me.'

'All right, I'll continue my train of thought. I know I'm flying by the seat of my pants here, so to speak, but suppose we go one step further and say maybe the four-by-four, the Range Rover, caused the accident *deliberately*.'

'Hang on a minute. Where on earth could you get that idea from?'

'I was looking at the cuttings file – you know, on you, Edge Farm, and all that. There wasn't much except bits and pieces from the sports pages, though a great deal more from the period after you won the Irish National, and there's also a couple of reports on the trial of some former owners of yours – the Sharps? It seemed to me that they could still have a pretty powerful grudge against you since you gave evidence at their trial.'

Jan relaxed a little. Farr was on completely the wrong tack now, she realized, and she rather preferred it that way.

'It's not possible. The Sharps are all in prison,' she said.

'But they could get someone on the outside to harass you. To make threatening phone calls, follow your car, things like that?'

*Christ!* Did he know about the phone calls? Just who had Farr been talking to?

'Look, I appreciate your concern, but this is really nothing whatever to do with you. I think it's best we leave it to the police.'

'But it would help Eddie, wouldn't it, if the responsibility was deflected away from him?'

'Look, he *wasn't* responsible—'

'That's what I'm saying and maybe I can help prove it. If this other vehicle was driven by a person whose registration is unknown, cloned even, then he or she will be almost impossible to trace. But if it was driven by someone who actively wanted to harm you, then it's not going to be too difficult to draw up a list of suspects. Look, here's my card in case you think of anything.'

Jan's heart sank again. Talk of a list of suspects was ominous and Tim Farr sounded gripped by the idea of playing the sleuth.

'I don't see how you can help or why I should want you to help. I've already said the police are investigating the whole kit and caboodle. It's their job, or hadn't you heard that? And the last thing I want is bad publicity for the yard.'

Farr shrugged. 'Sometimes, Mrs Hardy, publicity is inevitable. The trick is to make sure it's the right kind of publicity, and that it's honest. Come on, surely you must be interested in the whole truth emerging. I'm certain the family of William Moorhouse is.'

Jan looked him in the eyes, glaring. Then she pointed to the crushed butt end which lay on the ground between them.

'I hope you're going to pick that up and take it away with you,' she said. 'By the way, please don't ever smoke in my yard again, it's far too dangerous.'

She turned and joined Declan, who had already led Erin's Jet to his stable.

The wayward horse that A.D. was entrusting to Jan arrived a week later from Ireland, via the Holyhead ferry. Morning Glory was a rich chestnut with a star on his forehead, not a big horse by any means, but with enough size to impress the eye.

'He looks fit,' said Jan as Roz led him from the lorry. She noted with approval the broad, sloping shoulders, good feet and knees, and his well-rounded quarters. 'He's carrying his head a bit low, though, isn't he?'

'He's had a Mickey Finn,' said the grizzled lad who had driven the transporter, 'or we'd never have got him loaded. He usually kicks out like a maniac, you know, and it's odds on he'd have hurt himself if we hadn't doped him. That feller's as mad as the devil's dog.'

Jan looked closely into the horse's eyes and could see the effects of the tranquillizer ACP. Morning Glory was regarding her with a dull, uncurious gaze that was quite alien to any horse in a strange new environment. It would be impossible to make an accurate assessment of him until the tranquillizer had worn off completely. Jan decided to allot him a stable away from the other horses on the west side of the yard, where all the boxes were empty and where he could acclimatize gradually. It would not be until Morning Glory felt completely at home that she would expect him to take a full part in the stable's daily routine; only then would she find out the true scale of the task that A.D. had set her.

The next weekend was Easter, one of the busiest times of the year for a racing stables. Jan's yard was no exception as there were eleven National Hunt race meetings distributed between the Saturday and the Monday of the bank holiday weekend. These were very popular with owners, since the extra day off made it easier for *them* to see their horses run. Edge Farm was due to send out six runners, all with different owners – two on the Saturday and four on the Monday. In the middle of all this came the Children's Easter Parade at Chiselcombe.

Most of Good Friday, which is traditionally a day without racing, was devoted to creating Megan's and Matty's costumes. Megan's sudden desire to go to the parade on her pony dressed as Joan of Arc had to be swiftly quashed.

'I don't think animals are allowed in the rules, darling,' said Jan. 'And, anyway, some children might be nervous if you turned up for the parade on Monarch, and I'm sure some of the others would be jealous, which we should avoid. What about going as the Easter Bunny?'

'Yuk, no! That's *so* boring. If I can't have Monarch with me, I'm going to go as a great white shark. I'm going to be Jaws.'

Matty was equally resistant to the idea that he might be anything as easily constructed as an Easter egg. Instead he had to be an Egyptian mummy or he would be nothing.

Reminded of Megan's remark to her at the hospital, Jan burst into laughter.

'So you're not frightened of mummies any more? That's good.'

While Jan worked out the best way to wrap Matty from head to foot in crêpe bandages, Megan, helped by Annabel, created the top half of a great white. The nose and jaws, made of cardboard pointing upwards and fashioned like a helmet, fitted over Megan's head, but extended considerably higher. They were covered in fabric from an old umbrella and vividly painted with eyes, grinning mouth and sharp teeth. A dorsal fin, a tailored black bin bag, and a pair of rubber frogman's flippers completed the unlikely transformation.

'I'm rising out of the sea to grab my prey, so it doesn't matter if you can't see my tail fins properly,' Megan announced in a muffled voice, peering out through tiny holes drilled in the fish's lower jaw.

The parade was held, under an overcast sky, in the neighbouring village of Chiselcombe, and consisted of several circuits of the village green to the accompaniment of the local silver band and a lot of laughter. Then the judges conferred and the vicar handed out prizes at the war memorial. About half the children were dressed as Easter bunnies or eggs, while the other half represented a motley crew of cartoon characters, pop stars, robots and a sugar plum fairy. Jan stood in the centre of the green and agreed with Annabel that Megan and Matty were by far the best and most imaginative entrants.

Annabel laughed and pointed at the other mothers. 'They all think that about their little darlings, too, you know.'

Nevertheless Jan couldn't help being disappointed when the prizes went to a Michael Jackson lookalike and a Catwoman, with the sugar plum fairy getting a special mention. But the children did not seem to mind in the slightest and, as light rain began to fall, the silver band led them in a long, capering crocodile to the vicarage, where tea was laid on in a marquee.

For half an hour Jan chatted to fellow parents from the village school. She knew several of the mothers quite well, yet for some reason their conversation seemed unnaturally stilted, as if they were nervous of saying something offensive to Jan about the accident. At first she put this down to the difficulty some people have discussing the misfortunes of others, although several did eventually ask about Eddie, giving Jan the impression that news of their relationship had percolated more deeply into the local community than she had suspected. Jan also had the feeling that people were looking at her, discussing her even, and this became so uncomfortable and disturbing she suddenly decided it was time to leave. By now the rain had intensified and was drumming even more loudly on the marquee as Jan looked around for the children. Unexpectedly, Viv Taylor-Jones, the vicar's wife, a tall, youngish woman in a printed dress, bare legs hairier than Russian Eagle's and Jesus-creeper sandals, approached.

'Jan, look, this is a bit awkward. Do you think you could pop over to the house for a moment?' she asked in her clipped Oxford accent.

'Certainly. What for?'

'Something's come up, which the vicar and I feel you should know about.'

Unable to imagine what might have come up, Jan instructed the children to find their friends and play a while longer, before following Viv across the soggy lawn, and through French windows, into a large, sombre drawing room.

'This came last week. I think you should read it.'

Rain lashed the windows, and the wind moaned in the huge chimney above the unlit fireplace, as Viv handed Jan a sheet of paper. It was headed: PRESS RELEASE. EDGE FARM – A STABLE IN CRISIS? With growing disbelief, Jan read on.

The fatal road crash which involved the National Hunt trainer Mrs Jan Hardy of Edge Farm, Stanfield, and her close friend Eddie Sullivan, who occasionally rides her horses, has been the subject of widespread speculation in the tightly knit equestrian community of the Cotswolds. The accident happened after racing on Gold Cup Day at the Cheltenham National Hunt Festival, when two cars were involved in a serious accident on Cleeve Hill.

The driver of one of the cars involved, Mr William Moorhouse, died at the scene. Mrs Hardy sustained face and head injuries, and was detained in hospital overnight. Sullivan was more seriously injured and is now under treatment at the National Spinal Injuries Centre at Stoke Mandeville Hospital. Sullivan was at the wheel of a two-seater sports car, which neighbours say he was often seen driving at speed around the Gloucestershire and Oxfordshire countryside. He had earlier in the afternoon been celebrating the victory of Mrs Hardy's horse Magic Maestro in the Cathcart Chase. The death of Mr Moorhouse, and the serious injury to Sullivan, has cast a blanket of gloom over Mrs Hardy's racing operation, typified by her horse Arctic Hay's poor showing in the Grand National last weekend, where he finished in last place.

Sullivan's father Ron, the former wealthy property tycoon who now lives 'quietly' in Australia, said of his son's condition that it was 'typical of the boy. He's always enjoyed life to the full and that means he sometimes has to pay the price, doesn't it?' Release ends.

At the bottom was some small print, including a phone and a fax number.

This press release is issued by the Cotswold News Agency as a service to the community. It may be freely used whole or in part by news or broadcasting organizations, parish magazines and any other outlets giving news and information about the Cotswolds.

Jan had finished reading, but continued to stare at the sheet of paper. It was beyond belief. What was this news agency trying to achieve? Nothing here was actually untrue, nothing was libellous, though the insinuation was monstrous – that Eddie had been drinking heavily before the accident, that he was a well-known hell-raiser, that she and Eddie were being gossiped about throughout the countryside, that her yard was 'in crisis'.

'This is filthy rubbish. How did you get it?' Jan asked.

Viv was nervously smoothing her straight hair with the long bony fingers of both hands. Her wide mouth briefly twisted into an embarrassed smile.

'I'm the editor of the parish magazine. It just came in the post,' the vicar's wife answered nervously.

'Does that mean it's been sent everywhere in the area, to all the parish magazines?'

'I guess it must have been, probably the community freesheets and the local radio stations, and the established papers too.'

'And what the hell *is* this Cotswold News Service?'

Viv shrugged.

'It must be new. I've never had anything from them before, and I've been doing the mag three years now.'

Jan scanned the text of the press release again.

'This is bloody *outrageous*. Who the hell do they think they are? Why are they doing this?'

She sprang to her feet and folded the paper.

'Can I keep it?'

'Of course.'

'I'm going to find out who's behind this, Viv, and I'm not going to let this rest until somebody's issued an apology.'

The rain had cleared by the time the Shogun turned off the road, so the ribbon of tarmac leading up to Edge Farm gleamed as a few fresh rays of sunshine penetrated the cloud. Arriving at the house, the children pounded up the stairs to their rooms and Jan went straight to the kitchen, where she set about making supper. As she worked the insinuating words of the press release came back to her mind again.

'It's unbelievable,' she told herself, the anger charging her body once more. 'It's absolutely bloody *unreal*.'

Jan's back was turned to the kitchen door as she filled a saucepan with water, raised the cover on the Aga and slapped the pan down on the hot ring. A few spilled drops fizzled and spat as they made contact with the heat, but above the noise she was aware of a click behind her from the latch of the kitchen door.

'Is that you Megan? Matty?' she called out. 'Supper'll be ready in fifteen minutes, OK?'

'No, I'm afraid you're talking to someone else.'

Jan spun round and her mouth fell open. A woman of about her own age, a complete stranger, was standing in the doorway.

'Who the hell are you?' demanded Jan. 'And how did you get in?'

'The door was off the latch,' said the woman. 'I just pushed and it opened. Am I speaking to Mrs Jan Hardy?'

'Yes, you are. And who in blazes are you?'

The woman was as white as a ghost and very agitated, but obviously determined. She took another step forward into the kitchen.

'My name is Rachel Moorhouse,' she said. 'I'm the wife of William Moorhouse.'

# 11

'Can I offer you anything? Tea, coffee maybe?' Jan asked stumblingly, unnerved by the woman's sudden appearance.

Rachel Moorhouse shook her head and continued walking into the room. She pulled out a chair and sat at the kitchen table, placing her handbag in front of her like a defensive wall. She was a sturdily built woman, wearing jeans and a loose blue shirt, with an unkempt head of wiry black hair.

'Look,' said Jan, almost at a loss for words. 'I'm terribly sorry about what happened, I—'

'Well, don't be. I didn't come here for your sympathy.'

'Then why *did* you come?'

Rachel dug deep into her large shoulder bag and came up with a packet of gum. She folded a piece in half and shoved it into her mouth, then began chewing it with grim determination.

'It's difficult to say, really. To actually see someone who was there when he died, I suppose. And to find out what I'm up against.'

'Up against?'

'The police say it wasn't his fault. He'd never left his side of the road, not until he swerved to the left and hit the tree. He was avoiding an oncoming car, they said, in the middle of the road. Your boyfriend's car, as I understand it, yes?'

Jan shook her head.

'No, no. You've got it all wrong. It wasn't like that, it wasn't like that at all.'

Rachel sighed.

'Yes, of course. You would say that.'

'Look, if you really want to know how it happened—'

'No, no, please. Don't bother,' Rachel said, holding up her hand.

It was as if she was excusing Jan from a chore. She sat chewing noisily and there was an awkward pause. Rather than stand there like a nincompoop, Jan went back to preparing the supper, chopping an onion and then dropping the pieces into the frying pan sizzling on the hob. Rachel watched her stonily.

'You're a widow too, so I hear.'

'Yes. My husband died four years ago. It was a form of cancer.'

'But look at you now, with no problems at all.' Rachel chided in a monotonous voice. 'You're young, good-looking enough, and you've got a nice business. Train horses, don't you?'

Jan suppressed her annoyance at the woman's supposition that running Edge Farm was a complete doddle.

'Yes, that's right.'

'I've never had a career. Too late now. I'll be forty-eight next time. Forty-eight, and going nowhere.'

She exhaled, a shaky self-pitying sigh.

'Hey, come on,' broke in Jan, momentarily provoked. 'That's not old at all. And I don't think it's ever too late, anyway.'

'Huh.'

Jan scissored the rind off some rashers of bacon and chopped them ready for the pan.

'I expect you loved your husband,' Rachel remarked at last.

'Yes I did, and I'm sure you loved William too,' Jan risked, crossing in front of her to the fridge, where she rooted around for mushrooms.

'Me? Oh yes, I was besotted. Loved him to distraction.'

She watched Jan at work, almost suspiciously.

'But that was a long time ago, then it was him who got distracted.'

'Really? What do you mean?'

'Oh, the obvious. Younger flesh. Totty.'

It was not just the words, but the way she said them, that made Jan suddenly realize the truth about Rachel Moorhouse. The woman was not mourning or grieving. She was not even sad. She was angry – deeply, bitterly, corrosively angry.

There was a further pause, only filled with the noise of sizzling onions and the bacon Jan had just added, and the sound of her slicing mushrooms. Then Rachel spoke again. 'He shouldn't have been anywhere near Cheltenham that night, you know. He told me he was going to Cirencester to a funeral. Ha, ha! That's funny, when you think about it. He was a solicitor, you see. A lot of his business was tied up with nursing and retirement homes, so there was an endless supply of old biddies among his clients. They adored him – he had charm, you see, charm to spare for everyone except me. So he'd draw up their wills, that sort of thing, and when they died he said the least he could do was turn up at their funeral. It took me years to find out this was all a sham.'

'He was seeing another woman?'

'Women. Dozens, probably, for all I know. I've no idea how many or where he found them over the years. He was a world-class, Olympic gold-medal bastard, I do know that.'

Jan dropped the sliced mushrooms into the frying pan and stirred them into the bacon and onions.

'So you'd *think*,' said Rachel, 'that I'd be glad to be rid of him. Well you couldn't be more wrong there. He died leaving me completely in the lurch. Negative equity on the house, nothing in his bank account, investments disappeared, life insurance virtually worthless. His pension fund's the same. As for his bloody stamp collection – or rather, to be absolutely precise, British and Commonwealth covers – there were five books of them and he used to go on and on and *on* about how cannily he had bought them, and how they were worth a mint.'

'Weren't they?'

'I got eighty-five quid for the lot. I was told it was pretty standard, a child's collection. And to top that, the icing on the cake even, is that I've still got to look after Wendy.'

'Is that your daughter?'

Again, a bitter laugh.

'No, the kids are all right. Two teenagers. But Wendy lives with us. She's my blind mother-in-law.'

Suddenly Rachel pushed the chair back and stood up. She ran her fingers through her hair, pushing it behind her ears. She bent forward to pick up her bag from the floor, then moved towards the door.

'Well, I won't impose on you any longer. William's partner in the firm is being very helpful, I will say that for him. He probably feels guilty as hell because he knew all along that my husband was a total shit. So he's offered to represent me in the court case. It will ease his conscience, I expect.'

Jan's heart thumped a warning.

'Oh really? What court case?' she enquired, following her visitor out into the hall.

Rachel had hold of the front door. She turned and pointed her index finger at Jan.

'The court case where we sue *you* and your sodding *boyfriend* for damages. It was because you killed that swine between you that we can't meet the mortgage payments, the school fees, or the heating and light bills and frankly not even the bloody food we eat. And I'm telling you, Jan Hardy, I'm not going to let you get away with it.'

It was Rachel's parting shot as she gave a sharp pull on the door knob and let herself out, hurrying to her car in an unexpectedly businesslike manner, which gave the distinct impression of an assignment successfully achieved. Jan watched until she had gone and returned with a hollow pit in the middle of her stomach to the kitchen. The frying pan was sending up billows of black smoke as its contents burned to a crisp.

'Jesus,' she said, picking up the red-hot pan and hurling it into the sink. 'What a crap day.'

With four runners to send out on Easter Monday, Jan had little time to form an opinion about the Cotswold News Agency or the threat posed by Rachel Moorhouse and her solicitor friend. Yet both niggled at the back of her mind and, to make matters worse, she had a bad time at the races, which to others, Jan concluded, would seem to give substance to the horrible idea, enshrined in the press release, that her stable was struggling. Annabel had been at Chepstow, overseeing two lacklustre performances by horses that never looked threatening, and finished in midfield, while Jan was at Hereford, where both of the Edge Farm runners had the misfortune to fall, fortunately without damaging themselves.

After the last race Jan found Toby Waller and Johnny Carlton-Brown, her respective owners, in the members' restaurant, consoling themselves with an early supper and a bottle of Chablis. While JCB was at the bar getting her a drink, she tapped Toby's arm.

'Are you going straight back to London?'

'No, I'm staying the night in Malvern. We've a client living there who wants to get involved in the issue of junk bonds on Wall Street, the crazy fool. I've got to go tomorrow morning and try and talk him out of it.'

'You couldn't drive back via Edge, could you? There's something I want to show you, and I need a chat anyway. Things have been happening and I'm rather worried.'

Toby lifted his glass and winked.

'More developments, eh? Righty ho, m'dear. Will do. I'll be with you by teatime.'

Despite her sense of gloom, not to mention impending doom, Jan giggled.

'Toby, sometimes you sound ridiculously like Bertie Wooster. I hope you're not driving yourself, by the way.'

'No, no. The bank's laid on a driver so I can work while we are on the road. I'm very much their favourite son at the moment.'

On the Tuesday morning Jan decided to drive over before lunch to see Eddie. It was a month since the accident and he had only made limited progress. The temporary inflammation resulting from the shock to his spine was subsiding, but he still felt weakness in both legs and found walking extremely difficult. If there was any under-lying damage to his spine, it had not revealed itself.

The injury to his brain gave him even more trouble: he had recurring headaches which were severe and he was generally despondent and uncooperative. Memories of the weeks preceding the accident had been returning in short bursts, though he said he still knew nothing at all about the event itself, or of anything else that happened during the ten-day period before it.

Jan found Sue Sullivan sitting with her son, working with intense concentration on a piece of embroidery, which she quickly put aside as Jan came into the room.

'I had to have something to occupy me,' she said. 'It's great therapy, as I keep telling Edward. I think he should try it.'

'No way,' Eddie said sharply. 'You won't catch me stitching pictures. I'm not a poof. That's women's work.'

They talked about the weekend's racing. Eddie had seen the results in the racing paper that was delivered to him each day and was highly critical of the jockey and his tactics at Hereford.

'I don't know why you employ that clown, Jan,' he grumbled. 'He rides too short, and I bet he pushed Flamenco too hard approaching the hurdles. When I rode him on the gallops, what he hated most was being forced. He doesn't like the rider dictating to him. As a matter of fact, I bet he fell in protest.'

The idea that the horse fell deliberately was completely absurd, but even so Jan knew there was something useful in what Eddie was saying. Good horses are generally difficult customers or, at least, have minds of their own. Understanding them is half the success of training and riding can be, more often than not, a question of firm diplomacy.

The fact that Eddie had a point did not make it any easier to put up with, however.

'Eddie, Finbar is a good jockey and you know it. You're just being obnoxious,' Jan said, 'and I do mean that in a caring way.'

'If you say so,' he said, with a pout and a shrug.

This short outburst from Eddie was not typical of the whole visit. Jan stayed three-quarters of an hour, during which he was largely silent and uncommunicative, though at times he seemed to be possessed by an inner tension, which he showed by biting his lip and drumming his fingers on the counterpane. Jan became increasingly tense. She tried hard to remain good-humoured, but two or three times found herself speaking more sharply to Eddie than she had intended. When it was time to leave, she felt, if she was honest with herself, relieved.

Sue accompanied Jan back to the car park. She said she had been very comfortable in the bed and breakfast, but now it was time to go home.

'I've got a reservation on a flight back to Australia,' she said. 'The day after tomorrow. Poor Ron is in dire straits. Or maybe I should say diet straits. He's so bored with boiled eggs and tinned spaghetti that he's taken to eating out every night. It's costing him a fortune and it's terrible for his cholesterol – he just loves rich sauces.'

Privately Jan thought: *How pathetic is that? A man's wife has to fly halfway around the world to save him from having too many restaurant meals? Excuse me while I throw up!*

Jan would never dream of saying this to Sue. So instead she asked her if she was worried about leaving Eddie behind.

'Yes, of course I am. He's changed, Jan. I mean, as his mother I can still see he's the same person inside. Of course, I have the advantage of remembering him as a little boy who had tantrums when he couldn't get his own way, but there's no excuse for that in a grown-up, though we mustn't forget what he's been through and still is going through. He'll get over it, I'm sure, with our help.'

Standing beside Jan's car, Sue kissed her on both cheeks.

'Jan, I thank the good Lord Edward's got you. I know you'll always be there for him. If I didn't, I would be rather afraid. He's so down about his prospects. He won't talk about little Alice or about the future in any shape or form. He hates the hospital and he's terribly rude to everybody who's there when they are being so kind to him. He won't even discuss what he's going to do when he leaves. It's like a closed book.'

Sue shook her head.

'So you will give him somewhere to live and look after him when he comes out, won't you, dear? You wouldn't leave him to cope on his own, would you?'

'Of course not, Sue,' Jan replied fearfully. 'I'd never do that, not if I thought for one minute he couldn't manage.'

'He can't. He really can't, Jan. More than anything, I want to see Edward settled in life and I am looking to you, you know that, don't you?'

Ten minutes later, as she turned on to the A40 just east of Oxford, Jan was still thinking about Sue's parting remarks – they came across as a mother's protective feelings, which Jan, being a mother herself, knew were perfectly natural, inevitable even. But at the same time they were infuriating. Sue actually thought Jan would marry Eddie – that was what she was getting at – just because he might struggle to survive on his own, as his father was struggling now out in Australia. But what about Jan's own happiness and that of her children? And what about Edge Farm and all the people who depended on its success?

Jan was beginning to appreciate in her heart that these things were more important to her than ministering to Eddie Sullivan and his existential problems – if that was the right word for them.

Toby arrived in his firm's chauffeur-driven car promptly, as promised, at four o'clock. He found Jan working on race entries in her office.

'So, how did you get on with the junk bonds?' she asked.

Toby wafted a hand in the air.

'Piece of cake. I told him they're only for high-rollers, he'd be putting his alimony payments at risk and showed him a safer alternative. He folded like a concertina.'

'It's the kind of thing A.D. O'Hagan's into, isn't it – junk bonds?'

'Exactly. He's a high-roller. But *he* can afford to get it wrong occasionally. Now, what was it you wanted to talk about?'

As Toby sat down Jan began in reverse order with the visit of Rachel Moorhouse, giving a detailed rundown of the previous day's conversation in her kitchen. Toby listened attentively.

'Well, it's rather as I feared,' he said when she had finished. 'Only maybe it's worse. This woman doesn't just think she may be entitled to compensation. She's desperate for it.'

'At first I was only thinking of her as a victim,' said Jan. 'I mean, that's how she played it. But then, at the end, she just turned on me, you know? Came right out and threatened me with this legal action. I couldn't believe it.'

Toby scratched his head and considered.

'It's rather odd behaviour, I must say. And I'm not sure if it does her case any good, if she's seen to be harassing you in any way.'

'OK, fine, but Rachel Moorhouse was only the half of it. Look at this, Toby.'

Jan handed across the press release, issued by the self-proclaimed Cotswold News Agency. Toby fished a pair of half-moon glasses from his breast pocket and read it through, pursing his lips, then frowning as he came to the end.

'Where did you get this?'

'The vicar's wife gave it to me, believe it or not, and she said more than likely it's gone to all the other parish magazines, and everywhere else dealing in local news.'

'But this is a gossip-column story, stuffed with innuendo, though nothing you could actually nail as a lie, or libel. *A parish magazine?* That's unlikely in the extreme. This is not the sort of thing to put alongside the vicar's rehash of his Sunday sermon, or reports from the bring-and-buy sale.'

'But that's what Viv Taylor-Jones does. She runs the parish mag.'

'Well, it's very curious.'

He thought for a moment, pinching his bulbous nose between finger and thumb.

'I rather suspect skulduggery, Jan.'

He waved the paper in the air.

'This is the equivalent of a poison-pen letter. I think someone's trying to blacken your name and Eddie's, it's as simple as that. May I keep it? I'll do a photocopy and send it back, if you like. I'll see if I can find out who these people are, and if what they're doing is legal.'

'Could it be Rachel Moorhouse, do you think? Or Harold Powell?'

'I have no idea, but maybe. It might be possible to make a complaint to the police, though I don't know if that's advisable because it would just give the story more legs, if you see what I mean. It may just be better to let the thing run out of steam by itself.'

'But will it?'

Toby shrugged.

'If it's just a passing interest of some journalist scraping the gossip off his shoe, it might. On the other hand, if it's some sort of vendetta against you and/or Eddie, it probably won't.'

'What about the threat of legal action by the Moorhouse woman against *me*? Surely that's a vendetta!'

'I don't know. She's obviously a bitter woman, she has reason to be, and who can blame her? But the threat does need to be taken seriously if, as seems to be the case, she's obtained good legal advice. We shall have to do the same. But remember, the threat of legal action is one thing. Actually bringing an action is something else.'

'But she seems to think she can get *me*, not just Eddie. And you said I was in the clear.'

'I meant with the police. I really don't know how it would play in a civil case. I don't know if they've got a case or just a prayer. I'll look into it and let you know. You just get on with the job of training your horses and leave the worrying to your Uncle Toby.'

'But I can't help worrying. I had that journalist Tim Farr here the other night. I thought he was fantasizing because he said he had a theory that the accident on Cleeve Hill wasn't an accident after all, and that the driver of the Range Rover was deliberately trying to run us off the road. But I must say I'm more concerned now if everything I've been telling you ties in.'

'Well, Tim Farr's theory can't tie in with Rachel Moorhouse, since she only fits into the equation as a *result* of the accident. I suppose it could point to Harold Powell. You did say he drove a Range Rover, didn't you?'

He stood up.

'Well, in my opinion, it's useless to speculate too much. We must wait till we've got some more facts. Now, Jan, I think I've just about got time to pop down and pay a visit to my three heroes in the yard.'

🐎

Determined to follow Toby's advice, Jan concentrated on the horses for the next few days. High amongst her priorities was the progress of A.D. O'Hagan's Morning Glory, or MG as he was now known in the yard. She had let him get over the tranquillizer, and had spent as much time as she could with him, to enable them both to get used to one another's idiosyncrasies. Then she took him out on his own for some walking exercise along the quiet lanes surrounding Edge Farm, talking to him to reassure him. Each time MG got anxious Jan drew to a halt and patted him on the neck, encouraging him to pick grass from the banks. When she felt the horse relax she would walk on, and every time the horse 'boiled up' she repeated the process.

It was not until ten days later that Jan decided to give Morning Glory a canter. She was in the saddle, riding full jerk, as the horses left the yard that morning and walked in an orderly file up the track towards the gallop. Jan could feel MG's muscles begin to tighten, then his whole body stiffened as his head came higher.

'Christ, he's strong,' Jan called to Annabel as the horse made a loud snorting noise from his nostrils. Jan felt a huge surge of electricity run through MG's body as he fly jumped into the air, bounding forward like a crazed kangaroo. He veered to the left of the two horses in front of him, colliding with Roz on Arrow Star, then he was gone, accelerating like a Ferrari past the rest of the string. Jan shortened her reins, but with the bit firmly clenched between his teeth Morning Glory took not a blind bit of notice.

'Hang on, Jan, hang on.' Bel's voice could be heard in the distance. As the horse careered towards the gallop, Jan knew she was losing the battle. *We'll be safe when we get to the grass*, she thought. *He'll have run himself out by the time he reaches the top.* But MG had other ideas and a few seconds later he was bearing down on the railed fence which separated the gallop from the field next door.

'Shit,' Jan shouted as she realized she was about to find out what kind of jumper her new horse really was.

# 12

Morning Glory left the ground outrageously early. Jan felt he would certainly smash into the fence and launch her like a wayward missile, somersaulting over his ears. Instead he blasted off, tucking his forelegs tight up under his body, and threw himself to the other side of the fence in a beautiful arc, landing and resuming his gallop in one movement. It was a perfect exhibition of the art of hurdling.

The field where they landed, was flat for about two hundred yards then rose steeply, which immediately took the fire out of the horse. As Jan steered him in a series of ever-decreasing circles, she was at last able to take control, slowly bringing him to a standstill. But the horse was still keyed up, his ears pricked to catch every nuance of sound in this strange new field.

'Christ, MG,' said Jan, patting his neck to calm him. 'You're quite something, you mad bastard.'

The horse snorted as if he understood and took displeasure in the comment, the vapour streaming from his nostrils in the cool morning air.

'Are you all right, Jan?' Bel called when she and the rest of the string reached the top of the gallop.

'Jesus, Mrs H, I was bricking it and I was only watching,' shouted Roz. 'Are there any lumps in wind?'

'I'm not sure,' Jan gasped. 'I'll let you know when I get home.' She was blowing hard, her face as bright a Belisha beacon.

🐎

Later that morning Jan and Annabel were discussing Morning Glory's escapade and deciding what their plan of action should be.

'What made him charge off?' Bel asked.

'I'm not sure. I could feel his whole body start to tense the minute he set foot on the track,' replied Jan. 'And his head got higher and higher. I was talking to him, patting his neck the whole time, then he just exploded. It was bloody hairy, I can tell you. No brakes, no steering. I tried pulling the bit through his mouth from left to right, but it had no effect. I knew I was losing the fight well before we reached the gallop, so I decided to sit still until he ran out of steam. I've seen people jump off runaways, but I haven't the bottle to do that. I would sooner take my chances and stay on board. Mind you, I never expected him to jump that post-and-rail fence like he did; it must be at least four foot high. It was amazing, terrifying but amazing. If he jumps like that on the track he'll make a great chaser.'

They were a fortnight away from winding the stable down for the summer, when the horses would then be turned out into the fields to eat grass and grow fat in peace. It was their annual rest from the routine of stable life, and the development of the youngsters during that time was incredible.

Jan decided not to turn Morning Glory out with the others. Instead she would go on quietly working with him.

'I thought we'd take a few steps back and just walk him. Then every three or four days I can take him into the pony paddock and pop him over some of Megan's jumps. Hopefully the variety will keep him interested in life.'

'What about his tack?'

'I'll try a ring bit first, then a snaffle and hopefully, one day, we can move on to a nylon bit.'

'But they used a citation in Ireland, didn't they?'

Jan knew that a citation bridle would stop a runaway train, but the action of the bit inside the horse's mouth, which was to prise it open when the reins were pulled, was quite harsh and brought its own problems.

'Yes,' she agreed, 'I know they did and you've seen his mouth. Those big sores on the inside of the cheeks just add to his difficulties. The citation's only a last resort, if all else fails.'

Jan had put a call through to A.D. O'Hagan and, later that evening, he phoned back.

'He carted me good and proper into the next field, A.D., and I have to say he jumped the fence in between brilliantly. I had no choice. He stood off and sailed over as if he had been doing it all his life. If I hadn't been so petrified, I'd have cheered.'

'Would you say he's a fast horse, Jan?'

'Oh yes, he's fast all right. But I think he has a problem with other horses being alongside him. If we can cure him of that, we might have a hell of a racehorse.'

'Good. Well, I hope to see him out over hurdles in the autumn. I'm looking to recoup some of the punts I laid out to buy him, you know.'

'We'll have to wait and see if he's going to be ready.'

A.D. laughed. 'He'll be ready. I'm confident if anyone can get him sorted, you can.'

'I suppose,' Jan admitted warily, knowing it would not be a piece of cake.

'Keep up the good work. 'Bye.'

Toby called Jan from London a week after she had first shown him the press release.

'Right, I've got some information, but nothing positive yet.'

'And?'

'As you know, the press release provides no actual info, but it does gives a phone and a fax number. Unfortunately the phone isn't being answered, but it's a live number and the fax is receiving too. I've put a message on it asking them to contact me, but nothing's come back yet.'

'Do you think the numbers were just made up?'

'No, because I've found out they both belong to the same address.'

'How did you do that?'

'I talked to our friend Sandy Wilson.'

Sandy was a retired policeman and a member of a syndicate who had a horse with Jan.

Toby went on: 'Do you know what a reverse telephone directory is?'

'Not a clue.'

'It finds the names and addresses attached to every telephone number in the country. It's a restricted resource, not available to the general public, but of course the police find it very useful.'

'And?'

'Sandy got a friend to run these numbers through it and guess what? They both belong to the same subscriber in Evesham. It's in North Street.'

Jan wrote the address down. Evesham was only twenty minutes' drive away.

'Is there a name?'

'Strangway, initials G.S. That's it.'

'Look, Toby, leave that with me. I'll see if I can find out a bit more from this end. There's a limit to what you can do in London. And thanks. I can't tell you how grateful I am. Now, what about the business of Mrs Moorhouse?'

'It's rather complicated. The insurers, particularly Moorhouse's own vehicle insurers, are bound to become involved, and if it turns out Eddie had none, there's an industry scheme to cover victims of uninsured drivers. But the question of additional compensation may come on top of that. It would of course be in Mrs Moorhouse's interest to see a criminal conviction because she would then be able to prove liability; on top of that she could apply to the Criminal Injuries Compensation Board.'

'So it depends on what the police decide to do. Is that what you're saying?'

'Exactly.'

After Jan had hung up, she delved in her bag for Tim Farr's business card. She found it and dialled his number.

'Mrs Hardy,' cried Farr with welcoming gusto. 'How nice to hear from you.'

'I'm ringing you purely because I am hoping you can give me some information. I hope you don't mind.'

'Why should I mind? Information is my business.'

'Good. So tell me, is there such an outfit as the Cotswold News Agency?'

'The Cotswold News Agency? No. If there was, I'd definitely know about it. It doesn't exist.'

'Is there any agency covering this area, possibly located in Evesham?'

Farr thought for a moment.

'There's a local paper. But no news bureau. I'd say the area was too small to support such an operation.'

'Have you ever heard of any such agency or bureau, or whatever you want to call it, operating for the benefit of parish magazines, community news-sheets, things like that?'

Again there was a pause.

'No, in fact I think the idea's absurd,' he said. 'Outlets like parish mags don't pay for their copy. They haven't got the money, or even the desire, to subscribe to any kind of news agency. It just wouldn't happen, Mrs Hardy. Would you mind telling me what this is about?'

'Sorry, Mr Farr. I can't, not at the moment. Maybe at some point in the future I will enlighten you. 'Bye for now.'

❧

The next day, with no runners to take to the races, Jan drove to the market town of Evesham, determined to discover who was trying to blacken her name with their bogus agency. North Street was a minor residential road, and the address was an old flat-fronted terraced cottage, opening directly onto the pavement. The place didn't look as if it had received any maintenance in living memory. The paint on the door and window frames was flaking off and the single ground-floor window was covered in grime. A lace curtain, brown with dirt, prevented any view of the interior. It looked an unlikely address for a thriving media business.

A stooped, skinny man in his fifties answered her long blast on the doorbell. He had thin grey hair combed over a mostly bald pate, and wore a baggy woollen cardigan.

'Mr Strangway?'

'Yes?'

'Morning. My name's Jan Hardy.'

She looked him directly in the eyes, but saw no sign that the name meant anything.

'Yes? How can I help?'

'Could I discuss a professional matter with you?'

Strangway stepped aside and ushered Jan into the house.

'Please, go through into the sitting room. It's on your right.'

The room was gloomy and unkempt, like its occupier. On the mantelpiece a smouldering cigarette was balanced on the rim of an ashtray. Next to it a glass-fronted mahogany case contained a dramatic little tableau – a stuffed kestrel seizing a vole in its talons. Jan looked around. Other cases were distributed around the room, each displaying stuffed birds, animals or fish. She saw a fox, a large brown trout, a pair of budgerigars and what looked like a domestic cat.

Strangway shuffled in behind her, his breath wheezing. Reclaiming his cigarette, he took a long drag.

'So, Mrs Hardy, how can I help you?' He exhaled and let out a brief bronchial cough. 'It is *Mrs* Hardy? I like to be correct, you know.'

'Yes, Mrs,' confirmed Jan,

'So, is it about a two-legged or a four-legged friend? Or maybe you're an angler bringing me a prize fish?'

'I'm sorry?'

'To preserve.'

Jan glanced again at the display cases all around them.

'I'm sorry . . . I don't understand.'

'You said it was a professional matter.'

Then it dawned on her.

'You're not . . .? You don't . . .?'

'Yes, that's right. Come with me, I'll show you around.'

Strangway beckoned to her as he went back to the hall. He led the way through the kitchen and out into a narrow, uncultivated garden, at the end of which was a large shed. He released the padlock on the door and showed her in.

'This, you might say, is the nerve centre of the operation,' he announced proudly, 'which I rather grandly call my studio.'

Under the shed window was a scrubbed wooden table, harshly illuminated by a bright overhanging spotlight. On it was the cruci-fied corpse of a large white rabbit, with its body spread open from belly to throat, surrounded by an array of scalpels, clamps and syringes. Jars of chemicals stood on a rack to one side.

Jan put her hand to her mouth, suddenly feeling nauseous. The smell of formaldehyde was overpowering.

'Could we go outside, please?' she asked weakly.

Back in the garden, Strangway was looking quizzical. He dropped his cigarette and ground it out.

'So what is it you wish me to give immortality to? As a matter of fact I'm very busy at the moment, but I expect I can fit another job in, as long as it's not a rhino.'

His laugh turned into a fit of coughing.

Jan waited for this to subside before she continued. 'Mr Strang-way, I'm sorry to disappoint you, but it wasn't taxidermy that brought me here.'

She handed him the paper issued by the 'Cotswold News Agency'. He read it through, then looked up bemused.

'Oh, you train horses, do you? It's not something I follow, the turf, so you'll excuse me for not recognizing you.'

'That's quite all right.'

Strangway pointed to the paper.

'I can see this is about you, but I don't understand what it has to do with me. I don't think we've met before – or have we?'

Jan shook her head.

'I don't think so, Mr Strangway. But look at the phone and fax numbers given there.'

He studied the page once more.

'Oh yes! How odd. They're my numbers!' he said in amazement.

She was sure he was genuinely surprised.

'I can only think,' he went on, 'that it's some misprint, a typographical error perhaps.'

Jan shook her head.

'No, it can't be. Look, both your lines are given. We tried phoning, but didn't get a reply, so we sent a fax . . .'

Strangway slapped his brow.

'Oh yes, the fax! I chucked it. Just thought it was a wrong number. It was from a Mr Waller, if I remember right.'

He patted the pockets of his cardigan and pulled out a packet of cigarettes.

'Anyway, I wasn't here when it arrived. I've been away in Germany, working for a private collector. He'd got a tiger he wanted preserving. A very demanding job, that.'

'And you live alone?'

'Yes, alone,' said Strangway, lighting up. 'It's a kind of lonely job, mine.'

He shut and repadlocked the door of his shed and held out an arm to indicate a move back to the house.

'So how on earth did my numbers come to be on this piece of paper? I can assure you this Cotswold News Agency is completely unknown to me.'

'Me too, Mr Strangway. I'm trying to find out who they are, but they seem to be rather elusive.'

Later, outside the office at Edge Farm, Annabel's mouth hung open as Jan related the story of her visit to Evesham.

'You should've seen the place, Bel. Honestly, I've never seen anything like it. There were cases of stuffed animals everywhere, birds, fish . . . And when he showed me into his shed, known as the studio, I bloody nearly threw up.'

Annabel giggled.

'Thank God you didn't. There's nothing more humiliating.'

At that moment a thought hit Jan.

'Just a minute, Bel.'

She darted into the office and Annabel followed to find her boss leafing feverishly through the 'T' section of Yellow Pages.

'Takeaway Food . . . Tank Cleaning . . . Tattooists . . . here we are, Taxidermists.'

She ran her finger down the short list of names.

'Here he is! "G.S. Strangway. Taxidermal services by inter-national practitioner" – don't laugh, he told me he'd been working in Germany – "Preservation and restoration carried out. All species considered. Evesham." Then it gives the phone and the fax number.'

'Jan,' Annabel said deliberately, 'are you thinking what I'm thinking?'

'Well, it's obviously no accident that Strangway's numbers were in that poisonous press release. By the fact that the numbers correspond. The question is, why?'

'I'll tell you what I think,' interrupted Annabel, 'it's clear they got the numbers from there.' She was pointing to the volume of Yellow Pages on the desk. 'And I don't believe Strangway had anything to do with it, beyond innocently placing the advert for his business.'

'But I still don't see why they used him.'

'I think they knew you'd try phoning the number, Jan. They were sending you a message.'

'Get stuffed you mean?'

'Don't, it's not funny. It all sounds too like that scene from *Psycho* – you know, in Norman Bates's office?'

'Oh my God, Bel! I never thought of that. "A man should have a hobby"!'

'Yes, that's it, Jan. Can you think of anything else in the film that fits? Maybe we can get a handle on the villain here, if there is one.'

Jan was musing, trying to remember the plot of a film she hadn't seen for years.

'A woman travelling alone, murdered in the shower by a motel guy who thinks he's his own mother . . . I don't think I know anyone like that, as a matter of fact.'

Suddenly Annabel gasped.

'Oh shit, Jan. I've just had a thought. A very, very nasty thought. Who played the woman?'

Jan clicked her fingers, trying to remember the name and getting it at just the moment Annabel herself pronounced it.

'JANET Leigh!' they both said simultaneously.

🐎

Twice Jan had left messages at Cheltenham police station for DI Hadfield. Now at last, after a fortnight, he returned her call.

'It's about time, Inspector Hadfield,' she said tartly. 'I've been trying to reach you for at least two weeks.'

'I'm sorry Mrs Hardy, but I've been on holiday. Didn't the office tell you? South Africa, actually.'

'No, they didn't.'

'I must say, it's been the trip of a lifetime. Me and my wife. Wildlife safari for a week, then the beach near Cape Town. Fantastic. Saw the lot, lions, elephants, zebra, wildebeest. I've got some incredible snaps . . .'

He paused expectantly, as if anticipating that Jan would suggest she pop round to view the photographs.

'I'm glad it was a good holiday, Inspector,' Jan continued, ignoring the silent invitation. 'But I didn't exactly phone you to get a stripe-by-stripe account of the zebras.'

'Oh, right, of course you didn't . . . so what can I do for you?'

'Well, I faxed you a poxy and damning press release purporting to come from an outfit called the Cotswold News Agency. I wanted to know what you thought. Have you seen it yet?'

'No, er . . . I just got back today. It'll be in my in tray, no doubt.'

'Well it's already been circulated round the parishes in this area, community newsletters and that sort of thing. I see it as a poison-pen letter. But no one's heard of this Cotswold News Agency and the press release itself's completely unprofessional, badly put together. It seems it was just sent to spread nasty gossip, implying for instance that my stable is in crisis, and that Eddie was to blame for the crash.'

'I see. Does it identify itself?'

'Well, it's unsigned, but the phone numbers are those of a taxidermist in Evesham, would you believe?'

'A what?'

'Taxidermist. We reckon these people, whoever they are, want to send me a message of some kind – quite a nasty message, actually.'

'I see. Look, I'll go through my in tray and find it. I'll phone you back immediately.'

But Hadfield didn't phone back immediately and, as the evening wore on, Jan thought to herself he'd probably gone home to stick his safari photos into the family album. She decided to call him again in the morning and give him a piece of her mind.

Just after eleven, Jan was getting into the shower as usual, when she heard the phone ringing. She turned off the tap, quickly wrapped herself in a towel and padded through to the bedroom.

'Hello.'

The voice was muffled, like someone with a heavy cold.

'Hello, Jan. Or should I call you Janet?'

'Who is this?'

'Oh, a friend. Have you been in the shower, Janet?'

Jan shuddered and nearly dropped the phone.

'What?' she managed. 'What did you say? *What* did you bloody say, you bastard?'

But the line was already dead.

🐎

Jan ran downstairs, first bringing in the dogs, then after making sure with feverish, trembling fingers that every door and window was securely locked, she dialled 999. The squad car was with her in nine minutes and a sympathetic uniformed sergeant heard her out, nodding his head like a priest hearing a confession.

'Well, Mrs Hardy, I can appreciate this must have been an incident of some concern to you. You say you've had anonymous calls before?'

'Only twice, and no one said anything then either. But this was far worse. He knew I'd been in the *shower*, for God's sake.'

Jan did not mention the *Psycho* connection. Looking at the broad country face of the policeman, she did not think it would play very well with him, and she didn't want to get into convoluted explanations about Evesham and the poisonous press release. Not until she could talk to Hadfield at least.

When the sergeant completed taking his notes, he snapped shut his pocketbook and pushed it back into his breast pocket.

'Mrs Hardy, most of these calls come from lonely, repressed men who need an outlet for their fantasies. They generally come to nothing and stop quite soon. But some are more obsessive, and we do have to consider every possibility. Is there anyone else on the premises apart from yourself? Your staff maybe?'

'No, they're all living out at the moment. There's only the children.'

'OK, I'll arrange to have a car call round throughout the night, and then with your permission we might come back and install a recording device in the morning so we can monitor any more calls of this nature. But I'll have to talk to my inspector about that.'

'That's not Inspector Hadfield, by any chance?'

The sergeant clearly knew who she was talking about, but he shook his head.

'No, Mrs Hardy. He's CID. They may well get involved at some point, but for the moment it's Uniform you'll be dealing with.'

Knowing that there were two burly members of the Gloucestershire Constabulary keeping an eye on the place gave Jan the confidence to go to sleep that night. It was not a long-term solution, but for now it was better than a sleeping pill.

# 13

With surprising efficiency, Gloucestershire Police installed a device for automatically recording the telephone calls made to Edge Farm, as well as providing an emergency number for Jan. For several weeks neither was needed because there were no more anonymous callers and no unexpected visitors, so Jan was beginning to relax. They were coming up to the time of year, during June and July, when the horses would be turned out to grass and their empty boxes would be thoroughly cleaned by the skeleton staff and Gerry Harris, Jan's builder and handyman. Gerry had come to talk about the job with Jan, to discuss steam-cleaning and disinfecting the boxes and what equipment he would need. The two of them then toured the yard to note any repairs and repainting that had to be done.

As they came to Morning Glory's box, the horse was standing at the back and made no attempt to come and put his head over the half door as most did.

'He's staying in the yard all summer, is he, Jan?'

'Yes. It's a shame really, he's missing out on his summer break, but I'm having to work with him every day.'

Gerry looked serious.

'That won't be no hardship to him, I reckon.'

Jan smiled. Gerry's devotion to her was never expressed, except through oblique compliments like this.

'I bet if you asked him,' she said, 'I'm sure he'd say he'd prefer a bellyful of grass. But he's still as nervous and jumpy as a Jack-in-a-box, so I've got to persevere with him. Mr O'Hagan sees him as his star novice hurdler next season, but I'll have to get his head right first.'

'If anyone can do it, I'm sure you can.'

'Oh, Gerry, that's really kind of you to say that.'

One by one the horses still in training had their last racecourse outings. Even Russian Eagle, his off-hind leg fully recovered, ran once more and won, landing a nice gamble for A.D. – or Jan assumed he had. A.D. rarely discussed his dealings with the bookies, whether successful or otherwise, but he had phoned Jan about the animal's well-being every morning between the four-day acceptance and race day. Jan didn't think even A.D. would have been quite so interested if nothing except the prize money had been at stake.

During one of these calls he departed from his usual script.

'Jan, some policeman from Cheltenham's been trying to get in touch with me. Feller called Hadfield. Something to do with Eddie Sullivan's behaviour in my box on Gold Cup Day. What's going on?'

'It's about the accident we had on Cleeve Hill, I guess.'

'But that's ancient history, isn't it?'

'Yes and no. The police are still looking into it. Have you spoken to him?'

'No. I expect I shall have to eventually, though. 'Bye, Jan.'

A few days later, with a dozen of the yard's inmates already turned out in the fields, and several more gone home to their owners, Reg and Mary came over in the afternoon, Reg to tend the pea and bean rows he'd planted in a sheltered spot behind the house, and Mary for a chat. It was warm and sunny as Jan sat with her mother on the paved terrace that ran the full length of the house, drinking tea and sharing the home-made cake Mary had brought with her.

'How's Eddie?' asked Mary.

'Doing well. They say he'll be ready to leave hospital soon.'

'He must be delighted. It's been such a long time.'

'And how are you, Mum? How's the kidney problem?'

'Doctor says I'm holding my own. Anyway, I didn't come here to talk about myself. Are you OK?'

That was typical of Mary. She had never liked being the centre of attention, much preferring the subject of other people, which meant that she had a mild weakness for local gossip, and a subject she wanted to discuss a few minutes later.

'I've heard something about Virginia Gilbert,' she announced. 'I don't know if I should tell you.'

'Oh, Mum, please! You can't go all coy like that. What is it?'

'It seems she's seeing a lot of a certain estate agent.'

'Estate agent? Not Harold Powell?'

'Yes, that's the one.'

'As a matter of fact, I already know. I've seen them together at the races, they were as thick as thieves. I assumed he was trying to sell her a horse or buying one off her. I didn't realize people were talking about them. What's going on? Is she training a horse of his or are they up to something else?'

'They say the two of them are going together, you know, as a couple – if you see what I mean.'

'As a couple? Harold and Virginia, a *couple*?'

The idea seemed so unlikely that Jan almost laughed out loud.

'I shouldn't think the colonel approves at all,' Mary went on. 'His daughter must be fifteen years younger than that ghastly man, and he's married.'

'Separated to be fair – although I don't see why we should be.'

'Anyway, with you and her always being such rivals, and I remember what you went through with Harold Powell before, so I didn't think I should tell you.'

'Well, you have now and I'm glad you did. What's more, I think they deserve one another.'

As they went back into the house with their empty mugs, Mary spotted the black voice-recorder beside the telephone.

'What's that for?'

Jan had not mentioned the nuisance calls to her parents, not wishing to worry them unnecessarily. But, given that the unit had a sticker identifying it as the property of Gloucestershire Constabulary, now she couldn't avoid it.

'It's just that I've been having a few anonymous calls. The police say it's not particularly unusual. Some sad git with too much time on his hands, probably.'

Mary put her hand to her mouth.

'Oh, my goodness!'

'Can't they trace these calls, then?'

It was Reg, coming in from the garden and pulling off his boots.

'Oh, hi, Dad. I've been told they're probably from a call box. It's nothing, really nothing. Happens to hundreds of women. The recording's just for evidence if they do happen to catch him. How are the peas coming on?'

'Well. You'll be able to harvest them soon.'

Later, Jan took her father down the yard to look at Morning Glory. She wanted his advice, and there was nobody in the world whose opinion she valued more when it came to problematic horses. But as they walked slowly towards the stables, Reg was still mulling over the conversation they'd had earlier.

'Are these phone calls worrying you, girl?'

'Well, yes. I suppose they are, if I'm honest. They're making me really nervous, particularly at night. But the police have been bending over backwards to give me protection.'

'Who d'you think's at it? Sounds like it might be the same folk who's sent round that letter about the yard being in trouble.'

'Yes, I know it does. And, obviously, I've got to suspect Harold Powell. That's even more sinister if he's really joined forces with Virginia Gilbert.'

'Virginia won't do anything against you, I mean not like that. For one thing her father wouldn't let her.'

'Dad, she can do what she likes behind his back. Though you're right about the colonel. He's been a proper ally of mine all along, in spite of Virginia's hatefulness. He doesn't let it affect our relationship one bit. He's even asked me to buy a horse for him at the July sales.'

Reg trudged on, still pondering. At the yard gate he stopped, then turned to Jan and said, 'I don't care for the idea of Powell having any influence on Virginia. She's a vindictive one when she wants to be. Always was, even as a child. And we already know what that man can do when he turns his hand to it, don't we?'

'You're not kidding. In fact, Dad, I think it was Harold Powell who deliberately tried to run me and Eddie off the road after Cheltenham. I think it was him in the Range Rover that overtook us.'

'Hmm, I wouldn't put it past him. He's a bad lot, that's for sure. But have you told the police about all this?'

'Well, I hinted at it, but it's a monstrous accusation to make. Of course I told them how he tried to cheat me out of Stonewall Farm, and they know all about his trial over the death of poor Olwen. They also know it was me that corroborated the evidence against him. Do you think I should actually accuse him of trying to kill me and Eddie? Won't they think I'm paranoid?'

Reg mulled over his daughter's concerns.

'I don't see why they should. It's their job to take all the possibilities seriously. You've got to make them do just that, else something far worse might happen.'

By now they had arrived in front of Morning Glory's box.

'Now, Jan, let's forget about these vile matters for the time being and have a look at Mr Temperamental, shall we?'

Jan's opportunity to make an explicit accusation that Harold Powell had tried to kill her came with unexpected swiftness. The next day Inspector Hadfield arrived at Edge Farm to check the voice-recorder, so he said, though Jan suspected that reason was something of a smokescreen. Hadfield was checking on her rather than on the equipment, she believed.

'Here it is,' she said, showing him the set-up beside the phone in the hall. 'We call it the black box – my own personal flight recorder. Has this now become a CID matter, Inspector?'

'The Uniform branch alerted us to the fact that you have been getting nuisance calls. They do that as a matter of course, Mrs Hardy. And, given that I'm already in charge of the team looking into the death of William Moorhouse, I've been wondering if there's any connection between the two.'

'Well, that's me and you both. I have told you about Harold Powell already, haven't I? If you ask me, it's him behind it.'

'I've made some enquiries about Mr Powell since you suggested he might have been there on Cleeve Hill when Mr Sullivan's car crashed into William Moorhouse's car—'

'But I keep telling you, it *didn't*.'

Hadfield spread his hands.

'All right. Let's say it has been suggested by you that Mr Powell was there on the night of the road accident involving those two cars. He categorically denies it. He says he left the racecourse at least an hour before your accident, which I have confirmed independently, by the way, and that he was already at home in Hay-on-Wye by eight, which was just before the accident.'

'And have you confirmed that last bit independently?'

'No. It's not been possible because he lives alone.'

'Exactly. His wife's buggered off because he's such a toe-rag. He could easily have been waiting for us hidden in a gateway or something. It wouldn't have been difficult to spot Eddie's car.'

'All I can say is, we have no real evidence at the moment that Mr Powell was anywhere near Cleeve Hill at the time. Of course, I've been through his file and I can see he could have a grudge against you, after standing trial over the death of your mother-in-law. If we could establish it was him making the phone calls, that would make quite compelling evidence indeed.'

Hadfield sounded tired, distracted. Even his eternal smile was wilting.

'So what about the letter circulated by this Cotswold News Agency?' Jan challenged. 'Wouldn't you describe that as compelling evidence? The whole thing's a concoction. It's bogus. Tim Farr of the *Daily News* told me there has never been any call for an agency like that. He says the practice of sending news dispatches to parish newsletters and the like is unheard of in this area, and he should know.'

Hadfield gave her a sharp look.

'Has Tim Farr been sniffing around here?'

'Not specially. He's called in once and we've talked on the phone.'

'How interesting. He's been trying to talk to me, too. My

sergeant says he's been sticking his nose rather deep into the circumstances surrounding your accident.'

'I know he has. He thinks the Range Rover wasn't just a reckless driver, but someone who deliberately wanted to do me and Eddie harm. Which is what I've been saying to you all along.'

'Well, frankly, if there's no evidence—'

Jan interrupted, pointing to the black box.

'Excuse me, but why is *this* here? And what about the Cotswold News Agency then?'

'Well, Mrs Hardy, it will do no good getting all wound up about this, but yes, I agree that's a very interesting development. It may be coincidental, we'll have to wait and see. I gather you went to see Mr Strangway personally.'

'Yes, I did.'

'If I may say so, that was rather a rash thing to do.'

'Oh, I don't know. It was obvious he had never heard of me before.'

'As a matter of fact, I agree this time, though you weren't to know that. You need to be more careful. But after speaking to him myself I'm satisfied he had nothing to do with putting his phone number on the circular.'

'Which is already known around here as the poison press release.'

'Ha! That's very apt. It's a rather clever tactic, I admit – I mean, as a way of spreading gossip. There's nothing illegal at all on the face of it. The writer was very careful not to print anything that's not already been printed, or could be printed, in the press. There's nothing prejudicial or obviously libellous.'

'But isn't it libellous to write that Eddie was drunk? They can't possibly know that for sure.'

'But, you see, it doesn't actually say that. It says he'd been celebrating and if anyone chooses to interpret that as being drunk, well . . . Had he in fact been drinking, by the way?'

'Now come on, Inspector Hadfield. We've covered that topic already. He had just enough champagne to make a toast. He wet his whistle and that was it. Let's get back to the poison press release.

Are you saying that, even if you find who sent it out, you can't take any action?'

'Not directly, I fear. But, as you said, it might be used as circumstantial evidence.'

'It's a bit more than that, I think, with its dreadful innuendo about *Psycho*.'

Hadfield looked puzzled.

'*Psycho?* The Hitchcock film?'

'Yes. Didn't you hear what the anonymous shit said to me the other night?'

'I'm sorry, he said what exactly?'

'He asked if I'd been in the shower.'

'Did he indeed? I'm sorry, I didn't realize that.'

The Inspector was clearly put out that he did not know this important fact. He pulled a notebook and pencil from his jacket pocket.

'And you say there's a connection with this press release and *Psycho*? I don't think I follow you. Did he mention the film explicitly?'

'No, it's just obvious. He's wanting me to make the connection myself, which I have done. You see, it ties in with the taxidermist's phone and fax numbers being on the press release. You know what that was all about, don't you?'

Hadfield was staring at her bewildered. 'Hang on a second . . . taxidermy. I hadn't thought of that. *Psycho* . . . the room behind the office of the Bates Motel, full of stuffed birds . . . Janet Leigh saying, "A man should have a hobby." I must have seen the film ten times at least. I'm a big Hitchcock fan, you know.'

'So you'll know Janet Leigh played the victim. Don't you see the connection there?'

Hadfield seemed to flinch under the force of his realization.

'Oh my—! Yes, yes, of course. Jan, Janet. This is extremely interesting – *extremely* interesting, quite disturbing actually.'

'You can say that again.'

Hadfield shot a few more questions at Jan and jotted down some rapid notes. Then he made his excuses and, newly energized, retreated to the car. Now he had an unaccustomed spring in his step and at last Jan thought she was getting somewhere. Until this point in time, she was sure, he had not really believed in the third car on Cleeve Hill, and had been altogether too detached, reluctant even, about the crash, treating it as if he would much prefer to wrap it all up as a dangerous driving case, dump the blame on Eddie and go home to put his feet up. But now, at last, thanks to Hitchcock, Hadfield's interest had been whetted.

🐎

Jan continued to move the horses out into the paddocks, usually in pairs as they were less likely to fight. She only had space for half of them on her own pasture, but a neighbouring farmer was more than happy to host any spares in two of his fields, which meant she had the comfort of knowing where they were and easy visits.

Over the next three or four weeks, when they had settled, the horses would be caught and given their annual inoculations – something Jan preferred to do when they were out of training in case it affected their performance on the track. There was an art to this operation. She found that after a period of being footloose and fancy free, the horses generally became harder to catch. Every group developed a mini herd mentality, a hierarchy in which most things were done in imitation of the herd leader. For Jan and her staff, the trick was to identify the leader in each group – the chief mischief-maker as they called him – catch him first and put a head-collar on him. They then led him into a corner and the others usually followed, after which it was relatively easy to catch and inject them. In most cases, it was Jan who enticed the gaffer into his collar.

They were in the middle of the inoculation procedure when Jan heard the parp-paaarp of a motor-horn coming from Edge Farm. Having successfully collared the lead horse in the field where they were working, Jan left Annabel in charge and drove home as fast as she could. There she found an ambulance waiting outside the house, as the attendant pushed a single figure in a wheelchair. She regis-tered that the ambulance had the words Stoke Mandeville Hospital stencilled on the side and realized that Eddie Sullivan had finally arrived back.

She jumped out of the Shogun and rushed over to him.

'Hey! It's you. This is unexpected.'

'I went on and on and on at them until they had to let me go.'

'Well, it's fantastic, Eddie!'

'I don't know about that. I've nowhere else to go.'

She knew she should kiss him. If he had been standing, maybe she would have because it would have been the kiss of equals. But to go to him, bend over and place a kiss somewhere on his head or face, a helpless man in a chair with a rug over his knees, seemed awkward and false, it would be different from any kiss she had ever given him before. She recoiled, patting him on the shoulder instead.

'Welcome to Edge Farm, Eddie,' she said. 'Welcome back, Eddie.'

He simply nodded.

'I need to go in now,' he told her with matter-of-fact simplicity. 'I need the toilet, and you're going to have to help me. I can't even have a bloody pee on my own.'

# 14

'Oh, all right, Eddie . . . all right . . . if you need me to.'

But take him to the *toilet*. Could he still be as helpless as that? Jan was horrified until she saw Eddie's face. He was looking at her intently, studying the effect of what he'd just said. Then he laughed, not the old full-throated laugh that she used to find so attractive, but a more cynical one. Nevertheless, it was the first laugh she'd heard from him for more than two months.

'Eddie, tell me you can go to the loo by yourself, will you – please?'

Eddie shrugged and spread his hands innocently.

'You needn't worry, Jan. I can go by myself,' he said.

'Then why did you say that?'

'Just testing. You promised my mum you'd look after me – I was wondering how far that extended.'

'That's not very fair, teasing me like that. You're a bloody disgrace, Eddie Sullivan.'

Jan laughed too, from relief more than anything else. Then one of the ambulance crew produced a pair of elbow crutches, which he handed to the patient. Eddie took one in each hand and heaved himself out of the chair.

'As a matter of fact, I can do a lot of things by myself now – not everything, but we can't have it all, can we?'

🐎

Jan put Eddie in Megan's bedroom. The children were delighted to see him again, and happy to double up in Matty's room as they had done when Sue stayed.

But having Eddie around, with his crutches persistently lying in wait for the unwary to clatter into or trip over, certainly emphasized how small Jan's living space was. For the first time she found herself wishing for a bigger house – a feeling she resented because she loved the home Gerry Harris had built for her. One day, she thought, when she had some extra cash, she would get Gerry to extend it, so she could have a spare bedroom, at least.

Eddie got around well, manoeuvring himself through the rooms and up and down the stairs with surprising agility for someone who until recently had been claiming he would never walk again. But his legs were still too weak to support him unaided and they could not be persuaded to do precisely what he wanted. Sometimes, Jan thought, he exaggerated his helplessness, but then she saw him struggling to walk and saw too how quickly his energy drained away. At these moments she felt dreadfully sorry for him.

'Jan,' he said one night, soon after his return from hospital, 'can you talk me through the day of the accident? It's still a complete blank. I want to know everything, every detail.'

Patiently she traced what she knew of his activities that day. She described the race meeting, how the Gold Cup was won, Russian Eagle's success in the Cathcart and the celebrations afterwards. She told him how they had left the owners' and trainers' car park, driven up Cleeve Hill and been forced off the road by the Range Rover.

'And you think that car might have been driven by Harold Powell?'

'Well, yes. And even the police are beginning to get interested in the possibility. If only you could remember a bit more, Eddie. You were driving. You were in a much better position to see who the other chap was than me.'

Eddie gave a discontented grunt.

'Everything I've been saying,' Jan went on, 'doesn't it spark even the tiniest memory?'

'Not the tiniest. So the police are coming round to the idea of my innocence, are they?'

'A little. I don't think they're convinced yet, but certain things have happened. I wish they hadn't, but the plus side is that they support my theory of someone with a grudge against us.'

Jan told him, for the first time, about the poison press release and the anonymous phone calls she had received.

'It could be the widow Moorhouse, couldn't it? She has a grudge against us by the sound of it.'

'The last phone call was from a man. So, if it's her, she's got an accomplice.'

Eddie was specially intrigued by her visit to the taxidermist.

'Great movie, *Psycho*,' he said musingly. 'Do you know you never actually see her getting stabbed?'

Jan shivered. 'Ugh, Eddie, don't!'

'No, it's true. It's a cinematic illusion. You just think you see the stabbing from the way it's edited.'

Eddie relaxed back in his chair and focused on the wall, as if it was a screen. He began to quote, in the portentous voice of the psychiatrist who sums up the story of Norman Bates at the end of the film.

*'I got the whole story – but not from Norman. I got it – from his mother. Norman Bates no longer exists. He only half existed to begin with. And now, the other half has taken over – probably for all time.'*

Eddie turned back to Jan, who was impressed.

'My God, for a man with memory loss you've got amazing recall. And you've got something in common with Hadfield, by the way – he's another *Psycho* nut.'

Eddie shrugged.

'I admit I've seen the film two or three times. But I wouldn't call myself a nutter. To be honest, I didn't even realize I knew those words.'

Although there were evenings when Eddie and Jan talked together, they couldn't get back their old friendship, let alone the intimacy that had once been so special to them. There was a certain reserve now, a holding back, as if they were both waiting for the other to make a move. Jan could not make up her mind about Eddie. She was finding it extremely hard to get used to his different behaviour, with his unpredictable outbursts of anger and bitterness, particularly when they were aimed at her.

She was not sure how best to help him, and decided to telephone the consultant neurologist at Stoke Mandeville.

'I'm confident Eddie's on the mend, Mrs Hardy. It's still very early days,' said a reassuringly upbeat voice. 'But he's not so sure of that as I am, not yet anyway. He won't need a trip to Lourdes before he throws those crutches away, believe me.'

'He seems very depressed. Sometimes he's really volatile. Is this normal?'

'I've seen patients like that many times. It's really very complicated and can be hard to unravel. Depression and anger can often set in because of the slow progress of treatment and the fear of not regaining all one's functions.'

'You mean these dark moods will clear up when he realizes he's not going to be in a wheelchair for the rest of his life?'

'Well, that will help. But not necessarily, I'm afraid. The complication is that he had a severe knock on the head. That alone can bring on long-term depression, sometimes even personality change.'

'He still has amnesia about the day of the accident, Doctor. I don't just mean the crash – the whole day's wiped out.'

'And he may never recover those memories. That in itself can be behind a person's unhappiness. The recovery of memory is seen as important, as if it contains the only key to solving the problem. That's why a lot of uncertainty and anxiety can be focused on the memory loss alone.'

'So what can we do to help him?'

'Keep him busy. There's the programme of exercises he will have already learnt here; he should be doing those every day. And you should arrange regular visits from a physiotherapist through your GP. And if you can keep him active in other ways, that would be all to the good. Give him small tasks, play Scrabble, cards, anything that won't tire him out too quickly.'

At the end of June a fat A4 envelope arrived stamped with the logo of Tattersalls Sales. Enclosed was the catalogue for the auction at which Jan intended to find a horse for Colonel Gilbert.

That night she lay in bed, scrutinizing every page and marking the likely lots. After she'd read for twenty minutes, her eyelids began to droop. Sleepily she turned another page, the type dancing up and down as her sight blurred. She was just ready to let the catalogue drop from her fingers when Lot 214 came momentarily into focus. In an instant she was wide awake. Where had she seen that name before?

The pedigree described was of a well-bred four-year-old, whose sire had been a stayer on the flat, while the dam had progeny that included several National Hunt winners. The gelding's own exploits on the track, running for the Yorkshire flat trainer Clive Appleby, had so far been undistinguished. The description tried to make the best of his dozen or so runs, but to a pro it was clear this horse was considered a failure and Appleby was well known for firing horses out of his yard if they did not live up to his expectations. This particular damp squib was called Velvet Dynasty.

Then in a flash Jan made the connection – it was the race she'd watched on television in Eddie's room at Stoke Mandeville, when she had fancied the prospects of the bay with the squiggly blaze. Velvet Dynasty, she'd said to herself, could make a very nice National Hunt horse some day. Now she pencilled in three thick stars against the horse's name and closed the catalogue. He just might be the one, and he would probably be sold within the colonel's price limit.

The next day she phoned Clive Appleby.

'I've got a client who may be interested in Velvet Dynasty. What can you tell me about him? Is he sound?'

'He's a decent horse, all right, I've always thought a lot of him. He's been catching pigeons on the gallops at home, but he's never come good on the track. We don't know why. It's probably nothing to worry about, a touch of immaturity more like, but my owner, he's the impatient type and doesn't want to keep him on the off-chance.'

*And nor do you, I'll bet*, thought Jan.

'Thank you, Clive. That's very helpful.'

'He'll make you a nice jumper, in my opinion,' Appleby went on. 'There's some class hurdlers and chasers in the family, as I'm sure you already know.'

For a more independent view Jan got the number of Froggie Whelan, the flat jockey who often rode for Appleby's yard. Froggie could not have been more helpful.

'Oh yes, I've rode him in a coupla races. They all had a great regard for him, you know, the way he went at home. But he's been a let-down on the course.'

'But does he have any specific problems I should know about, Froggie? He doesn't break blood vessels, does he?'

'No, definitely not, there's nothing you can put your finger on. Give him a change of air and he might be a different horse.'

Jan knew Froggie was right. Sometimes when horses had problems it was just boredom, or they didn't like the regime they were living under. Another regime, another stable, and they could be utterly transformed.

The sales, held at Tattersalls' Park Paddocks in Newmarket, stretched over three days, but Jan decided to attend only on the second, when Velvet Dynasty was coming up. As a precaution she had marked a few later lots as alternatives for the colonel, but in her mind she had already decided the bay gelding would be her primary objective.

Reg always went with Jan to bloodstock sales if he could. Father and daughter thoroughly inspected Velvet Dynasty in the morning, getting Appleby's lad to walk him out of his box. The quality of his conformation, which had first impressed Jan on the small screen, was substantiated, and the liquid movement when he trotted was a complete joy. Reg walked around him twice, then looked him in the eye. He could see plenty of spirit, but no roguery.

'He's bonnie, Jan,' was Reg's verdict. 'A real bonnie one.'

Threading their way back through the many would-be purchasers who were coming and going on the lawns that surrounded the stables, Jan suddenly drew her father to a halt with a violent tug on his jacket.

'Look! It's them!'

Walking in the same direction, a dozen paces ahead, she saw the backs of a man and a woman. Jan knew the man's angular boniness so well, the tall frame in the tailored country suit and dark hair beginning to turn grey.

'My God, they're walking hand in hand, Dad! With all these racing people everywhere. Do you see?'

'Yes,' said Reg, 'and why not?'

'It means they're making it official, public, that they're together. How horrible. "Harold and Virginia." Yuk! In fact it's worse than sickening, it's sinister!'

Jan had a chance to study the couple more carefully in the refreshment room, where she and Reg went for a ploughman's. Harold and Virginia were drinking wine with a group of Virginia's rich friends, whose booming public-school laughter echoed around the walls and off the ceiling. Harold Powell, she knew, was not from this social background. He was self-made, the son of a Herefordshire farmer. But he showed no sign of discomfort amongst these grown-up children of wealth and reputation, smiling at their jokes, even contributing a few himself, while constantly exchanging fond glances with Virginia.

'Is her father here?' Reg asked, noticing the object of Jan's frequent attention. 'Didn't he say he might be?'

'He rang this morning to say he didn't feel up to it. I had already faxed him the details of the horses I was interested in, stressing that I thought Velvet Dynasty would probably be the best of them—'

'Which he is, to look at,' Reg interrupted.

'He said the pedigrees looked fine and he trusted me to get him something he would be proud of.'

'And so you will, my girl. Only maybe he's sent Virginia just to make sure.'

'That would be a complete waste of time,' Jan replied dryly. 'She wouldn't know Arkle from a pantomime horse.'

Reg popped the last bit of his cheese into his mouth and stood up.

'I just need to pay a visit to the gents,' he said. 'Us old men, you know . . .'

Watching her father make his way slowly between the tables, Jan was startled by the male voice close to her ear.

'You and your mouth, Jan Hardy,' he growled.

She whipped round and saw it was Harold. He quickly slid into the chair Reg had just vacated.

'Been talking about me to the police, have you? You never stop, do you? Will you never learn?'

Harold was speaking in a low, menacing voice, his mouth hard set, his teeth clenched. Jan was too alarmed to say anything as he drummed his fingers on the table.

'That copper Hadfield's been making my life an effing misery, poking around, asking questions, thanks to you.'

Jan looked across to the group Harold had just left. She saw Virginia take a sip from her glass of wine while, at the same time, shooting a swift sideways glance across the room at Harold.

'Look,' Jan interrupted, 'if the police are making enquiries, they must think they have good reason.'

'Yeah, because of your lies, you bitch. You destroy my reputation, my marriage—'

'Well, you seem to be consoling yourself on that score all right,' said Jan, tipping her head in Virginia's direction.

'That's none of your bloody business. Keep out of our way, or I'll see you crushed, you and your precious horses. Do you get me?'

With that parting shot he got to his feet and left.

An hour or so later it was Virginia's turn to have her say. Jan and Reg were sitting beside the sale ring, waiting for Lot 214, when she drifted by alone.

'I hope you're spending wisely,' she said in a sarcastic manner.

Virginia was smiling, but despite her pretence Jan caught the undertone of spitefulness.

'I always spend money wisely,' said Jan. 'I've never had enough of it to do otherwise.'

'But this isn't your money exactly, is it? It's my father's.'

'Your father has approved the lots I may be bidding for,' said Jan.

Virginia stood watching the horse currently being auctioned as it circled the ring, while the auctioneer called out the bids into his microphone.

'Six thousand, five hundred. Come on now, ladies and gentlemen. Who's going to say more for this attractive filly?'

'Oh yes, indeed, he told me,' Virginia said. 'He also told me what he was prepared to pay. It seems an awful lot . . .'

'*Seven* thousand. Thank you, sir. It's your bid. Who'll say seven five?'

Jan made a huge effort to control her increasing anger.

'It's about the right price for what he's looking for. I would have thought you knew that. Or, if you didn't, you must have twigged by now.'

'Well, yes, Jan, as a matter of fact I do know. After all it's why he has most of his horses with me, isn't it?'

The next lot was Velvet Dynasty. Jan desperately wanted Virginia to go away, but instead she sat down right behind her and Reg, literally breathing down their necks.

There were two early bidders. The auctioneer started at five thousand, while Jan stayed out of it until the offer rose past ten, then twelve. There was a pause after one of the bidders dropped out and the other, a well-known Lambourn trainer called Jamie Fuller, looked smug. His expression seemed to say that, at this price, the horse would be a bargain, but the smirk dissolved as Jan jumped in with a flick of her catalogue.

'A new bidder on my right! Twelve thousand five hundred. Thank you, ma'am. Do I hear thirteen, sir? Thirteen thousand guineas?'

Fuller looked pained. He raised his catalogue, then he and Jan batted back and forth in increments of five hundred until the bar stood at seventeen and a half thousand. The next bid was with Jan. She lifted her catalogue once more.

'Eighteen thousand guineas,' the auctioneer called. 'Now, sir, the bid is with you at eighteen thousand five hundred. No? This is your last chance. Won't you reconsider? You may regret it, you know.'

But the Lambourn trainer had had enough. He shook his head impatiently, clearly riled by Jan's unexpected intervention. The auctioneer looked around.

'Any more? No? Selling, then, at eighteen thousand guineas once . . . twice . . . SOLD to Mrs Jan Hardy.'

He banged his gavel.

'Thank you, ma'am, it's good to see you here,' he said, scribbling down a note of the price and the buyer. 'And now, Lot two hundred and fifteen is a four-year-old grey gelding by Shareef Dancer . . .'

As Jan watched her new purchase leave the sale ring, she turned to her father full of joy.

'We got him, we got him, Dad!' she whispered, forgetting Virginia's presence.

'Yes, and I don't think you'll regret it,' said Reg, equally pleased.

'Oh, but you will if what I heard this morning is correct,' said Virginia, leaning forward. Jan turned round.

'What was that?'

Virginia nodded to where Velvet Dynasty's rear end was disappearing from view.

'He's a whistler, so I've been told.'

Jan looked at Reg in alarm. A whistler was a horse with suspect breathing. It often followed an attack of pharyngitis, bronchitis, pneumonia, influenza or pleurisy and could seriously affect a horse's performance. Could Virgina be right? It wasn't something you could tell by just walking or trotting a horse up and down a stable yard at a sales complex. Only when the horse was galloping would the larynx make a high-pitched sound.

Reg just shook his head, as if to say he didn't think it a very likely story.

But on their way home the question of Velvet Dynasty's wind was still on Jan's mind.

'What if she *is* right, Dad? I'll have to return him.'

'Well, if he was, I don't reckon that Jamie Fuller would've been bidding for him. Didn't you talk to the jockey beforehand?'

'Yes, Froggie Whelan. He never mentioned it and he'd have had nothing to gain from keeping it from me, would he? I asked him if the horse was a bleeder and he said the horse was completely sound as far as he knew.'

'That's all right then,' said Reg. 'So stop worrying. You're not going to know for sure till you get him up on those gallops and the vet's had a listen to him. Virginia was probably just taking the Mickey. Like I said, she's got a nasty streak a mile wide, that girl.'

# 15

Jan couldn't stand the uncertainty of not knowing if Virginia's jibe about Velvet Dynasty was correct or not. As soon as she got home she rang Shirley the vet.

'Shirley, I need you here first thing in the morning to listen to a horse's wind. I bought him from Newmarket sales today and he had a clean certificate, but I've since been informed he's a whistler.'

Shirley detected the anxiety in Jan's voice.

'Jan, I'm operating on a horse in the morning, so I can't come then. You've got seven days to notify Newmarket, so surely it can wait a couple.'

'*Shirley!*' Jan said with an edge to her voice, 'I need to know. Not only for my sake, but I bought the horse for Colonel Gilbert and I need to let him know what's what.'

Shirley stood her ground. 'Well, as I said, Jan, I can't do tomorrow. But I do have a colleague over from America who's staying for a few weeks, he could come along instead. His name's Lance Clancy.'

'That's fine. Tell him to be here at seven-thirty, and by the way, Shirley, he'd better know his job.'

🐎

When he arrived to examine Velvet Dynasty in his stable, Lance Clancy first opened the horse's mouth and had a good look inside.

'Now then, little lady, everything seems OK in there,' he confirmed, letting go of the tight hold he had on the horse's muzzle, who snorted his disapproval. Lance then placed his thumbs and forefingers on the horse's throat in the area of his Adam's apple.

'Can't feel any problems there either. So we'll endoscope him now, then he can go out to exercise. I'll listen to him on the gallops and we'll endoscope him back here in his box afterwards.'

'Would you like a coffee while I tack him up?' Jan asked. 'Roz will get you one.'

'No thanks, little lady, we'll get the job done first.' The phrase 'little lady' was beginning to grate on Jan's nerves. Maybe it was just his southern twang. Other than that, she had to concede he seemed a very nice bloke.

'OK. If you go up the gallops in my Shogun with Annabel, my assistant, I'll let the horse stride on past you at the four-furlong marker and then I'll trot back to you.'

'That'll be fine, little lady,' said Lance.

OK, Jan thought, getting more irritated by the second, *just drop the little lady. It's worse than 'you know what I mean'.*

Jan eased Velvet Dynasty into a canter, steadily building up speed, until he zipped past the vet and Annabel. Jan listened intently to the horse's breathing as she eased him to a trot.

'That sounded perfectly clear to me,' she declared as she reached the place on the gallops where the vet, equipped with his stethoscope, was waiting to continue his examination.

'Sounded pretty clear to me too,' Lance agreed.

As he finished the endoscopic procedure back at Edge Farm, he declared, 'Apart from a bit of mucus, I can see no problem at all. Little lady, you have yourself a fine young thoroughbred and I'm sure he'll win plenty of races for you. Now, you mentioned some coffee. I sure could handle one if the offer's still open.'

'Sure,' said Jan almost imitating the Yank, 'come on up to the house. Fran will have some freshly made.'

As she entered the house, the red message light was flashing on the answering machine. Jan pressed the play button and heard the voice of a worried-sounding Reg.

'Jan, it's your dad. Give us a call as soon as you get in. It's important.'

Jan dialled and Reg picked up the phone almost before the ring tone started.

'Dad, you sounded upset. What's happened? Is it Mum?'

'No, your mum's all right. It's Colonel Gilbert. There's been burglars at the Manor.'

'Oh, no! Is everyone OK?'

'No, at least the colonel's not. He was there on his own and heard glass shattering in the night, three a.m. or something. Anyway, he thought it was the storm, so he went downstairs without thinking and found two men in his dining room, so they're saying. Helping themselves to his silver, they were. The colonel shouted that he'd got a gun and they took off through the French windows. Apparently, the colonel ran after them shouting, threatening them and then he just collapsed on the lawn. There was no one to help him. So he just lay there.'

'Oh, the poor colonel! How *awful*. How long was he out there?'

'They didn't find him till morning, when Mrs Whatsername came in between six-thirty and seven.'

'Oh, Dad! You mean he was out in the open for hours, in that dreadful weather?'

'I don't think he was conscious, mind. They say he'd had a heart attack, on top of that there was hypothermia, as he'd been lying in the wet. They took him to hospital, but he was more dead than alive. They don't expect him to recover, that's what I've heard.'

'Well, *they* can always be wrong. We've got to hope for the best, Dad.'

'OK, girl. I'm sorry to be the bringer of bad news. I thought you should know, you having two of his horses.'

Lance sensed the tone of the conversation Jan was having with Reg and silently mouthed, 'I'll catch up with you later for the coffee. 'Bye for now.'

Jan held up a thumb and mouthed back, 'I'm sorry, thanks very much.' As the vet left, she turned her attention back to the phone and Reg.

'Yes, Dad, thanks. Speaking of which, I've only just come in from galloping Velvet Dynasty.'

'What was he like?'

'Like magic, and what's more the vet gave him a clean bill of health – no wind problems at all. He's going to be good, Dad, I just know it. He's very willing and really fast, with fantastic acceleration.

Give him a bit of schooling and I reckon he'll take to hurdling like a good 'un – maybe a *very* good 'un.'

'Well, that's something anyway. We must hope the colonel will be here to enjoy it.'

'The first chance I get I'm going down to the hospital to tell him. It will do him the world of good to know we've bought him a future champion. It's the best possible medicine he can get.'

Annabel and Jan had coffee together in the office, as they did most mornings. Normally they would talk about possible races for the horses, training and veterinary problems, the staff, the feed supplies and the many issues that arise from day to day in a working racing stable. But at this quiet time of year, when most of the staff and horses were on holiday, there was little enough to discuss and Jan concentrated on describing the new horse's exciting gallop.

'Gosh, he sounds like a real prospect,' said Annabel.

'Potentially the best hurdler I've had,' Jan said. 'I can't think why he was such a flop with Appleby. He's got real speed. I haven't travelled so fast on a horse since MG carted me.'

'How *is* MG? From what I've seen at a distance he's still quite a handful.'

Jan sighed. 'No real progress, I'm afraid. God, it's frustrating. He's so tense, always keyed up. The enormous amount of energy he uses putting himself under pressure is such a waste. Once he sets foot outside the stable he's on such a high burn. I need him to trust me. But some days he won't do a single thing that I want him to do. The awful thing is I believe he could be every bit as good as Velvet Dynasty – maybe even better. But at the moment he's got about as much chance of going racing as a clothes horse.'

Annabel was sitting with her head and long neck bent back, gazing dreamily at the ceiling.

'But just think of it, Jan. If we can get him right, Edge Farm might have, not just one, but two brilliant novices. That would really bristle the moustaches of the tweed brigade. What a lovely thought.'

Jan drained her mug. 'There's nothing I'd like more, but there's a long way to go before that happens.' She chuckled, getting to her feet.

As the two women strolled into the yard to rinse their mugs under the tap, grunts and groans could be heard coming from one of the boxes on the opposite side, where Eddie's crutches were leaning against the wall. This was where Gerry, after consultation with Jan, had laid some threadbare carpet on the floor and brought in a couple of poles from the pony paddock, fixing them securely on trestles as parallel bars. Roz had borrowed a rowing machine from a friend in the village, while Declan contributed some old dumb-bells. Now it was Eddie's personal rehabilitation unit.

Jan and Annabel, like a pair of snoopers, peeped over the half-door of the loose box. Eddie was lying on the ground in his tracksuit, spread-eagled and breathing heavily, his eyes closed, sweat dripping from his forehead.

'Hi,' said Jan. 'How's the Arnold Schwarzenegger routine?'

Eddie opened his eyes. 'Bloody terrible. Help me up, you two. I've had enough.'

Jan unlatched the door and went in, followed by Annabel. Taking one arm each, with care they hauled Eddie to his feet. Once he was standing he shrugged off their supporting hands.

'Let go of me. I can walk to the door on my own.'

Grimacing at the effort, he moved with a drunken, dragging gait. The two women hovered nervously, one on either flank, ready to catch him should he crumple or lurch too far from the vertical. It was only half a dozen paces, but Eddie completed his task unaided.

'Eddie, you're so much better,' exclaimed Annabel.

'I don't know about that. I haven't noticed any improvement. It seems to me I'm just the same as when I left Stoke Mandeville.'

'No, you're not,' said Jan. 'You're definitely on the up.'

Eddie grunted cynically. 'On the up? If only you knew the half of it! Pass me those sodding crutches. I'm too knackered to go without.'

In the afternoon Jan rang Cheltenham General Hospital.

'I was wondering about Colonel Gilbert, and if I can visit him. He was brought in this morning.'

'Please hold,' said a female voice.

Jan was put through to someone else and repeated her enquiry.

'Are you a relative?'

'No, I'm a . . .'

What was she? Employee? Friend? Business associate? Not exactly any of these, and yet, in a way, all three. She settled for 'A family friend.'

'I'm terribly sorry, but I have sad news. The colonel died at about ten-thirty this morning.'

Jan gasped. Despite what Reg had said earlier, she was unprepared.

'I see. Did he . . . did he regain consciousness?'

'No, I'm afraid not. It was very peaceful.'

'I see. Thank you.'

Jan stood numbly by the phone listening to the tick of the hall clock. An airliner mumbled across the sky. Then, from what seemed like miles away, she heard a car draw up outside. She knew it must be Fran bringing the children home from school.

Now her feet felt as if they were glued to the floor. It was hard to believe that Colonel Gilbert was dead. She'd known him, as her parents' landlord, all her life, and though they were separated by both age and class she had respected and liked him enormously. All right, she admitted, he was a bit of an old codger, but a kind and loyal one, and he'd never been anybody's fool, that was for sure.

Jan was suddenly brought back to the present as the front door burst open and Megan raced into the house. She shouted a greeting and charged up the stairs.

'What are you doing?' her mother called after her.

'Changing, putting my joddies on,' came the answer. 'I want to put Monarch over a few jumps before tea.'

Monarch! He'd belonged to the colonel; he had lent him to Megan for her junior eventing. What would happen to the pony now? It would break Meg's heart if she had to part with him. And what about the other Gilbert horses in her care – the racehorses, including Wolf Rock and this brilliant new one Velvet Dynasty? Their training fees helped to pay the bills. If they left, she'd lose a crucial amount of her income at a stroke. Few businesses could take such a hit easily and certainly not hers.

Briskly pulling herself together, she went to the bottom of the stairs.

'Megan, you'd better come down. I've got something to tell you.'

Five minutes later her daughter was in tears. Jan explained that Monarch's fate would be decided by the colonel's heirs, his daughter Virginia and son Harry.

'But they won't take Monarch away from me, will they? They can't! They absolutely can't.'

'Sweetheart, they can. But that doesn't mean they will. We'll have to wait and see. I'm sure nothing's going to change for the time being. Anyway, this is no time to be thinking about ourselves. We must remember poor Colonel Gilbert, he's been so kind to us in the past.'

Megan pouted.

'I suppose so. But I *hate* those burglars – it will be all their fault if Virginia Gilbert takes Monarch away.'

A little later Matty came solemnly to his mother, who was sitting in the lounge, and crept onto her lap.

'Mum, is Colonel Gilbert in heaven? With Daddy?'

'Yes, darling,' Jan gulped, stroking his hair as he put his head on her breast. 'I'm sure of it. The colonel was a very good man. Daddy will look after him.'

🐎

The funeral was held a week later and, though Jan and her parents arrived in what they considered to be plenty of time, there was precious little room left in Riscombe's medieval church. The benches were packed with dignitaries and a high proportion of the village population, many of them tenants who depended more or less on the squire and his estate for a living. Harry and Virginia Gilbert sat in the family pew at the front. She was wearing a stylish black outfit with a string of pearls, while her twenty-four-year-old brother, her junior by seven years, wore an Italian-style black suit, the uniform of a young City slicker. But there was no sign of Harold Powell.

The colonel was dispatched according to the rites of the Church of England, with nothing added and nothing taken away. The hymns were sung, the vicar gave his eulogy and prayed over the body, and the coffin was carried out for burial in the Gilbert vault, which was surmounted by an ornate Victorian structure. Over the door the Gilbert coat of arms was flamboyantly carved in marble. Sniffles had been heard throughout the service, but there was no outpouring or other demonstration of grief even now as Virginia, dry eyed, followed her father's coffin down the aisle, though Jan thought she saw Harry surreptitiously wipe away a tear with a knuckle.

Outside, in a fine drizzle, the congregation watched as the colonel was laid to rest beside his late wife.

'I thought he was a lovely old gentleman,' said the postmistress later to a group of mourners, which included Jan. They were at the funeral gathering at Riscombe Manor in the already crowded ornate room known as the Great Chamber, which had been added to the medieval structure by an Elizabethan Gilbert four hundred years ago. Its walls were lined with linen-fold panelling, and the ceiling had a complicated patchwork design in highly decorative plaster, while the high mullioned windows were inset with coats of arms in stained glass. 'He liked to do things the old-fashioned way.'

*You can say that again*, thought Jan. Under Colonel Gilbert the Riscombe estate had in many ways been suspended in a time warp. The rent continued to be collected on the traditional quarter days – Lady Day, Midsummer Day, Michaelmas and Christmas. By modern standards the estate workers were poorly paid, but they received, in the colonel's opinion, considerable benefits in kind: free issues of scrumpy from the Riscombe cider press, fruit and vegetables from the kitchen garden and honey from the beehives, while the colonel played the part of country squire to the hilt. He had been very active in the community, opening the annual fete, judging dog shows, chairing the board of school governors and the parish council, acting as local magistrate and, from time to time, accepting various ceremonial county offices, such as the high sheriff.

'Yes, he was tradition-minded, was the old colonel,' said George

Machin, the village butcher, whose sausages were famed for miles around. 'And there's gunna be changes all right, with these young 'uns in charge, that's for sure.'

There was a lot of speculation about Harry Gilbert. It was thought he had little appetite for playing the squire and would probably cling to his well-paid City job, leaving the estate affairs to Virginia. This idea was not universally popular as Virginia was regarded with some suspicion for her high-handedness and apparent meanness. On the other hand, it was felt she knew a great deal more about country life than her brother, who was seen as little better than a flash City boyo. Everybody remembered how he'd once killed a heifer on the Winchcombe Road in his Mercedes sports car, and offered the farmer a twenty-pound note by way of compensation. The matter had only been resolved by the colonel's intervention.

Jan noticed a group of Virginia's stable staff standing together in the large window recess and made her way over. The head lad, Scottie Venables, was a small easy-going man whose knowledge of horses would have commanded more respect had he not been so fond of the bottle.

'Mrs Hardy!' he said, tossing back his wine and reaching for another from the tray of a passing waiter. 'I hear good things about this new horse you bought for the colonel, but I reckon he'll be coming to us before too long.'

'In that case you know more than me, Scottie. Miss Gilbert's said nothing about it either. The colonel's will hasn't been made public yet, has it?'

Scottie nodded, swaying slightly on his feet.

'That's right. The boss has said nothing to me about it. But we'll have him back at Riscombe before September, mark my words.'

'It must be right if you say so, Scottie,' Jan said with a forced smile.

They continued to talk about more general racing topics until Jan noticed her father signalling to her that he and Mary wanted to leave. Jan crossed the hall to the cloakroom to gather their raincoats. She was searching through the damp, higgledy-piggledy pile when someone came in behind her.

Virginia shut the door and leaned her back against it.

'I'm amazed you've got the bloody nerve to come into my home and chat up my stable staff,' she said with quiet menace.

Jan found her father's coat buried on a hook under six or seven others. After a struggle, she unhooked it and turned to face Virginia.

'I don't know what you mean,' Jan said as coolly as she could. 'I came here out of respect for your father, not to chat anyone up.'

'You're a common, underhand, conniving bitch, Jan Hardy. I don't want you here. You're not welcome in this house and you never will be.'

Jan coloured.

'I may be common as muck in your eyes, Virginia, but when it comes to conniving, it would be impossible to beat you and your new boyfriend.'

'What's *that* supposed to mean?' hissed Virginia.

'You and Harold. These games you're playing. It'll all come out, you know. Because I'll make sure it does, however long it takes.'

'Fuck you. You'll make sure of nothing. I'll see you in hell first,' Virginia raged. She turned and grasped the door handle.

'Oh, one more thing,' she continued, speaking more lightly, as if she had just thought of something juicy to hasten Jan's demise. 'You've got several horses you shouldn't have in your yard, including Wolf's Rock and Velvet Dynasty. They're *my* horses now and I'll be sending my transport to collect them the day after tomorrow. I'd be obliged if you'd have them ready to travel.'

'What about Monarch?' asked Jan, almost in a whisper. She wished she hadn't had to ask the question because to do so put her in a weaker position, almost like a petitioner.

'What?' Virginia sneered. 'That shitty little pony? What possible use would I have for him? Particularly since your daughter has no doubt been busy ruining him for the past year. My father, in his wisdom, realized this. He left the animal to her in his will.'

Virginia yanked open the door and marched out. As Jan searched on for Reg's tattered old golf brolly, she felt a bubble of relief rising inside her, which partially displaced the heavy black anger she felt towards Virginia. Monarch at least was staying.

'Thank you, Colonel,' she whispered devoutly.

# 16

Around the middle of July, Lady Fairford got in touch to say she was in need of six weeks' stabling for two hunters, and she wondered if Edge Farm could take them. It did occur to Jan that it was an unusual time of year for hunters to be exercised, but Lady F said they were youngsters and needed a bit more educating before she could go cubbing with them in the autumn. Jan thought it was more likely her ladyship had heard the rumours about Virginia Gilbert's treatment of her and wanted to apologize in a roundabout way. Though it meant exercising and schooling the new inmates, Lady Fairford paid generously, and this way Jan had a little extra money to help plug the hole and make good some of the training fees lost after Wolf's Rock and Velvet Dynasty's removal from the yard.

Most days Jan and Annabel had been taking the Fairford horses up to the ridge and onto the bridle path that ran along its length for four or five miles. It was a superb ride, which passed through a couple of small woods and gave them a chance to talk in the relaxed way that horse riders do when hacking through beautiful country. It was amazing that, however many problems you set out with, they soon got washed away, they agreed.

'But are you *sure*, Jan?' Annabel continued, as the horses picked their way along the sandy track that snaked through the first of the copses. 'There's so much going on at the moment and I'd feel a bit of a rat leaving you.'

Every year they had the same conversation about the pros and cons of Annabel taking a holiday in August.

'There's nothing going on I can't handle,' Jan said. 'It's the silly season. These two fellows are leaving next weekend. Most of the horses are turned out. The weird phone calls have stopped and no more nasty news bulletins have been sent out. I also think the police have Harold well and truly in their sights, and he's very unlikely to try anything on, not at the moment anyway. So I'll be all right, honest. You're entitled to a holiday, so get off and enjoy yourself while you can.'

'But what about you? How long is it since you went away with the kids?'

Jan sighed. How long? Actually, when she thought about it, she realized she'd never been away with the kids, not since John died. Not properly *away*.

'Well, we're all going over to stay a week with Mum and Dad at Riscombe. Gerry wants us out of the way as he's putting in a proper fitted kitchen. Ben's going to be home. It'll be great, all of us together.'

'Is Eddie going too?'

'Eddie? No. That'd be a bit too much for my poor mother. He'll be the caretaker at Edge. Gerry thinks he can probably make use of him, bending lengths of pipe or something.'

'They get on well, don't they? Surprisingly.'

'Why surprisingly?'

'Come on, Jan. You know how Gerry feels about you. You'd think he might be jealous, but not a bit of it. Since the accident he's been Eddie's best mate.'

'Not to mention his personal fitness trainer.'

They emerged from the wood to a place where the path followed the apex of the ridge. The views were sensational. From there they could see at least six counties. To the west was the lower Severn and beyond that the Brecon Beacons and South Wales, while, if they turned the other way, the fertile fields of Gloucestershire were spread out beneath them. They drew their mounts to a halt and sat in the early morning sun, breathing in the fresh, clear air, two silhouettes against the sky.

'So, anyway,' Jan continued after a few moments' silence, 'what are these holiday plans of yours?'

Annabel coloured slightly.

'I've been invited over to Barbados to do some scuba diving.'

'Wey-hey! That sounds sexy. Who by?'

'Johnny Carlton-Brown, actually.'

'Really? That's fantastic. Is it a big party?'

'No, it's not a party at all. Just me.'

'You mean just you and him?'

'Yes, I'm afraid so'

'No one else at all?'

'No. Not another soul.'

'Bel, is there something you haven't told me? Have you two been getting together on the sly?'

'Not on the sly. But we have been out a few times. I like him.'

'What happened to whatever her name was – Vanessa, that's it, the actress? I thought she was his girlfriend.'

'Not since she won that Oscar. She's dumped Johnny and decamped to Los Angeles. She's going out with some brawny action hero now.'

'So why didn't you tell me you were seeing JCB until now?'

'Oh, you know me. I didn't consider it was a big deal, and I don't want a big deal made of it.'

'Is it a big deal, though?'

'No, *definitely* not. As I said I like him – uhm, quite a lot, actually. But I'm not in love with him.'

'Not yet, but you wait till you get out there. Lightning can strike without warning, you know.'

'They say the hurricane season's over.' Annabel laughed. 'I expect I'll be safe enough.'

🐎

Jan started to give Eddie a briefing on everything that might occur during her absence at Riscombe.

'Yes, yes, Jan,' he interrupted. 'I know how it all works in the yard. Remember, I have worked here before. I've got your parents' phone number and anyway you're only a few miles away. Just leave everything to Gerry and me, we'll be fine. He's offered to stay in the house if I need him to.'

'It sounds like you'll be glad to see the back of us.'

'Rubbish. I want you to have a rest. You're going to need one before the start of next season. So I don't want you worrying about this place, or about me.'

'Well, of course, worry is something you can't control that easily when you have animals to deal with, whether they have two legs or four. Anyway I'm inclined to do it by myself, but you could help me out, maybe.'

Eddie shot her a warning glance.

'What do you mean, help you out?'

Jan sensed that they were swimming in deeper waters than they had been exploring recently, but she plunged on.

'It's just that . . . well, it's the way you are these days. You're so impatient, so critical all the time . . . so hard on yourself. I wish you'd ease up.'

'Ease up? I can't ease up or I'll be in that bloody wheelchair for the rest of my life.'

'Come on, I know you have problems. But you're not the only one. Everybody has them. I have stacks.'

'Yes, the most obvious being me, I suppose.'

Jan could not deny it.

'The point is, I expect you to get over your problems. You seem to feel that unless you are always fighting you will actually go under.'

'What do you expect me to think? I'm a sodding cripple.'

'That's crap, Eddie. Just look at the progress you've made. You were in a bad way, I admit. You couldn't speak properly, or take a single step unaided, or remember what year it was even, but look at you now. You have improved out of all recognition.'

Eddie gave a bleak smile.

'The trouble is I keep thinking of the things I still *can't* do four months on.'

He spread his fingers and counted. 'I still can't walk the way I could. I can't remember the accident, the worst day of my life. A man died and I don't even know for certain whether I was responsible.'

'Eddie, get a grip! You were *not* responsible—'

'Let me finish, will you? I can't ride or drive, play tennis, earn a living, sleep through the night, or have a bonk even.'

'*What* did you say?'

Eddie gave a tired shake of his head. Suddenly all the fight seemed to have gone out of him.

'You heard.'

'I've been wondering how long it would be before that subject came up,' Jan said gently, tears welling up in her eyes.

'Don't worry. It probably won't again. I'm not criticizing you, am I? It's not your fault.'

'Are you sure?'

'No, this is something I have to deal with alone.'

'Oh? And there's me thinking sex is better when there are two people taking part.'

'That's not funny. It makes no difference, Jan.'

'What's that supposed to mean?'

'It's supposed to mean I can't do it, not anyhow.'

He was staring fixedly downwards, apparently studying his shoes. In reality, he was unable to meet Jan's eyes.

'Tell me, Eddie.'

'All right. It's like this. I don't think I can have sex at all. It's a physical incapacity.'

Jan tried to hide her astonishment. It would explain a lot of his behaviour, but why had he not told her this before?

'Is that what the doctors are saying?'

'No, I haven't discussed it with them. Well, not since Stoke Mandeville, when it was mentioned as one possible effect of the spinal damage.'

'Temporary or permanent?'

'One or the other.'

'Why did you keep this from me?'

'I didn't, not deliberately. But it's not easy for a guy to confess to. It scares the shit out of me, if you really want to know. My eyes see you, I smell you, my mind wants you, but nothing happens.'

'So, it's this that's making you angry? I'm really sorry, Eddie, you should have said something before now.'

'Jan, I know I've been ratty, but that's because I feel so low. I can't seem to see any light or a way out of this black hole at the moment. I just wish we could, you know, get back to the way we were. As a couple I mean.'

'Do you, really?'

Eddie sighed and spoke very quietly. 'But anyway, it's just wishes, isn't it? And they don't come true very often, do they?'

🐎

The Pritchards had always been a close family, and Jan genuinely looked forward to returning with her children to stay in the house where she had spent the best part of her childhood. Particularly, on this occasion, because her brother Ben was staying too.

Jan felt Ben's life had something of the prodigal son about it. Years ago he'd left England as a mumbling nineteen-year-old with a backpack and a guitar, in flight from Reg's desire that he would knuckle down and they would work the land together. But Ben ended up in Australia, where slowly he began to fashion a reputation as a musician and songwriter. After four years maturing, Ben came back – a more complete, more articulate young man than seemed feasible – to land a job as a record producer in Johnny Carlton-Brown's rising company, Brit Records.

On their first evening reunited at home, the Pritchards had a big family meal, washed down with plenty of Riscombe cider. They played French cricket, then reminisced until late in the evening, when Ben got out his guitar and sang them half a dozen of his own delicate, bluesy songs. Halfway through one of the numbers, 'Wedding Tune', Jan found tears stinging her eyes.

'That's a beautiful song, Ben,' she sniffed as he played the last chord. Jan had to admit she was a little woozy from the cider. 'What are you doing writing about weddings, you sad old bachelor?'

'It's not about me, Sis. Actually, I was thinking of you when I wrote it, you and John, on your wedding day.'

It was then Jan burst into proper tears.

Next day brother and sister went off first thing to do their mother's big shop. When Jan returned, hauling in a cargo of bulging plastic bags, she knew instantly that something was wrong.

Mary was sitting at the kitchen table, her old face puffy from crying. Reg was on the phone, standing with the receiver jammed to his ear, his agitation visible in every action, by the way he held himself, tapping his foot, aimlessly fingering the telephone cord, and working his jaw as if chewing a bit of gristle.

'Mum? Dad? What on earth's wrong?'

Reg immediately hung up.

'They're just keeping me on hold until I give up, I reckon,' he growled. 'Bloody solicitors! Snakes in the grass I'd call 'em!'

Jan dropped the shopping and hurried to her mother's side. She took Mary's hand.

'Hey, Mum! Tell me. What's gone on? Why are you crying?'

Mary shook her head, her mouth twisted in anguish.

'You'd better ask your dad.'

'Dad, what is it? Please *say* something.'

Jan looked pleadingly at Ben, who was coming in behind her carrying the rest of the shopping.

'There's something wrong, Ben. Dad, tell us what it is, for goodness sake.'

Without saying a word, Reg picked up a piece of paper that was lying beside the phone. He handed it to Jan. The printed letterhead established it was from a legal firm in Evesham and it was dated two days earlier. Jan started to read the contents aloud, rapidly. But then, as she realized the actual meaning, she slowed down in appalled disbelief.

Dear Mr Pritchard,

Riscombe Vale Farm Cottage

On the death of Colonel Gilbert, the legal title to the house and thirty acres of land, previously leased by you, at a peppercorn rent, from Colonel Gilbert, has passed on to his daughter, Miss Virginia Gilbert. As I am sure you are aware, the current lease is due to expire next March. I am writing to inform you of Miss Gilbert's intentions regarding the above property.

On the expiry of the lease, Miss Gilbert wishes to take possession of the land and the dwelling house for her own use and your lease will NOT be renewed. You will therefore vacate the property on or before the due date.

Not wishing to cause inconvenience, Miss Gilbert has instructed me to make the following offer. Should you wish to leave Riscombe Vale Farm Cottage at an earlier stage, all outstanding rent from that period to the date Miss Gilbert receives vacant possession will be waived. Only on condition that the property is left in a habitable condition, and that the land is fenced and similarly cared for, will the money be waived.

We look forward to hearing from you on this matter.

The letter was signed by one of the partners, Arthur Snodgrass.

Jan's first reaction of complete disbelief gave way to reality when she thought about the person who had instigated it. This was Virginia Gilbert's revenge against her. It had nothing to do with Reg and Mary, or Ben, or anybody else. It was directed at her and it came from envy, snobbery, callousness – the full battery of dangerous qualities that Virginia possessed and had always possessed.

Somewhere into her memory flashed a vision from years ago of Virginia, aged about eight, coming into the Manor kitchen hand in hand with her father. Reg had been asked in for a cup of tea and a friendly chat about farm business. But during the proceedings Virginia had pulled Jan, who was a couple of years older, to one side and whispered, so that her father would not hear.

'I don't usually play with children from the village, they are common. I much prefer playing with my school friends, only don't tell Daddy. He gets cross when I say things like that.'

Jan had looked at Virginia, puzzled, then said in defence of her friends, 'Well, I heard Lady Fairfax telling my dad she really liked her new horse and that he was a bit common, but he had a lot more substance than a thoroughbred, so you really should like them, Virginia.'

🐎

Unnoticed by Jan, Ben had taken the letter from her hand and read it through again.

'Is it true that the lease expires on the twenty-fifth of March?'

Reg nodded gloomily.

'The old lease, yes, Lady Day. It's been in force for forty years or more.'

'But Virginia can't do this!' Ben spluttered. 'Didn't the colonel say you could live on the farm as long as you wanted to?'

Reg nodded.

'He did. He changed the lease, but I don't know exactly what it said.'

'You probably never read it, Reg Pritchard,' said Mary in an unnaturally high tone. 'You're far too trusting. I've told you that before.'

'I've got a copy in the bank,' Reg continued, ignoring the telling off. 'Anyway, whatever the colonel wanted, he's not here now. What a man does in kindness can usually be undone in spite.'

'Well, I'm not so sure,' said Jan grimly. 'And I'm not going to let her get away with it. Let's have that letter. I'm going to show it to Fred Messiter and ask him what the hell's got into Virginia.' *As if I didn't know*, she muttered to herself.

'Right. I'll come too,' said Ben, rushing after her. They jumped into his sports car and sped off to the manor.

🐎

Fred Messiter had been the Riscombe estate manager for a quarter of a century and liked to say he knew the colonel's land better than its owner did. He and his wife Gillian had always been good friends to Reg and Mary, and he was appalled when Jan showed him the letter.

'Oh my Lord,' he exclaimed, combing his hand through his thin hair. 'Look, I really don't know anything about this. It's . . . it's . . . well, I'm speechless.'

They were in the estate office, built into one of the old coach houses at the Manor. It was an orderly room, with a row of metal filing cabinets along one wall and a desk under the window, where they had found Fred sitting. The atmosphere was pleasantly spiced with smoke from his aromatic pipe tobacco.

'Have any of the other tenants had letters like this?' Jan asked.

'No, Jan, not so far as I know. Miss Gilbert's said not a dicky bird to me about it. What do they mean by "wishes to take possession of the land and the dwelling house for her own use"? As far as I know she's got the Manor to live in. Harry's got the house in Fulham. He's not bothering with the estate at all. Though he got a half-share of it, I do know that much.'

'Then why do you think Virginia's doing this?' asked Ben.

'Well, I can only think she's meaning to sell it,' Fred answered in her defence. 'There'll be the bill for inheritance tax to pay, you know.'

'But it doesn't say she's going to sell the farm,' Jan objected. 'She wants it for her own use, whatever that may be.'

'Something sinister,' said Ben, 'knowing her.'

'I'm sorry. I wouldn't know,' Fred continued, turning the palms of his hands upwards as a sign of defeat.

'Perhaps she doesn't want anyone to know she's selling it,' Ben said, 'not for the moment. She won't have a clue how big the tax bill's going to be just yet, will she?'

'Anyway, all this is beside the point,' said Jan impatiently. 'The fact is, whatever the real reason, Virginia's had this letter sent. The important questions are: what about Colonel Gilbert's promise to let my parents stay as long as they wish? And can Virginia do this anyway? Can she take the farm over and dispose of it if our parents refuse to move out?'

Fred laid his smouldering pipe in an ashtray on the desk and laced his fingers together, placing them across his chest.

'The original lease was drawn up long before I started working here. I probably read it when I first came, while I was rationalizing the filing system, but I can't remember any details. About ten years ago I do remember the colonel coming in to fetch it because he wanted it revised, he said. That was when they reduced the size of Reg's acreage from a hundred down to thirty, at the same time as his retirement.'

'So-called retirement,' commented Jan.

The estate manager unlaced his fingers, rose slowly from his chair and went over to the three filing cabinets. He hesitated for a moment, then seized the chrome handle on one of the drawers and drew it towards him. He riffled through the hanging files with his thick, strong fingers.

'Of course I had nothing to do with the revising. The colonel had his solicitors in Broadway do it.'

'Evidently not the same firm as Virginia's been using, then,' observed Ben.

'They were probably too honest for her,' Jan put in sardonically.

Fred flicked a look of alarm in Jan's direction. For all his employer's faults, he depended on Virginia for his livelihood and was none too comfortable hearing her being maligned.

'Now,' he said, 'we'll be on better ground if we know exactly what the terms are.'

Having no luck in the first drawer, he clattered it shut and slid open another. It was from here that he fished out a card folder labelled 'Riscombe Vale Farm Cottage'.

'Got it!' he said triumphantly.

He laid the file on his desk and flipped it open. Jan and Ben stood on either side of him as he leafed through the contents, most of it sporadic correspondence about leaky roofs and water supply. At last he came to an envelope spotted with age on which was written: *RISCOMBE VALE LEASE*.

The original forty-year-old document came out first. It was typewritten on heavy foolscap paper, its pages held together by green ribbon looped through punch holes in one corner, with blobs of sealing wax at the bottom of each page. It contained screeds of detail, defining exactly the land covered by the lease, and giving a minute description of the house and farm buildings. Fred found the paragraph which laid down the lease's duration and put his finger on where the expiry date was given: the coming 25th of March.

Fred laid the old lease aside and fished inside the envelope again, this time drawing out a copy of the revised deed, which, like the other, was typed and sealed with wax, signed at the bottom of each page by Colonel Gilbert and Reg Pritchard. He turned the pages slowly until he came to a numbered paragraph, which he tapped with his index finger meaningfully.

Jan and Ben leaned over to read what it said. Once disentangled from the undergrowth of legal jargon, and all the 'aforementioneds' and 'notwithstandings', the meaning of the provision was quite clear.

The revised lease said that the leaseholders should have the right to use the dwelling house and land for as long as they might wish, without let or hindrance, only providing that they gave three months' notice of their intention to quit.

Fred looked up, his mouth hanging open in surprise.

'Well, what do you make of that?' He shook his head in bewilderment. 'Miss Gilbert can't have read this. They can't have been aware that the old lease had been superceded. She must have been working from a copy of the old lease that she found in the house. It's the only explanation.'

Jan and Ben looked at each other as smiles of relief and triumph slowly creased their faces. They could think of another explanation, but they decided not to stretch Fred's loyalties by sharing it with him. What did it matter, anyway? The newly found lease looked completely watertight. Virginia's little scheme had been blown right out of the water, smashed to smithereens, Jan thought with glee.

# 17

By the time Jan came back to Edge Farm, drought had succeeded the earlier storms. Even where racecourses were equipped to water the ground, the tracks became bone-hard and Jan was forced to put all her racing plans on hold. Use of the all-weather gallop was invaluable and helped to keep the string fit. Some trainers kept on racing despite the conditions, eager to snap up prizes in fields that were generally smaller and less competitive. But Jan had seen too many horses ruined by this kind of greed and told her owners it was in their best interests to be patient, the rain would come eventually and give the ground a 'cushion'.

Although he was supposed to have twice-weekly physiotherapy at the hospital – timed to coincide with the afternoon lull in the yard's activities so Jan could drive him there – Eddie used every excuse he could to get out of the appointments.

'Eddie, don't forget it's your physiotherapy today,' Jan reminded him over breakfast.

'I think I'm getting a cold. I'd better not go.'

'Don't be daft, a bit of a cold's not going to make any difference.'

'I can't go to the hospital and sneeze virus everywhere. It's completely antisocial.'

Three days later there were more excuses.

'I've got to skip physio again, I've done my shoulder. Ricked a muscle or something on the rowing machine. It hurts like hell.'

'So now you need the attentions of a good physio even more.'

'No, Jan, I don't,' he contradicted sharply. 'The advice on this kind of injury is to rest it, and that's what I intend to do.'

Jan decided to ask Tony Robertson if he would talk a bit of sense into Eddie.

'It's undermining his recovery, Tony. He does work out here, but I think he needs to see the experts to keep him concentrating on the most beneficial movements.'

Tony agreed to drop in the next day. When he arrived, he spent half an hour with Eddie in the living room and emerged with an amused smile on his face.

'How's his shoulder?' asked Jan.

'I gave it an injection. He didn't like it much – he's pathologically terrified of the needle – but he submitted in the end. I also told him he had to keep up the physio or his problems will only get worse.'

Later, when Eddie felt the coast was clear, he looked for Jan in the kitchen, his face like thunder.

'That bastard doctor of yours is a nutter, completely unethical,' he growled.

'Oh, come off it, Eddie. What the hell are you talking about?'

'I'll have you know he deliberately tortured me with that injection and I've a bloody good mind to report him to the General Medical Council.'

'Oh, grow up, Eddie, for God's sake. Like everyone else he's only trying to help. Stop whingeing, people are walking on eggshells around you. Well, enough is enough.' Jan couldn't believe what she was hearing and that *she* was saying it.

Eddie looked shaken.

'We've all done the sympathy bit to death, Eddie. Now snap out of it, or not only will you not get any better, neither will our relationship.' Leaving Eddie with his mouth open and plenty to think about, Jan got to her feet and stormed out of the house and down to the yard.

🐎

By the end of August, rain was cascading down on Gloucestershire, turning the ditches into streams and the streams into rivers. Gerry invited Eddie to the pub and took him in his van, leaving Jan alone with the children. It was about half-past nine when through the sheeting rain she heard a knock on the door. She put on the security chain and undid the latch.

'Yes?'

'I'm looking for Mrs Hardy.'

It was a young, male, Irish voice.

'You've found her. What's it about?'

'It's about a job.'

Jan stole a cautious look at her visitor through the gap between door and jamb. Under the porch light, she could see he was a thin streak of a child, carrying a sodden, yellow, dilapidated rucksack. His hair clung to his scalp like a bath cap and glistened like wet seaweed. Rainwater trickled like tears down his drowned face.

'My goodness, just look at you. You need wringing out.'

'I walked from the station. It's seven miles.'

Jan hesitated. Then, with a sudden impulse of concern, or intuition perhaps, she unhooked the chain and swung the door wide open.

'You'd better come in. Quick. Go through there and wrap yourself round the Aga. I'll find a towel and some clothes.'

Only then did it occur to Jan what a silly move she had just made. The pasty-faced boy could have been anyone, dangerous even, and he could have been *with* anyone, for that matter. She was alone in this isolated house, with just Megan and Matty upstairs asleep and below in the yard close on half a million pounds' worth of vulnerable, highly tuned horseflesh. What chance would she have?

But, by the time Jan had thought all this through, she was sure her visitor was alone and harmless. Puzzling, but innocuous, and looking in desperate need of help.

The boy was trembling as he shuffled into the kitchen. His grimy, torn anorak dripped onto the quarry tiles and the trousers of the blue suit that he wore underneath were drenched and plastered with mud. His cheap shoes squelched. Jan ran upstairs and fetched a towel, a clean T-shirt of her own and a pair of Eddie's old jeans.

'Get out of those clothes and dry yourself,' she said, thrusting the towel into his arms. 'Then put these on. I doubt there's anything dry in that rucksack, is there!'

She dropped the clothes on the table beside the boy and smiled at his startled, unspoken question.

'Don't worry, I won't look.'

Turning her back, Jan hoisted the hob cover on the Aga. She unzipped a tin of tomato soup, upending it into a saucepan, then dropped two thick slices of bread into the toaster. Behind her, as she stirred the soup, she could hear her visitor laboriously exchanging one set of clothing for the other.

'You decent yet?' she asked with a faint smile.

There was a grunt and she turned. The boy looked more pathetic than ever, his black hair rubbed down and the clean clothes hanging off him, at least two sizes too big. He was just like a kid who'd missed his bedtime and was afraid of the dark, his eyes darting around taking everything in.

'Don't you know me, Mrs Hardy?' He turned a beseeching look up to Jan. 'That time we met . . .?'

Now, seeing him standing there clean and dry, Jan remembered. She clapped her hand to her mouth.

'Oh God, yes, of course! At Newbury. You did that thing with the horse. You're Patsy Keating.'

'Yes. An' you offered me a job.'

'I did what?'

'That's why I'm here. You said I could come and work for you any time.'

Suddenly she wanted to laugh, but stifled it because Patsy Keating was so plainly serious.

'Well, yes, I know what I said. But I didn't mean—'

She sat down at the table and scrubbed her face with her hands. This was ridiculous. She looked up again.

'Anyway, you had a job. What happened to that?'

Patsy Keating shrugged and looked at the floor.

'I run away,' he whispered.

As he spoke the tomato soup boiled over with a furious hiss onto the hot ring.

On that day at Newbury, six months earlier, Jan had had a
runner in the first race, Johnny Carlton-Brown's Supercall. As she
stood in the paddock with Annabel and the owner, watching the
gelding in his walking paces and discussing his future, the first of
the jockeys appeared from the weighing room.

The day had started fine with long periods of sunshine and high
silvery clouds, and warm air. But, as the runners for the first race
circled the parade ring, storm clouds began to mass in the west and
the sunlight lost its sparkle, dimming to glowering shades of old
gold. In this hectic light the atmosphere began to thicken so that
the thin file of brightly dressed jockeys glimmered like a string of
coloured party lights.

As they entered the paddock, the riders fanned out to find their
connections. Jan knew virtually all the senior members, at least by
sight. But these were conditionals and only a small number would
ever make the grade as professionals, though all were devoutly
convinced they could. Jan was only able to name a few, but among
the unfamiliar faces one caught her attention, a pinched, pale figure
who seemed tiny even among these diminutive men. He was
wearing the colours of one of Virginia Gilbert's notoriously demanding owners.

'That one looks like he's going to his execution, poor little sod,'
she murmured to Annabel. 'Probably the first time he's ever worn
Mr Kavunu's silks.'

Annabel nodded towards a large gelding, who was jigging round
the ring. 'That's nothing to how nervous his horse is. Look at him, I
wouldn't give him a snowball's chance, and he's fancied.'

Jan looked in her race card for the name of the horse, Canteloupe, and then read across to see who his tiny pilot was: *Patsy
Keating*. She looked up again at the horse. He was still on his toes,
yanking at the leading rein with repeated jerks of his head. His
flanks foamed with sweat and his eyes rolled.

'Bel's right,' Jan murmured to JCB. 'I doubt we've got much to
worry about from that one. He's boiling over.'

Virginia Gilbert, Canteloupe's trainer, was talking urgently to
her jockey. Then she took Patsy by the elbow and began steering
him towards their runner, apparently anxious to get him in the

saddle as quickly as possible. Suddenly, as Jan felt Albert Mines, her jockey, tap her on the arm to get his instructions, a nerve-shredding detonation of thunder ripped through the air.

It spooked all the horses; some of them snorted and shook their heads, but Canteloupe was just as if he'd been ignited like a firework. With a whinny of terror he reared, his front feet jabbing the air like a shadow boxer. Virginia's lad was caught off guard. He panicked and let go of the lead rein, then tried to snatch it back but only snatched at air. Canteloupe was loose and completely lost his head.

Snorting, he came back to earth and began to buck and kick ferociously, veering off the tarmacadam path surrounding the parade ring onto the grass, where the owners and trainers were gathered. Those nearest to him scattered in alarm, while the grooms leading the other runners stopped and tried to soothe their horses. Jan looked anxiously towards Supercall, who was being led by Roz. He remained typically unconcerned. But Canteloupe was beyond reason. He began to buck in circles, lashing out viciously before standing on his hind legs, rearing and squealing with fright. Suddenly the watching crowd gasped as they saw Patsy Keating stroll almost casually towards the frenzied horse. His tiny, brightly coloured figure stopped immediately under the forelegs of the huge, rearing animal. He opened his right hand, before raising it in the air beneath the horse's muzzle. Canteloupe's rage, or fear, or whatever it was, drained from him and he came back to earth instantly, planting his forefeet on the ground and standing absolutely still. He swished his tail once, nodded his head and flared his nostrils, but did not move one iota. Murmuring words that nobody could hear, Patsy rubbed the palm of his hand over the gelding's muzzle and Canteloupe, in a gesture that looked simultaneously grateful, loving and respectful, shoved his nose under his jockey's right armpit. Thunder cracked and echoed around the racecourse for a second time, more loudly if anything than the first. But it had no effect on the horse as Patsy took the leading rein and handed it to the groom.

Several members of the crowd broke into spontaneous applause.

Jan looked at Annabel. 'I can't believe what I've just seen. How on earth did he do that, Bel?'

Annabel shrugged.

'I don't know. But whatever that boy's got, if you could just bottle it . . .'

Virginia had checked the horse's legs and surprisingly – no doubt under pressure from Mr Kavunu – decided not to withdraw her runner. But word of the incident had reached the betting ring and Canteloupe's price drifted, so he started at relatively long odds. Meanwhile Supercall was shortened to second favourite.

The race took place in heavy rain. Jan was pleased with Albert, who gave Supercall a great ride, sticking to his instructions by keeping out of trouble on the outside of the field, and challenging with a smooth run from the two-furlong post. In truth, the horse was not really wound up for the race and, after clattering the last obstacle, finished not a bad third, ten lengths behind the winner. But the revelation was Canteloupe. Patsy Keating had him hacking round at the back of the field for most of the race, gently allowing him to improve his position as they reached the final bend. Weaving through beaten horses can be a tricky manoeuvre at the best of times, let alone on slithery ground. But horse and rider achieved it without fuss. As Canteloupe pinged the last two flights, he lengthened his stride to go past the favourite and won by three easy lengths.

An hour later Jan had run into Patsy Keating outside the weighing room. He was out of the riding gear and wearing his crumpled blue suit and cracked shoes.

'That was quite something what you did in the paddock,' she said. 'I thought the horse was going to have your head off for certain.'

Patsy gave her a thin, twisted smile.

'Sh-Jesus, he wouldn't do that.'

'How did you know he wouldn't? Weren't you afraid?'

The jockey looked up at her with big steady eyes.

'No horse would worry me.'

Jan laughed.

'Well, all I can say is, if you can do that, you can come and work for me any time.'

🐎

She hadn't meant it as a serious offer, of course. Poaching stable staff from any trainer, let alone Virginia Gilbert, was not the way to get on in the racing world. She had meant the remark as a compliment, a way of showing her admiration. But Patsy, it seemed, had taken her words literally. And now here he was in her kitchen.

'So why did you run away?'

'I couldn't put up with it no more.'

'With what?'

'Working for Miss Gilbert. They didn't treat me right.'

'Who didn't?'

'The other lads. They were always playing tricks on me.'

'How old are you, Patsy?'

'Nineteen.'

'Haven't you any family or friends that you can go to?'

'In Ireland, but I've no money. That's why I need the job, see.'

'Yes, I do see . . .'

Jan studied him carefully. He was shovelling the soup into his mouth hungrily, then snatching bites of the buttered toast she had placed on the table in front of him. He looked pathetic and vulnerable and suddenly, without quite knowing why, her heart went out to him.

When he'd finished, Jan gave him a slab of fruitcake and a mug of sweet tea. Patsy was terse and she couldn't get him to tell her in any more detail why he no longer wished to work in Virginia's yard. By ten-thirty she gave up.

'I really need to think about this, Patsy. The truth is, I don't need any more staff at the moment. But I'll tell you what I'll do. You can stay here tonight and I'll speak to Riscombe tomorrow. Will that be all right? They'll be wondering what on earth's happened to you.'

Patsy nodded. 'I don't mind if you talk to them, long as I don't have to go back.'

'OK. You can sleep in the caravan – did you see it down below? Come on, I'll take you.'

The old caravan, in which Jan and the children had lived for a year after first coming to Edge, was not particularly wholesome after its most recent tenants, Dec and Con, had vacated it, but at least it was weatherproof. Patsy appeared almost happy as he looked around, then dumped his sodden rucksack on the table. Jan found a stinky sleeping bag in the cupboard, but, as she left him, he gave her a wan smile, which she read as an expression of gratitude.

Jan walked across to the yard and let herself in, then went from box to box to check that all was well. When she came to Morning Glory the horse immediately backed away from the door, rolling his eyes suspiciously. She slid back the bolt and went in, talking to him in a quiet voice while stroking his silky smooth neck. MG had made painfully slow progress over the summer, but he had come to trust her to some extent. She had been riding him herself every day as no one else in the yard could get near him. That was a problem now since Jan had too much to do to devote herself to one horse. Tonight, no doubt, his emotional state was not helped by the storm, but Jan knew even on a quiet day his nerves were as tightly strung as a newly tuned piano. She also knew there was an awful long way to go before they could even begin to fulfil A.D. O'Hagan's ambitions.

Jan was still mulling things over as she locked the yard gate and made her way back to the house. She passed the caravan, its window now glowing with a pale yellow light, which seemed to wink in the rain. Thunder rumbled overhead and suddenly, as if it were a bolt of lightning forking from above, the thought hit her. She heard again the thunder of that afternoon at Newbury, saw Virginia's horse Canteloupe loose in the paddock, and Patsy's astonishing feat bringing him under control.

She remembered, too, Patsy's calm and utterly convincing remark to her afterwards.

'No horse would worry me.'

Next day Jan phoned Fred Messiter.

'I've got someone here at Edge Farm,' she told him, 'one of Virginia's lads from the yard – Patsy Keating. Do you know him?'

'I know of him all right.'

'Well, he just turned up here last night. He says he's run away.'

'Really?'

'You don't know what's been going on, do you?'

'No, I'm afraid I don't. I deal with their wages, but that's about it. You'll have to ask Virginia.'

'I'd rather not. Can you give me Scottie's number?'

A minute later she was dialling Scottie, who lived in one of the estate cottages.

'Patsy!' exclaimed Scottie. 'So that's where the little git is. We missed him at evening stables and he didn't turn in this morning. What's he bloody playing at?'

'I don't know the ins and outs of everything. He only told me he ran away because he wasn't very happy. Then he clammed up. He seems really upset. What's going on up there?'

The Riscombe head lad hesitated, while considering the situation. Then he cleared his throat.

'The lad's been with us since the New Year. Strange boy, fantastic with the horses, mind. In fact he's one of the best horsemen I've ever seen at that age. But he doesn't get on with people, if you get my meaning.'

'Go on, Scottie.'

'I don't know why for certain, but the rest of the lads took against him. I suppose that's why he says he's not happy.'

'But he seems harmless enough.'

'Oh, yeah, he's harmless. But he's a loner. Never joins in with anything.'

Jan could understand the problem. There was often a strong bond amongst stable staff, and they quickly came down on anyone who wouldn't try to fit in.

'So what would you like me to do with him?' she asked. 'Shall I run him back?'

'Oh, I don't know . . .'

Jan couldn't decide whether Scottie's caution was defensiveness or indecision.

Eventually he continued, 'What the hell took him to your place anyway?'

'He says he wants to come and work here.'

'Oh, does he now?'

There was a pause. She sensed Scottie taking a long draw on a cigarette.

At last he said cautiously, as if advancing a dubious proposition, 'Tell me, Mrs Hardy. How do *you* feel about the idea?'

Now it was Jan's turn to hesitate. She knew Patsy knew horses, but the worry was all the bits she didn't know about him.

'Well, I'm not really sure, Scottie. Are you saying Miss Gilbert would let Patsy go?'

'Yes, Mrs Hardy, I think she might. I'll have to talk to her, of course. But it'd be a weight off of my mind if she did, I *can* tell you that.'

'Scottie, there is just one thing – can you assure me that this boy is honest?'

'Oh, don't get me wrong, Mrs H. Patsy's straight all right, in fact he may be too straight.'

'Meaning?'

'OK. He's very religious. Catholic, if you know what I'm saying.'

'Tell me more.'

'Well, that's it. He's *very* Catholic.'

Jan could imagine why this might be a problem. Almost all the Irish lads had Catholic backgrounds, though it was not that often you saw them trailing off to Mass unless there was a particularly important religious celebration. Yet she could guess most of them had left home with the same parting words from their mothers ringing in their ears: 'Now promise me, Sean – Kieran, or whoever – you'll never miss Mass over there in England.'

Patsy's observance of his religion would be an uncomfortable reminder of their backsliding, and some of the more uncouth ones among them wouldn't like it.

'I'll need to think about this,' said Jan. 'Can you talk to Miss

Gilbert anyway? In the meantime I'll have another chat with Patsy.'

The rain, for the moment, had cleared and the Gloucestershire air was breezy but warm. After breakfast Jan went down with a mug of tea to the caravan, where Patsy had yet to emerge, though she did find him up and dressed. He was sitting at the table with a book open in front of him.

'I've been talking to Scottie,' she said.

'D'he say I got to go back?' His voice quivered with fear.

'How would you react to that?'

As if tasting a foul medicine, he screwed up his face.

'No way. There's definitely no way I'm going there ever again.' Now a tear watered his eye.

Again Jan was touched by his vulnerability. She went on softly, 'Come on now, don't worry. Scottie was very understanding. And he thinks Miss Gilbert might agree to you coming here, at least on trial.'

Patsy relaxed and that wry smile, the boy's only way of showing pleasure, appeared on his face.

'So I can stay?' he asked huskily.

'I can't say for definite, not at this stage. I will need to get clearance from the Jockey Club and your stable pass, if you do, but I'm thinking about it. You can stay today and, if you want to show willing, there's some mucking out needs doing. So come on. Get your skates on.'

Before they left the caravan she glanced at the book open on the table. It was a prayer book.

Jan took Patsy and introduced him to Roz Stoddard, then asked her to find him some boots and get him going. Annabel, who was just back from Barbados, was already in the office looking through the next week's entries when Jan appeared.

'Thanks to the rain it looks like we'll be able to declare most of these.'

Two mugs of coffee steamed on the desk in front of her.

'Yes.' Jan nodded in agreement. 'It'll be a huge relief to get started.'

Annabel handed one of the mugs to Jan.

'Who was that kid? He looks familiar.'

Jan sipped from the mug.

'Don't you remember him? That's Patsy Keating.'

Annabel frowned.

'Not . . .?'

'Yup. From Virginia's. Remember Newbury, the conditional race? That's him. He turned up late last night, soaked to the skin, almost hypothermic, looking like a ghost. He said he'd run away and wanted to come and work for me.'

'No! Just like that?'

Jan nodded.

'Yes, just like that. Weird, isn't it? I've just spoken to Scottie Venables. Of course, he wouldn't say, but I'm pretty sure Patsy's been bullied at Riscombe. Scottie said Patsy was *very* religious, making it sound like he'd got a screw loose.'

Annabel wrinkled her nose.

'Perhaps he's a religious maniac. Do you think he flogs himself with thistles and thorns?'

'*Bel*, stop it, this is serious. Patsy's come here and thrown himself on my mercy. He's desperately unhappy and it's not his fault, I'm sure of it. Remember when we used to take in horses that were resting and we discussed how some of them were probably only depressed. And how later on we realized that it was literally true. We said then they deserved as much of our love and attention as the ones with sore feet. Well, it's the same with Patsy, and I really don't think I can turn him away. I just can't.'

A brief silence fell between the two women before Annabel, staring mindlessly through the window, continued, 'Speaking of disturbed animals, they seem to be Patsy Keating's particular forte, don't they?'

Jan was in the middle of taking a sip of coffee and looked up at her assistant, expectantly.

'Go on,' she said quietly.

Annabel carefully set her mug down on the desk.

'I wouldn't be surprised if you were thinking the same me,' she said.

'And that is?'

The two friends looked at each other and spoke in unison.

'Morning Glory!'

# 18

Scottie Venables did not ring back until after evening stables.

'I spoke to Miss Gilbert about Patsy,' he told Jan.

'What did she say?'

'She's no very pleased. She doesna like the idea of Patsy pissing off to you like he did.'

'No, I can imagine.'

'So I claims if the kid's unhappy here, we won't keep him anyways. In the end she says, all right, Scottie, you handle it.'

'That's good,' said Jan. 'I've decided to take him on, anyway. Will you send over any paperwork?'

'I don't do paperwork, Mrs Hardy. That's Fred Messiter's department. I'll ask him to send you his P45, and all that kind of stuff.'

'Thanks, Scottie, I'm glad we sorted this.'

'Me too. You've got yourself a good horseman, that's for sure. I suppose you could call it a fair swap.'

'I'm sorry?'

'Patsy for this Velvet Dynasty we had from you. My God, Mrs H, that's a surprise package and I'm no joking.'

'What do you mean?'

Scottie laughed.

'No, no, you'll be finding out soon enough without me telling you.'

Jan was gutted by the way such a lovely, promising horse whom *she'd* picked out had been whisked away from her, not to mention the grievous loss of her old friend Wolf's Rock, who always managed to pull a race out of the fire when she most needed it. So she did not appreciate Scottie's crowing – if that's what it was.

Strolling out of the office a couple of minutes later, Jan saw Patsy's slight figure in the yard going from box to box talking to the horses, all of them coming forward eagerly to greet him and have their muzzles rubbed, even though he had no carrots or Polo mints as a bribe. She noted how confidently Patsy carried himself when he was around them, not with the bounce of a show-off parading his skill, but like someone relaxing amongst his own tribe. His mouth hardly moved as he whispered to them, but she was too far away to hear any magical words.

She smiled and went across to him.

'Patsy, I've got news from Riscombe. It's going to be all right. Miss Gilbert has agreed to let you transfer to Edge Farm, and I'll be happy to have you. So, is it a deal?'

She held out her hand and as Patsy shook it, his face lit up with pleasure and relief.

'Thank you, thank you, Mrs Hardy. That's great.'

'You can go on using the caravan for the time being. Is that OK?'

'Yeah, that'll be fine, I'll soon have it shipshape. It'll be like brand new, you'll see.'

'Now, about the horses, I thought I'd give you just the one to do for the time being. It's what you might call a specialized job, and Annabel and I have a feeling you're just the man for it. He's called Morning Glory and he needs some special TLC. He's from Ireland, so at least you'll be speaking the same language.'

'I seen him already, Mrs H, in his box,' Patsy said.

'What do you think of him?' Jan set off walking towards Morning Glory's box, with the lad stuck to her side like glue.

'I thought there was somethin' up with him, so I asked Roz. She said he's a bit mental. Well, I think he's just scared, but I let him know he could trust me. So I reckon we might work well together.'

For the monosyllabic Patsy, it was a long speech, but it was also just what Jan thought.

'Well, here he is. How are you, old boy? Meet your new lad. Patsy's going to be looking after you now.'

Morning Glory came cautiously to the door and as Jan raised her hand to stroke his muzzle he backed away, blowing sharply down his nostrils as he did so. She outlined the reasons for MG being at Edge Farm, as Patsy listened with close attention.

'Anyway,' she finished, 'whether he's a nutcase, a fruitcake or just a misunderstood genius remains to be seen. I want you to spend all of your time with him, ride him in his work and do him in his box. He's not easy, Patsy. He's even had the pluck to run away with *me*. Which was not very pleasant for either of us, I can tell you. But I did get a good feeling when he galloped, so he might just be the best horse we've ever had in this yard – with the right handling, of course. Do you think we can get him right for a novice hurdle in a few weeks' time?'

Patsy nodded, his face serious.

'It might take a bit longer,' he said, 'but I reckon we'll get there in the end, won't we, old boy.'

Once a week Jan had a half-hour conference with A.D. O'Hagan on the telephone. As usual, they went through each of his horses, discussing their general fitness and reviewing suitable races. A.D. always required a variety of options and made the final decision. It never ceased to amaze Jan how a busy international financier had time to study the conditions of a race at Fontwell Park or Newton Abbot. But A.D. was the consummate gambler, who never let the slightest detail escape his attention.

'Now what about Morning Glory?' he asked. 'I'm rather hoping he'll run before the end of October.'

'Me too, but I can't rush him,' Jan said. 'I've got a new lad, Patsy, working with him full time. He gets on with him brilliantly.'

'So have you marked out any possible entries?'

'There's a couple of novice hurdles at Warwick and Stratford that might suit.'

'And they are?'

Jan gave A.D. the details.

'Would you like me to enter him?' she asked.

'I'll get back to you on that. Now what about Russian Eagle?'

It was interesting that A.D. never put extra pressure on Jan by asking if she thought a horse would win a particular race. For that she was grateful. She knew what A.D. required of his trainers, which was to know how fit a horse was when it ran. Then it was down to him to decide what its chances were of winning.

🐎

Every year on the second Sunday in September a horse show was held at Cheltenham racecourse and this year both Megan and Matty were due to take part. During August Megan, with Monarch, had been at pony club camp in North Wales. By the time she returned home, her enthusiasm for junior eventing had been gushing. Matty, a beginner, and a great deal less confident than his sister, had at last started to enjoy his riding under the tutelage of his grandfather. He and his pony Rocket had already been entered in some of the mounted games. 'Then he'll have a target,' Reg had confided.

That morning the chaos at Edge Farm had been comparable to Grand National day. Reg and Mary had arrived early to help with final preparations and found the place in a state of high tension. While Reg worked with Matty, grooming Rocket and plaiting his mane, the keyed-up Megan rushed around, infecting everyone with her feverish excitement. Every detail had to be checked, every contingency allowed for. Mary, making sandwiches with Jan in the kitchen, observed it all with amusement.

'Mum,' shouted Meg breathlessly from the hall, 'I've checked the fuel in the lorry and I don't think there's enough to get us there. So we'll have to leave enough time to fill up on the way. And I *wish* people wouldn't go off with the clothes brush. I need it for my hat.'

'You used to be just like that,' Jan's mother said fondly.

'I still am,' Jan answered, grinning.

Despite Megan's anxiety, the party of five, with the two ponies, arrived at the showground in good time. Jan had tried to persuade Eddie to come with them, but he'd flatly refused.

'No way, Jan. I don't like going out while I'm like this. I don't want the sympathy vote.'

'You go out to the pub with Gerry.'

'That's different. Everybody knows me there.'

'Forgive me, Eddie, but that's pathetic. Until you're prepared to face the world, you'll never be able to consider yourself better.'

'I'm not better.'

'Please yourself, stay here, but you can't hide for ever, Eddie,' Jan responded, full of despair, then left without him.

❦

Jan was making her way from the parking area to the secretary's tent, where she needed to confirm the children's entries, when Tim Farr came into view, striding purposefully towards her.

'Could I have a quick word, Mrs Hardy?'

'If you can walk and talk at the same time you can, but I'm on urgent business. What's it about?'

'I was in the pub in Stanfield, your local,' said Farr. 'And Terry the landlord was saying you'd just taken on a new lad from Miss Gilbert's yard.'

'And?'

'Well, according to Terry, this lad had been complaining about mistreatment by the staff at Riscombe. I was wondering if you could confirm that.'

'No, sorry, I can't. That would be confidential. Anyway, who told Terry this?'

'It seems to be pretty much common knowledge, actually.'

Jan knew this often happened in a village like Stanfield, which was small and intensely curious about any strangers that appeared.

'OK,' she said, 'I can confirm I *have* taken on a new conditional. His name is Patrick Keating and he has transferred to me from Miss Gilbert. That's all.'

'The thing is,' Farr persisted, 'I'm working on a story about stable lads' working conditions and I've been turning up more and more tales of harassment and bullying in training establishments. It seems this is a serious problem.'

'Not in my yard it isn't.'

'What about Miss Gilbert's?'

Just for a second Jan was sorely tempted. Then she saw, in her mind's eye, the likely headlines: HARDY ACCUSES GILBERT YARD

OF BULLYING or even worse, in tabloid transformation, TRAINERS IN CAT FIGHT OVER STAFF. She shook her head firmly.

'Forget it. There's no way I can answer that because I honestly don't know what goes on in Virginia Gilbert's yard. You'll have to ask her. I'm sure she will be most obliging, she is with most people,' Jan added mischievously.

'I will, of course. But it would help if I'd already established some of the facts. Do you think Patrick would agree to talk to me?'

Jan stopped and turned to the journalist, raising her finger.

'No, Mr Farr, absolutely not. I won't have you pestering my staff just to feather your own nest, so stay away. Patsy's a very shy boy. You wouldn't get anything out of him anyway.'

'I could try . . .'

'I have already said it once, stay away. Keep off my property. If I catch you hanging around my place looking for a story I'll be onto your editor before you can say, "Hold the front page". Have you got that?'

Tim sniggered and ran to catch up as Jan strode off.

'All right, all right, you're the boss. But I'm not giving up on the story. It's a public issue, and important for the good name of the racing industry. If my editor agrees with that, why wouldn't you?'

'I would. But I'm not getting involved. My life's complicated enough as it is. Please just go away.'

By now they had arrived outside the secretary's tent. Jan turned to face Farr once more.

'Look, I've got to go and sign in, or my daughter will kill me. This is a very rare, but very important, family day for me, so please leave us alone.'

But Tim Farr hadn't quite finished.

'Oh, Mrs Hardy, there's just one more thing. On quite a different complication in your life, are you aware of any further developments in the case involving Eddie Sullivan? You know, the road accident?'

'No. Are you?'

'It's just that, well, I understand Inspector Hadfield is now preparing a case against him for causing death by reckless driving. It seems he's convinced Mr Sullivan had been drinking excessively.

Apparently he doesn't believe in the third car that you and I have spoken about. Nor does he believe there's any evidence against that certain person who we both think may have had it in for you and Mr Sullivan.'

'More fool him then,' said Jan, trying to control her increasing anger and frustration. 'So who does he think's been trying to blacken our names all over the West Country? And how would Hadfield know about this supposed *excessive* drinking by Eddie? Eddie was unconscious for four days. He couldn't possibly give a sample.'

'I know that. But I'm told Inspector Hadfield has statements from others who saw him drinking at the racecourse.'

'Malicious gossip. That would be enough for a prosecution, would it?'

'I don't know. But I guess it might be.'

'Who the hell's been giving these alleged statements anyway?'

'Well, I only know of one for sure.'

'And that is?'

'Are you sure you want to hear this?'

'Yes, of course.'

'It's Virginia Gilbert's head lad.'

🐎

They returned to Edge Farm in moderate triumph. Jan had been determined not to let Tim Farr's unwelcome news spoil the afternoon, and had forgotten it completely when Megan and Monarch won the dressage class and came third overall in the working pony. Later Matty and Rocket had a hilarious time, especially in the apple-bobbing contest, which involved riders trying to capture small russet apples floating about in buckets of water without using their hands. Matty had ridden Rocket to the bucket and stood him correctly beside it. Then, as the child struggled to get a hold with his teeth, his hair soaking, the pony decided to help him out. As quick as a flash, Rocket stuffed his head in the water right up to his eyes and drew the apple out in triumph, chomping on it with delight.

In the evening Toby Waller phoned to tell Jan that he had business commitments which meant he wouldn't be able to go racing on the Wednesday, when Flamenco was due to run at Worcester.

'Oh dear, I was hoping to have a chat, actually,' Jan replied. 'Did you know the police are still pursuing Eddie, the bastards? I thought the idea of getting him for death by reckless driving had gone away, but now it seems it hasn't.'

She passed on the information Tim Farr had given her.

'It still looks a bit thin, if you ask me,' Toby said, doing his best to reassure her. 'Is Eddie's memory still totally blank? Can't he remember anything at all?'

'He says he can't. Hadfield obviously doesn't believe him, though.'

'I know a good defence brief can try to convince a jury that the amnesia is genuine, and that Virginia's employee, the guy who made the statement, could be accused of acting against you maliciously, with some success, no doubt.'

'Well, he must be. Especially as his boss seems to be going out with Harold Powell now. Can you *believe* that? Why can't we nail that skunk once and for all?'

'Because there are no witnesses to his presence on Cleeve Hill. No proof that he did anything. But there's still time, and while there's time there's hope. So hang on to that.'

'I wish Eddie could. He seems close to despair at times. It's really worrying and such a struggle.'

'Oh, Eddie'll come through. It's a difficult time for you both, I know, but he'll come through.'

A few days later A.D. O'Hagan was on the phone.

'How's it going with Morning Glory, Jan?'

'Patsy's doing wonders with him. He's been working him on his own, so at last we're getting him into some sort of shape. We think he's made real progress these last few weeks. But I'm still worried about his attitude to other horses around him. The only way to sort that out will be to try him, I suppose.'

'Exactly. I'm sure you know what you're doing. So that's settled then. We'll aim him for the Stratford race you mentioned in October.'

Jan knew she now had to get serious with Morning Glory. She had given Patsy enough time to get to know her wayward inmate. They walked and trotted then cantered the horse on alternate days, working him on his own after the rest of the string had come in. Then, in the third week of September, they tried him once more with just a couple of others. On the way to the gallops MG was fully charged, but Patsy held him together, constantly talking to him, reassuring him, stroking his neck until they reached the end of the track and the start of the gallop.

Suddenly the horse exploded, leaping in the air like a kangaroo. Patsy sat still, as cool as a cucumber, until he regained control. He turned the horse in a circle and headed off after the others, who were waiting for him. Two more huge leaps placed him between them, and as they set off galloping Patsy's pale cheeks turned bright pink. After four furlongs the horse pulled away finishing ten lengths clear of his rivals.

'He's a quick horse,' was all Patsy said after he had brought MG under control and walked him gingerly back.

Later Jan and Annabel discussed the fairly disastrous gallop with Patsy. Annabel suggested they should return to the citation bridle, but Patsy said definitely not.

'I'm thinking maybe the biggest problem is the other horses,' he said. 'He doesn't even try to run away when he's on his own. He's just sensible then and you can get some serious work into him.'

Jan had been thinking along the same lines.

'I agree with Patsy. I'm sure everything the horse does, he's telling us something. Maybe he's saying he's not the sociable type. If so, we'll just have to accept it and go back to working him on his own.'

'But if he can't cope with a couple of horses at home,' objected Annabel, 'how's he going to manage on a racecourse with twenty odd banging and crashing over hurdles?'

'We'll worry about that when the time comes,' Jan said. 'What's more, I don't even know if we can get him into the horsebox to get him there yet. Still, at the moment I just want to get him fit.'

But the looming problem of MG's reluctance to load would not go away and one morning in late September Jan decided they would put him to the test. She had Dec bring the lorry to the yard gate and lower the ramp. The interior of the vehicle was divided so that four horses could travel together, each in its own stall.

'Why don't we try taking out the dividing walls, Mrs H? Maybe he just wants more room.'

'That's a good idea, Patsy,' said Jan.

It only took a few minutes to realign the partitions, which created twice as much space for the tricky horse to stand in, and meant he would be less likely to be spooked by the stalls touching his flanks. Jan knew that cajolery and kindness would be the only methods to work long term as the use of force and the drug ACP had already failed with him.

Talking to MG in a continuous stream of soothing words – something he'd never have been able to manage with a human being – Patsy led the gelding gently up the ramp. MG moved forward cautiously as the handlers held their breath. First his head crept up the ramp, sniffing it as he gingerly moved forward inch by inch, then the withers and finally the quarters passed inside the lorry. Dec and Con raised the ramp swiftly but quietly and waited for the sound of kicking. Jan got into the cab and peeked through the sliding panel into the horse compartment. MG was standing patiently while Patsy held his bridled head and gently stroked his muzzle.

'You all right, Patsy?'

'Yes, Mrs H. He's as nice as pie now.'

Jan saw MG blink and for a moment his eyes rolled upwards, the pupils almost disappearing. But as Patsy rubbed his nose, the horse lowered his head with a snort of acceptance. As Jan turned the key to start the engine she looked back, expecting to see a reaction. There was none. She slipped the transporter into gear and drove slowly along the tarmac that formed an access road between the yard and the house. MG was still unfazed.

'Let's take him for a trip down the village and see how he reacts,' she said.

🐎

'Well done, Patsy, that was a relief. It was a brilliant idea, moving the partitions. I really think we might have cracked him at last,' Jan said when the experiment was over and MG was safely back in his box.

At that moment the sound of cars being driven fast up the lane from the main road could be heard. The bulky horsebox, still parked beside the yard entrance, masked the view so it wasn't until the two cars swept onto the forecourt that Jan and her staff realized they belonged to the police.

Inspector Hadfield stepped out of the first vehicle and carefully placed his trilby on his head. He then flicked his jacket with his fingertips – like a dog scratching at fleas – before taking a deep breath.

'Mrs Hardy,' he said, his serious voice belying that incessant milky smile, 'is Edward Sullivan here? I need to have a word with him.'

# 19

Eddie must have seen the police cars from his bedroom window and he appeared at the front door without being summoned.

'What the hell's going on?' he bellowed, holding on tightly to a pair of walking sticks, which were replacements for his elbow crutches.

Hadfield beckoned a uniformed constable forward and strode towards the house. Jan hurried to catch up.

'Mr Edward Sullivan?'

The policeman's voice was formal, without a trace of his concocted geniality.

'I think you know who I am, Inspector Hadfield,' Eddie snarled.

'Mr Sullivan, this is a warrant. I am arresting you on suspicion of causing death by reckless driving. I must warn you that you are not obliged to say anything unless you wish to do so. Anything you do say will be taken down in writing and may be given in evidence.'

Eddie's resentful attitude was instantly dispelled as he looked wildly back and forth between Hadfield and Jan.

'What? You can't. I don't get this, you're *arresting* me?'

Hadfield nodded.

'Yes. You'll be coming back with us now to the station for questioning.'

He beckoned to a second constable and the two uniformed officers stood on either side of Eddie. One of them gently touched his elbow and Eddie yanked it away.

'Get your sodding hands off me,' he yelled. 'I don't need your bloody help.'

The two constables flanked him as Eddie hobbled between his

sticks, still protesting, all the way to the patrol car. Hadfield moved rapidly towards his own car, with Jan in quick pursuit.

'What the hell is this? You can see Eddie's disabled. He's in no condition—'

'He can walk, Mrs Hardy,' interrupted Hadfield, as he turned to face her. 'You needn't worry. I'll have a police doctor look at him when we get to the station to check if he's fit to be interviewed.'

Jan watched anxiously as Eddie clambered into the back of the second car. He gave Jan a look she had never seen before, an angry, glowering black look.

'Inspector Hadfield,' Jan pleaded, 'stop it. This is completely and utterly *ridiculous.*'

'I don't think so, Mrs Hardy. Now you can give the station a ring later on if you wish and I will tell you what has transpired.'

He opened the door, slipped into the passenger seat and motioned his driver forward as if he was mushing a team of huskies. The two cars took off at speed while Jan and her team watched in complete astonishment. The whole affair had taken less than five minutes.

It was three hours later when Jan phoned the Cheltenham police station and spoke to the desk sergeant. She was told Eddie had been charged and put in a cell. She then asked if she could speak to Inspector Hadfield, but was informed he had already gone home to Mrs Hadfield.

'So tell me, what happens next?' asked Jan.

'I'm told he'll go before the magistrates in the morning,' the sergeant continued, in a practised and kindly tone. 'They'll consider bail favourably, I imagine, but of course you can never be sure.'

'But where? When? Do you have any details?'

She quickly wrote down the address of the court alongside the time: ten a.m.

Eddie's time in custody was brief. Following hurried discussions with Tony Robertson, Eddie's doctor, Jan contacted a local solicitor, Bob Warren, who went to see Eddie promptly and agreed to represent him. Jan watched from the back of the court as Warren, a small ginger-haired forty-something in an untidy suit, successfully argued for the prisoner to be granted bail on Jan's surety. Outside, on the steps of the court house, Jan thanked him profusely.

'I don't know how we'd have managed without you.'

'That's OK, Mrs Hardy. It's what I do.'

'What happens now?'

'You take Eddie home and give him a bit of TLC. This ordeal is bound to have set back his recovery. I'll go back to the office and put in an application for legal aid. The police and the Crown Prosecution Service will now start to prepare their case.'

'Their *preposterous* case,' Eddie called out truculently from several yards away.

'So there'll definitely be a trial?' Jan asked hesitantly.

Warren shrugged.

'Not necessarily. That's for the CPS to decide when they have reviewed all the evidence. Of course, while Hadfield will be trying to persuade them to proceed, my job at this stage is to see if I can get the charges dropped.'

'Is that likely?'

'No, not very, I'd say. The police have clearly been thinking about this for some time. They must be reasonably confident they have a good chance of it going to trial or the arrest wouldn't have taken place. But we'll see . . .'

It was still morning as Jan drove Eddie back to Edge Farm. He looked like thunder and was reluctant to discuss events in the police station, or the police questioning.

'I just told them the truth – I've got amnesia and can't remember the bloody accident. Hadfield didn't believe me, of course. What is it with that man?'

'Oh, Eddie, I hope you didn't lose your temper.'

'Lose my temper, I was spitting blood a couple of times. But I realized it wouldn't do any good in the end.'

'Well, it wouldn't. What do you think of Warren?'

'Don't know. He's all right, I suppose.'

🐎

Bob Warren turned out to be far more than all right. He was a bull terrier. During the next three weeks he drove over several times for consultations with Eddie and Jan. He also spoke to everyone else in the yard and to all of Eddie's medics. At Jan's suggestion, he contacted Tim Farr and on his own initiative looked into the background of William Moorhouse, whom he already had knowledge of through the legal network. Again at Jan's insistence, and with her help, he compiled what he called a narrative account of Harold Powell's ventures, beginning well before the auctioneer had attempted to defraud Jan over the sale of Stonewall Farm. He regarded the fake press release as extremely significant, and took affidavits from the Taylor-Joneses at the vicarage in Chiselcombe, and hunted down several other recipients of the offensive document.

As Warren often stressed, there was nothing else either Eddie or Jan could add while the wheels of justice slowly turned.

'Just get on with your lives,' Bob advised. 'Leave the worrying to me.'

In the midst of this upheaval, Edge Farm Stables was doing well. Over the next month Jan sent out fifteen runners, and carried home two trophies, as well as getting a second and three third places. One of the winners was for A.D., on a day when he could not be present. As usual on these occasions, the Irishman sent Jan a bottle of champagne with a note, written in his own rapid scrawl.

> Sorry to have missed Wexford Lad. Congratulations to you all. We are looking forward to Morning Glory at Stratford. A.D. O'H.

The Stratford race was now only a week away and this was A.D.'s way of letting Jan know just how keenly he was following MG's progress. Jan did wonder why this particular animal was so important to him. She knew he had paid a lot of money for the horse, but A.D. was a very rich man indeed. On the other hand, she also knew for sure that he didn't like the idea of being taken for a mug. Perhaps now, having shelled out far more than the horse appeared to be worth, he urgently wanted Morning Glory to prove him right.

🐎

The days preceding the Stratford meeting had been showery, but the day itself dawned under a clear sky. The beautiful crisp autumn morning promised perfect racing conditions. By ten they were ready to load Morning Glory and Jan seriously hoped he wasn't feeling as nervous as she was. It was a huge relief when he went up the ramp calmly into the enlarged stall and then travelled to the course without incident. His race was a novice hurdle that had attracted so many declarations it had been split, with MG in the first division, which was the opening event on the card.

Jan and Patsy were settling MG into the racecourse stable when Annabel brought Jan a race card.

'Have you seen the runners in the other division?' she asked, pointing her finger to a name halfway down the list, a name Jan knew only too well: Velvet Dynasty, owned by 'executors of Col. G. Gilbert', trained by Miss V. Gilbert and ridden by F. Howlett.

'Yes, I saw it in the *Racing Post* earlier this morning. It looks like we've been spared an interesting clash,' Jan said.

For the time being she was too busy concentrating on MG to think any more about Virginia's runner. At first MG was keyed up and suspicious of his strange new surroundings, but Patsy had stuck to the horse's side like a limpet and managed to calm him down by degrees. The fine weather only added to the optimistic gloss. And the Edge Farm contingent felt they had done everything they could to give MG his best chance. Now it was all up to him.

The parade ring at Stratford was sited between the racecourse buildings and the finishing post, so the entire stand had a good view of the runners. This could easily have added to MG's emotional state, despite the reassuring stream of talk Patsy was directing towards his left ear as he led him round.

At last the jockeys dribbled into the paddock and a wave of anticipation swept through the crowd. A.D.'s usual jockey, Murty McGrath, had taken the ride. Although Jan had invited him to give

MG a spin on the gallops a few days earlier, the champion jockey had other commitments and couldn't make it.

'Murty,' she said nervously, her mouth as dry as chipboard, 'you *have* seen this horse before, haven't you?'

Murty rode hundreds of horses every year but, like most successful jockeys, he had total recall.

'Yeah, I rode him OK, if you can call it that. He was headstrong all right and always wore a citation bridle. He fought me like a wildcat, but I never gave him his head until two furlongs out. But he didn't quicken, burnt himself out, I reckon. To be honest with you, I didn't take to him. I thought he'd a phobia with other horses. Something must have happened when he was broken, I'd say.'

'Well, he's *much* better now, different altogether, thanks to a lot of hard work by young Patsy. That's the lad minding him.'

Just then Patsy and MG came wandering by. Murty's eyes lit up as he looked at the horse's head in alarm.

'Where's the citation, Mrs H? Surely you're not running him without one?'

'Yes I am,' said Jan firmly. 'He doesn't need all that gear in his mouth. In fact, I'm pretty sure that's been a large part of the problem. That bridle hurt him and I've been weeks sorting out the inside of his mouth.'

Murty was looking volatile.

'Mrs H, I'd not expect you to put me up on that horse without extra precautions being taken, that's for sure.'

'Now look, Murty,' Jan persisted, 'it's no good you going on about this. Anyway, we haven't brought the equipment with us. So we haven't got a choice. He runs as he is and that's the end of it.'

'I've got two more rides this afternoon. If this one puts me in hospital because you sent him out with the wrong bridle, you'll have the other owners to answer to and they're not going to like it.'

'Don't be bloody ridiculous, Murty. Are you telling me the champion jockey's afraid of the horse? Is that the case?'

'Afraid? Course I'm not afraid. I'm just not a fecking eejit.'

The bell sounded, signalling the jockeys to mount and Patsy brought Morning Glory to a halt.

'Now, Murty, look,' Jan said firmly, 'I know the horse has ideas of his own, and if you try and dictate to him he'll expend all his energy fighting you – as you found out over in Ireland. So you've got to go *with* him to some extent. Understand? Let him run the race the way he wants. As long as he's not pissing off and he jumps over all the hurdles, I don't mind.'

'You're saying it's a steering job then, are you?' Murty growled. 'Jesus, the horse is a novice. He knows no more than a dead cat would know.'

'Well, let's just see, shall we, Murty? Let's call it an experiment. But the point is he has to go to the start without getting steamed up. Don't canter him down with the others. Take him out on the course last, and go very steady. That's essential. You'll be fine, you'll see.'

At the very moment Murty was getting a leg-up from Jan, A.D. hurried over to join them.

'All right, Murty?' he said.

Murty tipped his cap.

'He's on his toes, Mr O'Hagan. But Mrs H's been telling me to let him do it his way.'

A.D. patted his horse's neck.

'Off you go then.'

Murty checked that the last of the runners had already left the parade ring, and moved MG off at a sedate walk towards the exit and the course. Only the odd sideways jink of his quarters betrayed the horse's nerves. A.D. watched them depart, then looked sharply at Jan.

'Do it his way, is it? You're not forgetting this is his first race over obstacles?'

'No, A.D., I'm not,' said Jan, suppressing her irritation. 'Don't worry. I know he can jump. He's a natural, you'll see. I'm sure the obstacles will help settle him.'

But as soon as the words were out, Jan feared she had been overconfident. She didn't like being taken for a mug any more than A.D., but if MG didn't perform and her 'experiment' failed, that was exactly how she would look.

The opposition was more formidable in numbers than in quality, or so it appeared. The noughts in front of MG's name, denoting his unplaced efforts in his races in Ireland, were uninspiring to the punters, and he was quoted at long odds behind a group of fancied horses who had more useful, and more recent, form. But none of them, in Jan's eyes, could be seen as an overwhelming threat.

At the start, MG began to show signs of his old temperament, sweating and tossing his head from side to side, but the jockey's excellent horsemanship held him together. As the runners were called into line, Murty had MG poised slightly behind the rest, and timed his approach to the tape so skilfully that MG was already on the move when the elasticated tape flew away. The horse immediately lifted his head and, lengthening his stride, he glided into a three-length lead.

The first few hurdles presented no problem and he soared over them like a gazelle. Following Jan's instructions to the letter, Murty sat as quiet as a mouse, allowing the horse to find his own stride into the obstacles. It was obvious, even to the apprehensive jockey, that MG was enjoying himself out in front. The horse pricked his ears and looked confident as they came past the stands for the first time. He led the field around the tight left-hand bend which took the horses on towards the back straight, where halfway along they briefly met rising ground. Now the pace increased and they were galloping downhill towards the final turn.

Watching through binoculars from the stand, Jan's heart was thudding loudly against her ribs – she knew the race was reaching its climax. Morning Glory was handling the sharp bend well, but, quickly scanning the field for dangers, Jan saw two horses take advantage of the downward slope and career past the tired runners in pursuit of Morning Glory. By the time they turned into the straight, with just two hurdles to negotiate, the pair had forced their way into second and third places. They were still four lengths off MG, but it was obvious the race was going to be between the three of them.

Morning Glory got too close to the second last and hit it hard. All around there were cheers for the more fancied runners, as MG's advantage was reduced to a length. Murty responded by crouching lower in the saddle and seeming to raise his whip.

'Don't hit him, please don't hit him!' Jan said out loud, without realizing.

Murty didn't hit MG. He merely glanced to the side to check on the opposition. He pulled his whip through to his other hand and rested his knuckles either side of the horse's withers. Jan thought this was a breathtaking display. Most jockeys would have panicked, waving their whips, thrashing their horses' backsides. Murty did neither. He simply concentrated on making himself part of the horse's own flowing movement. But the two pursuers continued to close inch by inch. Approaching the last flight of hurdles, the three animals were almost level. Clearly galvanized by the sudden proximity of two other hard-breathing horses, Morning Glory stood way off the jump and executed a breathtaking leap. One of the challengers blundered and tipped his jockey over his ears. The other hopped over well enough but, by the time his jockey had shaken him up for a final effort, Murty McGrath had gone beyond his reach. On the run-in, as Morning Glory extended his raking stride inch by inch, he won with seven lengths in hand.

In the unsaddling enclosure Murty was delighted as all his earlier anxieties were washed away.

'He just made monkeys of the lot of 'em! And he had a ton in hand. Mrs Hardy, you were right. No more citation bridle for this feller. He loved it out there.'

'Thanks, Murty,' said Jan, 'and you rode him perfectly. He obviously likes you better than he did.'

'It wasn't me that did it. It was the horse. Look at him. Just look at him now, he wouldn't blow a candle out.'

They all looked at Morning Glory in the golden afternoon sun. His breathing was already back to normal, and he was the picture of well-being.

So was Mr A.D. O'Hagan when he took the bridle and posed for the photographers, an unusually broad grin lighting his face.

Jan had no more runners and by now she'd have got her winner into the transporter and headed back to Edge as early as possible.

But today she couldn't leave, at least not until after the sixth race. She wanted to see Velvet Dynasty run.

To lose horses to other trainers, especially ones with potential that she had spotted in the first place, ones that she had personally schooled over obstacles and taught the rudiments of the game, was a physical pain to Jan. And when the other trainer was Virginia Gilbert the pain was doubled. But today Jan felt compelled to watch, even though it was likely to add to her torture. The last time she'd seen Velvet Dynasty compete on a racecourse had been on the flat while she was watching TV. He'd been given a miserable ride, and made no impression on the result. Since then Jan had ridden the horse herself so she knew how misleading that form would be. Even more recently Scottie Venables had bragged to her that the horse was a surprise package. Now she was itching to know exactly what he meant.

Finbar Howlett rode Velvet Dynasty in quite a different style from the way Murty had handled Morning Glory. For half of the two miles he kept him under tight restraint, placed nearer last than first. But once they'd passed the stands and begun the second circuit Finbar gradually released him, letting him carve his way through the back markers. At the top of the final bend the horse was contesting the lead and, with two to jump, he was already a couple of lengths clear. His leap at that second last gained him another length in the air and, after that, there was not another horse to be sighted as Velvet Dynasty skipped over the last and won as he liked. Jan felt like spitting rust, but an image of the colonel came into her mind and she knew how pleased he would be. Jan's eyes welled up – it was hard losing such a dear and loyal friend as the colonel. Her only connection with him was the horses and now her old friend Wolf's Rock, not to mention Velvet Dynasty, had left. 'Life can be so unfair,' she sniffed, but she had to steel herself for what lay ahead good, bad or indifferent.

The staff breakfast at Edge Farm the next day was a noisy affair. Annabel, who always collected the *Racing Post* from the newsagent's in the morning, had read aloud an inside story, printed under the headline,

## HARDY AND GILBERT UNVEIL HOT-POT NOVICES
## AT STRATFORD

It made good copy: two female trainers from different walks of life, each possessed of a novice hurdler of exceptional ability. The paper had made no bones about how it saw things working out. No doubt Velvet Dynasty and Morning Glory were going to be intense rivals throughout the season but, more than that, they were going to embody a larger rivalry between their two trainers. Which horse, which trainer, was the better? On the evidence of their respective debuts, both horses ran enticingly over the same distance and under identical conditions, and they could not be split. The issue would remain undecided until they met, possibly at Kempton over Christmas.

At the moment Jan rarely made statements to the press if she could avoid it, so she was not quoted. Virginia Gilbert had been rather less discreet. 'Mine would beat hers doing handsprings,' she was quoted as saying. 'It will be no contest. We're ready whenever Mrs Hardy is. I can't wait.'

Jan's staff, on the other hand, were equally positive that MG, with his raking stride, would never be caught by the Gilbert horse. Jan said little, allowing them their effervescence. But as she left the table to answer the phone, she knew in her heart that a front-runner was always a big target, vulnerable to any particularly fast-finishing opponent, and Velvet Dynasty looked all of that.

She picked up the phone.

'Hello, Jan, it's Virginia.'

Jan almost dropped the receiver.

'Yes?' she said, trying not to sound too peeved.

'I take it you've read the *Racing Post*.'

'Yes.'

'They seem to think we're rivals. I really can't think where they got *that* idea from.'

'From you, I would think.'

'My horse will smash yours into the middle of next week, you do know that, don't you?'

'That's not a very pleasant way of putting it, and I doubt it's true either,' said Jan.

'Well, *we're* up for it at this end. Are you?'

'I'm up for most things, Virginia, as long as they don't harm my horses. But I'm not going to let you or the newspapers determine my horse's entries.'

'Oh no, of course not, but I do have other priorities, and one of them is to show you I've got the better horse. Another is to stop you spreading snidey rumours about my yard. Goodbye.'

A continuous tone cut in, so Jan replaced the handset. 'Right, if that's what she wants, so be it. I'll take you on Virginia,' she muttered, 'and I'll bloody beat you too.'

She didn't understand what Virginia had meant by snidey rumours until a few minutes later when, breakfast over, she was leafing through the pages of the *Post*. A small diary story caught her eye: 'Tim Farr's crusade against stable bully boys'. It appeared from what she read that Farr's investigation was shortly to be printed in the *Wessex Daily News*. Despite all its efforts, the *Post* had been unable to discover any details, except for one. Which stated that one of the stables being investigated was Riscombe Manor.

# 20

Before leaving the racecourse, A.D. O'Hagan had told Jan that he and Siobhan were staying overnight at Stratford, where they had tickets for a performance at the Shakespeare Memorial Theatre.

'But I have some people to see in Bristol tomorrow evening,' A.D. had continued, 'so Daragh and I'll be down your way in the morning. You won't mind if we call in, will you? I'd like a chat.'

'Of course not. Come to lunch.'

🐎

Jan was considerably more relaxed in her dealings with A.D. than she used to be, but the prospect of his visits still made her quake a little. Usually A.D. would come to cast a critical eye over the stable and his horses, but his stopovers had at times heralded a change in his racing policy.

It was well over a year since he had invited Jan to dinner at the Queen's Hotel in Cheltenham to outline his plan to set up an English training operation at a modern stable complex, with Jan as his private trainer. She had been bowled over by this show of confidence, but so far she had resisted the idea. She knew it would give her the kind of financial security most trainers only dreamt of, but she was unwilling to give up the independence she had worked so hard to establish. While she had not heard the scheme mentioned recently, A.D. was not the kind of man who let himself be thwarted. So she assumed it was not a dead duck.

🐎

Siobhan had gone straight from Stratford to Birmingham airport before flying on to Amsterdam, where she was due to give a recital, so A.D. arrived accompanied only by his driver, Daragh. Jan had fretted about whether to give them something out of a fancy cookbook, but in the end they sat down in the kitchen, herself, Eddie and the billionaire, to peas, mash and grilled sausages washed down with cider.

A.D. ate methodically, cutting the sausages into small rounds and carefully pasting the slices with Colman's mustard before putting them into his mouth. Eddie ate slowly and was almost silent, though he responded politely to A.D.'s enquiries about his recuperation. The court case, however, was not mentioned.

A.D. talked mainly about the horses and went through the list, paying particular attention to Russian Eagle, who in three weeks was due to run in the Mackeson Gold Cup, the first big chase of the season at Cheltenham in mid-November.

'He'll struggle to go the pace, I suppose,' A.D. said with a quizzical look. 'I doubt he'll be one of the fancies.'

'I don't know about struggle,' Jan countered. 'It depends on what he's up against on the day. You needn't worry about his fitness. He's really sharp and as keen as that mustard you're putting on your sausage.'

'Excellent. And so are the sausages, by the way.'

When they'd finished eating and Jan was making coffee, A.D. looked at his watch and said unexpectedly, 'Jan, would you mind putting on that radio at all? Just briefly. Siobhan's got a new recording out and they're playing something from it in a couple of minutes. She wants me to let her know if they give it any sort of review.'

'Oh great, I'd like to hear it myself. What's it on?'

Jan eventually found the wavelength of the classical station and the presenter was highly respectful towards Siobhan. A.D. nodded his approval at the words: 'One of Europe's top mezzo sopranos at the top of her game, with a coloratura technique almost comparable to Callas's.' Jan did not have a clue what this meant, except that to be compared with Maria Callas was obviously a hell of a compliment.

One of the tracks, an aria Jan decided, was sung in French, but

she was at a loss to understand the words, though she fully appreciated the phenomenal control of the vocalist. She glanced from
A.D. to Eddie, who both sat in silence concentrating, with their
eyes cast down.

When the aria finished, A.D. switched off the radio and, for a
few moments, no one spoke.

A.D. gave a contented sigh before suggesting that he and Jan
take a tour of the yard, and then what he called a post-prandial
walk through the pine trees above the house, as far as the top of the
ridge.

'Your man, Eddie, has quietened down a lot,' he said on the
way.

'Yes, I know, but he's a lot better physically, I think.'

Suddenly Jan decided she ought to broach a matter that, so far,
she had been keeping from her patron.

'A.D., I hope you don't mind, but while we're on the subject of
Eddie, there's something I ought to tell you. I wanted to give him
something to work towards, some incentive, so I promised him . . .'

She swallowed hard. She had no idea how her 'boss' would take
this.

'Well, you see, I promised him he could ride Russian Eagle in
the National – if he made a full recovery, that is!'

A.D., possibly from complete surprise, said nothing. Jan hesitated, then carried on.

'I know I should have talked to you first, but it just came out,
you know, sort of spontaneously. I didn't even ask your co-owner at
the time.'

'And what does Annabel say now?'

'Oh, she thinks it's a great idea. She knows Eddie can, or at least
could, ride the course, and he gets on with the horse really well.'

'Hmm. I suppose if the pair of them can virtually win the
Foxhunters', then theoretically they can win the National. Is that
what you're both thinking? Well, not if Eddie's in the state I saw
him in just now he can't, that's for sure. He'll have to get rid of
those sticks and prove he's completely fit, *completely* fit, mind, or I'd
never agree. The National is not there for occupational therapy.

And he'll have to sort out this police thing. He can't ride a horse from the jailhouse, can he?'

'Oh!' said Jan, surprised. 'It won't come to that, I'm sure. It's all going to be cleared up. Eddie's got a very good lawyer now.'

'Did you know that feller Hadfield came to see me at Aigmont?' A.D. went on. 'He wanted to know was Eddie drinking in my box during the afternoon before your accident.'

'Blimey! I hadn't a clue. Did he go over to Ireland especially?'

'He did. And I told him I didn't see the man take a drop.'

'Thanks, A.D. I appreciate that. So will Eddie, I know.'

'It was the honest truth. But there may be others that saw things differently. Anyway, I don't want to talk about that now. I wanted to have a word about Morning Glory.'

He explained that there was a race in Ireland, a good-quality novice hurdle at Leopardstown in early January, and he wanted the horse to run. As a successful poker player A.D. never liked to reveal his hand, but he dropped a broad hint that he had already backed the horse to win.

'I'll send you the details. It wouldn't do for you to be putting him in the wrong race. Now, the question is what do we do with him in the meantime?'

'We're all keen to take on that novice of Virginia Gilbert's.'

'The one she pinched from you after her father's death, who won the last race so handily at Stratford?'

'Yes, that's the one.'

A.D. laughed.

'I thought so. I saw the *Racing Post* this morning, so I knew it was on the cards you'd be thinking along those lines. What race have you in mind?'

'The obvious one's next month at Cheltenham, on Mackeson day.'

The Mackeson Gold Cup was the feature race of the season's first major meeting, and the two-mile novice hurdle on the same card was a prestigious event, worth four times the prize money that Morning Glory had collected at Stratford. A.D said nothing to Jan's suggestion at first, as he was concentrating on the track and maintaining his footing. As they came out of the trees and saw the crown of the ridge just above, A.D. reached the top before Jan with a final scrambling effort, and sat on the ground, breathing deeply, waiting for her to catch up. He gazed reflectively over at the wide spread of country on the other side of the hill, with the Welsh mountains in the distance.

'Will you look at that?' he said in wonder as she joined him. 'You could probably see the Wicklow Hills from here if you had the eyes for it.'

Jan flopped down beside him.

'So, anyway, what do you think?' she persisted. 'I'd say that's possibly the race Virginia will be going for as well.'

'Yes,' agreed A.D., to Jan's delight. 'That sounds fine, let's go for it.'

They absorbed the view for a few moments longer until A.D. broke the silence.

'There's one more thing I need to tell you, Jan. I'm going to view a yard in the Lambourn area tomorrow. It fits the biography and it's what I'm looking for over here, at least on paper.'

He turned his head and looked steadily at her.

'So if I like it, I'm hoping you'll give it the once-over. It would be a great opportunity.'

Jan took a deep breath.

'Well, A.D., if you want my *advice* . . .'

A.D. chuckled.

'It's not advice I'm wanting. It's your agreement to come in with me.'

'But I've already said no to that. It's not that I'm not grateful or anything.'

'Well, the offer's still open, Jan, but it won't be for ever. As of this week, or this month, maybe this year, you can still change your mind. Now . . .' He glanced at his watch. 'I'd better be off to my meeting. I'll race you down, but no running, mind!'

That afternoon Jan completed the entry form for MG's next contest. Then, after a moment's thought, she telephoned Reg at Riscombe.

'That was a great win yesterday, girl,' her father enthused. 'He's maybe your best horse. I expect he'll need a few more races like that before he's proved it, mind.'

'Did you see the result of the other division?'

'Velvet Dynasty? Yes, won his by the same margin, didn't he? When do you intend taking him on?'

'Are you reading my mind, Dad? Virginia's actually challenged me, so I can hardly back down, can I? I'm well aware that hers is good too, but I do have the advantage because I've handled both horses. And we all think our chap's better.'

'So what's the plan?'

'I've entered him in a novice event on Mackeson day. I'm pretty sure Virginia will be considering the race, but it wouldn't go amiss if it got around Riscombe village that we were definitely entered. If you know what I mean.'

Jan knew her father well enough to know that he was smiling.

'Just leave it with me, girl. I'll make sure everybody knows, don't you worry about that.'

🐎

Tim Farr's story ran in the *Daily News* two days later. It was a subsidiary item in a small block on the front, but occupied all of the back page, under the headline: THE UNACCEPTABLE FACE OF RACING. Farr had secretly recorded conversations with stable staff from two different establishments. The piece detailed initiation rites and other humiliation games as well as sexual harassment.

The article ended with a ringing denunciation of the per-petrators.

> Of course, not all racing stables are like this. But it is an
> unacceptable fact that there are individual trainers, and senior
> members of staff, who allow such practices to continue. Many
> of the young men or women come into racing purely for the
> love of animals, their sole reason for working with them. It is
> shameful that such idealism is battered by workplace bullies
> to such an extent that some apprentices actually run away,
> abandoning their possessions. Which is already alleged to have
> happened at Virginia Gilbert's yard at Riscombe Manor,

where a member of her staff was forced to 'bolt' after months
of being harassed for his religious beliefs. There is no suggestion that Miss Gilbert knew what was going on at the time.
But the point is she should have known.

'Wow, I bet Virginia doesn't like the fact that her yard was
mentioned,' Annabel declared when she and Jan discussed the piece
later.

'Do you think so? The snippet about Patsy looks just that – a
snippet. But, God, I'm really uneasy about this kind of reporting.
It smears the whole of racing and there are so many good people in
the industry working their balls off for a pittance, including us.'

'Yes, I know, but Tim Farr's right about not betraying the
idealism of staff. People do genuinely care and they are quite
prepared to put up with the long hours and low pay. But to allow
them to be bullied, that's despicable.'

'I agree. If I found out there was anyone here doing that kind of
thing, even a hint of it, I'd have their guts for garters, believe me.'

The following Sunday afternoon Edge Farm was almost deserted.
Eddie had gone off with Gerry, to support his friend in a stock-car
race. Jan thought it seemed a strange therapy for someone who'd
nearly died in a car smash, but now that Eddie had a macabre
interest in it, Jan was even more afraid that his next step would be
to get the Morgan patched up so he could race it himself.

Megan and Matty had disappeared with some friends from school
for a ride on their ponies and none of the staff were around when
Jan went down to the yard to take stock of the feedstore. She'd just
made a note of what needed ordering, and was relocking the door,
when she heard a man's voice behind her.

'All *alone*, are we?'

The menace in the voice was immediately recognizable and Jan
knew instantly that she was about to come face to face with Harold
Powell.

He was striding with grim purpose across the yard towards her.

'I hope you've got a very good reason to be here, Harold,' she
said, trying to control her voice and stop it quaking.

'Oh yes, I've got a good reason all right. I've come to give you a final warning, Mrs bloody Busybody,' Harold spat out.

Jan did not feel the need to reply any more sweetly.

'Don't you speak to me like that. I won't take any warnings from you. Your threats won't work, so just sod off before I call the police.'

Now Harold was shaking his finger at her.

'I've got a lot more than threats, I've got actions. I've already done some things, and I can do more, you'll see. You'd better watch your step.'

'So tell me what you have done.'

Harold made quote marks with his fingers.

'"This press release is issued by the Cotswold News Agency as a service to the community." Remember that? "Have you had a *shower* lately, Mrs Hardy?" Remember that too?'

'I always thought it was only pathetic tossers like you who made anonymous phone calls, and sent unsigned letters full of malicious gossip. Well, now I know I was right, you jerk.'

'As a matter of fact, I did it for another reason. I did it to make you shit scared, you self-righteous little bitch. You've put the police on to me again, haven't you? Accusing me of things you have no way of proving, not ever. Now you're making allegations against Virginia's yard that are unsubstantiated. You won't be allowed to get away with all this. You will have to be *stopped*. One way or the other.'

'Are you going to try shoving me off the road again, is that it?'

'Next time there won't be a mistake. I'll make damn sure of it. That car put me off. If it hadn't suddenly appeared, I could have made a better job of you and *darling Edward*. I was hoping for a fire – in fact, an explosion would have been nice. Still, better luck next time, eh!'

Jan had been edging round, with her back to the line of boxes beside the feedstore. She maintained continual eye-contact with Harold, wondering if he had gone completely insane. His livid face had turned ghostly white, his eyes had become bloodshot and his lips were drawn tightly back around bared teeth. She felt that if she showed him a moment of weakness he would attack her with his clenched fists.

'Talking of which,' Harold snarled more gleefully as he jerked his thumb in the direction of the feedstore, 'that little lot in there would *burn* merrily enough, I dare say, along with your precious horses.'

'So you are going to turn into an arsonist now, Harold. Is that to go with the attempted murder?'

'Getting rid of you wouldn't be murder, Jan Hardy. It would be a service to humanity.'

He twitched and moved towards her. Jan felt perspiration on her brow and edged further along the wall. The horses looked curiously over their stable doors. Some pawed the ground and whinnied at this extraordinary confrontation.

Jan saw a muck fork that had been left against the wall just a few feet away, in the direction she was heading. Slowly she took a couple more strides. Grabbing it in a flash, she held it in the air, pointing the tines towards Harold.

'Go back,' she warned.

Making a gesture calculated to mock, he moved away, tut-tutting and shaking his finger from side to side in a sarcastic manner.

'Stick me with it, would you? Now what would your Inspector Hadfield have to say about that? He'd say you were conducting some kind of ruthless vendetta against Virginia and me, wouldn't he? And I think he'd be right, don't you?'

'Vendetta? That's you and your ghastly girlfriend. I was ready to forget that you tried to cheat me over that land. I was even prepared to accept that my mother-in-law had, in fact, died accidentally. But now you've admitted your crusade against me. I'm going to see you locked up. That's for certain!'

Harold seemed as though he was about to speak. But instead he took a deep breath and thought better of it. He looked at the horses ranged on every side; they looked back at him bewildered. Suddenly, for whatever reason – the staring horses, the brandished fork, the fact that he might have said too much – he unexpectedly lost his nerve.

'Well, fuck you,' he said contemptuously, 'you'll see where it all gets you!'

Harold moved swiftly towards the archway, and, as he reached it, he turned. Jan was standing in the same position, with the fork raised.

'I'll get you yet, Jan Hardy. You'll pay for this,' he hollered. Then he was gone.

# 21

Jan gulped in air, her heart still pounding. Gradually she lowered the fork, then finally dropped it to the ground as she sank to her haunches.

'*God, please help me!*' she said aloud, covering her face with both hands. 'Is this never, *ever* going to end?'

'It's all right, Mrs H.'

Jan snatched her head from her hands and looked up.

'Who's there?' she called to the voice coming from behind her. She turned and there was Patsy Keating, his moon face peering over the lower door of the stable.

'Patsy! Where in heaven's name did you spring from?'

'I was in here all the time. I heard everythin' that feller said, so I did.'

'You did?'

'Sure, I did so. He said he wanted to kill you.'

'You bet he did,' said Jan grimly. 'You sure you really heard everything?'

'Yeah. He said he made phone calls because he wanted to scare you shitless.'

Suddenly it struck home. This was it! The breakthrough she'd been waiting for.

'Patsy!' she cried, tears running down her face in relief, 'you clever, clever boy! I believe you're the answer to my prayers, I really do.'

Patsy was puzzled.

'Your prayers, Mrs H?'

'Come on, let's go in. We need to make an important phone call.'

She caught hold of Patsy's arm and ran with him into the office, where she immediately dialled Bob Warren's home number. The woman who answered said she was Nina Warren and sounded rather peeved when Jan said it was work, and an emergency, and please could she speak to Bob urgently.

'I'll have to get him,' said Mrs Warren primly. 'He's in the garden.'

Fretfully and unaware that she was doing it, Jan drummed on the table with her fingers until Bob came on the line.

'It's Jan Hardy. I'm sorry to ring you at home on a Sunday, Bob, but I thought you should know. Harold Powell turned up here. He's threatened me – again, viciously – though I suppose I should be getting used to it by now. But I'm still shaking.'

'Did he come alone?'

'Yes – at least, I think so.'

'How did he threaten you? Verbally? Or did he actually hit you?'

'No, yes, I mean verbally. But there's more. He admitted everything: it was him that tried to drive us off the road, and he made the anonymous phone calls, and he also sent out those fake news bulletins. And what's more he said he wasn't giving up and that he was quite prepared to kill me if necessary. For ruining his life, he said.'

'When was this? How long ago?'

'Not long. Ten minutes or so.'

'Well now, don't be too concerned about this, Jan. I've seen it all before, people lashing out in rage.'

'I'm not concerned. I'm delighted. Because we've got him, haven't we? Now we know for sure he was responsible for Cleeve Hill. Eddie's off the hook, isn't he, Bob?'

'I'm afraid not, Jan. Unless, by some crazy chance, you recorded Harold's remarks on tape. Otherwise he'll deny it, then it's just the same old story, your word against his.'

'But it's not. I didn't record the conversation of course, but somebody overheard it. Patsy Keating, one of my stable lads, was right here. He heard the whole lot.'

'Did he, by God? Well that certainly puts a whole different complexion on things. Is he with you now?'

'Yes he is. He lives here in a caravan by the yard.'

Bob covered the mouthpiece of his phone and Jan heard a muffled exchange between him and his wife. Then he was back on the line.

'Just give me a bit of time to get out of these gardening clothes and I'll drive straight over. I think it's important that I record what Patsy actually heard from his own lips while his memory's fresh.'

🐎

The solicitor duly arrived with a tape recorder and interviewed Jan and Patsy separately about Harold's escapade. Bob told Jan that he would prepare affidavits based on the recordings and inform Hadfield of the new evidence.

'And I'll certainly tell him that Powell admitted causing the crash on Cleeve Hill in front of a witness: and that the police have also charged the wrong man. Just for good measure, I'll lodge a complaint on your behalf against Harold Powell for threatening behaviour, just to show he wasn't here to play a game of pat-a-cake. All in all, I'm pretty hopeful this will be enough, particularly with the amount of circumstantial evidence we've already got about Harold Powell's animosity towards you. I can get the CPS to drop the charges against Eddie. Where *is* my client, by the way?'

As Jan told him, Bob burst out laughing.

'That man's something else, you'd think he'd have had enough of crashed cars by now.'

🐎

Bob Warren had left Edge Farm by the time the stock-car duo returned. Jan and the children heard Gerry's van drive onto the forecourt, pulling a trailer with an extremely battered car roped to it. The Hardys rushed out from the house to meet them.

Eddie stayed in the passenger seat as Gerry stepped out and came towards Jan. His face looked pained and anxious, a man bearing bad news.

'Gerry, what's the matter? Didn't it go well?'

'It's Eddie, Jan. I'm really sorry, I—'

'What about him? Come on, out with it.'

Gerry spread his arms wide helplessly to explain.

'I don't know how it happened. Well, I do. There was all this free beer, see, and while I was racing, well, he just went a bit over the top, if you know what I mean.'

'You mean he's drunk?'

'You'd better come and look.'

Eddie was slumped in the van with a stupid grin on his face. Over the past months Eddie had been temperate. He went to the pub regularly with Gerry, but actually drank very little. Today had clearly been a different story. There was no doubting he was completely plastered. With his shirt pulled out of his waistband, he was slurring his words and his eyes had that unfocused look of a man whose head was swimming in alcohol.

Furious, Jan yanked open the door and Eddie, whose head had been lolling against the window, nearly fell out.

'Hello, Jan,' he said woozily as he levered himself upright. 'How is the most beautiful racehorse trainer that ever lived? Are you all right, old girl?'

'Eddie, you're pissed!' said Jan, slightly amused by his comments. 'Get out. You can't sit there all night. Gerry wants to go home.'

'Good old Gerry,' said Eddie fondly. 'I've been telling him about my plan to ride Russian Eagle in the National next year.'

Jan took his elbow and gently but firmly pulled him out of Gerry's van. Eddie stood there swaying as she extracted his walking sticks from behind the seat.

'Come on, Gerry, let's get him into the house,' she said, beckoning Eddie's drinking buddy over. Cautiously they half walked, half dragged Eddie towards the front door, while he still rambled on about Russian Eagle.

'The Ger-rand *National*,' he was saying. 'The ambition of every jockey. C'mon, tell you what, let's go down and see my friend Eagle. C'mon, Jan, please. I want to pay a visit to my old friend Russian Eagle, future hero of Aintree.'

'No, Eddie, not now, for Christ's sake! You'll scare the living daylights out of him. I'm putting you to bed.'

They got into the hall and were manoeuvring Eddie up the stairs. Suddenly he wrenched himself free from Jan's and Gerry's guiding hands and spun around.

'But I don't *want* to go to bed. I want to see my *horse.*'

At that moment he reminded Jan of her five-year-old child whining close to bedtime. Then, all of a sudden, he seemed to step forward into the air and missed the tread, tumbling to the base of the stairs. He landed in a heap at the bottom in total disarray, in front of the horror-struck Megan and Matty.

'Oh God!' shrieked Meg. 'Is he all right? Is he dead?'

Jan had been a qualified first-aider for years and she had more than once tended fallen riders with broken bones – but most of those had been sober. Eddie would not respond sensibly to her questions about what hurt and what didn't and she was unable to see or feel a serious injury, so in the end she let Gerry carry him up the staircase and lower him onto the bed. Eddie did not seem to be in any pain and lay in the fetal position, already half asleep.

'Do you think he's hurt himself?' Gerry queried anxiously.

'I'm damn sure he has, going arse-over-tit like that. But he's so rat-arsed I really can't tell if it's bad. But it's his spine I'm concerned about. I'll just have to call the doctor.'

Tony Robertson appeared briefly that evening, behaving rather off-handedly when he realized why the accident had happened.

'Let him rest, sleep it off,' he told Jan. 'I expect he'll be pretty bruised and sore in the morning. Though I wouldn't think he's aggravated his spine. But you say he still had numbness in his legs – before this happened even?'

'He says so, he's still walking unsteadily.'

Jan lowered her voice.

'And he also told me – it's a bit difficult really, Tony – but he can't have sex, he said nothing's happening.'

Tony looked at Jan shrewdly.

'Is that so?'

For a brief moment Jan was worried that he was about to make a wisecrack, but he quickly pulled himself together.

'Eddie's a lot better now than when I first saw him, that's for sure, and he's well on the road to a full recovery. But one can't take any chances with spinal injuries like this. So he'd better have another assessment. I'll arrange for a visit from a physiotherapist I know. She specializes and lives in this area.'

'She?' said Jan.

'Yes, her name's Gloria Hooke.'

'And this Gloria, she specializes in sex, does she?'

For the first time since he'd arrived Tony relaxed and laughed out loud.

'No, silly. Spinal injuries and so on – which, of course, can include sexual dysfunction. In any case Ms Hooke is much better equipped to assess Eddie than I am.'

The next day, after they had worked the first lot of horses, Jan took Eddie a mug of tea in bed. He had evidently been awake for some time. She heaved him upright and packed a couple of extra pillows behind him.

'Does that hurt?'

'Everything hurts. I'm knackered, completely knackered.'

He was in a deep trough of gloom.

'Just look at me,' he went on. 'No good to anyone. Half-crippled, unemployable, *drunk* . . .'

'Eddie,' said Jan impatiently, 'we've been round this block before. Tony Robertson says you're probably fine, but you're to stay in bed for the moment. Anyway, he's arranging a home visit from a physiotherapist, who'll give you another assessment and work out the appropriate treatment. Tony is adamant you're making good progress and will fully recover. This is only a temporary setback.'

'A temporary setback before I go to jail, you mean,' Eddie reflected gloomily.

'No, Eddie,' said Jan, suddenly realizing she had not told Eddie about Harold's incriminating visit. 'There's really good news about that!'

She summarized the previous afternoon's events at Edge Farm.

'So you see,' she went on as Eddie listened without comment,

'Bob thinks the CPS will decide there's not much chance of a conviction, and Hadfield will be under serious pressure to arrest Harold Powell. If so, your problems will be over.'

Eddie let out a profound sigh.

'If only it was that simple.'

As Jan and Annabel stood at the yard entrance waiting for second lot to return from the gallops, a small hatchback drew up and out stepped a tall Nordic-style blonde, with a huge bosom that seemed likely to burst the buttons of her white tunic at any moment. Her left breast was adorned with the badge of the Chartered Society of Physiotherapy.

'Hi, I'm Gloria? The physio? I've come to treat a Mr Sullivan – right?'

Jan and Annabel exchanged bemused glances. From her accent, and the way she turned every statement into a question, she seemed to be a New Zealander.

'Oh, yes, right,' said Jan. 'Come this way. I'm so grateful you could give us a home visit. He's still in bed, I'm afraid. He had a bit of a fall yesterday and he's rather sore. Do you know his medical history?'

Jan explained the background of the road accident as she escorted Gloria up to Eddie's room. The physio was carrying a medical bag not unlike the one used by Tony Robertson, though Jan imagined it was packed with massage oils rather than drugs.

As they went in, Eddie was lying motionless under the duvet, his eyes still closed.

'Eddie,' said Jan brightly, 'this is Gloria, your new physio.'

Eddie groaned.

'Do I have to?'

Gloria looked at Jan and smiled sweetly.

'Mrs Hardy, I'm sure it would be best if you left me alone with Edward? You must have loads to do?'

With reluctance Jan left and made her way to the stable office, where she found Annabel.

'I think I can see why Tony said she was better equipped than him. The bastard! He's done this on purpose.'

🐎

An hour later Jan heard a voice calling 'Coo-ee, coo-ee?' She left the office and saw Gloria Hooke beckoning with one hand, medical bag in the other. Jan swiftly joined her and they strolled to the car.

'We've had a really good session,' said the physio. 'I'll send a report to Dr Robertson and call back in a couple of days?'

'Do you think Eddie's aggravated his back injury with that fall yesterday?'

'Oh no. I'm wondering if the acrobatics on the stairs have actually done some good?'

'What on earth do you mean?'

'Dr Robertson told me, in confidence, of course, that Eddie was reporting some dysfunction which he found a little er – embarrassing, shall we say?'

'Ye-es. I know about that,' said Jan cautiously.

'Well, it isn't uncommon for patients with spinal injuries to complain of these physical problems – or difficulties of a *sexual* nature?'

The physio sounded impeccably clinical. Reaching her car she slung the medical case across to the passenger side and settled herself in the driving seat. She shut the door, wound down the window and started the engine.

'But,' she went on, 'just to *reassure* you, in Edward's case I can positively confirm that everything appears to be in perfect working order now? Well, in *that* department at least?' She winked. ''Bye, Mrs Hardy.'

Jan stood with her mouth half open as Gloria drove away, shaking her head in disbelief. When she told Annabel about it afterwards the two of them cracked up.

'You mean falling down the stairs made him a bit stiff, and now he can—?'

'Yes!'

'When he couldn't before?'

'Yes! According to the Buxom Bombshell.'

'Oh dear, we shouldn't really be mocking the afflicted, should we?' said Annabel as she caught her breath between fits of laughter.

'I don't know that we are. Perhaps he's been mocking us,' Jan replied.

But over the next few days Jan began to appreciate the more serious side of it all. What did it mean? Was it significant that she had joked about Eddie's condition? Did it mean she had abandoned, or lost, her desire to have Eddie as a lover? When she reflected more deeply she realized it wasn't about Eddie's lack of potency, or otherwise. It was about reality. Her attitude to him had completely changed in the last seven months. It was not physical at all. It was not his disabilities, but his personality – his new, far more aggressive and impatient personality – that had brought the change. How cruel was that? As soon as she told the man she loved him deeply, the *person* she loved was taken away, maybe for ever. It was like having her lover abruptly and unknowingly substituted for his twin – identical in outward appearance, but inwardly quite different and far less appealing.

For the time being nothing would change, Jan knew that. But Eddie was still her guest and another dependent. A discussion about their more intense relationship – a discussion she knew would eventually take place – would have to wait for now.

For two weeks there was no more news from the police regarding the case against Eddie. Meanwhile the business of racing and, if possible, winning had to go on. Jan's training fees were barely covering her costs and extra prize money was an important means of making up the deficit. Her personal target was to average a winner every fortnight; it had looked quite feasible in the first two months of the season, but suddenly they dried up. Jan had the whole string scoped by the vet, but there was no sign of virus. She made slight alterations to the feeding regime. But in the end, reminding herself of a few very near misses, she reasoned the element of luck was the one thing she couldn't control and that was now weighing against her. Soon the scales of justice would dip the other way, and if she kept the horses in good condition it was only a matter of time.

'Don't panic and lose your cool,' Reg had advised. 'You'll just have to sit it out.'

Many of the stable's hopes for a reversal of fortune would be riding on Russian Eagle and Morning Glory at Cheltenham. As MG's race approached, the sporting press began to hype it up even more. Several diary pieces appeared hinting at a grudge match between two ambitious neighbouring female trainers, though the main focus was on the rivalry of the horses, and the sense that the race would provide one of those climactic head-to-head contests that were the lifeblood of any sport.

On the morning of the race Jan's stomach was churning with nerves from the moment she woke. Riding Dingle Bay out at exercise, she could hardly concentrate, her mind was only half on the job in hand. Would MG load in the transporter? she wondered. Would he boil over in the paddock or down at the start? Was he fit enough to take first prize? Or would his run be jinxed by the unknown factor that had prevented her other horses winning for the last three weeks?

Annabel was equally nervous about Russian Eagle's tilt at the Mackeson. Realistic counsel did not see an Irish Grand National winner triumphing over the faster two-and-a-half milers, though Bel was more concerned about his safe return in what was probably going to be a fast and furious contest.

The horses travelled in the same lorry, with MG occupying his usual double stall, while Russian Eagle, uncomplaining, remained in the single compartment. Roz and Patsy had hardly left their charges' sides during the last forty-eight hours. Now, after decanting them from the transporter, they led them towards the security boxes at the course and tried to suppress their nerves, as they both knew their edginess could be transmitted to the horses.

The Mackeson was the fourth race on the card. Eagle was easily the pick of the paddock, and Roz was crimson with pleasure when he was awarded 'the best turned out'. Impeccably behaved as he went to the start, Russian Eagle under Murty McGrath ran, Jan thought, an excellent race to get third, making only a couple of minor jumping errors, and ceasing to be competitive only after jumping the second last, when his two faster rivals quickened away up Cheltenham's notoriously demanding hill to the finish. Even though Russian Eagle completed at one pace, he did so to the unrestrained cheers of his connections.

As Annabel pointed out to Jan, a third in the Mackeson was worth a great deal more than most wins. Things were looking up, they were sure of it.

But for Morning Glory, two races later, the preliminaries went rather differently. In the paddock, despite Patsy's best efforts, MG grew more anxious by the second, and though it was a misty, cold November day, there were streaks of foamy sweat running down his flanks. His behaviour clearly affected the market. Overnight the two novices had been joint favourites, but now Velvet Dynasty edged ahead to be clear race favourite, with Morning Glory half a point behind him. The bookies, like the crowd, found it difficult to separate them.

The plan was for Murty to let him run exactly as he had at Stratford.

'Remember,' whispered Jan fiercely to him in the paddock, 'he's a free spirit. Don't cramp his style.'

'I'm hoping the hill doesn't do him,' said Murty pessimistically. 'I've seen it get the better of some real champions in the past.'

'No negatives, Murty,' warned A.D. O'Hagan, who stood beside Jan.

They looked across just as Virginia Gilbert was checking the girths of Velvet Dynasty. By contrast, the Riscombe horse looked cool and magnificent. As Jan watched Scottie Venables leg Finbar Howlett into the saddle, swarms of butterflies were fighting for space in her stomach. She told herself that MG's sweating was not too significant, that it wasn't necessarily a serious problem. In fact, she decided she would probably have been worried if MG had *not* sweated. It was just his way of behaving.

As before, Murty was last taking his horse down to the start, and stood him discreetly behind the pack while they jostled for position in the line-up. To begin with the race did not go well since Murty misread the starter's intentions and as a consequence mistimed his approach to the tape. He had just checked the horse's forward momentum the second the tape flew up.

Missing the break meant MG had to use far more energy to reach his preferred spot at the head of affairs. Murty had no choice but to accept the situation and let the horse's surging acceleration take him through the pack and into the lead. By the time the field streamed past the stands, Morning Glory was doing what he liked to do best, galloping and jumping, refusing to let any other contender claim equality.

As the horses turned left-handed and headed into the country, Jan was scanning the runners through her binoculars to check the position of Velvet Dynasty. Finbar had him sat at the rear, loping along. She searched for dangers. It was a big field, but nothing was travelling as well as MG and Velvet Dynasty; it was still, she thought, between the two of them, though the Gilbert horse was equally full of running.

Morning Glory's pace was breathtaking. He treated the hurdles as if they were invisible, taking them in his stride. The only problem with that approach was, no matter how confidently the horse was racing, she knew that if he hit one hard he would have the stuffing knocked right out of him.

Along the back straight Finbar Howlett started to drive Velvet Dynasty through the field. Blithely unaware, Morning Glory was still full of running as Murty let him stride on. MG was now seven or eight lengths to the good and, three hurdles out, Murty looked round. There were no dangers in sight, just a line of horses with their jockeys rowing away and getting little response. Murty turned back and, as he did so, Finbar drove Velvet Dynasty stealthily between two horses and emerged from the chasing pack. Slowly, relentlessly, unknown to Murty, he began to shorten the distance between them.

Watching Morning Glory's lead diminish, Jan told herself not to worry. She knew he had the ability to quicken and, as she watched him sweep over the penultimate flight two lengths ahead of Finbar and Velvet Dynasty, her belief in him was intact. Obviously still full of fight, MG hurtled towards the last. Suddenly, Virginia's horse found another gear and quickly reduced the lead.

It was not until they approached the final obstacle that Morning Glory sensed the other horse. Instantly he responded and pricked his ears. In a breathtaking show of defiance, he took off. It was brave, reckless even. But he was too low, far too low, and moving swiftly. His front feet ploughed through the timber frame and he was unable to get them back quickly enough to make a safe landing. He crashed into the ground on the landing side of the hurdle, crumpling and rolling, and torpedoed Murty McGrath like a bullet over his ears. The jockey hit the ground, bounced twice and instantly curled up to minimize the damage if he was trampled by the pursuing pack.

Jan felt extremely nauseous as she lowered her binoculars. At least half of the crowd were going wild as the favourite cleared the last with consummate ease and galloped to the winning line unchallenged. MG and Murty continued to lie on the ground, neither of them moving. She glanced at A.D. beside her. His binoculars still raised, he was staring grim-faced at his stricken horse.

# 22

'God, please let him be just winded,' Jan kept repeating to herself, her eyes filling with tears as she pushed her way from the crowded owners' and trainers' stand out onto the course, battling her way through the huge mob of racegoers who thronged the lawns in front of the stands. One group of men, dressed in tailcoats and T-shirts reading 'Kevin's Stag Party Boom-Boom' were doing a conga along the row of bookmakers' pitches.

Jan was in no mood for games and with the pressure soaring through her body she bulldozed her way past them and made it to the small gate leading onto the track, which was manned by a couple of security guards. As Jan tried to go through, one of them spread his arms to prevent her.

'Don't be a bloody *prat*,' she shrieked, blinking back her tears and waving her arm. 'I'm with that injured horse. Let me by.'

'Badge,' the guard demanded. Jan looked down at her shoulder bag and flicked it over. TRAINER the man saw and stood aside as she hurried through. Jan looked anxiously down the course towards the final hurdle, where she could see a St John's Ambulance Brigade vehicle and the horse ambulance. Men in green overalls were putting up screens around the stricken Morning Glory.

Jan's nausea was reaching a crescendo and the shoes she had chosen to wear for the races had raised heels – not pointed, but high enough to sink into the soft turf as she ran towards the dramatic scene. She stopped for a second and bent to rip them off her feet, taking the chance to gulp in some air. Members of the crowd who had anxiously remained in the stands, glued to their binoculars, as the horse lay still where he'd fallen, now urged Jan on as she sprinted down the track in stockinged feet, her shoes clutched in her hands.

As she got closer, she saw that Murty had hoisted himself into an upright position. He sat on the wet grass rubbing his arm, looking shaken but in one piece.

'Murty, you OK?' she called.

Murty nodded as he unfastened his helmet and smiled ruefully.

'Crashing fall,' he wheezed, stating the obvious. 'He took off a mile too soon. There was nothing I could do,'

'No, I could see that. Anyway, thank goodness you're all right. I'll catch you later. I must see to the horse.'

As Jan entered the circle of screens, she could see immediately that Morning Glory, though still lying on the ground, was breathing, his sides heaving up and down like bellows and his nostrils flaring. The duty vet, Peter Heaney, whom Jan knew slightly, was kneeling beside MG, his stethoscope on the horse's chest. He looked up and nodded a brief greeting. At the same moment, Patsy arrived, panting, his face a mask of distress.

'Will he be all right, Mrs H? He will, won't he?'

Jan shrugged, gesturing hopefully towards the vet.

'Are you the lad that looks after him?' said Heaney, rising to his feet.

'Yeah,' said Patsy. 'I do him.'

The vet motioned him towards the horse's head.

'Right, let's get him up then. I've checked him all over and he seems all right. Just winded, I think.'

MG struggled to his feet and stood looking rather bewildered. As Patsy stroked the horse's neck and whispered his magic, the animal soon regained his composure.

'He looks sound,' said the vet. 'You can walk him back, if you like.'

'Thank you, sir,' said Patsy. 'I'm really grateful.'

As the crowd saw the horse being led slowly towards them, they gave out a huge cheer and a round of applause. That, Jan thought, was what she loved most about racing: although many racegoers knew little about the ins and outs of a horse's life, they cared about the animals just the same. They were there for the horses, in the same way the horses were there for them.

🐎

The next day the hacks were reasonably encouraging. One headline simply read FIRST ROUND TO RISCOMBE. Another argued that Morning Glory's fall was not a result of tiredness, but that he was so full of running, he had been goaded into a disastrous take-off. There was no doubt in the reporter's mind that MG would have held Velvet Dynasty's challenge on the run-in. Most agreed that the fall had deprived the crowd of a pulsating finish and that the issue between the two talented horses was still open. Only a rematch would decide.

Virginia, of course, had other ideas. In her interview she said Jan's horse was already out on its feet coming to the last and would have had no chance, even if he had stood up.

'Mine's a superstar,' she claimed. 'As far as I can see, there's not another novice in the country that's capable of beating him. Mrs Hardy's horse certainly can't, as we've seen already.'

It was crystal clear MG was stiff through his loins, but he came out of the race well, considering, since he ate up his feed next morning. After discussions with A.D., Jan felt there was no need to alter the plan to go to Leopardstown in early January, but decided they wouldn't risk the horse in the meantime. Virginia, A.D. had heard on the grapevine, was aiming Velvet Dynasty at the Kempton Park meeting on Boxing Day, so a rematch would be unlikely until the Cheltenham Festival in March.

On the following Monday Inspector Hadfield telephoned. His voice was far more conciliatory than when he had come to arrest Eddie as he asked if he could come over to Edge Farm that afternoon. He arrived with a different female constable, who was introduced as WPC Kibble.

'I'm sorry we've not been in touch until now regarding your allegations against Harold Powell,' Hadfield began, as they sat round the kitchen table drinking tea.

'I haven't had time to think about it,' said Jan. 'I've had such a lot on, I've been more than happy to let Eddie's solicitor, Bob Warren, deal with it.'

'We have, of course, been continuing our investigation on the basis of the sworn affidavits from yourself and Mr Keating. So we're here now, basically, to give you an update. But first, may I ask if you've had any other visits from Mr Powell since he made the original threats?'

'No.' Jan answered cagily, wondering where this was leading.

'Not seen him anywhere, or had any phone calls or other communication from him?'

'No, nothing. I've seen him at the races a few times with Virginia Gilbert – that was earlier, though – but I haven't seen him on a racecourse since.'

'When you say "with" Miss Gilbert, what do you mean by that exactly?'

'I mean what I said: *with* Miss Gilbert. Really, Inspector, that's a daft question.'

Hadfield coloured and his ever-smiling mouth twitched.

'Sorry. I meant, are you aware of any personal relationship between Harold Powell and Miss Gilbert?'

'I'm aware there's talk of one, and I've seen them holding hands in public, once. So I suppose so, yes.'

'You don't sound very convinced.'

Jan considered.

'Well, it just seems so unlikely. Virginia's boyfriends always used to be Hooray Henrys of her own age, not middle-aged psychos like Powell.'

Hadfield gave a small embarrassed cough at Jan's description of Harold.

'And did Mr Powell refer to Miss Gilbert at all, or his relationship with her, when he came here and threatened you?'

'Yes, he did. It's in my affidavit, isn't it? He accused me of slagging off Virginia's racing stables to the press, which is completely untrue. But it was obvious from the way he said it that he wanted it known he took it as personally as she did.'

'Suggesting there was still a personal relationship between them at that time?'

'Yes, definitely. But why don't you ask them?'

'I have already put it to Miss Gilbert, but she declined to comment.'

'Oh, does that mean she's off the hook? What about Harold?'

'Ah well, that's the problem. Mr Powell seems to have disappeared. Which is why I was wondering if he's been in touch with you in any way.'

Jan felt unusually thirsty all of a sudden. She offered more tea to the police officers and then poured herself another mug, which she drained almost immediately. She was thinking that, if Harold Powell had gone to ground, he might be capable of anything, including carrying out his threat against her.

Hadfield, good policeman that he was, had gone ahead of her.

'Mrs Hardy, I don't think we should take Mr Powell's disappearance lightly, so I am here to inform you that we would like to increase your level of protection. This time we'll post officers on the premises, twenty-four hours a day.'

Jan nodded her head in relief.

'Yes, good. Thank you, Inspector Hadfield. Me and my children will sleep a lot easier knowing there's someone keeping an eye out.'

'They will also follow you discreetly when you go out, Mrs Hardy. It will not only protect you, but it may locate Mr Powell, should he turn up. Now we need to interview him in connection with several possible offences, including the threatening behaviour which you and Patsy Keating have alleged.'

'Is one of the other offences causing death by reckless driving?' Jan asked cunningly.

Hadfield gave another embarrassed cough.

'Yes, I can confirm that is the case. In fact, since we are here, I need to see Mr Sullivan. Is he around?'

'Yes, he's down in the gym. It's in one of the stables. I'll show you.'

Eddie defiantly rowed away on his machine, his face unchanging, while Hadfield told him he was a free man again: all the serious charges had been dropped and the lesser offences of keeping an untaxed, uninsured car, had been referred to the magistrates' court, from whom he would be hearing in due course.

When Hadfield finished, Eddie stopped rowing, reached for a towel and mopped his face.

'So it was old Harold who dunnit and not me. Well, congratulations, Inspector. Now bugger off, will you? I've got another five hundred pulls to do before supper.'

❧

The police took up their duties later that day, when an unmarked car arrived containing two young constables. They backed the car into the old stone barn, where it would be less conspicuous, and settled down to their guard duty, consuming quantities of sandwiches, soup and tea provided for them by Fran, but otherwise causing little trouble. After eight hours each detail would be relieved by another pair, and so it went on. More than once Jan wondered if they were armed, but decided she preferred not knowing and so did not ask. At first she was obsessively conscious of their presence behind her every time she drove to the shops, to Riscombe or to the races, but after a week she became used to it. After two, she sometimes forgot they were there.

The only trouble the police presence did cause was when Bernie Sutcliffe came to visit, turning up without notice in the middle of one afternoon. Jan was vacuuming the sitting room and didn't know he was there until he'd come stomping in, breathing hard.

'Jesus Christ, Jan, what's going on? I've just been turned inside out by two coppers in your forecourt. Phew, bloody 'ell. I thought they were waiting for me. Why didn't you tell me they were 'ere?'

Bernie's Brummie twang always became more pronounced when he was upset.

'That's simple.' Jan grinned. 'I didn't know you were coming.'

Thankfully, Jan gave up the idea of housework and wound away the vacuum's cable.

'Why on earth would you think they were here for *you*, anyway?'

Bernie bit his lip, his reptile eyes swivelling evasively.

'Oh, well, you know what it's like – usual problems. Blokes like me are always rubbing the coppers up the wrong way . . . Anyway, what's going on? Them two wouldn't say a word.'

'I'm not supposed to say, but they're on surveillance, part of an investigation into someone I once knew as an owner, so you needn't worry; it's got nothing to do with you.'

'Good, that's a relief. Who're they after then? Not that chap Powell?'

Jan was surprised.

'What do you know about Harold Powell, Bernie?'

'Oh, I 'ear things. He stood trial for the death of your mother, right?'

'Wrong. It was my mother-in-law. But now Harold's made threats against me personally. So I've been given round-the-clock protection.'

This impressed Bernie.

'Threats, eh? You should 'ave come to me instead of that lot, Jan. I could do better than them.'

'I didn't know you were into protection as well as scrap metal.'

'Security, not protection. There's an important difference. It's a little sideline I developed after a gang of scousers nicked 'alf a ton of roofing lead off me.' Bernie chuckled.

'Well, thanks anyway, but I think I'll stick with the constabulary,' Jan replied. 'So, what can I do for you? Thinking of buying another horse by any chance?'

'No way. Two's quite enough, thank you, especially when neither of them's winning. I'm not made of money. No, I was in the area, so I thought I'd drop in for a gander at my horses. But if you're busy, I can come back another time . . .'

It was very unlike Bernie to be so considerate or to be in any kind of a hurry, for that matter. But today he was positively jumpy, and continually looking out of the window to check the whereabouts of the police. Jan enjoyed prolonging his agony by insisting he come down to the yard to inspect his horses. Bernie slunk past the police car almost on hands and knees and kept looking back over his shoulder as he crept down towards the stable block. Just for a moment, as the horses were led out, his old habits revived and, despite a complete lack of equine knowledge, he made his customary critical remarks.

'This one's a bit thin around his arse, isn't he? And I should 'ave that lump on his leg looked at, if I were you, Jan.'

'That's normal, Bernie. It's his hock,' Jan giggled, refusing to be provoked. She had learned to handle Bernie long ago, including his periodic attempts to cajole her into going out with him. She strongly suspected that the real reason for his appearance today had been to renew these attempts. But the police presence had made him so neurotic that, within just twenty minutes of his arrival, he had made his excuses and scurried off back to Birmingham.

During the last few weeks Jan had been seeing rather more of another owner than she was accustomed to. The three Barbadian weeks spent with Edge Farm's assistant trainer had clearly left Johnny Carlton-Brown besotted, and there was hardly a weekend when he didn't show up on Saturday morning to watch the gallops – or in reality, as Jan privately thought, to watch Annabel with her shapely rear raised, go past him on the back of one of his horses.

As she reflected, Jan realized it could present an insoluble problem. If JCB married Annabel, he would very likely want her to quit her job at Edge Farm. This would be a terrible loss to Jan, who depended on her friend for so much. On the other hand, if Annabel and JCB separated because she preferred the job to the man, he would, in all probability, take his horses away. Knowing men as she did, Jan reckoned it would be much too painful for him to keep a connection with a yard that maintained a stronger hold over his beloved's affections than he did. But the real problem was to know what was going on in Annabel's mind. She was so damned secretive and reserved about her love life that it was impossible to second-guess.

The only answer, Jan decided, was to face the dilemma head on. In early December, while travelling with Annabel to Warwick racecourse, where one of JCB's horses was running, Jan manoeuvred the conversation to the point where she could delve a little deeper.

'Bel, you and JCB – what's the story?'

'Oh, you know—'

'That's just the point, I don't really and I need to. He's absolutely crazy about you, that's obvious, and he'd whisk you off at a moment's notice to live with him, in Barbados or somewhere else remote. But what do you feel? Do you love him?'

'I feel . . . the same as I've always felt.'

'You've told me before that you liked him, but you weren't in love with him. Is that what you mean?'

'Yes and no, I suppose.'

'Bel, please stop being such a bloody pain in the arse. Yes and no what?'

'Yes I like him, no I don't *think* I'm in love with him.'

'But how can you not know? I would.'

'I never do know. That's my burden in life. I mean I know I love horses, and I love this life. But with men I can never seem to work it out. Of course, that's a different kind of love, isn't it? And scarier.'

'Scarier?'

Bel nodded slowly, then changed the subject. It was as far as Jan got in her attempt at plumbing her friend's romantic soul. They were as open and frank with each other as two women can be – about everything except Bel's romances. At times Jan felt slightly angry. Here she was, feeling wretched about the hopes she had had for herself and Eddie, which now appeared to be doomed. And there was Annabel, with men queuing around the proverbial block to take her out, and she had not the slightest idea what she wanted.

One morning the post delivered a letter with an Irish stamp. It contained a brief note from A.D., written as usual by his own hand.

Dear Jan,

You remember our chat at Edge Farm regarding my search for a property in the Lambourn area? I have taken the liberty to enclose the agent's particulars of one that has recently come on the private

market. Could you possibly find the time to run your eye over it?
If nothing else, I would value your opinion of the place.

Yours,

A.D.

He had added a PS:

You should view the premises strictly on its potential. Though
I gather it's in a bit of a state at the moment.

Jan unfolded the stapled sheets, which offered a 'unique opportunity to buy' Tumblewind Grange, near Lambourn, 'an estate of
character'. She knew the property A.D. had looked at following
Morning Glory's race at Stratford had been rejected because it was
too small. Jan scrutinized the description of the new place and
could see instantly, on size, Tumblewind Grange would pass muster.
There was a large Jacobean house 'in need of restoration'. The
outbuildings included stabling, six cottages and four hundred and
fifty acres of land, mostly laid to grass and some woodland 'previously used for shooting'.

That particular day Edge Farm had no runners. So on impulse,
and without telling anyone except her police escort where they
were going, Jan loaded the children into the Shogun and drove
down to Berkshire to take a look. She already knew what A.D. was
contemplating when he requested her to make this visit. He was
hoping, expecting even, that she would be seduced. Jan was equally
determined not to be, whatever it was like.

Tumblewind Grange, though on a beautiful site in a fold of the
Downs, was at first glance not very seductive. The young agent at
the Lambourn office gave her the keys to the house and told her to
be particularly careful upstairs as the floorboards were rotten. The
police stayed in their car just inside the front gates, while Megan
and Matty raced, like a couple of wild ponies, around an overgrown
formal garden at the back of the house. Jan pushed open the
dilapidated front door and was met by an overpowering smell of
cats and damp. Fungus grew inside the hall and the walls were
covered in mould. Cautiously she ventured further, and found
several broken windows and fallen plaster. Water oozed from pipes

onto mossy floors and the electric cables must have predated the war. Jan decided the claim that the house had 'until recently been occupied' was the best bit of fiction she had ever read.

On the other hand, the report stated that it was a house of character, which was undeniable. To Jan's unpractised eye there seemed to be two styles of architecture. One half was reminiscent of Riscombe Manor, with low ceilings, mullioned and leaded windows, wooden panelling and stone floors. The other wing had sash windows and sprung floors – where there were boards! – high ceilings and marble fire surrounds. In one particular room, the display of decorative plasterwork was quite spectacular, though badly ravaged by time and damp.

She tried to imagine living here, but couldn't. It was far too smelly, gloomy and draughty. More Tumbledown than Tumblewind Grange she decided.

As Jan went outside she could hear the children laughing. *At least they like it*, she thought. As she crossed the yard there was evidence that the outbuildings had at some time been used as a sawmill, with rusty woodcutting machinery lying about and a huge mound of rotting sawdust. She walked round the old stables and outbuildings; though well sited in relation to the house – not too close, like a farmyard – they were structurally useless and would have to be demolished.

Jan gathered the children and drove up one of the estate roads towards a group of three cottages. They seemed empty at first, but she saw blue smoke curling up from one of the chimneys and went and knocked at the door. A youngish man wearing a woollen bobble hat and dirty overalls answered. Jan pulled the estate agent's particulars from her pocket.

'Hi, I'm pleased to meet you. I'm looking over the estate on behalf of a friend.'

'Oh yeah?'

They chatted for several minutes on the doorstep. At first the man was not very forthcoming, but in the end he mellowed and Jan found him quite informative. Apparently he lived in the cottage with his elderly parents and worked on a nearby farm. He said only one of the other cottages was occupied but the land was leased to various local farmers, and there had been a lease on the shooting until two or three years ago. Old Mrs Trent had lived in the house until she died last year aged ninety-two. After her death the local authority had removed thirty-three cats for humane destruction.

Driving home, Jan was deep in thought about what she would tell A.D. The estate would need a huge sum of money spending on it. The stables and outbuildings could not be repaired and extended; they would have to be completely rebuilt. The house and cottages, while not absolutely falling down, were in a perilous condition. But with adequate funds the house in particular could be spectacular.

As far as the land was concerned, there was plenty of scope for the modern training complex that A.D. had been dreaming of. Jan knew he also had the money to bring it about. The chalky, undulating land was ideal for gallops, and there was plenty of paddock space available for turning horses out. All in all, she decided, if A.D. was prepared to lay out the money, Tumblewind Grange would do him well. Whether it would do her was quite another matter.

'Mum?' enquired Megan, from the back of the car. 'Are we going to live in that old house?'

'Tell me, what do you think of the idea, Megs?'

In the driving mirror Jan saw her daughter frown.

'It's got a lot more room for horses than Edge,' she said at last, 'but I think it's a lot less friendly.'

'I know just what you mean.' Jan laughed. 'What about you, Matty? What do you think?'

'Well, it has got a secret garden,' he said. 'And a troll lives there.'

When Jan got back, she went straight to the office and wrote a note to A.D. about what they had seen and found out at Tumblewind Grange. She decided, however, not to mention the troll. She put the note in the fax machine and dialled his number, then riffled through the pile of unopened mail that lay in front of her. Most were bills, or circulars, but one envelope was addressed by hand and locally postmarked. She grabbed the paperknife and slit it open.

She recognized neither the writing nor the address neatly inscribed at the top of the page. Flipping the sheet over, she looked at the signature in amazement. It was a letter from Rachel Moorhouse.

# 23

Dear Mrs Hardy,

I felt I must write to you. Yesterday the police informed me they had dropped the charges against Eddie Sullivan regarding the death of my husband. They said they are now seeking another man in connection with the crash, so it seems I was wrong when I accused Mr Sullivan, and you, of being responsible for my husband's death. I don't know what you must think of me, bursting into your house uninvited and accusing you like I did, and blurting on about my husband and his affairs. I was at a very low ebb, and I didn't have anyone to confide in or advise me. I was doing a lot of things impulsively without thinking about the consequences. Anyway, things are much better now and I am on a more even keel. I have met a kind-hearted man, who has done more to restore my faith in human nature than I would have thought possible. Even my kids like him!

I am sorry if my actions and words caused you distress. You too know what it is to be a widow. The difference between us is that I have been released by chance from an unloving, brutal marriage, while you probably lost the love of your life. Stupidly, I failed to appreciate that you had more to complain about in your widowhood than I did. Bitterness and envy I now know are a dreadful disease that can eat you alive. I hope you can find it in your heart to forgive me and wish you every happiness and success in the future.

Yours most sincerely,

Rachel Moorhouse

Jan read the letter through twice. It must have been hellishly difficult to write and Rachel Moorhouse had her wholehearted admiration for having the guts to do it. She did wonder, however, if it had been done at the prompting of some therapist or perhaps the 'kind man' the letter mentioned.

Jan opened the letters drawer of her filing cabinet. She had separate folders, which held the correspondence with each of her owners, and two for letters from members of the public, one labelled 'Fan Mail' and another marked 'Nutters'. The Moorhouse letter didn't fit either category, so she dropped it into a third file labelled 'Miscellaneous' and closed the drawer.

In early December, for no obvious reason, the fortunes of Edge Farm began to pick up when Supercall and Teenage Red both won at Wincanton to give Jan a double, while Tom's Touch found his form with a scintillating victory at Hereford and even old Arrow Star got his head in front in a mud-spattered four-horse finish at Leicester. Then A.D.'s hurdler, Gyllipus, travelled all the way to Ayr to record his first win of the season.

That night A.D., who usually combined his racing in Scotland with a few rounds of golf on the Ailsa course, gave Jan dinner in the luxury surroundings of the five-star Turnberry Hotel, where he always stayed, and where Jan had dined with him nearly a year ago.

'It's almost déjà vu,' A.D. smiled, greeting her in the lobby with a light kiss on the cheek. 'Remember last year? Our horses had been going through a terrible patch, I was chafing about the results. Suddenly you pulled out a surprise hurdle win at Ayr, then we dined here. Snap.'

He clicked his fingers.

'The only difference being that this year we won't eat in the main restaurant, I think. The food's excellent, but on the rich side, and I've got my cholesterol to consider.'

They strolled through to the hotel's Terrace restaurant, where the cuisine was far less extravagant.

When they were seated, Jan told A.D., 'Gilly's by far the nicest horse to train. We love him to bits.'

'Yes, I admit those horses we took over from Gary West have

been a success, or two of them certainly. When am I going to see
Holy Mist on the track, by the way?'

Between ordering food and a bottle of Chablis, they talked horses
and about their prospects for the big Boxing Day and New Year's
Day fixtures. But Jan guessed her owner was skirting around the big
issue and that it was bricks, mortar and green fields rather than
horseflesh that A.D. really wanted to discuss. She had noticed
earlier he had a large brown envelope with him. Now he drew out
the estate agent's glossy prospectus for the sale of Tumblewind
Grange estate and laid it on the table. He tapped the black rectangle
representing the house.

'Thank you for having a look at this for me. On the basis of your
report, I went down there myself last weekend.'

'And?'

'The buildings are, as you say, in a terrible state. But the land is
very good indeed, which is the only thing that really matters.'

He traced some lines on the plan with his forefinger.

'I thought we would establish some gallops here and here, and
possibly here, and an all-weather track over here. The stables and
most of the outbuildings will come down and a new stable block
will be built for a hundred or so horses on roughly the same site.
I've also earmarked a place for an equine pool, and a horse walker
just here, behind the walled garden. There's a lot of room for
turnout paddocks on either side of the drive. Of course, I'd have
the cottages renovated for use of the staff.'

Even though she knew A.D. acted decisively when his mind was
made up, Jan was completely taken aback at the speed with which
he had moved on this.

'Goodness, A.D., this is all very quick. Have you bought the
place already?'

A.D. closed the prospectus, slipped it back into its envelope and
turned his attention to the food in front of him.

'Not yet, though I have put in a bid.'

'I see . . . Well, it's certainly an exciting project. Something you
can get your teeth into.'

Jan felt torn. The old nagging but crucial doubts about her

independence remained. And the still fresh memory of the big, smelly, decaying house at Tumblewind made her feel queasy. Yet she had seen the land for herself and she had to admit it really *was* an exciting location for a racing stable. Furthermore A.D.'s legendary acumen and thoroughness were not a myth. Jan knew, under his direction, all he had described was set fair to become a reality. She couldn't help it – her pulse had undeniably quickened during A.D.'s brief presentation.

His clear, steely blue eyes met hers with the focus and aplomb of a completely self-possessed man.

'Yes,' he said quietly. 'It *is* an exciting project. I myself would have around forty horses in situ, and we can make up the numbers to another thirty or forty from other owners on a commercial basis. But, with a hundred boxes, we'd always have the capacity to expand our business if we wished.'

He reached for the bottle of wine and refilled their glasses.

'You know it's been a dream of mine for many years, and I still want you to be part of it.'

Jan had just forked some seafood into her mouth. As it contained octopus, which required chewing, it gave her more time to think. She munched – for slightly longer than necessary – then said, 'A.D., you know my feelings about being my own boss, keeping my independence.'

'But now you've seen the potential of Tumblewind I find it difficult to believe you're not tempted. Just a little, perhaps?'

'I've already turned you down once.'

'And you may again, I know that.'

'And what then?'

'I'll have to find someone else.'

'Who?'

A.D. shrugged.

'No one specifically, not at the moment, anyway. It's you I want, Jan.'

'I suppose if I say no, you would withdraw your horses from my yard?'

A.D. nodded. 'Yes, I'm afraid that would be on the cards, but not until the new yard is up and running.'

'So how much time have I got?'

'Supposing my offer on Tumblewind Grange is accepted, it will take between eighteen months and two years to complete the makeover. I'd hope to appoint a resident trainer before we're into the latter stages of the work, let's say by the end of next year. There, you've got twelve months before you make a final decision. After that I will need to go ahead – reluctantly, of course – without you.'

Now Jan decided to put her own cards on the table.

'A.D., you're a hard man to say no to. And I must say it was a very smart move to get me to look this place over. I admit to being a tiny bit tempted. But there are so many other important considerations. I will probably need all that time before I'm really sure about this, one way or the other.'

A.D. sat back and took a sip from his wine.

'That'll be all fine,' he said, his eyes twinkling in expectation.

🏇

Edge Farm's run of success looked set to continue when Supercall made a quick return to action in the A. F. Budge Gold Cup at Cheltenham, destroying his field in a classy chase. So, after six victories in just over three weeks, Jan and her staff were on a high until – in spectacular fashion – Arctic winds brought wintry storms down from the north-east. The snow lay thick on the hills and surrounding fields, and drifted to clog the woods, fill the ditches and cover the hedgerows. Temperatures continued to fall and the air became still and cold as a very hard frost set in, making horse racing impossible anywhere in Great Britain. The National Hunt yards were all in the doldrums and bookmakers filled their empty satchels by taking bets from Australia and on whether there would be a white Christmas.

Everyone knew that racing would resume as soon as a thaw allowed and trainers like Jan, with their all-weather gallops, had a distinct advantage. For the rest, there wasn't much to be done except sit it out. Horses remained in their boxes or old bedding from the stables was used to make small exercise rings. A lucky few within striking distance of a beach could canter horses at the water's edge.

Just before Christmas, with frost still holding the landscape in its iron grip, a carol service was held in Chiselcombe church. This annual event, with mince pies and hot punch served afterwards in the village hall, was always supported by farmers and people from well beyond the boundaries of the parish. The proceeds were usually divided between local causes and the Injured Jockeys Fund.

Jan drove over via Riscombe, in order to pick up her parents and a huge tray of mince pies baked especially by Mary for the occasion. Megan, as a member of the school band, was due to perform a carol and from the moment they set off she began to practise her recorder piercingly. Matty's class was scheduled to recite one of the lessons, and he had a few verses to speak solo. Not to be outdone by his elder sister, he started to rehearse his lines at the top of his voice:

'For UNTO you is born this day in the city of David a SAVIOUR, which is Christ the Lord.'

'Shut up, Matty!' said Megan. 'I'm trying to rehearse.'

'So'm I,' said Matty. 'And THIS shall be a sign unto you; ye shall find the babe wrapped in SWADDLING clothes, lying in a MANGER . . .'

Megan blew louder, and Matty shouted louder.

'AND SUDDENLY THERE WAS WITH THE ANGEL A MULTI—, MULTI—, MULTITUDE OF THE HEAVENLY HOST PRAISING GOD AND SAYING . . .'

Finally, Megan blew the recorder as hard as she could into her brother's ear, which made him scream in pain. Grimacing, Jan spotted a lay-by ahead and pulled in, checking in her mirror as she did so. Her police escort drew in behind her. Jan leaped out and yanked opened the rear door of the Shogun.

'Out! Out you get, young lady.'

Grabbing her arm, she dragged her daughter out, still holding the recorder, and marched her towards the 'escort'.

'Since you're going the same way,' she said, as the driver wound down her window, 'I thought you might like to make yourself useful, so can you give this one a lift? She's dying for a ride in a police car, aren't you, Megan? And she's driving the rest of us up the bloody wall.'

The young constable looked confused as Jan pulled open the rear door and pushed Megan onto the back seat.

'And don't forget your seat belt,' she warned, before turning back to the police officers. 'I hope you two like music. See you later. And thank you.'

Clambering back into the Shogun, Jan spoke soothingly. 'It's all right now, Matty darling, Megan's in the other car so you can practise without having her recorder blasting away in your ear.'

She heard Matty filling his lungs to capacity before belting out the last line at maximum volume.

'GLORY to GOD in the HIGHEST, and on EARTH PEACE, GOOD WILL TOWARD MEN . . . Mum? Why are you laughing?'

🐎

As always, Jan thoroughly enjoyed the service. The church was beautifully decked out with a crib and a tree, while a huge Christmas candle stood close to the altar. The congregation over-flowed the pews and people were packed into the back of the nave. 'God Rest You Merry, Gentlemen' was as rousing as ever and the choir's rendition of 'The Holly and the Ivy' was sparkling. The instrumental music, though not always exactly in tune, was applauded and the reading from St Luke's gospel by Matty and his friends passed off without a hitch. By the time the vicar had spoken and offered up prayers, a warm Christmassy glow was felt by all and, as the choir slid quietly into 'Silent Night', Jan thought of the timelessness of it all. For centuries people, in many cases the ancestors of *these* people, had come to sing or listen to these carols, and to recite or hear these words and prayers.

After a finale in which everyone joyfully roared out the chorus of 'O Come All Ye Faithful', they crunched through the snow to the village hall, which stood across the road surrounded by its own car park. Jan had parked the Shogun there after offloading Mary's mince pies. Now the congregation made hungry inroads into the piles of country fare, with punch and orange squash in paper cups dispensed by the Women's Institute.

With the Shogun fully loaded, Eddie arrived in Gerry's van, and as Jan entered the hall she saw the two men already in conversation with a blonde girl. The woman turned her head slightly and revealed herself as Gloria Hooke, the pneumatic physiotherapist. Eddie was able to walk with the help of just one stick now, and they were obviously discussing this development since Jan saw Eddie raise the stick and point to it. Following Gloria's first couple of visits to Edge Farm, Jan had asked Tony Robertson to call her off, and a highly skilled male physio had taken her place. But the reunion tonight seemed to be warmly welcomed by Eddie, who was smiling and talking to her with considerable vigour, at least when compared to his recent standards.

Jan did not have much time to dwell on the matter as Viv Taylor-Jones, the vicar's wife, spotted her and came over.

'Hello, Jan. I thought you might like to know that we never had any more of those unpleasant news thingies.'

'I know, it just seems to have been a one-off. I think the police effectively put a stop to it.'

As they chatted, Jan noticed the ghastly Virginia Gilbert with a small group of her equally ghastly friends on the other side of the hall, knocking back the punch in large quantities. She kept glaring towards Jan, shooting her dark looks. When Viv Taylor-Jones had been gently detached by one of her husband's parishioners, Virginia seemed to make up her mind. She pushed through the crowd towards Jan, who was now standing on her own.

'I suppose you think it was pretty clever,' Virginia said venomously, 'getting Harold into trouble.'

'I don't know what you're talking about. I didn't get him into trouble. He managed that all by himself.'

Virginia was plainly inebriated. She drained her cup of punch and snatched another from a passing tray.

'Yes you did, you common cow. You bloody snitched on him,' she hissed.

'Virginia, please, not here. Take my advice . . .'

Jan found being anywhere near Virginia usually brought down a red mist, but tonight it seemed strangely easy to keep her temper under control. Perhaps it was the spirit of Christmas.

'You'll find Harold's got no principles,' Jan went on. 'He doesn't care who he hurts. He'll hurt you in the end, that's for certain.'

'Oh, your bleeding heart?' Virginia sneered, as she took a hefty pull from her drink.

'No, Virginia, this is a fact. He's no good, no good at all, not in *any* way – unless he's OK in bed, on which subject of course *I'm* not qualified to speak.'

Jan hadn't been able to resist the gibe, which instantly caused Virginia's expression to switch from sarcasm to outrage in the blink of an eye.

'How dare you, how *dare* you, you snidey, disgusting bitch.'

Virginia hurled her cup at Jan's head, spun unsteadily on her heel and walked away in a haughty fashion. One or two people in the immediate vicinity looked in consternation at Jan, who groped in her bag for a tissue. Luckily Virginia had already drunk most of the contents, and only a few sticky drops had reached their target. Jan wiped them away and hurried off in search of Reg and Mary before anyone could approach her.

After half an hour people started to drift away. Jan rounded up the children and her parents and headed for the car park. She had just loaded them into the Shogun when she remembered Eddie. If Matty sat on his grandfather's lap there would be room for him, and it would save Gerry the trouble of driving an extra six miles to Edge Farm before going home. She decided to return to the hall to see if the two men were still inside.

She was just crossing the deserted apron of tarmac in front of the hall, and had still not quite reached the circle of light made by the overhead lamp, when she heard the scrape of a footstep behind her.

'Don't say a fucking word, you bitch,' a man's voice growled.

A gloved hand had clasped her upper arm, as another clamped over her mouth. She could smell the man's sweat as she was pulled against him and then bent round in the direction he wanted her to go. Seconds later she found herself being forced towards the shrubbery that fringed the perimeter of the village hall's car park. She knew instantly it was Harold Powell.

Despite her struggles, he was far too strong. He had almost manoeuvred her, slipping and sliding on the underfoot ice, into the bushes. Suddenly they both became aware that someone was standing in their path.

'Hey you! What the *fuck* are you doing? Let her go. Let her go, *NOW*.'

It was Eddie. He had been coming out of the bushes, zipping up his fly. When he saw Harold and Jan he had stopped momentarily to assess the situation and shouted out his challenge. Then he charged forward, raising his stick for the attack. Harold was taken completely by surprise. For a second he slackened his grip on Jan's arm, and by twisting her body she was able to slip his grasp and duck to the ground, glimpsing, as she went down Harold's face, blanched white, his teeth set and the eyes narrowing.

Jan crawled out of the way as Eddie launched himself, thrashing wildly with his stick. Harold gave a cry and raised his arms to ward off the ferocious attack. Slowly, under the rain of blows, he sank to his knees. After several moments, as Eddie landed another three or four cracking shots, running footsteps were heard and Jan's guardian angels, the two police constables, launched themselves into the fracas, pulling Eddie away and helping Harold, bruised and bloodied, to his feet.

Jan struggled to her feet, her legs weak with fear. She dusted the snow from her clothes and continued to shake violently, but was otherwise unhurt.

'That's Harold Powell,' she panted. 'That's the man who threatened to kill me. Thank God you were here.'

# 24

It was much later that night as Eddie sat with Jan by the fire in the lounge at Edge Farm. They were drinking hot chocolate made with added cream and heavily laced with brandy, an Eddie special. The air hung heavy with the scent of pine from a tree the children had festooned with garlands and fairy lights.

'What were you doing in those bushes anyway?' asked Jan.

'Having a pee, what else?'

'Ah!'

'And it's lucky I was – the bastard – or God knows what might have happened.'

'Yes, I realize it could have been a lot worse.'

The fire crackled as a chunk of log fell into the grate.

'Thanks for saving my life, Eddie,' Jan said meekly. 'Or my virtue. Or from whatever Harold thought he was doing.'

'You've nothing to thank me for, but you can thank my stick.'

'Thank you, stick.'

A long pause followed as they sipped from their mugs and stared into the fire, which periodically flared up only to die away again. Both had a sense that they had turned a corner in their relationship, but Eddie was the first to say it, in his usual moody, despondent way.

'We haven't ever got it back, have we, Jan? Not since the accident.'

'I know. It's been pretty awful.'

'That's all I was thinking as I flogged that bastard. Not only has he put us both through nine months of sheer hell, but he's actually taken away what we had together and at that moment I honestly didn't care if I killed him.'

There was another long pause before Jan, staring into the dying embers and feeling close to tears, whispered, 'I did love you, Eddie. I really did. But you've changed so much.'

There, she'd said it. She looked straight at him to see how he would react.

'I know. The weird thing is –' Eddie sighed – 'I've even noticed it myself. I actually *feel* different and I can't fathom it out.'

'That can't be very nice.'

'It wasn't. It still isn't, but I'm getting used to it now – the new me.'

'Oh, Eddie! I just wish—'

But Eddie had pulled himself out of his chair. He came over to Jan and reached for her empty mug.

'It's late. I've got to go to bed.'

He limped out of the room. A moment later she heard him washing up at the kitchen sink. It was something he would never have done a year ago.

'Yes,' she thought to herself. 'It's late – probably too late.'

Christmas Day was getting ever closer, but the freeze did not relent. The whole racing industry held its breath for the big Boxing Day meeting at Kempton Park, where many National Hunt stars would be on show. By Christmas Eve the meeting was in grave doubt and it was eventually called off the next day. Ireland, on the other hand, had been largely clear of snow and ice, and Morning Glory's date in the Fitzpatrick Castle Hurdle at Leopardstown, on the Saturday after New Year, was still very much on the cards. Jan and Patsy – still the only human beings MG would trust – were working diligently to keep the horse fit and ready to run.

To avoid the long journey by road and ferry, A.D. had decided the horse should take the much quicker route via Dublin airport.

'But A.D.,' said Jan fretfully, 'I really don't think MG would travel in one of those horse crates, not if it's like the one we sent Russian Eagle across in for the Irish National. He'd probably be packed in a narrow stall with a lot of strange horses on board, both of which he hates.'

'OK, I'll find a way around that,' promised A.D.

What he found was a deal with a friend who owned an Irish freighting company that specialized in transporting livestock. A.D. wangled a flight for Morning Glory in a specially adapted TNT jet that would otherwise be flying back empty from Luton to Ireland on the day before the races. Jan, who planned to travel with the horse, along with the obligatory Patsy, spoke to A.D.'s friend and was assured all would be well.

A week before they were due to travel, as Jan scanned the *Racing Post*, she read an item that almost made her drop the paper. As everyone knew, Virginia Gilbert had originally intended to run Velvet Dynasty on Boxing Day at Kempton; now she had switched him to contest the Fitzpatrick Castle Hurdle. The Leopardstown authorities were delighted. As the *Post* put it:

> Virginia Gilbert's Velvet Dynasty and Jan Hardy's Morning Glory have already established themselves as two of the best novice hurdlers around. The resumption of their rivalry on Irish territory is set to capture the imagination, especially of the English fans, deprived by the weather of their usual racing programme.

This was a complete understatement. The rematch had become the talking point of racing folk from the Sussex coast to the borders of Scotland.

Later that day Jan took a call from Fred Messiter in Riscombe. He sounded embarrassed.

'Hello, Jan. Look, I hope you don't mind but I'm calling on behalf of Virginia. She feels she can't speak to you directly because of what's happened recently.'

'What does she want?'

'It's about getting to Leopardstown. The thing is, she can't get Velvet Dynasty on a transporter. Everything's full and she's at her wits' end. She's read you're taking your horse over in a plane on his own, so we were wondering—'

'If we can give hers a lift, I suppose.'

'Exactly.'

Jan's first inclination was to laugh at the cheek. Her second was to turn the proposal down flat. With difficulty she suppressed them both.

'I'll have to ask my owner,' she said cautiously. 'A.D.'s gone to a lot of trouble over this flight, so I couldn't agree without his permission.'

It took Jan several calls to locate A.D., who had been spending the Christmas break in Monte Carlo. He listened to Virginia's request without any show of surprise.

'I wouldn't say there was a problem in principle,' he said judiciously. 'But I wouldn't want to take the horse across only to be beaten by him. You are confident that won't happen, aren't you?'

Jan didn't think confident was quite the right word. Very hopeful would be nearer. But she'd already told A.D. that she considered Morning Glory the better horse, and wavering was not what he liked. Involuntarily shutting her eyes, she took the plunge.

'Yes, barring accidents, I am.'

'I gather there's a lot of interest over there in the two horses meeting again. Is that so?'

'All the papers are talking about it.'

'Then I think the sporting thing to do is to say yes to Miss Gilbert's request, don't you? I'll talk to my pal who owns the transport.'

'How much would we charge her?'

A.D. considered the question.

'I'd say a hefty fee would be in order, wouldn't you? At least that's one way of covering my bet.'

So it was arranged. Early on the Friday morning, the day before the Leopardstown race, Declan drove Jan, Patsy and MG to Luton airport. They drove straight onto the tarmac to where the plane was waiting. Another horsebox with *VIRGINIA GILBERT RACING* emblazoned on the side was already parked beside it. Scottie Venables was talking to a tall, silver-haired man, who introduced himself to Jan as Simon Lacey, the pilot.

Scottie invited Jan to load Morning Glory first as his own lad hadn't arrived yet. Jan climbed the steep ramp to inspect the interior of the plane's livestock compartment, where she found a stall had been formed for Velvet Dynasty, and a larger space, more like a loosebox, had been laid out for Morning Glory.

'I'd better warn you,' Jan said to Simon Lacey, 'my horse is very nervous and I don't really know how he'll react to being shut inside a roaring and throbbing tin can.'

'What I usually do is taxi to the end of the runway,' the pilot told her. 'If everyone inside's still smiling, I'll take off. Of course, if your horse throws a wobbly, I'll have to take *him* off.'

Jan had no choice but to agree to this alarming procedure and went back to her lorry to get on with loading.

No sooner had Jan and Declan lowered the horsebox ramp than MG – covered in a light sheet and already booted up for the journey – started to fret. As Patsy led him out, he jerked at the lead rein and whinnied, hating the hard, unfamiliar surroundings of the airport, with nothing green anywhere in sight. The steep ramp that led up into the dark, cavernous belly of the aircraft seemed to have even less appeal. MG tossed his head and whinnied again. His skin shivered, rippling his rug.

Patsy hung on for dear life and continued talking to the horse, stroking his neck as Jan packed MG's ears with large chunks of cotton wool and placed a hood over his head to stop him shaking the wadding out. Then she fitted a piece of headgear, known as a poll guard, which made him look like a four-legged rugby player with a scrum cap. The device had a special function. It would protect MG if he reared up in a space with very limited headroom and the hood would muffle the sound of the jet engines.

Watched by Jan, Declan and Scottie, Patsy led him forward. As his hoof touched the bottom of the ramp, Morning Glory jinked and backed away. Patsy turned him in a circle and approached again. Jan was holding her breath with her teeth clenched, as this time MG inched further up the ramp, but the unfamiliar smell of the aircraft's interior overwhelmed him and he backed down again.

'Would you take him, Mrs H, and bring him up yourself?' suggested Patsy. 'I'm thinking maybe he'll come in after me.'

Patsy jogged into the plane and waited just inside the shadow of the interior. When Jan presented MG to the ramp, the horse hesitated and then walked onto it like a novice skater stepping onto the ice. A few feet up the incline he stopped again, dipping his head then stretching it forward. He knew Patsy was near. After making a few more hesitant steps towards the lad, he picked up the direction of his scent more strongly and immediately climbed on until he was inside the plane. Patsy retreated to the interior as MG advanced, almost casually now, into the loosebox. Reunited with his handler, MG gently shoved Patsy with his nose, asking for it to be rubbed.

'He's all right now,' said the lad. 'I'm only nervous about the devil getting into him when the engines start.'

Now it was Velvet Dynasty's turn.

'My bloody travelling lad's late, he's been in London for a few days off. The bastard promised he'd be here on time,' Scottie said.

'If you're sure he's coming,' Jan replied, 'Declan can help you load.'

Just then a young man with long black hair curling up at the back of his collar emerged from the terminal building. Lighting a cigarette, he began strolling nonchalantly across the tarmac towards them.

'Michael, put that sodding fag out and get your arse over here, ya bloody great lummox,' bellowed Scottie. 'You're late.'

As the Gilbert lad approached, Jan noticed that Patsy had left Morning Glory and was standing at the top of the aircraft ramp. When he saw who was approaching, his jaw dropped and his eyes widened. In a second he vanished into the belly of the plane.

'What's the matter with him?' Jan whispered to Declan.

'Shit, Mrs H,' said Dec more seriously. 'That's Michael Fahey. He's one of the lads who gave Patsy such a hard time when he was at the Gilbert place.'

Jan shut her eyes and held them shut for several moments.

'Oh God. That's all I bloody need.'

Though frightened initially by the engines' roar, Morning Glory did not go berserk as Jan had feared, and Simon Lacey radioed the control tower for clearance to take off. Patsy stayed with the horse throughout the flight, with Jan in the forward seating, and they landed in better order than any of the team had dared hope. At Dublin airport Patsy brought MG down the ramp to a gleaming modern horsebox, supplied by A.D. Entering it in much the same way as he had boarded the plane, MG seemed to be learning at last. Meanwhile the behaviour of his travelling companion was as sweet as a syllabub.

Leopardstown was about twelve miles from Dublin airport but, with most of the city lying directly between, the journey took considerably more time. So it was not until early afternoon, some six hours after they had left Edge Farm, that they finally settled the two horses in the stable block at the racecourse. It was not a race day and the area was quiet and businesslike, with horseboxes coming and going as some of the next day's runners arrived to be boxed, groomed, watered and fed by their attendants.

Jan was booked into the Shelbourne Hotel in central Dublin, where she was due to have dinner in the evening with her friend, the bloodstock agent Sean McDonagh. She had equipped Patsy with a flask of tea, three packets of sandwiches, chocolate and a bag of Irish coins for the phone. After giving him instructions for the horse's evening feed and the phone number of her hotel, she gathered her belongings ready to leave.

But Patsy was very quiet and looked anxious.

'You're sure you'll be all right? That guy from the Gilbert yard's not been bothering you, has he?'

Patsy hurriedly shook his head.

'Good,' said Jan. 'Phone me at the hotel at six. Don't you forget now.'

He assured her he wouldn't.

Leaving the stable area, she looked up at the sky, which was just beginning to darken. The wind had got up and a few black clouds had blown in from the west. Pulling her woollen jacket more tightly around her, she passed six or seven young men, obviously overnight stable staff, kicking a football between them. Seeing Jan, they stopped to watch her go by and she saw them nudging one another and passing remarks. They were too far away for the words to carry, but she could imagine the content. Fixing them with a defiant glare, she thought she recognized the mullet hairstyle of Michael Fahey amongst them.

❧

Later, as she lay on her hotel bed, Jan dialled A.D. O'Hagan at Aigmont.

'We've arrived and the horse is safely ensconced at Leopardstown with Patsy,' she told him.

'Good, I'm glad to hear it.' A.D.'s voice sounded as calm as ever. 'You'd no trouble with the flight?'

'Not to speak of, thanks to Patsy. Without him I don't know if we'd have got MG on the plane even.'

'How's our rival?'

'Good as gold, like I knew he would be. But don't worry, A.D. I'm sure we can beat him. Ask Murty.'

'I have done and he's not as confident as you.'

'I didn't say I was *confident*. I am optimistic, though.'

'The forecast says more rain. I really don't want to see the ground softer than it is already.'

'No,' agreed Jan. 'That's out of our hands, but it wouldn't be ideal.'

'Well, we're committed now. I'll see you tomorrow. Perhaps it would help if you said a few Hail Marys.'

Jan hung up and lay still for a moment, wondering if A.D. had really meant her to pray. At first the only noises penetrating the room were the wind and Dublin's incessant traffic. But after a few moments she heard a new sound, that of the first spots of rain spattering against the windowpanes. Hoping this would be no more than a light shower, she closed her eyes and, without meaning to, fell asleep.

Jan woke with a jolt. What time was it? Her watch read five past six. She rubbed her face and grabbed her bedside phone to dial the stables office.

'Sorry, Mrs Hardy, your man's not about at the moment,' said the official who at her request had gone to look in Morning Glory's box. 'That horse of yours is all right, though. There's nothing to worry about.'

'Please would you tell Patsy he *must* call me, immediately. I gave him the number, but I'll give it to you again in case he's lost it.'

Jan recited the number and hung up. Patsy had probably gone to the toilet or something. She decided to take a bath, but with the bathroom door ajar so she could hear the phone. It did not ring and twenty minutes later, still damp and wrapped in a hotel bath sheet, she called the stable office again. Patsy had not shown up.

Jan was due to meet Sean in the hotel bar at seven-thirty. As she dressed she tried to imagine what the hell Patsy was up to. She had given him specific instructions not to leave the horse for more than a few minutes. But, if the man in the office was to be believed, he had been away from MG now for at least an hour. By quarter past seven, as she took the lift down to the lobby, she felt a sense of dread. Before leaving the room, she had made a last-minute decision. Changing out of the dress she'd put on for Sean, she got back into her jeans, jumper and jacket. She would have to go out to the racecourse immediately and find out what was wrong. There was nothing else for it.

Recognizing the greying head of Sean McDonagh, as he stood with his back to her talking to the barman, she hurried towards him.

'Jan!' he cried, raising his glass of whiskey to salute her approach. 'Sure it's great to see your shining face.'

He lightly touched her upper arm and gave her a peck on the cheek, then looked at her clothes.

'Have you just arrived?'

'No, Sean,' she began, 'I'm terribly sorry, but I'm afraid dinner's off. There's a bit of a crisis and I have to get back to Leopardstown immediately.'

The bloodstock agent's delighted grin dissolved into a look of concern.

'What sort of a crisis?'

'You know I've got this temperamental horse we're running tomorrow? Well, the lad who is supposed to be staying with him at the racecourse stables isn't coming to the phone or calling in even. He's usually so reliable, I don't know what's happened.'

Sean drained his glass.

'I can see why that would be a worry. Come on, I'll drive.'

'Oh no, I couldn't possibly impose—'

'Nonsense. Haven't I the car outside? And Leopardstown's on my way home anyway.'

Jan felt some of the weight lift from her shoulders. She looked gratefully at Sean's weathered, kind, dependable face. She had someone with her now and, whatever was going on at the race-course, at least she wouldn't have to face it on her own.

The rain was still pouring down and the roads were slick, but Sean drove fast and skilfully. On the way Jan summarized the situation.

After hearing her out, Sean said, 'I saw the horse run on TV, at Cheltenham when he fell at the last. Looked all over the winner to my eyes, but I gathered from what the commentator was saying he's no Goody Two-Shoes.'

'That's one way of putting it,' Jan agreed.

'Anyway, I wouldn't be worrying too much about your man at this stage. He's probably just gone off with the rest of them to the pub and forgotten the time.'

'I wouldn't have left him alone with the horse if I didn't think he was dependable. He loves that horse – in fact, I think he'd probably die for it. He's usually very serious about the job. He wouldn't just go off to the pub. I don't even think he drinks. He's a very devout Catholic.'

'Ah well, piety doesn't stop you drinking, unfortunately. Quite the opposite, some would say.'

Sean sighed and shook his head, as if he had privately decided alcohol must be at the root of the problem. Threading through the early evening traffic, he took the main Wicklow road to Ballsbridge, Donnybrook then Stillorgan, where he turned right off the national road towards Leopardstown itself.

'I only hope we're in time,' Jan prayed.

'In time for what?'

'In time to stop a disaster.'

'Ah sure, the horse'll be all right for a couple of hours, even if he is a bit lonesome. So don't you worry about that now.'

The racecourse stables were enclosed by a high mesh fence, with the stable office next to the gated entrance. Jan and Sean walked in to find the two security guards watching television.

'The horses have been a bit noisier than usual,' said the older of the two. 'But you'll often get that with stopovers. Otherwise it's been quiet enough here.'

'Have you seen my lad yet? Patsy Keating?' asked Jan.

'No,' the other one stated. 'But a lot of the lads went off in a gang to the pub down the road a while ago.'

'When?' asked Sean.

'About an hour or so, I'd say.'

'That's where he'll be,' said Sean. 'I'd bet on it.'

'But he can't be, that's *after* I phoned the first time,' Jan protested. 'And he wasn't here then. What the hell is he playing at? He's damn well supposed to be *here*.'

Jan produced her racecourse pass.

'I must go in and take a look at my horse,' she said.

'OK, Mrs Hardy,' said the senior man, after carefully scrutinizing the pass. Oddly, he made no comment when Sean, who had no pass, followed as she headed towards the row of boxes, each housing one of tomorrow's runners.

Patsy was not at Morning Glory's box and it was obvious to a blind man that the horse was distressed. He was continually calling out, walking round and round in circles, and in the process winding up the horses on either side of him. Jan examined the box carefully. Patsy seemed to have made a nest for himself in the corner. Jan saw an indentation on the bedding, and the sandwich wrappers and the tea flask were hidden in a corner behind the water bucket. But the tatty yellow rucksack that Patsy had been carrying with him was missing.

While Jan stood by MG's head, stroking his neck, doing her best to calm him, Sean offered to find the large group of visiting lads and see if Patsy was with them. Jan heard the tyres squeal outside as her friend turned his car and drove away fast in the direction of the bar mentioned by the guards.

Jan continued talking to Morning Glory. She knew she was no substitute for Patsy, but at least he knew her.

'Oh MG, MG,' she whispered. 'What's happened? Where on earth's Patsy gone?'

The horse blew down his nostrils, snorting loudly, and pawed at the bedding.

# 25

The rain had stopped by the time Sean returned to Morning Glory's box around twenty minutes later, where he found Jan sitting outside on an upturned plastic milk crate. But there was no sign of Morning Glory, who had turned to face the back wall in sullen fashion and was taking no interest.

'I don't suppose you found him?' Jan questioned, without much hope of a positive response.

'They say he's not been in the bar at all,' Sean said, breathing hard, 'but I spoke to some of them other fellas.'

'They haven't seen him?'

'No, and if they have they're not saying. I couldn't get a peep out of 'em, but I've a lead on him anyway.'

He pulled a crumpled, torn piece of envelope out of his pocket and showed it to her. Jan saw some scrawled details, and even made out the name: Michael Cusack.

'Who's Michael Cusack?' she asked.

'I believe he founded the Gaelic Athletic Association.'

'Sorry, Sean, I'm lost. I don't get it.'

'It's simple – they named a block of flats after him, and in that block of flats lives Patsy's family.'

'You mean this is the Keatings' address?'

'It is. How important is it that you find him tonight? I mean, do you need him right now?'

'Yes, absolutely. Without Patsy, the horse drops to pieces. Just look at him, he's already gone into an almighty huff. I doubt we'll be able to send him out tomorrow, not without Patsy being here, that's for sure. And if we did, it's highly questionable whether he'd run a worthwhile race. How far away is this place?'

'Not far. It's here in Dublin, just a few miles up the road.'

Jan sprang up, suddenly filled with renewed energy.

'Sean, can we go in your car?'

'But what about the horse?'

'He'll manage until we find our boy. Come on, big fella, you can't desert me now!'

'Tally ho!' said Sean with a broad grin.

They returned to the security gate, where Jan called in at the office.

'If Patsy Keating, the lad who looks after my horse, turns up, tell him I'll be right back.'

'Right y'are, Mrs Hardy,' said the guard.

As he drove, Sean explained what had happened in the pub.

'There was about a dozen of the boyos in there. I asked after Patsy, which they thought was quite amusing – I mean amusing that I was looking for him. "What would you be wanting with the quare feller?" said one and, "He's after going to confession," said another.

'It wasn't till I left the place that one of them came chasing after me in the street. He said he knew Patsy, they were kids together. I asked him where the Keatings lived and bingo! He gave me the address, simple as that. It's the obvious place for him, especially if he's been frightened off by those lads.'

'Unless he *is* at confession,' said Jan drily.

During the twenty minutes' drive, the cityscape changed to one of housing schemes and suburban squalor – grey blocks of flats interspersed with windswept and derelict open spaces.

'You have to be very careful driving on the roads here,' commented Sean.

Jan looked around. Compared to the city centre, there seemed relatively little traffic.

'Why?'

'You'll see.'

A few moments later the rump of a shaggy-coated grey horse,

his long mane and tail matted and clogged with sludge, suddenly appeared in the car headlights. He was wandering along the road, totally unfazed, and appeared to be following the centre line. Sean slowed to a walking pace until they had passed the bedraggled animal, then accelerated.

'That's why,' he said. 'These estates are crawling with semi-wild horses, a lot of them owned by kids. Some are just abandoned.'

'Where do they come from?'

'The first Sunday of the month there's a horse fair at Smithfield Market, in the city centre, where the youngsters go and pay a few quid for a pony. They bring it back to whichever of these rackety estates they live on and either tether it or turn it out on some old patch of scrubland.'

Jan looked from side to side, and every now and then spotted the ghostly form of a horse or pony standing in the dark, cropping whatever grass it could find. She even saw a mare with a foal at foot.

'But why on earth do they do it?'

'Status. Excitement. In the evening they round 'em all up and go out and race one another. Dubliners call them the urban cowboys. I bet Patsy was one of them, in his early days. Many of them are travellers' kids, who at least have some idea how to look after a horse. But a lot are typical skangers, who haven't a clue, and don't even give enough water to the poor beasts. It's rumoured they actually keep them in the apartments, like you would a pet dog. Would you believe that? Apparently they take them up and down in the lifts, horse shit everywhere. I read about one kid that wanted a zebra, so he painted black stripes on his pony with some old paint he found. Of course the poor sod became real sick with the poisoning.'

'But it should be stopped,' protested Jan, horrified. 'Aren't there any controls?'

'This is Ireland. You need to get a licence for a dog, but even a baby in nappies can own a horse. They're talking about legislation now to bring in licensing and an age limit, but of course it'll take a few years.'

'Well, the sooner the better.' Jan sighed with relief.

At last they approached the estate, where the apartment blocks stood in line a little back from the road. Sean slowed right down to scan the names on the weather-beaten display boards. The dilapidated concrete structures were rust stained and densely scrawled with graffiti, each displaying a few boarded-up windows. Sean moved gently on, then pulled up.

'This looks like the place,' he said, squinting at the ramshackle building.

They left the locked car and approached a door, which stood half open. Jan led the way, reading the name of the block on the board above: Michael Cusack House. She pushed through into a damp, smelly hallway, from which a concrete stairwell rose to the upper floors. By the dim light of a single bare electric bulb dangling from the ceiling, they began climbing the stairs.

'I wouldn't fancy doing this on my own. Thank goodness you're here,' said Jan. 'Do you have the flat number?'

'Yes, it's thirteen.'

'It would be,' she answered grimly.

Standing outside the flat, they could hear the mumblings of a television. Jan tapped on the door, then hammered louder. Eventually a quavering voice was heard.

'Who's there?'

'It's Jan Hardy.'

She heard her name reverberate around the stairwell.

'I'm Patsy's boss in England. Is he there?'

They heard the security chain rattle and a second later the door jerked open. A watery old eye inspected Jan through the crack.

'I'm his grammah. What do ye want at this hour of the night?'

'I need to speak to him. I don't wish him any harm. We're friends.'

With a whumph, the door was shut. Jan grimaced and shot an anxious look at her companion.

'Shit!' she mouthed silently.

Then they heard the security chain sliding out of its groove and the door opened again, wider this time. A small woman with tangled grey hair gave them a fuller inspection. She pointed at Sean.

'Who's that?' she demanded gruffly.

'He's a friend. He drove me here. I don't know the area. I would never have found it on my own.'

The woman swung the door wide. 'You'd better come in.'

Compared to the grime of the stairway, the flat was pristine. The carpets and curtains, with their bright swirly patterns, were well worn, but immaculately clean. So were the holy pictures that seemed to cover every square inch of the wallspace, and the white lace doilies laid on the gleaming table and sideboard. The whole atmosphere carried a powerful smell of furniture polish.

'Sit down there.'

Patsy's grandmother gestured at the settee, which was placed against the wall opposite a television. A spaghetti Western was blaring from its screen.

Obediently they perched on the edge as the old woman shuffled out of the room. A moment later they heard her calling out, 'Patsy, Patsy, you there?'

Jan closed her fists and lifted them in front of her.

'Yeesss!' she whispered.

Sean jumped up and stationed himself by the door, his face tilted upwards, listening. Elsewhere in the flat they could hear the sound of an urgent conversation, though the words were initially drowned out by a long burst of gunfire from the TV. Then the old woman came back in, followed slowly and reluctantly by a very hangdog, very nervous Patsy Keating.

''Lo, Mrs H,' he said.

'For Christ's sake, Patsy,' Jan exploded, 'what the bloody hell are you doing here? I need you, so get your things right now. You're coming back with us.'

Patsy knew he had a snowball's chance in hell of standing up to Jan that night. So he collected his yellow rucksack and mumbled something to his grandma. She kissed him and grunted a reply as she opened the door of the flat.

Jan sat with Patsy in the rear of the car while Sean drove back to Leopardstown, and gradually Jan extracted the boy's story. Michael Fahey had been his chief persecutor at Riscombe, and after Tim

Farr's article in the *Wessex Daily News* he had been disciplined by Scottie Venables. Although Fahey already despised Patsy, the punishment had redoubled his loathing and, during the flight to Ireland when the two of them were alone in the horse compartment, Fahey had threatened all sorts of evil retribution.

But it was much later, when he met up with a few of the boyos at Leopardstown, that things became far more serious. They had already heard the rumours concerning Morning Glory and his total dependence on Patsy Keating. As they all liked a wager, Michael Fahey had seen a way of discrediting Patsy, while at the same time making sure that Velvet Dynasty was an attractive betting proposition in Saturday's race. Backed up by his pals, he'd gone round to MG's box and told Patsy that the animal would be blinded if Patsy didn't scarper.

Jan gasped. Some of those lads had already been questioned by Sean in the pub. They knew a search was on. If they guessed Patsy would be found and brought back, would they carry out their brutal intention?

'Ah, don't you worry too much about that,' Sean reassured her. 'It's all cod. They wouldn't risk actually doing anything to the horse. There's too much security at that place. It's empty threats.'

'But I couldn't take the chance, mister,' said Patsy plaintively. 'I wouldn't mind what they did to me, but I had to save MG. Isn't that right, Mrs H?'

'I can see your point, Patsy,' said Jan. 'And I don't blame you for being frightened. But you should have told me instead of buggering off like that.'

It was almost midnight when they arrived back at the racecourse and Patsy was reunited with Morning Glory. The horse had come to no harm and was visibly delighted to see his lad, spinning round in his box and nickering with pleasure.

🐎

There was no way Jan could go back to the Shelbourne, not that night. After a big warm hug from Sean, who then left for his home in County Wexford, she dropped in to the stable office. There she found the two guards hypnotized by the same Western that Patsy's grandma had been watching in Michael Cusack House.

'I've had serious threats made against my horse,' she told them, raising her voice to compete with the volleys of frenzied shooting from the TV. 'You will be extra-vigilant, won't you?'

'Right,' said one of the guards, lifting a finger but not taking his eyes off the screen.

'Did you hear what I just *said*?' Jan shouted.

The two men turned to her, blinking.

'Sorry, what was it?'

'I said, I have reason to believe my horse may be got at. So I'm staying here tonight, with the lad, if that's all right with you. Is that clear enough?'

'Right you are, Mrs Hardy,' said the older man. 'No problem at all.'

For the next six hours Jan and Patsy were always near MG's box, taking it in turns hour by hour to keep watch while the other catnapped.

As she poured the lukewarm remains from the flask into a beaker at what seemed like their darkest hour, around three a.m., Jan asked, 'Was it your grandma who brought you up?'

'Mostly she did.'

'So where's your mother?'

'In England.'

'When did you last see her?'

'I dunno. Four or five years ago, maybe.'

'And what about your father?'

'I never seen him in my life.'

*Poor little sod*, Jan thought. She could only imagine how hard his life must have been.

After what seemed an eternity, daylight came and life resumed in the stable complex as more horses began to arrive for the day's racing. With plenty of people around, Jan thought it would be safe to return to Dublin for a quick shower and change while Patsy saw to the horse – a good lead-out, a ten-minute pick of grass, a sip of clean water, a thorough grooming followed by a small feed would set him up fine.

When Jan got back to Leopardstown around ten, she went straight to the stables, where to her horror she saw the Riscombe thug leaning over the open half-door of MG's stable with a cigarette in one hand, speaking to Patsy inside.

Jan stormed up to him.

'Get away from here, Fahey! Don't you dare hang around the box door with a lighted cigarette. You're not supposed to smoke in here anyway. Are you so thick you don't know anything about the rules?'

Fahey sprang from the loosebox door and jogged backwards away from Jan, showing her his open hands, shrugging his shoulders and grinning impertinently.

'You're a bloody disgrace,' Jan went on furiously. 'Don't think I don't know what you've been up to, because I do – everything.'

Fahey curled his lip and raised two fingers.

'Stuff you, you old bag,' he sneered, before turning on his heels and marching away.

Jan was crimson and shaking with rage. 'What did he want? What was that bastard saying to you?'

'Nothin', Mrs H,' said Patsy, who was polishing the bridle the horse would wear in the race. 'Just the normal gab he always gives me.'

'About what? Did he threaten to harm you or the horse again?'

'No, he said he was only havin' a dig, like.'

'What else did he say?'

'Same as usual, he took the piss out of me for going to church. And said I shouldn't be involved in racing because it was, you know, a sinful type of business, so.'

'Do you really think it's sinful, Patsy?' she said more calmly.

'A lot of it is so,' he replied with sincerity. 'But the horses wouldn't be, would they?'

Jan couldn't help laughing.

'No,' she agreed. 'Naughty, bloody difficult, sometimes impossible, yes; but sinful? I don't think so, not even nearly.'

❧

Later, in the owners' and trainers' bar, Jan gave A.D. O'Hagan a summary of the previous night's drama, highlighting the role taken by Virginia's travelling groom. It seemed to give the great man less cause for concern than she expected.

'We do get these threats from time to time,' he said unflappably. 'It's usually just a blast of hot air.'

'You're taking it rather lightly, A.D. They talked about *blinding* the horse, you know!'

A.D. gave a wry smile.

'Ah well, *you* never take it too lightly. In my time I've had two of my horses threatened with being shot. Here in Ireland, can you believe? So there it is, you just take the necessary precautions, as you did last night – very effectively, if I may say so.'

'But what can we do now? We can't just let them get away with it, can we?'

'What we do is simple,' said A.D. 'We go to the races and our horse gives theirs a good licking.'

For all A.D.'s apparent indifference, Jan could not restrain herself from tackling Virginia in person. Small clusters of owners and trainers were beginning to gather, as the runners for the Fitzpatrick Castle Hurdle circled the parade ring, still wearing their sheets. By sheer coincidence Jan happened to enter immediately behind an unaccompanied Virginia, and she increased her pace to catch up with Velvet Dynasty's trainer.

'Virginia, are you aware your lad threatened to blind my horse last night?' she demanded.

Somehow Jan prevented herself from raising her voice. On a racecourse, not just the walls, but every blade of grass could have ears, and she did not want this feud with Virginia to get more publicity than it already had.

Virginia smiled. 'Horrible sense of humour some of these young men have, don't they?'

'I don't think a criminal offence is a laughing matter. What are you going to do about it?'

Virginia looked at Jan with indifference.

'Well, I don't see why we should care what *you* think, so nothing. Now, if you'll excuse me, I have a horse to see to.'

As Virginia stalked off, A.D. appeared in the ring with his entourage, quickly followed by Murty McGrath and the other jockeys. Caught up in the vital business of last-minute preparations and racing instructions, for the time being Jan brushed aside Virginia and her cruel sarcasm.

Previously Jan had taken runners to the Cheltenham Festival, Aintree and Fairyhouse's Irish National and no one could describe the Fitzpatrick Castle Hurdle, with its 25,000 Irish punts in prize money, as being remotely in the same class. Yet she felt, if it were possible, even more tension now than on those distinguished occasions. Of course, the previous night had left her exhausted, but that didn't matter. It was how the horse came through it all that was much more relevant, and he seemed absolutely fine, although Jan wished Reg had been there to reassure her. In her experience, when it came to assessing a horse's well-being, Reg's keen eye was second to none.

Jan told Murty to ride Morning Glory exactly as he had done before.

'Only don't fall at the last this time,' she said with a twinkle in her eye.

The ground was a little sticky after the previous day's downpour, which would to some extent cramp MG's free-running style. But, on the other hand, it would also blunt the finishing speed of Velvet Dynasty and the other 'flat yokes', as A.D. so succinctly put it. The debates that raged on the course, as the horses made their way to the start, were as to whether this was going to be another duel between Jan's and Virginia's yards, or whether some other pretender would emerge to take them both on. The betting market at this stage suggested the former. MG and Velvet Dynasty were joint favourites at seven to four, with the next in the list standing at five to one.

The two-mile start at Leopardstown was a couple of furlongs away, to the left of the stands, and Jan and A.D. took up a position that gave them a good view of the line-up. Jan thought Murty handled MG beautifully on the way to the start, and once again she marvelled at his cool, controlled horsemanship. Now, through her binoculars, she could clearly see the O'Hagan colours moving around at the back of the pack as the champion jockey attempted to position MG so that as the tape flew up he would already be moving forward. She also caught sight of the Gilbert colours, worn once again by Finbar Howlett on Velvet Dynasty.

Murty judged the start perfectly and MG immediately pulled into a clear lead, his tail streaming proudly behind him as he surged up the incline. As the horses thundered past the stands, and through the flying divots, Jan noted that Velvet Dynasty had taken up a position nearer to last than first. Finbar was using his familiar waiting tactics.

The crowd let out a huge roar. They loved Morning Glory's devil-may-care hurdling, gasping and cheering when he skimmed over the obstacles at full speed. His jump at the fourth, around the halfway mark on the far side of the course, heralded a mammoth groan as he hit the willow, but this time he never even broke stride. All the way along the back straight Jan could see Velvet Dynasty and Finbar Howlett deftly picking their way through the field. As they swung round the long final bend and downhill towards the start of the home straight, he had moved into fourth place and was travelling better than any of the runners, with the exception of Morning Glory.

Jan's mouth was bone dry, her heart thumped like a jackhammer, and her teeth were clenched as Velvet Dynasty powered into second place and began determinedly to close on the leader.

*Here we go again!* she thought, her mouth too dry to speak. She flashed a glance at A.D. He had never told her the size of his bet, but she could see from the way the muscle in his jaw was twitching that, for him, a whole lot of cash depended on the outcome of the next few seconds.

This time, unlike Cheltenham, the horses rose to meet the last flight in unison, with Velvet Dynasty on the outside. As Morning Glory's forelegs touched the ground, he pulled his hind legs under his body to give maximum power to that all-important first stride away from the obstacle. At the same time, right alongside, Velvet Dynasty screwed in the air, landing at an angle. The two horses collided shoulder to shoulder.

Completely knocked out of his stride, Morning Glory came off far worse and Murty, for the first time that day, had to earn his riding fee. He yanked violently at the reins to avoid colliding with the rails, and to get the horse back on an even keel. For a couple of strides he let his mount regain his balance, before giving him a dig in the flanks with both heels to restart his run. MG responded wholeheartedly, though by now he had lost considerable ground. Even worse, he had conceded his position on the rails as Virginia's horse barged across in front of him.

MG acknowledged his jockey's desperate call and lowered his head to dig in, as Murty steered him away from the rails to tackle Velvet Dynasty on the outside. With the furlongs ever-decreasing to the winning line, MG began to make steady progress. It was agonizing. Step by step, with every reach of his forelegs, he took a few more inches off Velvet Dynasty's lead. As they raced past the stands both horses were at full stretch, their ears laid flat back as their jockeys pumped away like a couple of madmen. Morning Glory was edging closer to Velvet Dynasty. The crowd went ballistic as he reached the other horse's quarters, then his neck, both jockeys pushing, pushing, trying to lengthen their mount's stride, refusing to give in.

In the last few lung-bursting strides the horses' heads rocked back and forth, with first one and then the other getting his nostrils in front. Finally they flashed past the post and there was only a nod in it.

Jan went bright red, flushed with excitement and emotion. Not since winning the Irish National had she seen a horse of hers fight back so bravely. She looked at A.D., but he was still watching as the horses careered on round the bend, their momentum taking them several hundred yards further along the course before their jockeys could begin to pull them up. As they did so, A.D., slowly and deliberately, lowered his binoculars.

'Half a stride after the post, we were in front.'

'But . . .?'

'At the line itself, I just don't know, I couldn't be sure.'

Jan saw a microscopic bead of sweat nestling in the wrinkles of A.D.'s brow as they waited for an announcement.

'Photograph, photograph.' A voice bellowed over the loud-speaker a few seconds later.

Now the result of the race was in the hands of the judge.

🐎

There was absolutely no way of knowing which way it would go, who was the victor or who was the vanquished. The noise from the crowd had fallen away, but the course still buzzed like a gigantic hornet's nest as everyone debated the outcome. The bookies were busy quoting prices on the result of the photograph, with an apparent even split between those who thought Morning Glory had got up to win and those who maintained that Velvet Dynasty had held him off.

Jan pushed her way through the throng of racegoers moving around the stand, mesmerized and electrified by what they had just witnessed. She was halfway to the unsaddling enclosure when the announcer's voice boomed out from the PA again. She stood still to listen.

'Here is the result of the photograph. First number six, Velvet Dynasty; second number ten, Morning Glory; third number twelve . . .'

The lives of drowning victims are said to flash before their eyes. Now Jan had a similar experience. It was as if all the stress and problems of the last six months had come back to haunt her in a concentrated form.

Jan made her way to unsaddle her horse. She found Velvet Dynasty already standing in the winner's slot. His connections were triumphant, with Virginia already posing for photographs as Michael Fahey went about his business wearing the smuggest of smug smiles. Patsy, on the other hand, looked shell-shocked as he led Morning Glory into the number two position. Jan could find nothing to say as Murty slipped to the ground and faced her, his face grim.

'Did you see that at the last?' he growled. 'I'm fecking sure he did it deliberate.'

Murty undid the girth and removed the saddle and weight cloth before stomping off towards the weighing room. Then Jan saw her owner emerge from the crowd to intercept him. A.D. listened attentively as Murty talked, gesturing angrily. The owner nodded just once, before Murty touched the peak of his cap with the whip he was carrying and hurried off to weigh in. As Jan was about to fling a cooler across Morning Glory's steaming back, A.D. arrived to rub the horse's nose.

Jan swallowed the hard lump that was still lodged in her throat.

'A.D., I'm so sorry—' she began.

A.D. held up his finger.

'Shhh! Listen!'

The public-address system crackled and the announcer's voice was heard again.

'Objection. Objection.'

Instantly the crowd buzzed at the prospect of another twist in the tale. A hush descended and you could have heard a pin drop as the announcer continued.

'The second has objected to the winner on the grounds of bumping and boring and taking his ground after the last. Patrons are advised to retain all betting tickets until the stewards have made their ruling. Thank you.'

Jan's hand was over her mouth as A.D. murmured, 'It's not over yet, Jan. It's not over yet, my girl!'

🐎

When the stewards sat to adjudicate, they considered nothing but the video replay and the evidence provided by the jockeys concerned. So, although Jan went with Murty to the stewards' room, which was across a corridor from the weighing area, all she could do was stand outside. Finbar Howlett was already waiting at the door as they got there. To Jan's relief, there was no sign of Virginia.

Murty mouthed something uncomplimentary at Finbar as they lingered.

'McGrath, Howlett, come in!' the steward's secretary said as he opened the door.

At that moment Jan was reminded of a summons to the head teacher's office at school. She caught a glimpse of the scene inside.

It was a large room, in which three male stewards were sitting behind a polished table. To one side, on a trolley, were a television set and video recorder. As the two jockeys entered, the steward's secretary marched to the far end of the table and stood to attention – it was his job to advise the stewards on the rules of racing.

There was a loud 'clunk' as the door closed.

The voices inside the room were audible, but not the words. Jan knew roughly what was going on. Firstly the tribunal would hear what the objector, McGrath, had to say, followed by Howlett's defence. Then they would all look at the video recordings of the race, most importantly the head-on, but also views from the side and rear. Jan had already seen a television replay of the two horses jumping the last and was in no doubt that Morning Glory would have crossed the line first if he hadn't been bumped. But was the bump deliberate or accidental? Murty was absolutely convinced of Finbar's guilt, and though Jan, in her heart of hearts, was not quite so sure, she knew the stewards would have to reverse the placings if they agreed with her jockey.

She wandered into the weighing room and chatted with the clerk of the scales, then wandered back. She chewed her lip, bit a fingernail, and studied the framed ancient sporting prints lining the corridor's walls. At last, after almost ten minutes, the door of the stewards' room opened again and the secretary ushered the jockeys out.

'Wait there a moment while the stewards deliberate. I will call you back when they have reached a decision,' he said.

Before closing the door firmly again, he gave Jan an icy stare, which did nothing for her confidence in the outcome. Finbar was glowering, and Murty seemed edgy as they waited by the heavy highly polished outer door. Jan looked at her watch. The next race was due off in twelve minutes. If the stewards didn't produce a verdict quickly, the session would have to adjourn. Nobody wanted that, certainly not the punters who would be anxious to re-invest.

Suddenly the door swung open. It was the secretary dressed in his traditional tweed suit and bone-polished shoes.

'McGrath, Howlett, please come back in.'

It took the stewards less than a minute to deliver their verdict.

Murty bounced out of the room followed by Finbar, looking decid-edly sour, and the secretary, who strode off hurriedly with a paper in his hand.

'What's happened?' Jan whispered. 'What's the result?'

But Murty, with a mischievous smile quite different from the scowl he had worn earlier, was already off.

'I'll catch you later, Mrs H. I'm riding in the next. Listen for the announcement.'

Jan went outside, where a spell of watery sunshine had now brightened the winter afternoon. She stood with her back to the wall near the weighing-room door, content to be by herself. Then she heard the PA system crackle into life.

'Ladies and gentlemen, following the objection by the second to the winner in the previous race, the stewards found that Velvet Dynasty interfered with Morning Glory at the last flight, and thereby gained an unfair advantage. Finbar Howlett has been sus-pended for foul riding and number six, Velvet Dynasty, has been placed last. Here is a revised result: first, number ten Morning Glory, second number twelve . . .'

Jan felt very calm. She shut her eyes and rested her head against the brick wall of the racecourse building, as the sun's warmth bathed her face.

# 26

The trial of Harold Powell, on the double charge of attempted murder and causing death by reckless driving, was held in the second week of March before Judge Laurence Bancroft, sitting at Gloucester Crown Court. Harold's brief was Charles de Courcy QC, a well-known London silk, while the Crown was represented by Benjamin Jeffreys, a senior barrister practising on the Western Circuit. When the clerk of the court asked the defendant how did he plead, Harold said firmly, 'Not guilty,' to both charges.

As a witness for the prosecution, Jan was excluded from the early stages of the proceedings. Bob Warren had explained to her that a jury had to be selected, and then the preliminary submissions of prosecution and defence would be made before Jeffreys could open the case for the Crown. Which he did on the second day, when those waiting in the witnesses' room began to thin out as they were called to give evidence. One by one, the police officers, including Brian Hadfield, stepped up to the witness box to describe the scene on Cleeve Hill almost a year ago. A pathologist gave the results of his autopsy on the body of William Moorhouse. Members of the forensic science team provided details of skid patterns, impact analysis and paint fragments. As she and Patsy sat, awaiting their turn, Jan did not feel overly nervous, except on behalf of Patsy. He was clearly tortured, sitting there pale as a glass of milk.

Jan was called to the stand immediately after the expert evidence. She took the oath, then looked across to the public gallery, where Reg and Mary were sitting, so close together she knew they were holding hands. Nearby, she could see both Toby Waller and Annabel. There was no Eddie – he'd said he couldn't face it. But sitting detached from the others, Virginia in a typical 'look at me' pose, glanced at Jan. Next, Jan looked across at Harold, who was standing in the dock. Flanked by two stony-faced prison officers, he was staring menacingly back at her.

After the preliminaries, Jeffreys courteously invited Jan to lead him through the hours preceding the accident on Cleeve Hill. She gave details of the race meeting and A.D.'s party, and of Harold threatening her. She went on to report how she and Eddie had left the course, and how they were being overtaken by a car on Cleeve Hill as another car was speeding towards them; how they had been barged off the road by the overtaking car, which sped away leaving mayhem in its wake. Finally, she detailed her injuries and Eddie's long and painful rehabilitation.

Jeffreys went on to ask about Harold Powell. How long had Jan known him? Would she tell the court how he had acted in the sale of Stonewall Farm? Did anything subsequently occur to suggest someone might have a grudge against her? What had happened when Harold visited Edge Farm on that afternoon back in October?

'No more questions,' said Jeffreys at last. Jan was feeling relieved and rather good until she saw the figure of Charles de Courcy rising to his feet to cross-examine her. She steeled herself, remembering Bob Warren's advice: the man was a highly skilled advocate; she must keep her answers brief and be as decisive as possible.

'Mrs Hardy, I won't detain you very long,' the QC began suavely. 'Now I understand that, on occasions when one has had a success at the races, it is usual to celebrate with champagne and other alcoholic drinks. Is that so?'

'Yes,' Jan agreed, 'many people do.'

'Prior to your road accident, you yourself had been celebrating with your owners at the Cheltenham racecourse, after the win you so admirably described to the court. Is that so?'

'Yes, I had a glass or two.'

'In the hospitality suite of your horse's owner, A.D. O'Hagan?'

'Yes.'

'Was Edward Sullivan present in Mr O'Hagan's box?'

'Yes, he was.'

'And did he celebrate the victory?'

'Yes, of course. He was delighted.'

De Courcy looked at her over the top of his half-moon glasses.

'I mean, did he drink the champagne or any of the other alcohol on offer?'

'I didn't see him.'

'But he was with you, was he not?'

'Not all the time. When he was with me he didn't drink.'

'And when he offered to drive you home, did you ask him if he'd had a drink during the day?'

'Yes, I did.'

'What did he say?'

'He said he was fine to drive because he'd had no more than a gnat's bladderful.'

A ripple of laughter ran around the court, quelled by a glare from the bench.

De Courcy continued, 'Which means, I take it, that he *had* had something to drink?'

'Yes. It means a very little.'

'Indeed? Though a gnat's bladder is not, I think, a term recognized in the Weights and Measures Act.'

There was another wave of giggles. De Courcy was clearly enjoying himself.

'On that same afternoon at the races,' he went on, 'you allege that you met the defendant by chance and that he threatened to make sure that you would, I quote, "get what's coming to you". Is that right?'

'Yes.'

'Was anyone else present when, as you allege, he said these words?'

'No.'

'No witnesses at all?'

'No.'

'I see. Now, can we move on to the accident itself? Mrs Hardy, how well can you remember it?'

'I remember it well. I'm not likely to forget it, am I?' Jan responded, feeling a little flustered as the memories were brought back to life.

'How well did you remember it immediately afterwards – the next day, for instance?'

'Not very well, not then. I'd had a bang on the head, I was concussed. It was fuzzy, broken up, like a dream.'

'Were you suffering from what is sometimes called transient post-traumatic amnesia?'

'That's what I was told by the doctors, yes. It took time to get all my memory back.'

'How much time?'

'Days. A week or two.'

'A *week* or two, really? And did it all come back at once, in a complete picture?'

'No, it didn't. It was bit by bit.'

De Courcy glanced at the jury meaningfully.

'And when these fragmented memories of the accident *did* come back to you, was it only then that you remembered seeing the car that you say overtook Mr Sullivan's on Cleeve Hill?'

'Yes, it was.'

'Did you remember recognizing that vehicle at the moment it came alongside you?'

'Well, I saw what sort of a car it was.'

De Courcy consulted the bundle of papers in front of him.

'A four-wheel drive, yes? But you never at any stage during the recovery of your memory thought that you had recognized the individual car? Something specific – that you knew, for instance, who owned it?'

'No. I didn't, not then, but I—'

De Courcy cut in.

'Only that it was some kind of four-wheel-drive vehicle.'

'Yes.'

'What colour was it?'

'I don't know, it was dark.'

'The car was dark?'

'No, no . . .'

Jan was getting more flustered. She consciously pulled herself together.

'I meant the *night* was dark, obviously.'

'I see. And did you, when you recovered your fragmented memory, remember recognizing – in the dark – the driver of this vehicle, which you allege pushed Mr Sullivan and you off the road?'

'No, I didn't see him, I—'

'You didn't even *see* this driver, did you? Not at all, not even in silhouette?'

'No, because I—'

'Thank you, Mrs Hardy, yes and no will be fine, unless I ask for elucidation. I have just a few more questions.'

De Courcy adjusted his half-moons and turned a few pages of his bundle.

'You have told the court that things began to happen to you subsequent to the accident, suggesting that someone had a grudge against you – a few anonymous phone calls, and this mysterious press release that you have described. Was there anything in those reports that told you the defendant was their author?'

'I suspected him.'

'But there was nothing specific about them that told you that it could, in fact, *only* be him?'

'No, I guess not.'

'So the instigator of these unpleasant events might have been someone else entirely?'

'No, I don't think so.'

'Oh come, come, Mrs Hardy. Don't tell me public trainers of racehorses don't sometimes provoke the wrath of disappointed racegoers and gamblers – for instance when their horses unexpectedly lose a race.'

Jan glanced anxiously at the judge, who was busily writing notes.

'Well, yes, it does happen occasionally. But to my knowledge that was not the case here.'

'To your knowledge, to your *knowledge*,' de Courcy repeated, surveying the jury before going on. 'But you decided at some later point, did you not, that the defendant was responsible?'

'I began to suspect him, yes.'

'Even though you had no real evidence?'

'I had good reason—'

'But no hard *evidence*? No facts?'

'No,' agreed Jan reluctantly, 'I suppose not.'

Again the barrister rifled through the pages of his bundle.

'I turn to the episode you have described to the court when, as you allege, Harold Powell came to your stables and admitted responsibility for the accident, among other things. Apart from yourself and your employee, Patrick Keating, did anyone else actually hear him threaten you? Or see him even?'

'I don't know.'

'You did ask around, surely?'

'There was no one else there, except Patsy and myself.'

De Courcy asked a few more questions about the stable routine on Sunday afternoons – who wasn't there, who might have been there – then suddenly he snatched his glasses off his nose, rose to his full height, raised his voice and went on the offensive.

'Mrs Hardy,' he boomed, 'were you extremely worried at the time that your friend Edward Sullivan was himself being investigated by the police over the death of William Moorhouse on Cleeve Hill?'

'Well, yes, I was worried, but I—'

'I put it to you, Mrs Hardy, that Harold Powell was never at your stables on that day, any more than he had been on Cleeve Hill when the accident occurred.'

'No. He *was* at the stables.'

'And that you made up this story of his confession, and asked your employee Patrick Keating to confirm it, in order to get Edward Sullivan off the hook. That's it, Mrs Hardy, isn't it?'

'Mr de Courcy, Harold was *there*.'

'Mrs Hardy, would you tell the court why, after training my client's horses for several years, and with some success I might add, he removed his horses from your care and sent them to Miss Gilbert?'

'Because I asked him to remove them after we had a disagreement and I recommended Virginia Gilbert as an alternative,' Jan replied sharply.

'Why Miss Gilbert in particular?' de Courcy countered.

Jan was already getting irritated by de Courcy's demeanour. 'Because I thought they were a pair of sh . . .' Jan choked back the

288

expletive. 'Because I thought they would be a good match temperamentally.'

'Really!' de Courcy intoned. 'I put it to you, further, that you knew that Mr Keating had a grudge against the defendant's friend, Miss Gilbert, for whom he once worked. You yourself had a grudge against my client because you believed he had cheated you over a land deal. So, between you, you conspired to implicate Harold Powell and exonerate Edward Sullivan, your friend. That's right, isn't it?'

Jan knew she was red in the face, not from embarrassment, but anger. How dare this man call her a liar? How dare he accuse her of conspiring against Harold, when it was Harold who'd conspired against her? She took a deep breath. *De Courcy's doing this on purpose*, she thought. *He's hoping I'm going to lose control. I can't let them get away with it.* She inhaled deeply and knew it would be fatal to start shouting.

'No, no,' she continued as coolly as she could. 'It's me telling the truth and Powell who's lying. You've got it arse about face.'

'Now, Mrs Hardy!' said the judge sharply, looking up from his notes.

But her retort was enough to shut de Courcy up. He bowed and said, 'Thank you, Mrs Hardy, no further questions.'

🐎

Jan had not expected to be branded a liar by the defence though she realized it was the obvious tactic – the best chance for Harold to win. Now, after de Courcy's vicious cross-examination, she began to appreciate how uncertain her entire future looked in the light of this case. Suppose Harold was acquitted. Would that mean she was in the frame for perjury? Or conspiring to pervert the course of justice? It didn't bear thinking about.

Once her evidence had been completed, Jan was able to sit in the public gallery. She was more concerned about Patsy than she had been for herself. How would he stand up to any rough treatment from de Courcy? Surprisingly Patsy was an effective witness, answering Jeffreys's questions quietly and with conviction. But when it was de Courcy's turn, he simply waved his hand.

'No questions, your honour.'

'Thank you, Mr Keating,' said Bancroft. 'You may step down.'

Harold's defence team had decided to rely on the argument that the Crown's case was too flimsy. Tellingly, they did not want to risk exposing their client, with his tendency to flip his lid, to Jeffreys's questions. So Harold did not give evidence and de Courcy confined himself to calling one of the drinks' waiters at Cheltenham, who said he thought he'd seen Eddie 'supping'. Then came two not especially persuasive character witnesses and a scientist, who stated in tortuous terms that anyone who'd had a head injury might not be all there, mentally, for several months after the event. This last evidence was an obvious attempt to back up de Courcy's attack on Jan, but the scientist was so circumspect, and used so many 'maybes' and 'possiblys' that, as Bob Warren said later, he tended to strangle his own theories at birth.

De Courcy's closing statement was short. He hammered home the fact that no one except Jan, the victim of a serious head injury, had seen the third car at the scene; that no one except Jan and Patsy had heard Harold Powell confess to being responsible for the accident; and that both might harbour grudges against Harold, either directly or because they didn't like Virginia Gilbert, who was Harold's closest friend. A much more likely explanation, the QC argued, was that Eddie Sullivan had been intoxicated, and had caused the accident himself. With that poisonous suggestion, he sat down.

Benjamin Jeffreys countered strongly with the fact that there was no evidence of Eddie's inebriation, that skid marks in the road and paint traces on the Morgan might have been from Harold's Range Rover, that Harold had made obvious and demonstrable threats against Jan, and what was more, he could produce no alibi for the night of the accident. It was a good closing speech, confident and uncomplicated.

By lunchtime on the third day the evidence and the judge's concise and impartial summing up were over and the jury retired to consider their verdict. During the recess, Jan had a light lunch with Bob Warren in the court cafe.

'Why did de Courcy not cross-examine Patsy?' she questioned.

'He didn't think it would help his case. He sensed that Patsy was a sympathetic witness, that the jury liked him – quite rightly, by the way – and wouldn't want to see him attacked.'

'What about me? Wanted to see me attacked, did they?'

Bob smiled broadly.

'They enjoyed that. You gave as good as you got, mind.'

'Did I? Bloody cheek, that man accusing me of lying.'

'De Courcy's been quite clever, actually, but I think he may be feeling he's met his match in you. And by the way all this about Eddie drinking is rather clutching at straws. The forensic reports make it virtually certain a third car was there, and the fact that Harold could produce no alibi is very damaging.'

'So what do you think will be the verdict?'

Bob sighed. Years of experience had taught him not to second-guess juries.

'We can only wait and see. Keep your fingers crossed.'

Jan was thoughtful, remembering how she had waited outside the stewards' room at Leopardstown for the verdict after a very different kind of trial. The outcome there had gone in her favour and now Morning Glory was due to contest the Supreme Novice Hurdle at the Cheltenham Festival in a couple of weeks. For the yard these were exciting times. But if Harold Powell got off they wouldn't be, that was for certain.

The jury were out for two hours before coming back to ask for clarification about the forensic evidence. They then retired again and another hour dragged slowly by. Jan was sitting with Reg and Mary on a bench outside the court when they noticed the atmosphere had grown more hectic. Bob Warren bustled up to them.

'*Quick*, the jury's coming back,' he said. 'I think this is it.'

'All rise,' came the cry as Judge Bancroft entered.

Two minutes later they watched as the jury filed in. Jan squinted and tried to read the verdict in their faces but could see no clues. They all looked uniform and serious.

The clerk of the court cleared his throat.

'Would the defendant please stand?'

Harold did so, his eyes flicking from one member of the jury to the next. The clerk turned to the jury's foreman.

'Would the foreman please stand? Have you reached a verdict on which you are all agreed?'

'Yes.'

'Do you find the defendant guilty or not guilty of attempted murder?'

There was a minute pause as the whole court held its breath.

'Guilty.'

There was a loud whoosh as the onlookers breathed out and the tension was released. Someone in the public gallery blurted out, 'Yess, yess!' Jan closed her eyes from pure relief as Mary, sitting next to her, squeezed her arm. Jan slowly opened her eyes and looked at Harold. The muscles in his jaw had tightened, but he appeared otherwise unmoved.

The clerk continued, 'And do you find the defendant guilty or not guilty of causing death by reckless driving?'

'Guilty.'

'And are these the verdicts of you all?'

'They are.'

For several seconds Judge Bancroft allowed the buzz of the excited court to die away. Then he spoke firmly and without hesitation.

'Harold Powell, you have been found guilty of two extremely serious offences, the more serious of which is attempted murder. For this offence I sentence you to a term of imprisonment of ten years. On the charge of death by reckless driving, I sentence you to a term of five years. These terms are to run concurrently.'

Bancroft looked down from the bench at Harold Powell and his words rang out with crushing finality.

'Take him down.'

# Epilogue

The short dark afternoons of midwinter were behind them now and there was still light in the sky as Jan, her family and friends emerged through the swing doors of the court house and gathered on the steps.

Jan felt totally drained after the emotional helter-skelter of the trial and closed her eyes as she breathed deeply. Even the taste of the traffic fumes, which hung in the cold damp air, was preferable to the musty atmosphere of the court room. Jan was still trembling as she thanked Benjamin Jeffreys for a job well done.

'Don't thank me, Mrs Hardy, that's the man you should be thanking.' Jan half-turned and saw a smiling Bob Warren walking towards her.

'That was a good result,' he said.

'Not in my opinion,' contradicted Toby. 'The sentence was too lenient.'

'Don't you worry about that: to a weak man like Harold Powell it will be more like twenty years; he'll suffer all right.'

'Good,' Annabel said brightly, 'I hope he does.'

'And so say all of *us*,' agreed Toby.

But Mary, usually a quiet presence in any group, put a warning hand on Toby's arm.

'No, Toby, we must hope he learns how much harm he's done, and how much suffering he's caused. Maybe he'll come out a better person then.'

'Not much chance of that,' growled Reg.

But Mary insisted.

'Reg, that's what we must hope will happen,' she insisted. 'Otherwise, what's it all for?'

Jan felt a sudden surge of love for her ever-optimistic mother, and a pang of regret that this strong-minded, yet gentle woman should have been put through the strain of this trial when her own health was not particularly good.

'Yes, Mum,' she said. 'I want him to come out a better person, too.'

*But only after the bastard's been to hell and back* was the thought she kept to herself.

'Well, is anyone up for a glass of something?' asked Toby brightly. 'I noticed a decent-looking little wine bar up the road.'

Jan made her excuses. Reg and Mary wanted to go home and she had to get back to the children and the horses. She was just guiding Reg and Mary down the steps when they heard a clatter of heels behind them. She glanced back to see who was coming down.

'I suppose you think you'll get away with this, you bitch!' hissed Virginia Gilbert from the side of her mouth as she swept past.

'What did that woman say?' asked Reg, as Virginia reached the pavement and stalked off up the road.

'It wasn't congratulations, Dad.'

'You'd better keep an eye on that woman, Jan. She's not going to let this rest despite what your mother might think.'

'I always do, Dad.'

They had just reached the pavement and were turning towards the car park when they heard a shout from the road behind them. Jan turned. Belching smoke from its exhaust, Gerry's van drew up at the kerbside. Eddie climbed stiffly from the passenger seat and leaned inside to pull out a rather bedraggled bunch of flowers wrapped in cellophane.

'Just wait here for a moment,' Jan told her parents and went over to meet him.

'These are not much, but—' Eddie began.

'Garage, I suppose?' She chuckled.

Eddie gave her a slight, self-mocking smile.

'We stopped for diesel. What I'm saying is, I'm really sorry. I got them because I wanted to apologize for leaving you to sit through the trial, and all that. I know I should have been there. I was just being a sodding wimp.'

Jan gestured to Reg and Mary.

'My mum and dad were with me. So were Bel and Toby. I was all right really.'

Eddie took her hand and placed the flowers in it. All of a sudden, his eyes seemed larger and more tender than usual.

'I don't want to lose you, Jan,' he murmured. 'I know some things were said before Christmas, or implied, at any rate. But I've been thinking a lot in the past few weeks and I can't believe what has happened to us this last twelve months. I want to try again.'

Jan clutched the flowers with both hands. She shut her eyes, squeezing the lids tight, then opened them again. He was still there in front of her, waiting for a response.

She sighed.

'Eddie Sullivan, you're bloody impossible. We've had one good result today. I suppose we'd better go home and get our lives sorted out, hadn't we?'